In the beginning,
there was Planet Earth.

In the end,
there was nowhere to go
but the stars . . .

REGENESIS

The future has arrived—with a vengeance.
Planet Earth is no longer a suitable environment
for sustaining life. Every creature great and small is
on the verge of extinction. Their only hope: Noah's Ark,
a scientific mission to find new homes for the last
surviving species of Earth . . .

An odyssey that will take both human and beast to
strange new worlds across the galaxy . . .

An epic journey to a new beginning.

REGENESIS

JULIA ECKLAR

ACE BOOKS, NEW YORK

Sections of *Regenesis* have appeared previously in *Analog:* "Blood Relations" (June 1992), "Ice Nights" (October 1992), "Tide of Stars" (January 1995), and "The Human Animal" (April 1995). They have been revised for this edition.

REGENESIS

An Ace Book / published by arrangement with the author

PRINTING HISTORY
Ace edition / June 1995

ISBN: 0-441-00189-0

ACE®
Ace Books are published by The Berkley Publishing Group, 200 Madison Avenue, New York, NY 10016.
ACE and the "A" design are trademarks belonging to Charter Communications, Inc.

PRINTED IN THE UNITED STATES OF AMERICA

10 9 8 7 6 5 4 3 2 1

To Stan,
for giving Rahel Tovin her first job

ACKNOWLEDGMENTS

Few things in life are ever done all on their own, but science fiction novels seem to utilize a wider variety of interesting people than most other projects I can think of.

First and foremost, I have to thank Dr. Karen Rose Cercone from Indiana University of Pennsylvania for her invaluable research assistance, support, and encouragement in all stages of this project. She first indoctrinated me into the world of the female scientist, and helped me to recognize what a brave and thrilling place it is. Without her enthusiasm and honesty, this book would never have come about.

Special thanks also to Dr. Susan U. Linville, Cheryl Smyth-Kiser, Dr. Jane Robinson, Jennifer Protzman, and all the other women scientists and technicians who convinced me there was more to be done with Rahel, and that there were readers out there eager to see it.

Thanks to Chris Laughery of the Pennsylvania Geological Survey for his invaluable assistance with the scuba and diving portions of this book; Dr. Stanley Schmidt for trusting me; and Ricia Mainhardt for knowing when to nag me and when to leave me alone.

Special thanks, of course, must go to Kurtain Kraft, Ron Popeil, and the Psychic Friends Network for keeping me company throughout more sleepless writing nights than I care to think about.

And, finally, thanks to Rusty for all the usual stuff. Food is good. Friends are good. Friends who can cook are best of all. I appreciate your being there.

The last word in ignorance is the man who says of any animal or plant: What good is it?

—Aldo Leopold

REGENESIS

⚡Blood Relations⚡

Basa hated everyone. Rahel always assumed Basa only tolerated her because she let him ride in the lower pocket of her field vest when she pursued animal study groups across tundras and woodlands. He seemed to like bobbing along, hip-high, with no responsibility except to keep himself from falling out. Black terrier eyes surveyed myriad worlds with malicious interest, and one broken-down terrier ear drooped just enough to give Basa an expression of comical confusion. That expression, of course, was a lie. That's why Rahel hated to take Basa around other people; some well-meaning idiot always felt the need to approach the little dog, hand outstretched, and ask:

"Is he friendly?"

Rahel glanced up from the scatter of reports and photos on the table in front of her. A meter away, Colony Prelate Killean Wels waited with his hand suspended just above the terrier's head. Basa, seated half-atop Rahel's work pile, had already started his dance of anticipation, toenails clicking frenziedly on Wels's wooden tabletop.

"Depends on what you mean by friendly."

Wels seemed to find that amusing. Rahel turned her attention away from his porcelain face and political smile to run long fingers over the plasticast footprints in her hands. Tall and rawboned, she knew what a contrast she must make beside the dapper Wels—dark-haired, dark-eyed, even her

rough bush suit and vest in various colors of khaki. She was
a monochrome person, all drawn in shades of brown, with
her straight, jaw-length hair pulled back into a simple
ponytail. Compared to Wels's elegantly tousled and braided
blond mop, she must look like she had the fashion sense of
a farmer. Which, really, she did.

"I mean will he bite me?"

Ah—the persistent type. Rahel shrugged and set the
plasticast prints aside. "He hasn't bitten a Colony prelate
yet."

The rough, distorted pugs looked as much like tiger tracks
as anything else, so Rahel flipped through the reports again
while Wels tried to make friendly with her dog. Tigers had
been on New Dallas since its colonization fifteen years
ago—twenty-three variegated adult Modern Sumatrans,
according to the Ark records she'd studied on her way here.
The geneticists at Noah's Ark had scrambled the mix
enough to make it safe for the tigers to pick their own mates,
so—except for a few routine checkups on the four hundred
species of various this-and-that originally seeded on New
Dallas—nobody had really spent any time with the tigers
before now.

Of course, the tigers hadn't killed anyone before now,
either.

Basa exploded into a gravelly avalanche of snarls, and
Rahel's paperwork went everywhere as the terrier launched
himself across the table at Wels. The prelate swore, jerking
his hand back behind him, but didn't erupt into shouting, or
run away as if in fear of his life. He just stood with his hands
held close to him, his cheeks high with color, while Rahel
scooped her dog up in one hand and tucked him under her
elbow. "Sorry about that," she said automatically, not really
sorry at all.

Wels tried on another smile, but it faded too quickly.
"You said he didn't bite."

"I said he'd never bitten a prelate." Basa hung patiently
enough under her arm, but his wiry white-and-black body

still trembled with growling. "I guess the other prelates were just faster."

Annoyance tangled Wels's pale eyebrows, but humor toyed with the corners of his mouth. Neither really won out; he finally sighed and crossed his arms in efficient dismissal. "I stand corrected." His fashionably long braids gathered about his shoulders when he dropped into a seat. "So, tell me about our tiger."

His sudden redirection toward business suited Rahel just fine. Shifting Basa to her other arm, she shuffled the reports together with one hand. "Your *alleged* tiger." The stack of flimsies and paper hit center table with a slap. "Is this all the information you have?"

Wels's mouth twitched into that phantom grin again. "I thought you safari types could tell an animal's species, weight, and blood type just by the look of the leaves where the animal passed."

Rahel scowled and rocked back in her own chair. "Then you thought wrong." She hated the sarcastic ones. "Tell me what you know."

"Only what you've got there."

It figured. Pushing Basa into a sit on her lap, Rahel basketed her hands around the little dog to keep him from lunging at Wels again. "Well, all you've got here is a list of who was killed, where, and when. You give names and addresses, who they lived with, when they were last seen, how long you figure they were dead before your Cop Shop found their bodies. You've got pictures, the one good plasticast, and a bunch of speculation from a lot of local yokels who seem to have picked on the tigers 'cause they were the biggest thing around." She wished they were outside, where there might be something nearby to throw. "Even us 'safari types' can't get jack-shit out of that."

Wels toyed with one earring and stared at the pile, but Rahel could see the line of his jaw bunch and move while he chewed over what he should say. She wondered if these "Colony types" knew that safaris would end a lot faster if colonists would just spit up what they knew and get out of the way.

"I gathered whatever information I could think of," Wels said finally, slowly. "We haven't had to call Noah's Ark back to New Dallas since the animals were originally seeded here. I didn't know what kind of information you'd want."

Honest, at least, if stupid. She sighed and tried to keep her voice neutral. "I want a lot of stuff you probably can't tell me. But let's start with why you're so sure it was a tiger killed those people."

Wels laced his hands in his lap and squared his shoulders, as if planning to carry some heavy load for a long way. "There have always been tigers in Melissa Pass. They showed up sometimes on our bioscans, and my miners reported seeing them now and then. But we were set up fifty kilometers outside the Pass, so the tigers never got anywhere near our outposts. But there was once . . ." He shifted a little in his seat, and embarrassment made his eyes glisten. "One of the fellows got drunk while they were surveying the Pass a few months ago," he explained awkwardly. "He got drunk with one of the cops and a couple of the other miners, and they all ran around in the brush 'big game hunting.'" His eyes glanced away from her, to the paper pile again. "They shot one of the tigers."

Her ears rang with a surge of anger, and familiar self-hatred snarled up inside her until she wanted to kick the prelate's office to pieces. Frustrating—so goddamned frustrating to try and uphold anything fair and right when all it took was one thoughtless primate to shatter anything she and the others could do. "You signed an agreement with Noah's Ark," was all she could make herself say—and that not even politely. "You can lose your Colony Charter for killing even one protected animal."

"I know that." His hand drifted up to play with that earring again. "They only managed to wound it, and I fired all of them and shipped them offplanet immediately. Everyone else understands that nothing like that is to happen again. We've had no further incidents."

God, she wanted to backhand the look of contrition off his face. In her lap, Basa grumbled and circled three times before lying down. "You still should have reported it."

He snapped a brave look into her face. "I didn't want to lose my Charter. Not over one wounded animal."

But you want to break contract with Noah's Ark over a couple of dead people. Rahel traced the soft inside of Basa's ear, listening to the tiny, tick-tock growl that meant something pleased him. "So what has all this got to do with your killings?" *Stick to business,* she chastised herself. *You'll never get to leave if you don't solve their problem.*

"Those tracks look pretty scarred up." Wels pointed at the plasticasts in front of her. "We got those at Melissa Pass, where I sent a man just two weeks ago to scout out a new vein. When the follow-up crew arrived four days later, he was dead. We thought maybe it was the tiger who'd been injured before, that maybe it couldn't hunt like normal anymore. That"—the prelate cleared his throat with some embarrassment, but went on—"that maybe it hated people."

Rahel snorted. The only thing worse than a human who had no respect for other animals was a human who assumed all other animals thought and felt just like he did.

She glanced down at her notebook to check on Wels's facts. The surveyor would be Del Harbin, age forty-seven. The Cop Shop estimated he'd been dead since shortly after reaching Melissa Pass, since between tiger damage, decay, and the amount stolen away by scavengers they'd only been able to identify him via DNA. "It says here there were other deaths," Rahel said. "What happened to them?"

"Pretty much the same. A couple days after I left the miners alone in the outpost, they 'linked us to say one of them had been killed—apparently by tigers." His gaze dropped to his hands, and he rubbed at one thumbnail as if trying to scrape something away. "By the time I got a flyer out there to pick them up," he went on, very steadily, "the other two were dead as well."

Somewhat against her will, Rahel felt a sting of sympathy as she tried to imagine that little surprise. She pushed the feeling away. "How well did your people clean up the attack sites?"

"Pretty thoroughly," Wels admitted with a sigh.

Rahel ground her teeth. "Well, what about during the autopsies? Did anyone run a protein match on the bodies? Any leftover tiger biology should stand out dandy on a human corpse."

Wels continued staring at his fingernails.

The prelate's guilty silence burned on the air. "Hair?" Rahel persisted. "Didn't you even think to collect hair samples? Or photograph bite signatures?"

When Wels finally looked up, it was at some vague distraction to his left, not at her. "We didn't perform autopsies."

Didn't perform autopsies. Didn't collect samples. Without any data, they just expected her to come in and wave a magic wand to solve the problem. "You didn't perform autopsies," she guessed, "because you already knew the killer was a tiger."

Wels at least had the grace to nod miserably.

To channel off some of her frustration, she wrapped her hand around Basa's whole head and shook it gently, fondly. The terrier sighed and thumped his stumpy tail. Seeing him happy soothed her into a tiny smile. "The problem," she said to Wels at last, "is that we still don't know *which* tiger. Assuming my investigation even agrees with your tiger hypothesis."

She bobbed forward just far enough to snag the pile of reports and pull them back in front of her. "As an employee of Noah's Ark, it's my duty to figure out which Ark-bred animal is causing your difficulty, and why. Then I can use my discretion"—she cocked a nod toward Wels—"and your suggestions"—that was the most deference she was willing to grant him—"in deciding how best to rectify your situation. I think I should warn you, though, I'll opt for relocation of the animal over killing it. If you can't live with that, get yourself a new proctor now."

Wels studied her for a long while, lips pursed, brow knit. Just when she'd decided not to wait around for his answer, the prelate announced, "I just want the killings to stop. Any solution that promises my miners' safety, I can live with."

Rahel nodded; that was one less fight, then. "Consider this contract in action." She slid one hand under Basa and got to her feet. Basa growled and snapped at the paperwork as she shoveled it up with her other hand. The plasticast footprints disappeared into Basa's favorite riding pocket; he'd have to rough it back to their quarters. "Come morning, I want to sniff around the Melissa Pass mining outpost. I've got my own equipment—all I'll need from your AI is directions."

Wels stood with her, obviously caught somewhat off guard. "Do you think it's safe for you to be up there alone?"

"I guess we'll find out, won't we?" Rahel stepped around him to head for the door; Basa snapped at him, as well, in the passing.

"I'd really rather you take someone with you," Wels insisted, staying close behind her.

Rahel paused in the door, holding it open so that the unprocessed smell of outside could wash over her while they talked. "Have you got robots?" she asked without turning around. "I don't even care if they're Newborn—just plain robots are fine."

Wels was silent for a moment. "No. Only human colonists. But I'm sure someone—"

"Forget it." She stepped all the way outside, and the bright midday sunlight hurt her eyes. "I'd rather go alone."

"Ms. Tovin, I already have plenty of proof that tigers are dangerous without you getting killed, too." Wels caught the door before it closed, his hand stopping the sculpted metal with a soft slap. "Do you really trust animals that much?"

"No. I hate people that much." Rahel produced a thin smile, and half-turned so he could see her expression for the truth. "See you when this is all over, Prelate."

She left him still standing in the doorway, the shadows of a tree painting tiger stripes across his eyes.

Melissa Pass was smothered under a calico blanket of treetops and mist. Looked like tiger country to Rahel, for all that was worth. She pushed Basa off her lap and down-throttled the pachyderm to glide the ship under the gnarled foliage. Tall, heat-brittle grasses bowed aside, and a herd of native jembels bounded out of sight as she flew by, flashes of their frantic white tails the only remnant of their disappearing act.

A glimpse of glossy, slate-colored rocks spoke of a spring or pool less than three kilometers from New Dallas's mining outpost. Tigers liked water. Rahel thought back over all the studying she'd crammed in the night before, trying to remember what (if anything) she'd learned about territories, den sites, and numbers. All she could remember was that tigers almost never killed people and always lived alone.

Frustration forced a groan from her, and she put her hand down where Basa could chew on her fingertips. She was not the best choice Noah's Ark could have made for this safari, and she knew it. Saiah Innis—perhaps the Ark's wisest jungle feline specialist—had supervised the original seeding of the New Dallas tigers; he was twice Rahel's age, but still had to be a better proctor than an irritated canine specialist who hadn't looked at tiger spins since school. When she'd bitched about this last night to Saiah, though, he told her, "You were closer, Rahel. Don't worry—you'll do fine."

Easy for him to say. He got to stay on Eden.

Which was where Rahel would rather be right now. Not that she didn't trust the journeymen proctors assigned to replace her; she just believed in instincts above and beyond what a proctor learned from schools and tapes. That sense

grew out of innate talent and experience—neither of which
she had for Sumatran tigers. Saiah Innis would have smelled
the solution to this safari fifteen minutes after bumping port;
Rahel Tovin had a feeling she wasn't going to smell
anything until she stepped in it. A string of murdered people
that resulted in a murdered tiger might solve the problem as
far as Killean Wels was concerned, but it wasn't the solution
Rahel hoped to settle for.

The Melissa Pass outpost bubbled up from the jungle
floor like a blanket of bulbous white mushrooms. The place
must have stood out like a diner's club, even to a color-blind
tiger. Any tiger dining on humans in the first place was
undoubtedly either sick or injured, making humans the only
prey too slow and stupid to avoid it. Rahel had to admit that
if her only choice was between stalking an outpost and
starving, she'd probably opt for munching miners, too.

Circling the outpost on low-throttle, she activated the
pachyderm's chameleon to mask the transport's sight and
smell, and set down as close as she could to the outpost's
wide-open hatch. Basa twirled about the floor in an orgy of
excitement.

Rahel kept trotting back to check the open hatch between
sorting together sample slides and testing gear. Oh, these
miners were pips, all right—too weak-kneed with their
phantom tigers to even think about dogging the hatches
behind them when they abandoned the post. They might not
be able to hard-lock them from the outside to prevent human
entry, but they could at least latch-lock them to keep
animals out. Who knew what sort of things had moved into
the premises in the week since? On top of further corrupting
an already ruined attack site, such second-hand tenants also
meant Rahel couldn't feel safe inside the compound.

She toed Basa away from the pachyderm's hatch, ignoring the terrier's attack on her boot. "Back. Back!" He
minced back from the hatch by four precise steps, grum-
bling doggy complaints. "Sorry, Basa—you've gotta stay
here. Don't want the big, bad tigers to eat you." She slipped

a snooze pistol out of the cabinet and squeezed out the hatch while Basa pouted. "I'll let you know when I've decided all's clear."

A mantle of jungle heat pressed against her as she darted across the distance between pachyderm and outpost. She paused at the doorway, checking the snooze pistol's charge and deliberately slowing her breathing. Her soft-soled boots shushed against the flooring as she crept inside.

The interior wasn't nearly so humid and foul-smelling as she expected. Work surfaces sat neat and undisturbed; chairs and lounges still possessed all their stuffing; a faint, brittle scent of industrial cleaning chemicals hung like spider's silk on the air. She didn't know how the place got open now, but she'd just about decided it must have been locked all week, when she edged around the last open hatchway to find Wels waiting patiently inside.

Her fingers twitched on the handle of the snooze gun, and she jerked the muzzle toward the ceiling by reflex, just in case it went off. It didn't, and even that irritated her. "I ought to shoot you," she told the prelate.

Wels seemed remarkably unperturbed by the threat. "I thought proctors didn't carry guns."

"You think a lot of things that aren't true." She abandoned him long enough to trot back to the entrance and dog the outer hatch. Stupid of him to leave it hanging open when he didn't even have a gun of his own; he couldn't guess what might wander in here any more than she could, and he was a lot less likely to know how to deal with it. When she got back to him, he still waited patiently, both hands folded in the lap of his neat, new-bought bush suit. She felt remarkably earthy and competent by comparison.

Wels made a show of leaning over to peer around her. "Where's your rabid sidekick? Do I have to get ready to run?"

"I left him in the pachyderm." Shoving the snooze pistol into her trouser pocket, she demanded tartly, "What are you doing here?"

He straightened and shook back his elaborately braided and bound blond hair. "Waiting for you."

Rahel snorted, wishing she'd brought Basa in after all. "I already told you—I don't want your help."

"Oh, I don't intend to help. I intend to observe."

As if his presence would somehow prove too beneficial for her to resist. "Great." Rahel swung her pack onto the nearest work desk; it landed with a satisfying *clunk*. "Just fucking great."

Wels's mouth drew tight with annoyance, but Rahel gave him credit when he didn't fidget or twitch. "This Colony is my responsibility, Ms. Tovin," he told her in a flat and reasonable tone. "The people who live and work here expect me to take care of things so they don't have to. I'm not about to sit twiddling my thumbs at Colony Central while you do whatever it is you do out here. I want to know what's going on."

Rahel dumped a handful of sample slides onto the table. "Like you're going to understand everything just because you see it."

"You can explain it to me."

"Yeah, sure. That'll make things go *so* much faster." She turned with her hands full of sampling gear, and sighed. "You're just going to get in my way."

Wels stood, poised on his toes as if ready to leap in any direction she chose. "I'll try not to." He flashed his faint, cutting grin. "What's first?"

Kicking him back to Colony Central was a now or never thing, Rahel knew. Assuming, of course, he didn't just run back out here to harass her some more. Sighing, she decided she'd rather take control of both the situation, and him, right now. "All right, then. Let's get started." She sorted her slides into order and stepped toward the center of the room, already suspecting she'd regret her capitulation. "First, I scour the attack sites to see if your people left me enough in the way of samples to do any good." She flipped through the screens on her notebook. "Says here two of the attacks occurred outside the outpost." She glanced a question at him over the screen.

Wels nodded. "The very first one—the surveyor who was alone, Del Harbin. We airlifted his body out when we dropped off the start-up team, then shipped his remains homeward." Rahel added one more lost data set to her tally. "The first casualty among the start-up crew was also killed outside," Wels went on. "They kept her body in the infirmary awaiting pickup. We, uh . . ." He crossed his arms suddenly, and cleared his throat. "We found her still there when we came to lift them out."

So Wels had been with the group who cleaned the outpost. No wonder he wanted this tiger thing solved so badly. Bending her attention to the notebook again, she asked, "So the other two were killed inside?"

He nodded, pointing toward the center of the room. "There, and there. We found them here with the outside door still open."

She grinned with amused disgust. "And you left the same door hanging open while you waited for me? Brilliant."

"I only just opened it when the outpost system said you'd arrived." Wels bristled, pulling his chin higher. "I'm not that stupid."

They'd have to see about that. "How many hours have we got till planetary dark?"

The apparent change of topic caught Wels unprepared. He blinked in confusion, and brought his arms back to his sides. "Four or five. Why?"

"I want to check the outside sites first. They're probably next to useless, but I'd rather know that than guess." She paused to glance over her surroundings. It struck her for the first time that this must be a rec room, small though it was. She wondered if the miners had fought the tiger at all, and if the furniture might retain bloodstains or saliva.

"If you show me how," Wels interrupted her thoughts, "I can collect some samples in here. Just until you get back from outside."

Rahel made a face at him. "You told me you'd stay out of my way."

The expression on Wels's patrician features was too ingenuous to be sincere. Rahel wanted to smack him. "I won't be in your way—I'll be in here while you're outside. And I'll stop as soon as you get back, I promise."

Save the time, she told herself. *It's not like there's anything in here for him to find anyway.* Motioning for him to join her, she moved toward the segment of floor scarred by the colonists' zealous cleaning.

"I still need an ID on this tiger," she explained. "The more data I can get from each of the attack sites, the better chance I'll have of crapping together a DNA model. Especially since you guys didn't leave me much to work with." She crouched at the edge of the scarring; Wels squatted beside her. "If this is where the killings took place, there must have been a lot of blood spread around here. We'll take some samples from here, just in case there's enough left to compare against the slides we pull elsewhere."

Wels pressed his hands to the floor between his knees. "How will we know that the . . . blood and things we get here aren't . . ." Taking a huge breath, he rushed on ahead. "That they aren't from my miners?"

Rahel shrugged, counting her slides. "Do you still have any of those bodies at New Dallas?"

"I'm afraid not." Wels's very tone was apologetic. "We shipped them back to their homeworlds as soon as we were able."

"Shit."

"Sorry . . ."

Rahel waved his apology aside; they'd already wasted too much time just determining that they didn't really know anything. "Doesn't matter. We'll just have to use their medical records, is all." Would have been nice to have the fresh comparison, though.

Taking his hand, Rahel turned it palm up and spilled

several slides into it. "I need samples from all over this area—the floor, the furniture, any place you think the tiger might have touched. If we still had those bodies, I'd check their skin and clothing, too, but there's nothing to be done for that."

Wels obviously checked himself from apologizing again. "What are we looking for?" he asked, stacking the slides together.

Rahel peered at him sidelong. "*I'm* looking for biological traces of our alleged tiger. Saliva, blood, skin. Saliva and blood would be best, since they'd also tell me if we've got a sick tiger on our hands." Not that she really expected to find usable samples of either. Didn't hurt to try, though. "Here—this is how you get a sample."

Wels didn't interrupt her throughout the quick lesson, and he caught on easily enough. She made sure that he had enough slides to get him started, then pushed to her feet to collect her own gear. "You can't get into the pachyderm without me, so just wait here till I get back."

"I wouldn't want to try and get past that attack beast of yours, anyway," Wels assured her, smiling.

Rahel swung her pack over one shoulder, not smiling in return. "With that in mind, do yourself a big favor—keep the outside door hard-locked from the inside while I'm gone." Much as she would have liked to have samples from a fresh tiger kill, she didn't think Colony Central would approve of how she got them.

Rahel imagined she could hear Basa wailing while she felt her way around the camouflaged pachyderm. Interior sound couldn't travel outside, she knew, and she'd never had any proof that Basa either barked or howled in protest to her absence. He sometimes tore up her belongings something fierce, though, and had once peed all over whatever of her clothes he could find. So it seemed likely he bitched aloud at her heartless abandonment. She considered it a blessing that she was usually able to take him along when she hiked; otherwise she could never have afforded to keep him.

Not today, though. Not when Wels and his yahoos had left so little physical evidence for her to recover at any given site. Basa's very presence could drop enough dander and hair to corrupt a site beyond use; hell, her own presence probably ran that risk as well. At least she was fairly certain she could identify her own head hairs without having to run them through the sequencer. She didn't want to depend on that with Basa's.

As she stepped beyond the pachyderm, air warm and gamey as a carnivore's breath frumped her clothing and feathered her hair. It felt good for the briefest moment, lifting away itchy, ever-present sweat; then the jungle seemed to run out of breath, leaving her in sweltering stillness again.

Not that the jungle was ever truly silent or still. Rahel flipped her notebook open to the Cop Shop's description of Harbin's murder site, following those directions with one eye while slipping between foliage into the deeper darkness beyond. Her senses expanded without her having to think about it, listening for the scratch and chatter of every leaf, watching for any movement not explained away by sunlight, shadow, or breeze, sniffing the air for the telltale spike of musk or urine that sometimes meant a large predator nearby. The bioscan on her wrist could tell her much the same things, but she resented trusting equipment for information she felt her instincts should be able to deliver; not feeling and not seeing didn't necessarily mean "not there." She knew that, and she suspected the tigers did, too.

She wondered if Harbin had been wearing a bioscan.

Her notebook beeped when she reached the murder site. Stopping, she confirmed the location with a quick look around and grumbled (much like Basa) to herself. The week had done its work; a cairn of soggy leaves marked where the tiger had probably tried to conceal Harbin's body for later eating, and a burned-yellow patch at the base of a tree hinted that territorial spraying had dripped down the trunk to the ground. Rahel fished three clean sample slides from her vest pocket and moved to kneel beside the urine-stained tree.

The smell of ammonia prickled faintly at her nose, sunk too deeply into the bark to tell if it were fresh or long-standing. Wiping three samples from various stinking areas, she promised herself she'd collect more if time and light allowed. The slides clicked together in her pockets as she shuffled on hands and knees around the edge of the site.

Drag lines, trampled sticks, splayed and scarred-up tiger pugs. She sniffed the ground at the clearest print, drinking in the thick, living smell. But it smelled of hot earth, nothing more, so she moved on. Eventually, she wrestled the magnification gear out of her pack and let it scan the ground ahead of her, showing her sand grains as big as finger bones, beetles as large as birds. She found a blade of grass with blood on it (probably Harbin's), and a single long, lovely whisker lying white against the ground. All the oversize sample slides had been left in the pachyderm, but the beauty of a whisker was that it wouldn't lose its informative value by being introduced to pocket lint. Thumbing open a tiny breast pocket, Rahel slipped the single whisker inside and patted her treasure proudly.

A wicked sting raced suddenly along her radial nerve, making her hand twitch against the air. Adrenaline pounded into every fiber, and she clutched at the bioscan on her wrist to silence it; a ghost memory of the warning still made her fingers tingle. Around her, colors had deepened like wet cloth, dusted over with shadow by evening's approach. She rose slowly to her feet, probing the jungle with eyes and ears and nose for any sign of the big life-form detected by the scan. She felt as though her attention might cut her, it had narrowed so pointed and sharp.

But, of course, she heard and smelled and saw nothing—the bioscan picked up on life-forms at a far greater distance than she could possibly be expected to sense. Slipping the snooze pistol from her pocket all the same, Rahel crouched very slowly to retrieve the last of her gear, all the while darting her gaze among the foliage and the shadows.

"If you're out there," she whispered, to no one but herself, "I'll find you."

The tiger didn't have to answer. She had a piece of it, intact and in toto. That would tell her everything she needed to know.

Basa greeted her inside the pachyderm's hatch, wheeling and prancing and whining with desperate delight. "Back!" He skittered dutifully away from the hatch, and Rahel scooped him up without slowing, bouncing him from hand to hand as she picked her way through the minor destruction he'd wrought on her dirty clothes. It seemed he could ferret out her laundry no matter what she did to stow it. "You've been a bad bud," she said without conviction. Basa apologized for his behavior by gnawing on her pocket flap.

The testing station AI came up without greeting her (Rahel had disabled that annoying little courtesy years ago), and accepted her slides and notes without comment. When the last sample was logged and labelled, Rahel cleared the unused slides from her pockets to make room for Basa. "I need a DNA map and search," she told the station. "Reference: Sumatran tiger, Saiah Innis." Basa slipped into his accustomed pocket with much squirming and sighing. "Primary match code: Genetic set Number 8737, New Dallas subset. Secondary code: Likely genetic combinations of Number 8737 descendants. Give me sex and age."

"Okay."

"If any results come up with human DNA, disregard them."

"Okay." The AI shuffled both samples and parameters with a string of muffled clicking. "I can have results for you in approximately nine hours, thirty-seven minutes."

Rahel glanced over the bioscans and kicked her scattered clothes into a pile. Nothing had come near the pachyderm except a string of confused birds and something ankle-high that waddled. "It takes as long as it takes. Knock yourself out."

"Okay."

"And file those samples for reference when you're done."

"Okay."

Darkness had clogged the jungle quickly since Rahel ducked inside. Sealing the pachyderm behind her, she waited in the recessed hatchway until her eyes adjusted to the dimness. A tapestry of insect songs and night wings repainted the jungle in colors of sound, showing her the path from pachyderm to outpost as clearly as any light could. Even the air that hugged her face like warm wings smelled of a new and different life than graced this world in the daytime. Rahel breathed in these secret stories and let them swell her spirit. Sometimes, when the workings of nature pressed in so close around her that she could stand at their edge and almost feel like she belonged, Rahel could believe humanity still had some useful place in it all. Besides scrambling to repair its old mistakes, that is.

She punched up the latch-lock at the outpost door, and pulled a severe frown when the hatch slid obligingly aside. That little dance of technology combined with the stark white interior to sever her connection with fleeting native peace. Once again, Rahel's stomach burned with a hatred of all things human, and Basa picked up on her rage just enough to growl at Wels when they found him in the rec room.

The prelate, seated on the edge of one of the empty work desks, jerked his head up at the sound. A cool, cynical smile curled his lips, but honest fear flashed across his eyes as he asked, "Is it safe to be in the same room with him?" He aimed a slim finger at Basa.

Rahel shrugged, tugging at the dog's flopped-over ear. "Probably not." *It wouldn't be if I was him.* "Didn't I tell you to hard-lock that door?"

Wels shrugged, unconcerned. "Tigers can't work latches, Ms. Tovin. I figured it was safe enough just closing them."

"Tell that to your miners." She motioned him impatiently toward her. "So what did you do in here besides pick your nose while I was gone?"

"I didn't pick my nose." Wels slid off the desktop, the pockets of his trendy bush suit clinking with slides. "I figured that would contaminate your samples." He fished a handful of slides from each pocket and held them out to her, smiling. "Not that I found too many. I think the ones I found are good."

Rahel snorted, but kept Basa pinned with her elbow when she reached for the slides. Squirming his butt deeper into her pocket, Basa grunted with disappointment at not being allowed to make a lunge for Wels's fingers. Rahel understood his frustration.

No matter how many Wels had tried to collect, only four of the slides actually listed samples retrieved. She figured that was expected, since he'd admitted they'd cleaned up the post before leaving with the bodies. The first slide was supposed to be a blood scraping (probably useless); two others didn't look like much of anything (almost definitely useless), but the last, wonder of wonders, contained a single ebony hair.

Rahel raised one eyebrow and peered at Wels over the slide. "You're not shitting me? You really found this?"

The prelate shoved his hands into his pockets, pursing his lips in prim annoyance. "I really found it. On the floor. Over there." He pointed at a corner behind him without turning.

"It's not one of your eyelashes?"

"My eyelashes are blond."

His face had flushed coral pink at the suggestion, his annoyance quickly supplanted by good old-fashioned anger. He reminded Rahel of Basa when she took away anything he was particularly intent upon mauling. She couldn't help grinning while she pocketed the slides.

"Then pat yourself on your downy little head." She tossed Basa a couple of times, enjoying both the dog's happy grunts and Wels's accompanying frown. "If your slides match the ones I got outside, we've got a positive ID on your attacker. Which means we get to go out tomorrow with a nice nucleic acid sequence and a tag signal to keep us company."

Wels didn't follow right away when she turned for the front entrance. "Where are we going tomorrow?"

"Into the jungle." Rahel opened the hatch with one hand, not even pausing to let her eyes adjust to the dark before striding away from him into the open. "Hunting scat."

Wels had to jog as far as the doorway, then, to call after her, "What's scat?"

"Tiger shit. You're going to love it."

Rahel plugged Wels's slides into the testing station under the same parameters she'd used on her own. The AI promised to spit up some results by mid-morning tomorrow, latest. A little later than Rahel had hoped for, but the best it could do. "We can let our Colony kid sleep in."

"Okay."

When Wels finally made the short jaunt between outpost and pachyderm a little while later, Rahel let him make up a bed for himself in the cockpit, while she promised to keep Basa in back with her. Then she keyed the pachyderm's interior to reflect the jungle setting outside, just so she could feel like she was sleeping with nature even though the thickness of machine walls stood between them.

Lying on her side, staring into the foliage, she pushed Basa onto his tummy near her waist when he wouldn't settle down on his own. Slick black fronds swayed outside the pachyderm's walls, and Rahel couldn't see what moved them. Bright, tiny eyes glittered beneath the underbrush, only to blink once or twice, then vanish. Once, an invisible flock of day birds exploded into shrieking when something deeper in the jungle disturbed their sleep. Even Rahel's dreams that night were fractured by the sound of distant, coughing roars.

Three or four times before morning, Basa woke her by

dancing on her stomach and growling at things he could see beyond the walls. Whenever she rolled over to look, though, she never saw anything there.

FILE # 834287

RESULTS: MATCH TEST 1

                      RAHEL TOVIN, NEW DALLAS SAFARI 7

                      SLIDES 1418–1424

REFERENCE: SUMATRAN TIGER [*PANTHERA TIGRIS SUMATRAE*],

                      SAIAH INNIS

****

GENETIC SET #8737, NEW DALLAS SUBSET: SEE "DESCENDANT: #8737"

DESCENDANT: #8737:   99.9% CONFIDENCE

SUBJECT #55, "ARJUNA," MALE, 4 STAND YRS: 98.899% CONFIDENCE

(SUBJECT #55 TAGGED BY SAFARI 6, DAY 9. SEE RECORDS FOR SAFARI 6

FOR FURTHER INFORMATION)

Rahel switched functions on her notebook, checking Arjuna's tag signal against their coordinate map while she waited by the outpost hatch for Wels. The tiger was apparently still stationary at less than four kilometers away. That unnatural stillness intrigued her, made her ready to be up and on their way. Wels's lateness only made her want to cut off into the jungle and leave him to find his way out on his own.

Through the outpost door behind her, Basa protested his confinement with intermittent attacks on the hatch. The skitter scramble of his toenails carried to her almost as clearly as his wails. Rahel kicked back against the door in hopes the sudden boom would startle him into silence.

"Back!" she called over her shoulder when that tactic didn't work. "It's your own fault you're in there." She didn't dare leave the terrier alone in the pachyderm, not with Wels's gear scattered all over the vehicle with her own. If Basa mauled and ruined her own things out of love, she could just imagine what he'd do to Wels's. She couldn't say she blamed him, though. "Wee-wee your little heart out, bud. There's nothing in there I care about."

"I hope you're not talking to me." Wels appeared in a doorway that seemingly floated in midair. The pachyderm's open hatch was the only section of the vehicle currently unable to reflect the jungle surroundings.

Rahel snorted and hefted her pack to her shoulders. "You can wee-wee your heart out, too, if you want to. It'll probably attract the tigers." She motioned irritably for him to step down. "Get out of there and let me dog the hatch so it doesn't look like such a goddamned window."

Wels scooted obediently to one side, then stood and plaited his hair into a cap while she sealed up the door behind him. "The outside of this thing makes me feel so antsy. You've got it fit with a repulsor, don't you?"

"Yep." She turned to push past him, ready to be on her way. "It irritates most animals enough to keep them away. That way, the little birdies don't bash their little pea brains out while I've got the chameleon on. Too bad it doesn't work on Colony prelates."

Wels smiled in appreciation, then fell in step beside her. "So what with the repulsor and the chameleon, are we actually going to be able to find this thing when we get back?"

"Sure." Rahel checked Arjuna's signal again without slowing or looking behind. The pachyderm might be invisible to Wels—and maybe even to the thousands of color-blind animal eyes that overlooked it every day—but Rahel had long ago adapted to spotting it in all sorts of terrain. Like the photocells' reptilian namesake, the chameleoned pachyderm stood out against its surroundings like a silhouette cut from same-colored cloth—matching in pattern, but easy enough to spot. She focused her attention instead on the static tag signal on her notebook, frowning.

Wels matched her pace easily enough, studying the jungle all around them with interested eyes. He didn't need a testing pack, but Rahel had consented to letting him carry a charged snooze pistol, just in case he proved too stupid to graft himself to her hip. So far, he kept obediently within range, sometimes bumping shoulders with her when the rhythm of their movements fell out of sync. That unasked-for contact nettled her more than if he'd just run off into the trees and gotten killed. Rahel wondered if the Ark would pull her off this safari for snoozing Wels and locking him in the pachyderm with Basa. She got to spend three uninterrupted years in research after doing that on Resus. It might be worth an encore now.

"So." Wels broke into her thoughts with an idle, make-talk sigh. For all that his hands stayed in his pockets, he seemed alert enough, and watchful. "Are we really out here looking for tiger droppings?"

Tiger droppings. Like it was something they did by accident while trying to get from one place to the next. "Well, with such nice results off my slides, and yours yet to confirm them, we don't really need scat anymore." Rahel glanced at the tiger's signal again. "If you see any, though, you can always let me know." Christ—not even ten meters away.

"I don't know what tiger scat looks like."

"Then it's pretty pointless to ask about it, isn't it?"

A flush of brief anger brightened Wels's eyes. He pursed his lips around it and sighed. "I'm doing everything in my power to cooperate with you—I haven't even poisoned your lovely little dog, much as I've been tempted. You don't need to go out of your way to aggravate me."

Rahel fished her snooze pistol out of her pocket, trying to believe the twitching in her stomach was because she knew they were close to their killer and not because Wels's insight into her behavior bothered her. "You don't even know me." She slowed to a stop, her voice dropping to a near-whisper. "Don't tell me what I do or don't need to do."

When he took breath to argue further, she clapped a hand over his mouth to silence him. Wels's eyes narrowed, and Rahel felt his lips pull tight against her palm. Leaning close to breathe in his ear, she whispered, "Time to shut up and climb a tree."

Blue eyes widened beautifully, and slim fingers wrapped around her wrist to pry her hand away. "Where is it?" Wels mouthed.

Rahel nodded over her shoulder, deeper into the brush. It was nice to see him speechless for a change. She decided not to tell him that Arjuna's signal hadn't moved all morning, or that her bioscan didn't flutter even now. She already had a good idea what that meant, but didn't want to spoil the moment. "Get in my way now, Prelate," she said, checking the charge on her pistol, "and I'm perfectly willing to let him eat you. Nature's way, and all that. Got it?"

He scowled and stepped away to put his back against a tree. "Got it." Knuckles white, he slipped his own gun from his pocket and clenched it between both hands. "I'm kind of willing to let it eat you, too."

Rahel quirked only the slightest smile before turning into the brush to leave him alone. Sometimes, he displayed more character than she gave him credit for.

Tangled vines and rotten leaves padded her footsteps, filtering the stench of rich, wet dirt up into her face with each step. No challenging roar interrupted her approach, and she brushed heavy leaves from her face with a growing certainty about what she'd find. When the notebook said she was only five strides away from Arjuna, she looked between the trees to where the notebook pointed and wasn't the least surprised at what she found. Only that there was so little of it.

"Hot damn." She kicked the bone closest to her, and it tumbled among the undergrowth to land near the picked-clean skull.

Her pack clattered when she flung it happily to the ground. "Tovin?" Wels called from behind her. "Are you all right?" She ignored him, stuffing both notebook and pistol into her pockets while she knelt among the scattered remains.

It didn't take a paleontologist to recognize a tiger skull, given the circumstances. Vertebrae littered the ground nearby, cracked slabs of cartilage flaking to pieces between them. Few other bones remained; those that did bore the cracks and gnaw marks of various teeth. Digging through the loam where the shoulders should have been, Rahel found the thumbnail-sized chip with little difficulty. Once the dirt was blown away, she could even make out the silvery etching along one edge: ND8737-55 "ARJUNA." She pulled out her notebook to verify the signal, but a grin already tugged at her face before the code flashed greenly across her screen. Paydirt.

"What is it?" Wels had managed to get right behind her without her even knowing. She was too delighted at the prospect of leaving him and New Dallas to care.

She slipped the tag into her notebook, then reached back for her pack. "This is Arjuna's signal tag."

Wels nudged her gear closer with his foot. "What's it doing here?"

She rapped her knuckles on the skull, chuckling. "This is Arjuna. I'd say we've found your tiger, Mr. Prelate." Technicalities—everything from here on in was technicalities. She could even be pleasant without resenting it too much.

Wels watched her harvest samples from the one remaining long bone, a rib, a vertebra, and the skull. Then—for the sake of completeness, and nothing else—Rahel scanned the immediate site on hands and knees, taking whatever samples struck her as potentially useful, trying to pretend there was still some mystery so she wouldn't be sloppy. Only after she'd logged each sample, stowed them in her pack, and stood, did Wels move forward into her line of vision to frown down at the remains. "So what happened?"

She shrugged. "Something ate him." She slipped into the jungle, headed back the way they'd come. Maybe when she was finished here, the Ark would let her go back to her coyotes on Eden for more than a few weeks at a time.

"Actually, a lot of somethings probably ate him, but it was probably another tiger that did him in. Males fight over territories, and sometimes one of them dies. Not often, but often enough. There certainly isn't much else around here that can kill an adult tiger."

At this stage, she didn't much care how Arjuna died, truth be told. She knew it hadn't been Wels's people—they'd abandoned Melissa Pass more than a week ago, and Arjuna's remains weren't any older than that. The colonists wouldn't have dared call Noah's Ark if they'd already killed the tiger themselves. There'd also been no signs of traps or poisons around the remains. If nothing else, Rahel gave Wels credit for basic honesty—she couldn't believe he'd attempt something so stupid as calling for a proctor while planning to sic Colony Cops on the animal while said proctor was onplanet. Which all meant Arjuna had died from natural causes—nature, in this case, taking the form of some bigger, meaner tiger who needed more room to do his tiger stuff.

Either way, Rahel was out of here.

After all, they'd placed Arjuna at the murder sites. Arjuna was now dead. While that cheated the case of its neat little sense of closure, Rahel didn't mind. She wasn't in this job to create aesthetically pleasing scenarios; she was in it to solve them. Or, at least, to recognize when they'd been solved for her.

"So does this mean we're finished here?"

She smiled at Wels, jostling him with her elbow. "It means *I'm* finished here."

Wels fished out his pistol and handed it across to her. "I guess I won't need this anymore, then." He stuffed his hands in both pockets. "What happens now?"

"I go home." Rahel spun the pistol in the air in front of her face, then caught it between her palms. "You stay here. We never see each other ever again."

"Are you taking your dog with you?"

Rahel flashed him a curious frown. "Of course I am."

Wels smiled without turning to look at her. "Then I can live with that."

Not if they talked a whole lot more, he wouldn't. But he was smart enough to stay silent throughout the rest of their walk, so Rahel didn't have to kill him before they got back to the pachyderm.

Rahel saw the open outpost hatch through the pachyderm's chameleon, and all her pleasant feelings boiled completely away. "God *damn* it!"

Wels slammed to a stop, letting Rahel's momentum carry her past him. "I didn't—" he stammered. "It was closed! I swear, it was closed!"

"*I* closed it!" She thundered one fist against the all-but-invisible pachyderm as she rounded it. Wels's image flickered and warped at the edges of her sight, reflected through the chameleon from further and further away. "I even latch-locked the damned thing! No wonder the tigers thought you guys were easy prey, what with your god-damned glow-in-the-dark outposts and your doors that won't stay closed. Basa!" Her calls and whistles startled shrieks from the birds all around them. "Basa!"

Wels hung back near the pachyderm's nose while Rahel circled the outpost, calling and swearing. Since she'd never in all his little life left Basa alone outside the pachyderm, she had no idea what he might do or where he might go in alien terrain. This was her own damned fault for trusting in anything besides herself and her own Ark equipment.

When she pushed past Wels again, aiming for the open hatch, he called helpfully, "We weren't gone for long. I'm sure he didn't get far."

"You'd be surprised how far those stumpy little legs can get him." She barrelled through the hatch and nearly skidded onto her butt on the smooth indoor floor. "Basa?"

She noticed the ribbon of blood before she noticed the smell.

Beyond the second doorway, only the crooked smear of

red and a bouquet of tiny, bloody footprints gave any indication what had happened. Rahel shuffled two steps into the room, feet suddenly numb and heavy. A scrap of black, white, and pink lay tumbled in the blood, but she had to crouch beside it very slowly and turn it over with one finger before she could recognize it for a tiny canine jaw.

"What happened?"

Wels's question so closely matched the ones churning in her own brain, she didn't even realize he'd said anything at first. She climbed to her feet and stumbled back toward the door, trying to make her mind pin down the next steps she needed to take. But her thinking had gone as numb as her hands, and it fumbled around in her skull like a drugged bear. She collided with Wels in the doorway, frowning in confusion to find him blocking her. "Get out of my work area."

The prelate shook his head and moved to intercept her when she would have stepped around him. "We still don't know what happened to the doors. I think I should—"

"Get out!" She stiff-armed him in the chest, slammed him with both hands, and propelled him clear out to the main entrance. He caught himself in the outside doorway. She left him there, snatching up her equipment pack and retracing her steps to what was left of Basa's corpse. Every minute passing stole a data point from her chain, and she'd kill Wels for real if he squandered too much of her time.

"I could wait here with you." His voice echoed flatly from the other room. "I won't get in the way—I'll just watch the doors."

Sample slides slipped and clicked as she dug them out in shaking hands. The blood—the blood was Basa's, she was nearly positive of that. The jawbone, too. But there were hairs yet to be collected, and saliva traces, and tiny dead skin cells from the soles of the killer's feet. And the blood, too, she decided. Just to make sure. A hundred little informational bits that could be used to trap any killer in the universe, all no more than an hour old.

If only she could keep from crying long enough to harvest the samples without contaminating her field.

Rahel spent three hours in the room with Basa's remains. Everything that might possibly be useful found its way onto a slide and into her pockets. Once she was certain nothing more of value remained, she checked all through the outpost for any other exits. There were four—all still hard-locked from the inside. Only after she'd made sure of the hatches, sealed the rooms behind her, and stowed her equipment by the front door did she set about carefully mopping up the red-brown blotches crusted onto the outpost floor.

When she was done, she retrieved the only part of Basa that couldn't be sopped up with a rag. The terrier's tiny jawbone wasn't even enough to fill her palm. Cupping it between her hands to save it from any further harm, she carried it gently outside, to the trees beyond the pachyderm's nose. There, she found a sun-flecked spot among a froth of bobbing ferns—a spot with just enough twigs and leaves for a little dog to chew, and just enough dirt for digging and happy rolling. Then she plowed a deep trough with her fingers and snugged the tiny body part inside.

She could have kept the jaw for cloning, but she refused to do that to any creature that had been as unique and independent as Basa. She'd picked him special, the runt from a litter of live-whelped puppies, not from a list of vat-cloned blastulas. There was no other dog exactly like him, and there never would be again—he was the glorious result of the random magic of genetics, never the same trick twice. Rahel wouldn't lessen his place in life by commissioning a replacement as if he were a broken piece of equipment.

"You were a lousy little predator," she whispered gruffly. Then, gripping Basa's favorite pocket in both hands, she ripped it from her vest with a series of hard jerks. It stuffed clumsily into the oblong hole, but two handfuls of dirt packed it down well enough.

When she'd patted the dirt in tight and made the grave as invisible as her pachyderm, Rahel knew Basa was well and truly gone. Bowing her head to rest on her knees, she pressed her hands against the bulge of sheltering earth, and cried.

The pachyderm's interior was leaf-cluttered and sun-splashed, just like the jungle outside. Rahel paused inside the hatchway, caught off guard by the exterior display when she'd wanted the comfort of human-made darkness. She couldn't remember if she'd left the walls reflecting the outside, or if Wels had called up the display in some misguided effort at sympathy. Either way, it wasn't what she'd hoped for, and left her feeling all the more angry and out of control.

Tossing her pack onto the seat in front of the test station, she dug into her pockets for two attack sites' worth of slides. They piled onto the station with a great sliding clatter, one careful handful at a time. The AI beeped in welcome, lighting its screen in response to her presence.

MATCH TEST 2
** JOB ABORTED **

Gene lesion load: Structural-5/Regulatory-8
Primary viability default: Collagen a-chain truncation;
                               helix formation prohibited.

Speculation: Post-mortem embryonic sample;
                              Severe teratogenesis
Recommendation: Reharvest and reevaluate

Staring, Rahel touched a finger to the newly wakened screen, flipping past pages of supposedly helpful text to study what charts it had compiled from the actual spins.

"It said that when I got in. I didn't touch anything."

She looked for Wels's voice over her right shoulder. He

sat in the pilot's seat, the chair turned toward the rear of the craft instead of toward the front. Catching sight of the jungle through the viewport behind him, Rahel wondered if he'd spied on her private burial. The apologetic stoop of his shoulders told her more than she really wanted to know.

Cheeks burning with embarrassment and walled-up tears, she turned back to her AI and her samples. "What was I running?" Right now, the bands of color and rows of numbers refused to punch through the cotton webbing of her brain.

Wels boot heels clicked quietly on the deck as he came down to join her. "My samples from inside the outpost." He appeared at the edge of her vision, chewing on his lower lip. "What does it mean when it says that? It didn't do that when you ran your samples."

Little by little, the dim wrongness she sensed in the spins congealed into almost-recognizable chaos. She pulled up the results from her first set of outside samples, then split the display to run those spins alongside Arjuna's file and Wels's indoor samples. Sandwiched between clean bands of tiger DNA, the aberrations in Wels's samples leapt out like lightning in a stormy sky. Her shock dissolved under a wash of slow amazement. "Oh, hell . . ."

"'Oh, hell' what?" Wels fidgeted unhappily, jittering with apprehension. "What's it saying?"

"It's saying your slides probably came from aborted fetal tissue that lay around for a day or two before we sampled it." She made the station spit up Wels's slides. "Which is bullshit. Fetal tissue never attacked anybody, and fetal tissue doesn't have hair."

Wels glanced down at the hair sample she tossed to the desk in front of him. "So did I ruin the samples? Did I collect them wrong, or something?"

"No. It isn't you." Dumping the tiger files, Rahel set the station on searching up a whole new data pack.

"Then what's the matter?"

"What's the matter is, your samples don't have Terran DNA."

Frantic AI prompts reflected in the prelate's blue eyes. "Meaning?"

"Meaning"—Rahel fanned out her slides on the station, picking through them like a hand of cards—"whatever killed your miners isn't Terran native, and it didn't come from Noah's Ark."

"Oh, my God . . ."

"Yeah." She started flipping the slides she needed from one hand to the other. "Oh, God."

The AI said it would need two hours to verify whether or not Wels's samples contained New Dallas DNA. Forty minutes of that, of course, would be loading and sorting the Ark's New Dallas genetic data for comparison. Twenty-three hours after that, Rahel could pull a specific species match and know for sure what they were after. Until that time, Wels seemed determined to pace the pachyderm from stem to stern, blurting questions to which Rahel didn't always know the answers.

"Is this outside our Charter with the Ark? Are you obligated to see this through?"

"I'm not obligated to do shit, but I'll stick around long enough to sort everything out."

"Is this the same thing that killed your dog?"

"I don't know, Wels. Shut up."

"Can we still relocate this thing once we find it?"

"Wels, you ask me one more goddamned question, and I'm gonna hang your skinny ass out the door and drag you halfway across the continent!"

That shut him up, at least, and gave her a chance to check New Dallas's indigenous records for large predators before crawling off to bed. Wels's pacing about nervously wasn't the same as having Basa around to grumble and chew, but it beat the hell out of Wels's fretting out loud. Rahel floated into sleep that night frustrated by her fruitless search, and missing the warm little body that used to snore against her hip.

She jerked out of a sleep made nonexistent by lack of dreams to find Wels's white face hovering in front of her in the dark.

"I'm sorry to wake you." The jungle still filled the pachyderm wall behind him, looking as wild and restless as his sleep-tousled braids. "But there's something outside."

"This is a jungle. There's always something outside." Still, something about the rapid rise and fall of his breathing told her he wasn't just talking about some snuffling insectivore or a drape of overlarge fly-by-nights. So far, Wels had been a lot of things, but he wasn't a coward. "Okay . . ." She kicked off her covers and swung her feet to the deck. "Show me."

He padded barefoot into the main compartment, where the display walls offered the widest view of the unbroken jungle. Rahel stumbled to a stop next to him, rubbing the sleep from her eyes. He ducked a little to point beyond a webwork of strangle vines. "There," he whispered. "It comes and goes."

She couldn't see anything in the dark—not that she'd expected to. Leaning around him, she tapped the AI awake. "Night-sight. Light enhancement." She didn't know why she was whispering. Probably because Wels was. It wasn't as if anything outside the pachyderm could hear them. "Okay."

Dawn seemed to flash across the walls, sweeping detail through the outside display. Leaves and limbs and ground clutter suddenly sharpened to an intricate black-and-white, carving the nighttime jungle in images normally reserved for animal eyes. Peering into the grey-shaded chaos, Rahel forced herself to see what was really shaped by the patterns, not just what her lazy eyes would tell her. Even so, she might never have spotted their visitor against the jungle if it hadn't stood and moved.

When it broke cover to trot a few steps closer to the

outpost, something about its stiff-legged gait punched Rahel
in the stomach with dizzy recognition. It was Basa, she
thought. The same fidgeting feet, the same eager shake of its
head. Then she noticed the heavy, square muzzle, the trim,
rounded ears, the flat back and misjointed limbs, and she
wondered how she could possibly have mistaken this
waist-high monster for her little three-kilo terrier. Light-
gathering eyes—forward-facing and nearly as big as her
palms—flashed fluid and white when it scanned the artificial clearing.

"I'll bet it sees us."

Wels scowled at her, one eyebrow arched with skepticism. "All the way in here? I doubt it."

Rahel grinned despite herself. "I don't mean *us*—I mean
the pachyderm. With eyes like that, it's got to have kick-ass
night-sight." She turned to watch it stalk around the
pachyderm's nose. "Looks like an all-around good design."

Wels kept tight to her right shoulder as she moved. "What
is it?"

"Haven't the faintest." She crossed the pachyderm to
press her nose to the wall beside the hatch, watching their
visitor sniff around the closed outpost door. "External
visual: Give me an ID on that thing against New Dallas
indigenous life."

"Okay." The AI's conversational tone sounded suddenly
loud in all the quiet. "I can have a visual match in five
minutes seventeen seconds."

"Go for it."

"Okay."

Wels kept his questions and comments to himself while
they waited for the AI's results. Rahel stayed as close as she
could to the display wall, drinking in every hair and muscle
on the creature; she felt like she'd been drawn out into the
darkness beside it, close enough to hear its snorts and smell
its hide. Flat nostrils whuffled nose-prints back and forth
across the outpost hatch, and camouflage shadow-patterns
swirled over the shoulders and squared-off hips. Grey and

black, she guessed. Maybe brown. Its rump rounded off to a tailless slope, and the joints on its rear legs bent forward instead of back, unlike most Terran quadrupeds. In keeping with its leg structure, all four feet splayed flat to the ground, heels and toes pressing handlike prints into the grass. Rahel focused on the four blunt digits, studying how the toes gripped the outpost walls when the creature climbed into an awkward standing position against the hatch. Fascination clung to her, right up to the point when the creature closed clumsy fingers on the door's locking mechanism and deftly punched up the "open" code. Her skin chilled clear to the bottoms of her feet.

"Oh, shit!" Wels slammed both hands against the display beside her, swearing at the creature's reflection dropped again to all fours and as it disappeared into the outpost. "How did it do that? How did it know how to do that!"

Rahel didn't know. She didn't care. All that mattered now was that she suddenly knew precisely what kind of thing had killed her dog. Shoving back from the wall display, she turned and darted up into the cockpit.

"Where are you going?"

The AI interrupted with typical bad timing: "Results: I'm unable to find a visual match for the subject outside the pachyderm."

"Shut up!" Rahel aimed the command at both Wels and the AI. As usual, only the AI obeyed her.

"What are you doing?" Wels bounded into the cockpit beside her. "We're not just going to leave it here, are we?"

"Keep out of my view." She flopped into the pilot's chair and woke the external snooze gun, telescoping the turret. Glowing cross hairs appeared on the wall display, centering on the lower third of the open outpost hatch. "Come on," she whispered. "Come out to Mama."

Wels crouched behind her chair, carefully not touching her or the console. "Just what is it you're intending to do?"

"Shut up."

A flash of light, dark, then light again, appeared in the

outpost hatch. The creature's dinner-plate eyes blinked slowly against the inside darkness. "Come *on* . . ." Rahel gripped the trigger until her hand shook.

The creature slipped from the outpost with long, languid strides. Rahel's cross hairs rode it silent piggyback, sitting its shoulders like a high-tech firefly. It paced beyond the pachyderm's nose, then paused above Basa's tiny grave to dig at its ears with one hind foot. Rahel dropped it with a single pulse, but squeezed off a second shot just to make sure it was snoozed. She wished it hadn't toppled onto Basa's grave, though.

Wels nearly fell over when Rahel shoved out of her seat and ran into the back for her clothes. Her pants were still crumpled at the foot of the bunk, her boots tumbled nearby. While she yanked trousers on right over her night clothes, Wels rose to his knees and leaned over the console to stare outside. "Is it dead?"

"Of course not." She stamped into her boots, then snatched up her pack and a vidcam on the way to the door. "But I've got about two seconds to get out there and collect my samples, or we might never find out what's going on around here." The snooze would last a lot longer than that, but she didn't want to waste even a moment of it explaining anything to Wels.

Wels rolled to his feet as she hurried past. "I'm coming with you."

"The hell you are." The hatch popped open with a hiss, bathing her in wet jungle air. "You even try, you goddamned amateur, and I'll give up and leave you here with it. I swear I will." She muscled the door shut before Wels had a chance to answer.

No need to pause and let her eyes adjust to the night, not with the real-time display on the inside. Dashing across the floor of rotten leaves, she slowed to tiptoe near the creature's hindquarters. Ribs rose and fell like heavy hammer blows, and grunting breath scattered the loam in front of the thing's blunt muzzle. Rahel circled it silently, finally sinking into a crouch behind its shoulders. This way, she could at least see the pachyderm while she worked and still have a half-clear shot at running for it if she had to.

Hair samples. Tissue samples. She would have killed for detailed fluid samples, but didn't dare take the time to harvest them. The vidcam roamed from ears to tail, drinking in more information than Rahel could have hoped to gather by sight alone—from the cap of black fur between its speckled ears, down its dorsal stripe, and back across its glossy chest and sides. Its half-lidded eyes sparkled a striated amber, with no interior lid to obstruct her view of them. She'd just pocketed the last of her slides and dug into her pack for a signal tag, when the one visible pupil bloomed an iris-swallowing black, and air flooded the creature's lungs with a wakening roar.

Rahel scrambled back as the creature lurched to its feet. Too soon—it came around far too soon for her to trust that the snooze pistol in her pocket could put it under again. She dug out the weapon anyway, not intending to fire unless the creature moved on her. If it was like almost every other animal in the galaxy, it would just as soon vanish into the jungle as face a human scientist. Unfortunately, there was only one way to find that out for sure.

"Tovin!" Wels burst into existence beside the chameleoned pachyderm, a snooze pistol gripped in both hands.

The creature dropped its head and spun toward the prelate with a speed that kicked Rahel's heart into her mouth. *"No!"* Her voice sent night creatures crashing off into the jungle all around them. "Get back, damn you! Get back!"

Wels stubbornly stood his ground—

—and the creature flinched with a guilty groan, mincing backward by four unhappy steps.

"Back" was four steps. "Off" was keep your feet on the floor. "Down" he never listened to anyway.

My dog, Rahel caught herself thinking. *That's my dog!* Her hands suddenly trembled as if the snooze pistol were too heavy to hold.

The creature grumbled, fidgeting, but didn't try to move forward again. Wels's wide eyes met Rahel's over the thing's hunched shoulders. Did he see it, too? she wondered. Or did she only imagine it, caught between interrupted sleep and missing her dog? Wels's face spoke only of fear and confusion, his stiff body stance saying he wanted to take action but had no idea what to do. Rahel wished inspiration would strike and burn some special certainty into her brain. Instead, her lungs felt hot and empty, and all she kept seeing was her dog's belligerent expression and broken-down ears against a backdrop of amber eyes and patterned stripes.

"Get back in the pachyderm." She tried to keep her tone even, hoping the gentle volume would carry across the distance between them. "Just move smooth and calm, and step back inside." Wels opened his mouth to say some-thing—she didn't know or care what—and she cut him off in the same level tone. "Don't say a word. Don't try to shoot it. Just get back in the pachyderm, or we're both dead. Now go."

Nodding faintly, Wels still fingered his snooze pistol as though considering a spate of last-minute heroics. His left hand reached behind him, though, tracing the pachyderm's contours in the air. When his arm disappeared through the open hatch, he shuffled backward very slowly.

Rahel flicked her gaze to the creature when it grumbled and shifted its weight. Its front feet jigged a little dance, chewing up fistfuls of rotten dirt in anticipation. Rahel darted forward on the strength of her instinct alone. "No! Bad dog!" Wels flung himself inside the pachyderm, leaving her alone while the creature swung to face her, cringing. She scowled as fiercely as her thundering heart would allow, shaking her finger in its face. "Bad dog bad dog *bad dog*!"

Each shout seemed to smack the animal like a physical blow. It retreated from her steady advance in a panicky scrabble, finally turning to flee when its front end overran its rear and it tumbled over itself. Rahel waited until she heard it crash headlong into the undergrowth before bolting for the pachyderm herself.

At least Wels had wit enough to keep the hatch open until she got there. Rahel slammed the door, pressing her forehead against the metal and breathing deeply through her mouth to try and ease her twitching muscles. Behind her, Wels dissolved into swearing, seeming to vent her fear as much as his.

"What did I just see out there?" he finally blurted, stomping back and forth in the cramped hatchway lock. "What was that?"

"A big, huge, ugly native." The thought of volunteering anything else made her stomach knot. "I don't know what it was."

"But am I right?" He paused right behind her to lean over one shoulder. "Was that your dog? In a big, huge, ugly body, but somehow still your little dog?"

Hearing him admit that lanced new fear straight through her. She didn't like feeling so suddenly drowned by a flood of uncertainties. "Yeah," she sighed, pushing away from the door. "I don't know how, but I'm pretty sure that's at least partly my dog." Except that Basa wouldn't have known how to hide in a jungle, much less open an outpost door. There were still plenty of questions to be answered.

Sliding down the wall to squat on the floor, Wels groaned with shaky laughter. "I don't think I'm going to enjoy this. He didn't like me very much the first time around."

Rahel snorted, sliding past him to dump her gear on the testing station. "If even half of what I'm thinking comes up true, Wels, he's gonna like both of us a whole hell of a lot less."

Rahel didn't get back to sleep that night. Wels surprised her by catching another five hours in the cockpit—she hadn't given him credit for such steady nerves. Or maybe he just wasn't used to keeping screwy hours.

The AI spit up its match test results a couple of hours

after their midnight visitor disappeared into the trees. "No Adequate Genetic match on file." Small wonder. Rahel spent nearly an hour flipping through all the test results, drinking in details along with cups of lukewarm coffee. Wels's sample slides from the outpost were definitely of New Dallas origin, but the Ark had nothing on record to match those genes.

Nothing? She snorted and set the station on comparing her samples from Basa's attack site with the results of Wels's match test. How in hell could Noah's Ark survey an entire biosphere and manage to miss something as large as this predator? Could it be there was only the one? Then where the hell had it been all this time?

"Split screen. On one: Display full-body still of last night's intruder."

"Okay." After a moment, the AI gave her a full-body shot—color adjusted for daylight viewing—of the thing snoozed-out on the ground for sample taking.

"No, no—give me one of it standing up, moving around. I want it to look like it's alive, for crying out loud."

"Okay." This time, the creature was caught in mid-stride as it paced beyond the pachyderm's nose, huge eyes glowing.

"Better. All right—On two: List and queue all still visual records on New Dallas carnivores that aren't obviously reptilian, aquatic, or avian. Display in descending order, by size. I'll page through them manually."

"Okay."

Lots of variety, lots of lovely examples of how any ecological niche might be filled, but none of them resembling Rahel's new-found predator in even a cursory manner. And none of them, really, suited to be capstone predator in New Dallas's jungle environs. That's why Noah's Ark had agreed to seed the tigers—lots of prey, not much competition. Rahel wondered if anybody had ever put much thought into the *whys* of the New Dallas food chain, instead of just the *whats*.

Although, come to think of it, the *whats* were the major problem here.

By the time she got down to a voracious little predator slightly smaller than a Terran shrew, Rahel was ready to start all over again, this time with the healthy prey population. Maybe looking at what there was to eat would give her some ideas.

Wels interrupted her partway through by rolling awake and groaning at the light. "What time is it?"

"Dawn." Rahel glanced at the chronometer above the station. "A little after. I left you some food in the back."

He grunted a reply, then shuffled past while knuckling sleep from his eyes. Rahel pulled aside the records for the current continent and started comparing picture to picture, spin to spin. Wels reappeared just as she started the comparisons again, this time among the species most populous around Melissa Pass.

"Jembels." Wels grinned, recognizing the spindly legged herbivore on the station screen. He leaned back against the doorway to the cockpit and swept his unbound hair over the front of one shoulder to finish brushing it. "I can guarantee that's not what attacked us."

Rahel flashed him the corner of a scowl, not turning her attention from the screen. "How would you know? You're a city boy." She brought up two more samples, and the spins lined up exactly as she'd thought they would.

"City boy I may be," Wels allowed. "But the jembels are also getting pretty citified." He tossed his brush behind him into the cockpit, then set about separating his hair for braiding. "There must be a billion jembels in the Colony quarter alone. They even come into Colony Central and trample our flower beds."

Thoughtful, Rahel spun her chair to watch his fingers whisk his hair into a tight rope. The braid coiled as it grew, its own little DNA helix of blondness and length. Suddenly conscious of the tightness in her neck, Rahel rubbed at the back of her shoulders with a sigh.

"I'm not a scientist, but . . ." Wels sank onto the cockpit steps, finishing off his braid by wrapping it into an out-of-the-way bundle at the nape of his neck. "I've been thinking."

Rahel smiled a little, chasing away thoughts of DNA and tigers. "We don't have a corner on thinking, you know. We just do it better than you."

Settling back with his hands around one knee, Wels didn't smile back. "That thing we saw last night— It remembers stuff about the other animals it eats, doesn't it?"

Serious time, then. Rahel nodded, straightening in her chair. "Something like that, yeah."

"Well, here's what I'm thinking." He pursed his lips and frowned thoughtfully. "One of the tigers from Noah's Ark killed and ate Del Harbin." He flicked blue eyes up at her. "You found enough physical evidence at his murder site to prove that, right?"

When she nodded, he echoed the gesture, his gaze fixed in the imaginary realm of thought. "Okay. So then our new monster comes along. It eats the tiger, and because of that it remembers that people taste pretty good. So it eats one of the miners, and suddenly it knows how to break into the outpost and eat everybody else. Including your dog. You following so far?"

Rahel was beginning to sense where this was leading. "Considering you're only just making this up, I'm interested. Go on."

Wels shrugged and settled back against the steps. "What happens if we feed it something else? Like a rabbit, or a herd animal?"

She acknowledged the suggestion with thoughtfully raised eyebrows, rocking back in her own seat. "It might just decide it only wants to chew on carrots and trample marigolds." She nodded. "Not a half-bad idea, actually. But why hasn't it happened naturally? What's the damned thing been eating since your miners?"

Wels frowned. "I don't know," he admitted. "Maybe nothing. What does it eat normally?"

"Don't know. The Ark hasn't ever heard of it before. But I'll take a guess." Rahel swung around to tap a finger on the AI screen behind her. "The jembels."

Wels pushed to his feet to stand behind her, face blank with surprise. "What suggests that?"

Rahel combed her own dark hair away from her eyes, wishing she'd thought to shower before putting in her all-nighter. "When the Ark initially surveyed New Dallas, they listed a moderate but healthy jembel population— nothing like the numbers my AI gives me now, and nothing approaching what would be needed to push jembels down into Colony Central. I just figured jembels had suffered a population explosion. But look at this—" She magnified the jembel spins already on the screen, peering back at Wels to gauge his reaction.

"By now I know that those are DNA." He leaned so close over her shoulder she could see the pale stubble on his cheeks. It was a little strange to think of Wels unshaven.

"They're graphs of DNA spins." She tapped the screen, drawing his attention to the three striped diagrams in front of them. "See anything different from this one, to this one, to this one?"

Squinting, Wels leaned in far enough for the screen light to tinge his hair with grey. "No."

Rahel smiled. "That's the point." When Wels angled a frown at her, she stabbed a finger at the screen again. "Three different jembels, but almost identical DNA. You hear all about this in genetics classes."

Wels shook his head, straightening. "What's this got to do with our problem?"

Rahel turned her chair again to face him. "This sort of genetic closeness in a species usually means that, at some point in the past, that species was within a few animals of extinction. With only a handful of progenitors to choose from, the gene pool boils down pretty quickly to the two or three DNA combinations that are actually any good. You end up with a new population of animals who are closer in gene-type than most brothers and sisters."

"The punch line?" Wels asked.

"A good third of the prey animals on this continent exhibit the jembels' genetic closeness."

He frowned, toying with one earring. "I still don't understand."

Rahel clapped her hands to her knees, sighing. She knew he wasn't trying to be stupid—he was just a politician, he couldn't help it—but finding words to explain this to him wasn't proving easy. "Okay, let's play make-believe. We've got evidence that a large part of this planet's zoology has come very close to extinction at some point in the past. The proctors who first surveyed New Dallas guessed that some sort of natural disaster must have stressed this ecosystem to the point of near collapse—earthquakes, fires, plagues, something—and thus almost wiped out a lot of the life here. But what if it wasn't any of those things? What if their natural disaster was our predator?"

Wels pulled back with a skeptical scowl, crossing his arms over his chest. "*One animal* could do all that?" He paced back to the steps and sat. "Give me a break."

"Not one animal," Rahel admitted. "But I'll bet a decent population of them could."

"We don't have a decent population of them."

"Maybe we do." She stood to stretch her arms over her head. "Where did the one that's terrorizing you guys come from? Why didn't any of the Noah's Ark safaris ever notice them before?" She shrugged and swigged the last of her coffee. It was hopelessly cold; she spit it back into its cup. "What if they prey on an ecosystem until they almost destroy it, then go into hibernation or something until the prey populations can renew themselves? That could take years and years, both ways."

Wels watched her head toward the bathroom stall, stripping out of her vest and boots on the way. "Does this mean you think I'm right—that feeding it a jembel or two might fix things?"

"It means I think it can't hurt." Lifting up one foot, then the other, she yanked off her socks and tossed them randomly toward her pile of laundry. She quelled an automatic impulse to hide the laundry from Basa. The little blossom of grief that followed left her wondering if, after all these years with the dog beside her, she would ever get used to having him gone.

"All we have to do now," Wels called as she stepped into the stall to finish stripping, "is figure out where to get a jembel."

Rahel cracked the door to throw her pants back at him. "Oh, for God's sake, Wels—the way you talk, we should be able to run outside and stumble over one."

"True."

"So what we really have to do is figure out how we're going to find the damned predator." The first burst of water felt fine and hot. "I didn't get a chance to tag it last night."

Wels waited for the water to stop before yelling, "I've thought of that, at least." When she didn't answer right away, he added, "I'm just full of surprises, aren't I?"

Finished with her soaping, she yanked the water on again to rinse. "So it would seem. What's your plan?"

"You're not going to like it."

"I don't like anything about you, Wels. How bad can it be?"

"You might be surprised."

He was right—she didn't like it. But it made a certain amount of sense, and she had to grant him that.

"You can't blame me," Wels pointed out while they hauled the dead jembel back to the pachyderm. It hadn't taken more than an hour to find a herd worth gleaning. "It's not my fault the damned thing thinks it's *your* dog."

Damned if he wasn't right about that, too.

Back at the pachyderm, Rahel talked Wels through the

short list of things she most wanted him to remember. She made him practice telescoping and shooting the snooze cannon, and told the AI how to get Wels and the pachyderm back to Colony Central without her.

"But don't wake up the cannon, don't come outside, don't do *anything* unless that thing comes for me. And then *all* I want you to do is snooze it and get out of here." She hefted the jembel to her shoulder, its horned head flopping limply against her back while she pocketed a tagging gun. "The Ark can send somebody to fetch my pachyderm and my records."

Wels followed her as far as the pachyderm hatch. "Can I at least retrieve your body? I hate like hell to imagine that thing pretending it's you."

"I hate even more to think it might end up being you." She opened the hatch one-handed and stepped outside. "You just leave my body and get. There'll be nobody to report this if it kills both of us, and that'll make this whole damn safari a bust." Peering at him severely, she pressed, "Now, I know it's hard to tell the truth when you're a politician, but you either promise to leave me if it comes to that, or I'm taking us both out of here now."

He drummed slim fingers against the edges of the hatch, his brows tied into fretful knots. "All right," he sighed at last. "I promise."

Politician or no, she decided to take him at his word, and let him close the door.

Sunlight cut a ragged swatch out of the jungle, bleaching the grass in the outpost clearing a flaxen to match Wels's hair. Rahel paced clear of the pachyderm with the dead jembel warm and heavy over her shoulder. Their alien predator had returned to the outpost at least twice now — whether driven by memories of food or by memories of human companionship, Rahel couldn't say. She only knew that the thing she'd encountered last night was at least partly her dog, even if it was also partly something else. If Wels was right, that meant she also had some control over it.

At least, as much control as she'd ever had over Basa.

Stuffing fingers between her teeth, she loosed a whistle loud and high enough to shiver the leaves on the trees. She gave Basa a chance to answer, and the jungle a chance to recover, before whistling a second time, louder. Quiet gathered around her while native chattering and rustling died away. "Basa!"

Buzzing carrion flies crawled from the jembel's carcass onto her cheek, tickling her hairline, tasting her sweat. Rahel swiped at her face and realized her hands were shaking. *Not good,* she thought. *Dogs can sense fear.* Then, feeling a hysterical laugh coming on, she fought the impulse down. If she'd known she was going to be out doing something stupid like this, she'd have made sure she got some sleep last night.

"Basa!"

The creature barrelled out of the undergrowth with a great cracking and crashing of branches. Rahel stumbled back a few startled steps, fear swelling inside her until it crowded out all breath and thought. When the thing skidded onto its rump in front of her, a dense curtain of heat and body odor swarmed around her. It all felt so weird and wrong; Basa's breath had always smelled like dog food.

". . . good dog . . ." Her voice, tight and breathless, sounded like a prepubescent choirboy's. "Good bud." The creature gazed up at her with eyes as flat as cracked glass, its tailless hind end quivering. Rahel couldn't have fit both her hands around its muzzle, yet she still found it queerly easy to slip one hand along its skull to rub at the back of its ears. "There's a good boy."

Its fur felt soft and slick beneath her touch, not at all like Basa's short, stiff coat. Working her hand along a cording of thick muscle, she reached up to her shoulder with the other hand and dragged the jembel forward. "You want a yummy, bud? God, I hope you want a yummy." Basa certainly didn't know how to hunt—she hoped this thing was starving.

It jerked nervously away when the jembel thumped to the

ground. Rahel lowered her hands slowly to her sides, trying not to jitter with anxiety. "Come on, dummy. Do you want to eat or don't you?" She crouched to slap the jembel's flank. "Lunchtime."

Basa's quirky expression of interest—head cocked, one ear upright, one ear down—looked perverse on the massive features. It minced forward again to snuffle the carcass. Reaching for its scruff with one shaking hand, Rahel fumbled for the tagging gun in her vest pocket. "Yummies, bud," she whispered. "Eat up."

It didn't even flinch when she injected the tag beneath its skin. The crack of its teeth through bone, though, brought a growl up through its throat too deep and liquid to belong to Basa. Rahel jerked away, gasping, and startled them both. The eyes it rolled up to glare at her seemed wider than before, but still oddly doglike and frightened. She remembered Basa the one time they'd fought over a slab of raw steak he'd stolen from the Ark commissary—she'd managed to take the meat from him, but not without earning a five-centimeter tear in her hand. She shuffled backward slowly, torn between whether she should encourage its ill behavior or somehow discipline it.

The creature saved her from a decision. Sinking its teeth into the jembel haunch, it scuttled awkwardly backward, still growling. The limp little body dragged a trail through weeds and grass on its way toward the trees. Rahel put her own distance between them, not stopping her backward drift until she collided with the chameleoned pachyderm. By then, the creature had vanished into the jungle with its dinner, leaving only the agitated plant life to wave a silent goodbye.

For a long while after it left her, Rahel stayed pressed to the pachyderm, staring after the monster. She just couldn't make herself go back to Wels, not with guilt raising such a ruckus inside her. Wels might be right, after all. The jembel might just do the trick, and their predator might soon retain no memory of Rahel Tovin or her little Jack Russell terrier.

As close as that was to letting her dog die all over again, it seemed only right she stand silent vigil for as long as she felt it safe.

The sun crept slower across the sky that day, dragged at by both the hungry jungle treetops and Rahel's impatience. She fought off insanity by inspecting and filing every scrap of data they'd collected on the creature so far, noting videos and stills while Wells paced around the cockpit and fidgeted by the front viewport. She listened to the crisp metronome of his boot heels and his long, fretful silences until she thought she'd have to hamstring him just to make him sit down. Instead, she took pity on his frustration and cleared the pachyderm walls for an outside view. He responded by pacing to the rear of the ship and stretching out on the bunk with his head propped up on one hand, staring out at the jungle.

Rahel poked through a clatter of sample slides at the station. She had to give Wels credit for not jabbering at her the way he had yesterday. He was a politician, after all, used to being able to change things whenever he wanted, make things happen, know whether or not he'd won a battle just by the climate in a room. Taking things at Nature's pace was well outside his range of experience. She wondered if she ought to suggest he go camping more often.

"How long before we go looking for it?"

Rahel glanced up from her marking. "We give it a chance to come looking for us first. If it still thinks it's a tiger, it's probably nocturnal anyway. And if it thinks it's Basa . . ." She turned back to the AI, suddenly embarrassed. "If it's Basa, it'll come back here looking for me. How else is it gonna get food?"

She heard Wels stir on the bed, mussing the covers. "Is that what we're going to call it?"

She looked over her shoulder to find him rolled over to face her. "Is what what we're going to call it?"

"Basa." He pushed up on his elbows. "We've got to call

it something, and I haven't heard you suggest anything better." His shrug bounced the bunk more than him. "Why not call it a basa?"

Rahel surprised herself by blushing. "Sure." She nodded stiffly, not really wanting to talk about this right now. "Why not?"

Apparently sensing her discomfort, Wels went back to watching the jungle, not talking again until long after sunset.

By that time, Rahel had entrenched herself far away from him in the cockpit, wearily eyeing the darkness for some sign of movement. She hoped nothing came—she hoped the basa was out somewhere bounding through underbrush and trampling marigolds.

The basa, however, seemed determined to disappoint them.

"Here it comes." Wels crawled to his knees on the bunk, both hands pressed to the wall display like a little boy with his first hologram. Rahel moved quietly up behind him, caught again by the illusion that silence was a necessity.

The basa trotted into the open and halfway around the clearing before some sound or memory seemed to confuse it and brought it to a stop. Whistling a puzzled, doggy sound of distress, it bounded to the outpost and danced to a stop in front of the closed hatchway door.

"Don't open it," Wels whispered, tapping his fingers on the display. "Please, don't open it."

Some infinitesimal adjustment rippled through the basa's muscles, and the eager, doglike brightness receded. Rocking upright, it manipulated the lock and pushed the heavy door inward. As it disappeared inside the building, a lonely, canine wail echoed through empty halls.

Rahel swore and kicked the side of the bunk.

"It didn't work." Wels sank onto his heels, his expression numb. "I don't understand. Why won't it take the jembel memories?"

Rahel scrubbed her hands through her hair, feeling stupid

and slow and disgusted. "Because the basa's a predator, and the jembels are prey."

He twisted a startled look back at her. "What do you mean? That this thing only kills and eats other predators?"

She shook her head. "Just that it only remembers what it learns from other predators." God, it made so much sense, she could slap herself for not seeing it sooner. "Depending on how long these things hibernate, a lot of things can happen in their environment. If they wanted to find a successful niche real soon after coming out, they'd have to short-cut trial and error. So they munch a couple of whatever's currently the dominant predator, absorb what that predator knows about the current environment, and bang! Instant top of the food chain." She paced to the back of the pachyderm, drumming her hands against her thighs in thoughtful rhythm while the basa slunk away from the outpost to disappear, howling, into the trees. "They must go back to hunting prey after that; otherwise the jembels would take over and the basas would leave behind an environment with no predators when they went back into hibernation. It hit the tigers this time out because the tigers were the biggest predator around. Dammit!"

Wels scooted around to sit on the edge of the bunk. "If they only remember what predators tell them, then why do we have this problem to begin with? Tigers eat other animals, not people."

"Yeah, but the tiger this thing ate had already eaten Del Harbin. Remember?" She paced up into the cockpit. The whole pachyderm now seemed suddenly small and restrictive. "The basa may very well believe that people are all the New Dallas predators eat nowadays." She paused at the front viewport, listening while the basa's wail faded with distance.

"Except?"

When she turned to scowl at him, Wels rose and walked halfway to the cockpit. "I hear an 'except' in your voice. What is it?"

A politician, she reminded herself. "Except people are predators too, Wels. Only the thing we prey on the most is each other."

With people once more in the equation, Wels's leadership habit bubbled to the surface again. "So unless we figure out how to reeducate it, this thing is going to go around looking for other humans to eat?"

"Seems likely, yeah."

"Well . . ." He clenched his teeth and crossed his arms, straightening with sudden certainty. "Then I can think of one way to solve this right now."

Rahel leaned back against the console, unimpressed with his decisiveness. "We're not going to kill it."

He exploded into a sigh of frustration, slamming the heel of one hand against the testing station seat and sending it into a mad whirl.

"It was here first, Wels," she said, anticipating his next flurry of predictable, politician questions. "It owns New Dallas more than we do, and I'll be damned it I let you take the kind of liberties you're suggesting just because—"

"Dammit, Tovin, we're talking about *people* here!"

"We're talking about *animals*!" She shoved away from the console, down the steps and into his face before he could do more than jerk back in surprise. "People are *animals*, just like anything else! We think we've got more rights just because we have a bigger brain case, but we're wrong! If anything, we gave up our rights to fair treatment when we killed the last passenger pigeon!"

He shook his head, concern carving a furrow between his elegant brows. "If you really believe that," he said, very quietly, "then you're less human than that thing out there."

"Yeah . . ." This coming from a man whose very profession formed a menagerie of all that was human and vile. "Yeah, maybe I am." *And thank God for that.*

She swung about and found his sleeping gear stuffed into one corner of the cockpit. Wels didn't catch it when she threw the bundle at him, but she slung his spare clothes after without even giving him time to gather the scattered bedding.

"What are you doing?" he cried, snatching a shirt out of the air.

Rahel muscled past him to fling open the hatch. Jungle stench flooded the pachyderm. "Get out."

He froze, his arms loaded with his belongings. "What?"

"Get out!"

"And go where?"

"I don't care." She lunged forward to grab him by the collar and haul him toward the hatch. "Into the outpost, into the jungle." He stumbled out when she pushed him, but somehow managed not to fall. "You're the human—you decide."

"Tovin . . ." He backed into the outpost's open hatchway. Not enough moonlight penetrated the canopy to truly light his features, but she could still see the pale smudge of his face and hair against the darker inside. "You know I respect Noah's Ark, and I respect you. But what you're doing here—it isn't right."

"We'll see." She slammed the hatch, checking by habit to make sure she didn't trip over Basa, then flushed with anger and grief when she remembered that no one else shared the pachyderm with her now. "Maybe it's time we animals started sticking together."

As soon as Wels had locked himself inside the mining outpost, Rahel powered up the pachyderm and lifted clear of Melissa Pass.

"Find me a signal for all the tags from New Dallas genetic set Number 8737. Show me subject locations on my flight map, and update every five minutes."

"Okay."

She had to cover more than half the continent before she found a tiger demesne with no people within 100 kilometers. It wouldn't do to introduce another tiger who preferred eating something besides the jembels that clogged this entire continent. According to previous safaris, only six of the original signal tags still led to living tigers anyway, and one of those had been Arjuna. So she hunted out an aging female, well beyond cub-bearing years, and killed her quickly and neatly.

By the time she landed back at the outpost, the sun was tall above the canopy, and the inside of the pachyderm smelled strongly of tiger musk and blood.

Wels's voice answered sleepily from inside the outpost when she pounded on the door. "Who is it?"

Rahel snorted and kicked the bolted hatch. "Oh, for God's sake, open the door. If I were a basa, I'd have just let myself in."

A moment of silence; then Wels cracked the hatch to peer out at her. A wisp of cool air swirled between them. "You would not. I hard-locked the hatch from inside."

"Good for you." She pushed past him, scanning the interior for his gear. "Come on—we've got places to go, things to do." She wound up his bedding without asking, leaving him to grab his clothes.

Wels followed her into the daylight. "You're not taking me back to the Colony." It wasn't quite a question, but suspicion made it nearly so.

Rahel waited for him to dog the outpost hatch. "I'm not taking you back to the Colony."

"Then where are we going?"

She climbed into the pachyderm and pitched his things toward the bunk, letting them fall where they would. "Hunting."

Wels wrinkled his nose as he came through the hatch, but didn't say anything. Once he'd piled his own armload with the rest of his gear, Rahel sealed the door and waved him into the cockpit. The tiger lay stretched out between the testing station and the bunk. Even with her handling equipment, it had been a bitch getting the 100-kilo carcass inside.

"Find me New Dallas signal tag Number B-1, and plot me a point on the flight map."

"Okay."

Wels frowned as Rahel woke up the engines. "Off decimating the wildlife, I see."

"More like judicious pruning." She lifted above the treetops while keeping half an eye on the map. "Sometimes, a few have to die to preserve the whole."

He stared into her face for a long moment, the trail of his thoughts showing clearly in his eyes. "Are you actually planning to feed that thing another tiger?"

Her peace with this decision actually moved her to smile faintly. "I'll even feed it two, if I have to."

Wels jerked a look behind at the carcass, then back at her, eyes wide. "Dammit, Tovin, tigers are what started this problem! I don't see how feeding the basa more of the same is going to fix things."

She grinned, looking ahead rather than at Wels. But she knew he could see her. "Of course you don't."

Wels settled into his seat, his chin coming up in that way Rahel could already recognize as his stubborn prelate mode. "Ms. Tovin, we brought you here to resolve this situation so that my people could continue to do their jobs in safety."

Rahel shook her head, grinning. "Wrong. You brought me here to evaluate an imbalance in your ecosystem that was making tigers eat your miners."

"What's the difference?"

She laughed. "A politician, of all people, should respect the importance of fine-line distinctions." When he only pursed his lips in reply, she said, "The difference, Prelate, is that I got tricked into thinking that what needed solving here was the danger to human life. And that was all wrong. What needed solving was the imbalance. All I'm bound to do is get the basa back to eating the wildlife—which we have every reason to believe a brief diet of tiger will take care of."

"Even if it means you'll leave an entire Colony in

danger?" Anger prickled at the edges of his tone, the first hint Rahel had that he was beginning to understand.

"In a word?" She shrugged. "Yeah. The basas were here first, Wels. It's your job to get along with them, not the other way around. Stupid human arrogance is the only thing that makes you think otherwise."

Wels stared ahead at the jungle tumbling past below them. A trace of red stood out along the arch of each cheek, a legacy of the temper Rahel knew he thought himself too civilized to lose. "Noah's Ark won't let you do this."

"Don't count on that. The Ark exists to protect whatever we can of the big picture, not just single animal lives. How human beings fit into other worlds is part of that big picture. Humans took over Earth because a fluke of genetics gave them the ability to alter their environments. Well, the basa's an animal that a fluke of genetics has allowed to alter itself to suit its environment. If the tigers are going to survive here as predators, they're going to have to evolve to fit the basa's environment."

Wels nodded, very slowly, lips pressed tight with unhappiness. "And so are we."

Rahel glanced over at the flight map without answering, noting the slight movement in the basa's tag signal.

"You don't think we can make it work, do you?"

She studied Wels in silence, tried to imagine this coiffed and earringed dandy surrendering himself to the forces of natural selection. "Why should I?"

He laughed shortly, a darker, more cynical laugh than Rahel had heard from him before. "Because we really are better than simple animals, Ms. Tovin. We can think, we can change. We can do things because we choose to, and not just because Nature forces us to."

"Can and do aren't the same things." Snapping free the buckles on her safety harness, Rahel slid out of her seat. "Hold us here," she told the AI. "I've got a delivery to make."

"Okay."

Wels turned to watch her light-weight the tiger and drag it toward the hatchway. "You don't know that the basa will eat it."

"I rubbed it down with dog food. It'll get hungry enough, trust me."

"And if it gets hungry enough for people?"

She wrenched open the hatch, shrugging. "You cope."

Wels stood and joined her, taking hold of the tiger's rear end to help her heave it out the door. Then, leaning out to watch the carcass crash through the foliage toward the waiting wildlife below, he laughed sourly. "At least, I hope we cope."

She pulled the hatch closed, sealing New Dallas alone with itself. "Yeah, Prelate, I hope you do, too."

Only time would tell.

⚡Ice Nights⚡

Saiah Innis once remarked, "Any landing you can walk away from is a good landing—so long as nothing outside is waiting to make a lunch of you." Rahel herself had no time to consider this possibility when her pachyderm struck Reyson's Planet with a slamming blow that sent ship and passenger skidding across the icy surface like boiled mercury. Chip ice, blown to crystalline powder, curtained up around the ship to patter and hiss against the battered sides. Rahel had managed to wrest enough control to slow her descent to only a couple of meters per second after she'd plummeted into less-rarefied atmosphere. Belted into her seat, arms and legs pulled tight to thwart instincts to brace herself, she hoped she'd live to regret jettisoning the pachyderm from her jumpship to begin with.

Bumps and jolts stole momentum in jarring spasms, until the tail of the pachyderm languidly overcame its front and the whole craft nearly heeled on its side as it bumbled to a groaning standstill. The hull ticked and popped—Rahel couldn't tell if the ship actually shifted directionlessly around her or if she only insisted on the phantom movement as a result of the wild ride. Thinking about friction heat and damaged systems, though, she decided that out on the ice sheet might be a safer location from which to wait out the pachyderm's death throes.

Popping her safety harness, she stumbled down from the

cockpit on legs still weak-kneed from too much adrenaline and not enough time. The door to the equipment locker came open on her first bang, and she was stripping out of her boots and trousers even before her hand closed around the orca-slick fabric at the rear of the cabinet.

The suit was supposed to be one-size-fits-all, or one-size-fits-everything-reasonable, or something like that. Rahel didn't worry about it much as she struggled into the waste-elimination shorts and tried to tug everything into proper alignment. She wouldn't be able to strip down and adjust things after she was outside, but the pachyderm's alarming groans and shifts made her loathe to spend too much time analyzing the garment in here. A loud, popping buckle—in the ice sheet or the pachyderm itself, she couldn't tell—dropped one end of the craft a good half-meter and threw her against the locker. She dragged the insulation suit over her legs without bothering to straighten. First order of business was to survive; she could worry about being comfortable in the i-suit later.

The suit front sealed with one swipe of her hand, and the hood fit tight around her throat and head. Holding the breath filter away from her mouth with one hand, she used the other to jam her hair beneath the edges of the suit. The tactic only partially worked, and a few errant strands of dark bangs tickled her eyebrows as she stamped into boots, snapped on skintight gloves, and snatched protective goggles from the floor of the locker. "Power down," she shouted to the AI, fitting mirrored lenses over her eyes. The system responded by plunging the pachyderm into darkness, loss of inboard noise suddenly elevating the hiss and spittle of blown ice to a level even louder than her breathing. She snagged the pack with her testing gear by habit as she bounded out the door.

Wind caught her like a rough tiger, tumbling her to the ice and challenging her to gain enough traction to scramble farther away. Fractures and upthrusts cracked a crazy-quilt pattern in the ice around the listing pachyderm; she wedged both hands between broken plates and pushed up on all fours. If the ice plates meant to shatter and drop her ship to the bottom of Reyson's polar ocean, Rahel wanted to be as far away from the event as possible. She could always find out later how well an i-suit took to soaking.

A few hundred meters away, where the icescape was no longer jumbled and canted, Rahel turned to look back at her pachyderm and survey the damage. The wind still pushed at her, and her equipment pack bumped her hip with a numb, persistent rhythm, but the i-suit really did keep out the cold, so neither her eyes nor her lungs had frozen solid upon dashing outside. She supposed she should be grateful for such little things right now.

She couldn't tell how far back the pachyderm had actually touched down. A twisted scar of melted ice trailed the ship, its surface already milking up a glossy white as melt water refroze. Not good—that would no doubt be visible from orbit, a long, sparkling ribbon that snaked from one end of the ice sheet to the other. The Colony patrol wouldn't even need IR equipment to pinpoint her crash site, and the impacts made by her jettisoned cargo were probably just as visible.

She chucked at the ground beneath her with one heel. Ice sprayed around her leg in a twinkling of sudden diamond, whisking away on the ever-present wind as quickly as she'd kicked it up. Rahel grunted. The wind might just scour the evidence away, given the time and snow to do it. It was like a desert out here, all dunes and ripples and ghost siroccos that flashed between grey and brilliant white in the weak sun. A whole world, sketched in extremes. She tapped on the IR function in her goggles and looked down at the sleek white i-suit sheathing her hand and arm. Snow-spattered rock and ground showed up only as patchwork puzzles of nearly-black; the outline of her equally dark hand barely registered against that heatless chaos. That meant both color and insulation would conspire to render her invisible to a search, almost as if she didn't exist.

Not an encouraging thought, all points considered.

Switching back to standard visual, she checked out her lonely crash site. The pachyderm rested nose-downward in ice as dirty and rumpled as a rucked-up sheet. Steam feathered around its edges, but it didn't seem to be sinking, and the ice showed no signs of lessening its hold and letting the pachyderm go. In fact, the blossoming frost on the ship's hull looked like the possessive beginnings of ice-lock. Rahel felt the same frigid tendrils creep through her chest, playing with her breathing.

What if they didn't bother to come looking for her? What if the Colony or the mazhet only hunted down her cargo of *eisborne* coffins, snatched up what they wanted of the booty, and left Rahel alone out here to fend for herself? It wasn't like she'd given them any reason to want her back. But how would she get offplanet without their help? And who would know to come look for her here if the Colony authorities denied her arrival?

Shivering from more than simple cold, she dropped the pack to the ice beneath her and sat down on it to think how stupid she'd been to get into this mess in the first place.

When she'd landed at the Colony on Reyson's Planet yesterday, it was not quite 0400 according to her ship time. She'd squinted against the sun on her way off the people mover from the spaceport, combing overlong bangs away from her eyes. It was hard not to entertain thoughts about how Colony Central would react if she waited until her own version of "business hours" to apply for their asinine permit instead of coming over right away like this. Running these kinds of stupid errands was the only thing that ever made Rahel wish she had a travelling companion.

Not far down the street stood the real-wood building she'd been told was Colony Central. Garish, angular storefronts—most of them empty—bordered a main street far wider than the meager foot traffic required. It was almost as ridiculously oversized as the spaceport. Obviously, Reyson's Planet had thought they'd see a lot of visitors when they designed their Colony layout. The facilities looked mostly unexploited, though, an uneasy mixture of clean, well-kept façades without the friendly wear-and-tear of human usage.

Colony Square, as the spaceport mech had described it, apparently didn't exist anymore. (So much for updating electronic memories.) A sculpted artificial landscape took its place—a jumble of off-kilter slabs and water-filled depressions, surrounded by a ditch some good ten meters across. Rahel recognized it as an old-style containment habitat even before she glimpsed the pair of matched vertebrates sharing it. It was the animals, though, that actually made her slow down to take a look.

Externally, they appeared to be felids, although Rahel doubted they were of Terran origin. Both stood a good meter at the shoulder, with fine, square heads and short, nervous tails that flashed white when flicked. Velvety hides paled from sand to cream where they approached bellies and leggings, and cheek ruffs matched the thick white fur that spread across their feet between their toes. The only darker markings on them were the kohl streaks sweeping from eyes to somewhere beneath their ears.

Rahel guessed they'd been somebody's pets for a while. Midday sunlight glinted off hock-cuffs and toe rings; huge, tapered ears jingled from lobes to black-tufted tips with various sizes of gold and silver jewelry. They blinked eyes the same dusty brown as their coats, studying her without the slightest sign of interest or alarm.

"You guys are desert cats," Rahel informed them, leaning her elbows against a chest-high railing that had no doubt been put there to keep spectators from falling into the pit. "Somebody ought to tell your architects you aren't going to do much lounging around in water holes or climbing on slimy old rocks."

One of them flicked an ear. The jangle of its motion sounded like a handful of loose change.

"Not that either of you seem worried."

Someone laughed from a good distance behind Rahel. "I wouldn't bother if I were you." Rahel turned to find a pudgy older woman in a well-cut suit crossing the wide thoroughfare to join her. Although faded, her tightly curled hair was still red, her eyes still a friendly grey-green. "I think they're trained not to give up caravan secrets."

Rahel didn't waste time glancing back at the habitat. She knew the difference between thinking aloud in front of an animal and actually communicating with it. No sense encouraging some layman's anthropomorphizing just for the sake of small talk. "These yours?" she asked, hooking a thumb back at the exhibit.

"You could say that." The woman offered her hand, then seemed more amused than flustered when Rahel made no motion to take it. "I'm Meis Danoph," she said, returning her arm to her side, "Colony prelate. Welcome to Reyson's Planet."

Well, that was one thing taken care of. Digging into her field vest for the permit chit she'd gotten at the spaceport, Rahel asked, "Do you greet all your visitors personally?"

Danoph shrugged. "Only the ones I meet on my way to lunch. That isn't a lot anymore."

Glancing around, one would suppose not. Rahel handed across the permit chit in lieu of further niceties. "One of your spaceport mechs told me I had to file for a parking permit if I was going to stay planetside longer than two hours."

Danoph took the chit with a smile, thumbed on the display. "Here to do some shopping?"

Don't you wish. "Here to get a ship fixed. You guys had the closest mech 'port when my system went down." She leaned back against the containment railing, fingers drumming on the metal. "Seems a bit chintzy to charge a person for planetside parking when you're already charging them for time and parts on a ship repair."

Her insinuation was wasted on the prelate, though. "Is

this information correct?" Danoph's eyes flicked over screens of registration data.

Rahel shrugged. "Far as I know."

"So this ship doesn't actually belong to you." Danoph lifted her gaze from the chit, taking in Rahel's khaki-brown outfit, field vest, and leather boots as though only just noticing them. When she said, "You're a proctor for Noah's Ark," she made the words a statement, not a question.

"Which brings us back to where we started." Rahel jerked her chin back toward the in-progress enclosure and its bored feline occupants. "Are these yours?"

Danoph leaned a little to one side so she could peek past Rahel's narrow frame. "The habitat?" She shrugged. "Of course. The duacs, no. They're with the mazhet caravan."

Rahel remembered the daisy chain of gaudy transports taking up most of the slips at Reyson's 'port, and nodded. "Do the mazhet have to pay for their parking?"

Danoph smiled—a harmless politician smile that neither cut nor burned. "The mazhet have a special arrangement."

Somebody else always had a special arrangement. "So why are you building a shoreline habitat for some merchant caravan's desert cats?"

"Because the duacs aren't the intended tenants." The older woman folded her lips into a somewhat more satisfied smile. "And I'll bet you're wondering who is."

Rahel snorted, but took back the chit when Danoph offered it. "The thought had crossed my mind."

"Then I'll tell you what—" Danoph shoved her hands into her suit pockets in that calculatedly casual way politicians had when trying to bond with the masses. The gesture always made Rahel want to dump out their pockets to prove there was nothing really there. "Why don't you let me buy you lunch? We've got a native sea bird here that tastes like a chicken except that it's the size of a pony." She smiled winningly. "You can't come all the way to Reyson's Planet and pass up on a hesper fillet."

It was too early in Rahel's subjective morning to think about food without her stomach rolling. "No thanks."

"Then let me at least show off our latest zoological acquisition for you. You'll get your curiosity satisfied, and I'll see what I can do about your parking permit."

Never look a gift politician in the mouth. "Why do I get the feeling there's more to this invitation than meets the eye?"

Laughing, Danoph flapped the front of her expensive suit when she spread her pocketed hands in a conciliatory shrug. "Because, my dear, you're a smart girl who learned a long time ago that nothing in any world comes for free." She pulled one hand from her pocket to gesture back the way she'd come. "Shall we?"

Rahel had never actually seen a mazhet, although she'd heard of them, of course. Color swept in a garish cacophony from floor to mazhet skull, swathing a seven-foot-tall body in fabric enough to clothe a small circus. What Rahel could see of the mazhet beyond the robes and bangles looked basically humanoid, but cadaverously thin, and brown as the mud after a rain. He—she? it? Rahel wasn't sure—turned when Danoph opened the door, and huge, whiteless eyes glistened like black oil amidst otherwise minimalist facial features. Its face and spiderlike hands were the only parts of it not hidden beneath a magenta under-robe and an overlay of rainbow-striped silks and clashing ribbons. It raised one hand, five fingers spread, and the ringing of its caparisoned sleeve nearly drowned out the rapid tick-clicking of its voice.

"Is there some problem, Prelate Danoph, that you return so soon?"

The human words hadn't come from the mazhet, but from the slim human male who hurried to join them from within the mazelike collection of equipment that filled the room. Despite a head shaved to sport only a silky brown topknot, he was still more conservatively dressed than the mazhet, his simply cut outfit spun in shades of turquoise, aqua, and peacock-blue.

"There's no problem, Oro." Danoph aimed her smile at the mazhet, effectively ignoring the small man now positioned just behind and to one side of the alien. "I just ran into a friend I thought might like to see our setup."

Rahel snorted. Only in politics could you go from "stranger" to "friend" in the course of crossing a Colony plaza.

The mazhet rickety-clicked another string of pops and glottal sounds. Beside Oro, the human stood as still and impassive as marble for all that his voice radiated enough distinct emotion for the two of them. "Friendship has no place in business dealings."

Danoph quirked a little grin. "That's all a matter of syntax, I'm afraid." Then, more formally, "Oro, this is Rahel Tovin, a proctor from Noah's Ark. Ms. Tovin, meet Oro, Speaker of Prices for the mazhet caravan." She indicated each of them with a polite nod, but gave no hint that something like shaking hands would be appropriate.

Willing to live with that, Rahel instead waved toward the mazhet's human companion. "Who's this?"

The mazhet blinked its huge eyes slowly, and Danoph glanced between Oro and Rahel as if trying to gauge the right moment to intervene. Rahel waited, not sure what was so hard about this question, until the human himself finally flushed and volunteered in a whisper, "I am *dhaktu*. Ignore me."

Danoph angled her head closer to Rahel, keeping their communiqué human-to-human now that the other side had started it. "The *dhaktu* are the mazhet's translators—'the invisible voices.' You're supposed to pretend like they aren't there."

"Ah." Rahel saluted the small *dhaktu*. Leave it to people to build whatever little ego-holes they needed. "Keep up the good work."

"Ms. Tovin is here to see our cell cultures," Danoph

continued to Oro, as though the little interruption had never occurred. "She deals with things like this all the time in her work, and I thought she might be able to give us some pointers."

Rahel eased forward a few steps, leaning around the mazhet to peer at the equipment behind it. Oro slid fluidly in front of her to block her view, but not before she had a chance to identify at least two full banks of cell cloning chambers.

"This is not advised," the *dhaktu* announced in translation of Oro's clicking.

"Don't get your burnoose in a knot." Rahel ducked around the tall mazhet, pretending she couldn't recognize that its explosion of jewelry-bright gestures meant it was unhappy with her boldness. "I won't touch anything."

"You work for a company which often seeks to restrict mazhet trade," the *dhaktu* translated, mimicking Oro's strident protest. "Damage might be caused without your touching."

"Noah's Ark only restricts your trade when you try to mess with animal populations." The cell cultures ranged in age from brand new to almost sixteen weeks. Because she'd promised not to handle anything, Rahel didn't try to call up projection data on the reader. It was obvious they were shooting for a mature animal, though, and not just a sheet of organ cells.

Oro made a noise remarkably like a human sniff. "Colonies should have the right to barter with whomever they choose."

"Except for when they're bartering with goods that don't belong to them." Rahel straightened, and turned to face the mazhet. "Noah's Ark *owns* those planets, Mr. Mazhet—the Colonies we stop you from trading with only have Charters there. They don't have the right to sell off animals we seed there, and they don't have the right to bring in animals we haven't approved."

Oro cocked its head; the bells dangling from its headpiece

chimed breathlessly. "Mazhet deal in many things besides animals."

Rahel returned its comment with an un-belled shrug. "But it's only the animals we interfere with."

"Reyson's Planet has no such Charter with Noah's Ark. You cannot—"

"Look . . ." Danoph stepped up beside Oro with one hand extended as though she might touch the mazhet's sleeve for all that she didn't. The smile she flashed Rahel came no closer to making contact. "Much as I love a good debate, Proctor Tovin, I didn't bring you here to argue trade restrictions with the mazhet."

Just as well. Rahel wasn't in love with the subject, either. "Then why did you bring me?"

"For this." Danoph abandoned Oro and the *dhaktu* only long enough to rummage a nearby desktop and shake loose a wrinkled flimsy. The mazhet's immobile face looked no different than it had the moment Rahel walked in the door, but its hands had drifted up to chest height, pressed together as though in prayer except that the fingers drummed arrhythmically.

Rejoining them, Danoph shook out the flimsy and extended it to Rahel. "That's the spin from a mazhet *eisborne*." The unfamiliar DNA laddered its way up the sheet, a dark data stripe running straight and slim down one side. "We've bought the rights to clone and distribute the *eisborne*, pending success with what we're doing here."

Rahel looked up from the spin, a prescient suspicion of trouble tingling at the edge of her ever-present annoyance with humanity. "You can't just sell animals to planets like they were pieces of art."

"We won't sell them to planets." Danoph took the flimsy back from Rahel and rolled it into a tube in one hand. "They'll go to private owners."

"That isn't the point." Rahel wound her hands into fists and jammed them into her vest pockets. At the time, that seemed a better course than using them to lay into every small-minded primate within range. "Planetary ecosystems are balanced things—the ones set up by the Ark just as much as the ones set up by Nature. You can't just ship in foreign animals because you think they're exotic or cute. Ask me about rabbits in Australia."

"No, no, no—you don't understand. Pets." Danoph flashed a smile rehearsed to be both mollifying and confident. "We're selling the *eisborne* as pets. They won't be able to reproduce, and they won't be fit to take care of themselves if turned loose anywhere." Apparently taking Rahel's hateful glower as skepticism, she bent to level a hand at about knee-height. "We're scaling them down—about one one-hundredth their current size, to make them feasible as household companions. They're just too expensive to maintain otherwise."

"How do you know how expensive they are?" Rahel shot a searching glare first at Danoph, then at the mazhet. What she couldn't read on both their faces was enough to make her stomach burn. "Have you got a full-sized specimen?"

Danoph's gaze flicked sideways toward the mazhet, almost as though she hadn't meant it to. Oro moved not at all.

"The mazhet do," the prelate finally admitted. Oro creaked some broken sound that the *dhaktu* didn't translate. "Right now, we're working off specs and collected samples. We'll take possession of the existing *eisborne* after work here verifies we can get what we want from them. Within agreed cost parameters, of course."

Of course.

"The mazhet have promised us these are the only animals in existence, so no one else will be able to do what we do. We'll have a solid monopoly."

A surge of focused anger burned all along Rahel's bones, finally cracking free as words. "I'm not going to help you destroy an entire genotype just so you can supply pets to any idiot who wants one."

Frowning, Danoph said, "That's all right. I don't want your help."

Caught off guard by the prelate's confused admission, Rahel felt her insides coil the way they always did when she got cornered by anything. "Then what am I here for?"

Danoph shrugged, her hands coming primly together in front of her. "To see what we're doing, so we can show off." Another shrug lifted her broad shoulders. "I thought you might be interested."

Rahel snorted, folding her arms and leaning back against the counter behind her. "Bullshit. Anybody who wants something that simple is either stupid or maneuvering. You don't seem very stupid."

Her mask of polite attention never wavered, but the prelate at least had the honesty to blush. "I think that's rather cynical, Proctor Tovin."

Rahel grinned at her, not meaning it to seem friendly. "Is it?" She jutted her chin toward Oro. "Where did you get it?"

Danoph stirred a little uncomfortably. "Get what?"

Leave it to the politician to answer while her cohort the businessman only blinked wisely. "The *eisborne*," Rahel persisted, not taking her eyes off Oro. "The full-sized specimen you're using for downsizing and the mazhet are using to procure samples. I want to know where they got it."

Oro clicked sharply, briefly.

"That is not your concern," the *dhaktu* said.

Rahel shrugged. "That depends." Pushing away from the counter, she leaned toward Danoph with her arms still folded across her chest. "The one loophole in your plan, Madam Prelate. The Ark owns a lot of animals who are struggling as the last few of their kind. If the mazhet lifted this *eisborne* off an Ark-owned planet, that's poaching. That's stealing. That's *illegal*. We can confiscate everything you have here." She twisted a look back at Oro. "Including your full-sized original."

If the mazhet considered that a threat, it showed in neither its own muted clicking or the *dhaktu*'s translation. "It came from nowhere you would know."

"Prove it. Let me see it."

"No," Danoph interjected sharply.

Oro's single click translated simply as "Unacceptable."

Rahel tossed her hands in the air. "Then I'll look for you all on the legal net." She slipped past Danoph and the mazhet without touching either on her way toward the door.

"Wait a minute." The prelate moved quickly to cut her off, still composed and in control despite a face made almost honest with concern. "We don't have possession of the *eisborne* yet." Her voice came out low and grudgingly, as though she didn't want Oro to hear for all that the small room assured it would. "The mazhet are storing it in a neutral location until we finish negotiations—that's their rule, not ours." She met Rahel's dark eyes unflinchingly. "It isn't fair to punish Reyson's if it turns out the mazhet have lied."

"Mazhet barter. Mazhet do not lie." Oro didn't leave the rack of equipment to join them, but its body trembled with agitation, multihued vestments shivering with whispered ringing. The *dhaktu* stood in a near perfect imitation of his mazhet's stiff stance. "Noah's Ark should not be here, should not interfere."

"What's the matter, Oro?" Rahel wondered if reading emotion into any of the mazhet's gestures was any different than people thinking their cats were happy because they appeared to smile. "Don't you trust me?"

The mazhet blinked at her, black eyes glossy and unreadable. "No deal has been constructed between us. Trust is irrelevant."

"Good point." Slipping the permit chit from her pocket, Rahel flicked it to Danoph. "Well, I kept up my end of the deal—I looked at your stupid zoo project. Now you keep up yours." She nodded toward the *dhaktu* and Oro, and couldn't help scowling. "I can't say it's been a pleasure doing business with you."

The mazhet click-popped a quiet answer, and the *dhaktu* bowed almost double in reply. "May it be so before the finish."

After an hour or so of sitting out on the arctic ice sheet, Rahel finally decided the pachyderm wasn't going to sink beneath the tundra. Standing, she picked her way across the rumpled ice and let herself back inside the ship. She had a lot of things to do before she let Danoph or the mazhet find her—it was time she started doing some of them.

The pachyderm's chameleon came up without protest. She ducked outside to make sure the layer of photocells was operational, though, not willing to trust the inside readings. Confident her craft would be mistaken for another chunk of ice amidst many, she left the outside hatch hanging open while she collected what she needed of her gear. Any heat leakage from inside—not to mention the external dissipation still steaming up the cracked ice plate—couldn't be prevented, so she might just as well try to equalize what temperatures she could before walking away. With luck, nobody would search these ice sheets for at least another several hours.

She snapped on a bioscan bracelet, took her testing pack, her notebook, a snooze rifle, and the grav-dolly. She stuffed the dolly in her pack and swung the rifle over one shoulder, keeping the notebook in hand for the sake of following the signals from the cargo's tags. The closest coffin was still more than ten kilometers away. She kept the notebook tucked under her armpit in a vain attempt to protect it from the cold, and occasionally tipped her face toward the sky in case something in its dusty, watery brightness could guide her. No such luck. She had to satisfy herself with believing the notebook's instructions while threading a path among blow-holes and dunes of snow.

Trust—even of some hand-held machine and its data—didn't come easily just now.

*   *   *

She'd gone back to her ship after meeting Danoph and the
mazhet, burning to be able to slam the jumpship's sliding
hatch. Instead, she tore off her field vest and slung it across
the bridge toward the passenger's chair. It struck the edge of
the seat with a soft, unsatisfying sound, then slid into a heap
on the floor.

The Reyson's mechs had 'linked her while she was
in-Colony. They'd finished their tinkering, her jumpship
was operational, she could leave any time she chose—just
'link traffic control for clearance whenever she was ready.
Oh, yes—and they'd debit the repairs to Noah's Ark, along
with any slip rental fees necessitated by late departure. She
erased the note with a snort, not even bothering to acknowledge.

Behind that, she found a message from the mazhet. Rahel
assumed the face on the screen wasn't Oro, but didn't know
for sure how to tell. Scarlet and vermilion scarves poured in
brilliant waves from its tight, turbanlike headdress, and a
veil of woven chains and ribbons fastened at cheekbones
and nose to hide every feature but its eyes. No audio—
neither mazhet clacking nor *dhaktu* words—accompanied
the image for all that the comlink indicated a full AV
channel. Sounds of distant industry occasionally invaded the
signal, though, rumbling an unknown counterpoint to the
mazhet's silence. After some forty-five seconds or so, the 'link
was simply broken. No follow-up message had been received.

Rahel swore and erased that message, also. Let the
mazhet have their fun being mystic and alien; she had other
things to worry about.

Punching up the quick-code for Noah's Ark, she threw
herself into the pilot's chair and let momentum spin it while
waiting for her call to go through. She only made a rotation
and a half before friction slowed her to a stop.

"Impatient and angry, as always."

She kicked off with one foot, swinging the last half-turn

to face the comlink. Her mentor, Saiah Innis, smiled in a show of even white teeth. "How goes life in the land of safaris?"

Rahel didn't bother plastering on a pleasant expression for him. In the years they'd known each other, Saiah had seen her smile genuinely at least a dozen times or so. That should be enough for anybody. "People suck."

He laughed, probably the only person in the world who could do so without annoying her. "So you've told me. What is it now?"

She explained about Danoph, the mazhet, and the engineered *eisborne*. All the while, she twiddled with the jumpship's slumbering guidance controls, glaring through the ship's front viewport as though there was something there besides the various robot mechanics who whirred and fretted over someone else's repairs, running up a stupendous bill while their colonist-owners no doubt jerked the ship's owners around.

"You're sure they intend to destroy the original specimens?"

Rahel shrugged, an answer she meant to be almost as good as a nod. "They say it's too expensive to keep them, and the prelate talks a lot about preserving her monopoly. Once they've designed perfect genetic material for their midget model, what will they need the originals for?" That would mean yet another animal irretrievably erased by humanity's headlong rush for short-term profit over long-term gain.

She didn't need to say that to Saiah, though. He understood. "I don't suppose they could be convinced to sell the full-sized originals to us?"

"Not a chance. They'll worry we intend to threaten their business by designing mini-*eisborne* of our own."

Saiah's white brows slashed down into a frown. His skin color fell between Rahel's dusty olive and the mazhet's polished walnut, making his scowls impressively severe when his eyebrows came into play. "Noah's Ark doesn't work that way."

"They're businessmen." Rahel kicked the edge of the control panel, to no particular effect. "They don't care how we work."

"Did they let you see it?"

Rahel shook her head.

"Then I don't understand what you want the Ark to do." Saiah folded his arms—frustrated, Rahel knew, with the situation, not with her. "They say they didn't poach it; they aren't going to introduce it into a natural environment; they're following regulations for household pets." He spread his arms, palms up, in a gesture of hopelessness. "If they destroy the original *eisborne* genotype, it's going to be a damned shame, but the Ark can't stop them if the *eisborne*'s not a Terran animal."

Planting both feet on the floor, Rahel leaned over the console to confide in the comlink. "But it is."

Saiah reared his head back, eyes narrow with skepticism. "You said you never saw the animal."

"I didn't have to. I saw the DNA. The prelate showed me a spin—"

"They let you keep it?" he asked eagerly, and Rahel had to shake her head with an aggravated frown.

"No, they just showed it to me. For about a minute. That was enough, though—I *know* a Terran sequence when I see one."

"Oh, Rahel . . ."

She pushed upright again and scowled at him. "Don't 'Oh, Rahel' me. I'm not some first-year journeyman who's never had to sequence a spin on my own. I *know* what I saw!"

"All right, fine," he allowed. "But we can't very well get a restraining order on the strength of 'Tovin's sure about this one.' Get me facts, Rahel. Get me evidence, and I can do something."

She felt her cheeks burn with a mixture of anger and

something she didn't care to try and name. "But in the meantime you won't do shit."

"I can't." She knew the remorse in his eyes was genuine, but it still made her want to spit. "I'll check the Net for evidence of poaching at any of the Ark's planets, but if that comes up negative, there isn't much else we can pursue." He sighed, a deep, paternal sound that she'd grown used to through the years. "I'm sorry, Rahel, but the law is the law. Just like Nature, it's for the good of the overall, not the individual. You're old enough to know that. So finish your ship repairs and—"

She slapped off the 'link with the back of one hand, watching Saiah's image implode on itself and vanish. She'd cut him off enough times before not to worry about how he'd take it. Still, whether he knew it or not, he'd given her the guidance she'd needed.

"The good of the overall," she mused at the empty screen, drumming her fingers on her thighs. What if the overall was only one animal? And an individual was the only thing spanning the gap between continuance and extinction?

She locked up the jumpship so the repair mechs couldn't wander inside, then headed back for Colony Central with a snooze pistol in her pocket. "Evidence," she grunted.

Fine. If evidence was what Noah's Ark wanted, that's what they were going to get.

Rahel knew the *eisborne* had to be nearby. Danoph's people would have noticed if the mazhet were constantly hopping to some other continent, and the cost of obtaining test samples alone would have prohibited anyone buying the beast if the mazhet had stored the *eisborne* out-of-atmosphere. Realistically, that left only the mazhet caravan and the Colony itself.

The mazhet had insisted the hiding place was neutral, though, which ruled out the caravan. Within the Colony, there was only one place Rahel could think of where someone could hide something 100 times the size of a dog and not have the locals know about it—in the zoo habitat constructed to house the creature when it was finished.

She backed the pachyderm out of the jumpship's cargo bay and returned to the Colony in the middle of planetary night. The suspension coffins were in the hollow chamber beneath the unfinished habitat, just as she'd suspected. Temperature control, water circulation, feeding, and waste removal equipment filled the circular chamber. Nothing active, nothing set, just enough machinery to hint at what everything would one day be. Rahel wove between boxes and reinforcing columns, aiming for the oh-so-faint hum of electronics on the other side of the chamber.

Four silver-grey suspension coffins, in stacks of two and two standing taller than her head, were crammed against the farthest wall. She stood off to one side, trying to let as much light as possible leak in from the outside door as she felt along the chests for something familiar. Except for a flat readout screen—too faint to read in the dark, even with a pair of night-sight goggles—the coffins were identical and featureless. Most likely not of human manufacture, then. "Damn." She'd been hoping to at least identify which poachers were working with the mazhet.

Untangling a small grav-dolly from her belt, she fitted it to one of the upper coffins and carefully lifted it clear of the others. It torqued strongly to one side, and she was forced to stop and readjust the dolly in search of a better balance. That done, the path through the cluttered maintenance chamber required surprisingly little rearrangement. Apparently, the mazhet wanted to leave themselves convenient access, too.

The coffins stacked not at all neatly down the pachyderm's center aisle, two of them aligned head-to-foot, two wedged kitty-corner atop the others. Shoving the final coffin into place, she dogged the hatch, made sure the chameleon was running, and applied for launch clearance while still on her way back up to the jumpship.

Reyson's spaceport bloomed, flat and empty, at the brim of the horizon. The mazhet caravan made a ruddy smudge of the slips far to Rahel's starboard, but the rest of the field was as white and empty as a salt flat. Rahel grudgingly let the 'port automatics take the pachyderm's controls, folding her hands together into a single fist beneath her chin and waiting for launch control to give her jumpship clearance.

As she arrived at her parking slip, the 'port let her fly the pachyderm again. She eased the smaller craft past her jumpship's bay doors and bumped the hitching bolts that served as the pachyderm's dock. It clunked into place with a rough shudder, and the jumpship's comp 'linked through to announce, "Docking complete. Launch request noted. We have not received required clearance. Shall I begin pre-launch tests?"

Rahel popped her safety harness and bounced to her feet. "Do that. Buzz me as soon as clearance comes through."

"Aye aye." The jumpship's comp may have been programmed for a bit more formality than the pachyderm's, but that didn't make Rahel like it any better. "Request on queue. Pre-launch sequence begun."

Wrestling the suspension coffins out of the pachyderm proved easier than jamming them in. Rahel moved as fast as the bulky crates would allow, floating them to hitching positions and bolting them into place in preparation for a hasty launch. If she had time between securing her cargo and getting that damned clearance, she could start downloading whatever the brains in the coffins would give her. That way, even if Danoph or the mazhet showed up to thwart her escape, she would have enough data squirrelled away in her own systems to give the *eisborne* genotype a fighting chance.

Thoughts of the mazhet reminded her of the caravan half a 'port away and made her stomach twinge. "Clearance?" she shouted to the jumpship.

"Not yet."

"What's going on outside?"

A monitor mounted near the ceiling danced to life. On it, shreds of mazhet color drifted from various points of their caravan to gather together like autumn leaves around a twig. Rahel wondered if they'd received word already about what she'd done. The image was too small to tell if the *dhaktu* was among them, but who knew what other ways the mazhet had of obtaining and disseminating information.

"Shit."

The jumpship, at least, knew enough to ignore that.

"Get us ready to back out of the slip. I want to be on the field when that launch clearance comes."

By the time she reached the jumpship's bridge, the mazhet had strung a scrambled Joseph's coat of color all over their end of the spaceport. Mechs and admin robots hurried to intercept them, boxy bodies intermixed with slender aesthetes. Rahel wondered if the robots intended to deflect any sign of mazhet aggression, or if they'd just as quickly turn to help the traders once informed of Rahel's actions. She had a feeling she could kiss her launch clearance goodbye once that happened.

The first of the machine folk hadn't even come within clicking distance of the mazhet, though, when the jumpship broke through Rahel's worries to announce, "Launch clearance accepted. Prepare for departure."

Her already thrumming nerves zinged with fresh tension. She snapped into her safety harness without even bothering to seal the inner cargo bay doors. "Standard approach on first available gate." Launch pressures pushed her back into her seat as the jumpship coursed steadily upward. "Get me out of system and onto a down-and-dirty route to Eden, quickest you can find." To Eden, she sighed, and the Ark's political immunity.

Watching the mazhet recede from specks, to ribbons, to cloud-obscured visions of nothing, Rahel allowed herself a tentative pat on the back. After all, she'd managed to snatch the *eisborne* offplanet. At the time, that seemed like more than half the battle.

Then, in Reyson's lower stratosphere, the jumpship's systems failed.

The winking of a dozen scarlet lights seized Rahel's attention with a silent terror somehow more frightening than sirens. She slapped aside the monitor she'd been using to review jump gates and talked herself through a board diagnostic. Nothing came up—nothing ran. Like someone had pulled the ship's brains and forgotten to put them back in again.

Fear and anger clenched a bitter taste in her back teeth. She brought up one foot to kick the console edge so hard it twinged her knee. "They told me you were fixed." Leaning back in the pilot's chair, she drummed both heels against the panel, visions of the upcoming surface collision lending vehemence to her useless gesture. *"They told me you were fixed!"*

Yes, they did.

When the thought bloomed, she froze, both feet braced against the panel. "They did," she said aloud, and the sound of her voice startled her into standing. The 'port mechs had told her the ship was fixed, hours and hours before she even acted on her cock-and-bull plan to steal the *eisborne*. The bastards had given her launch clearance after she broke into Colony property, had held off the mazhet long enough to let her get out-Colony. Hell, Danoph handed her the *eisborne* puzzle in the first place, for no reason any politician or businessman would consider reasonable.

A new surge of fury made her punch the empty chair. Somebody had just located and stolen a commodity from somebody else, and a certain Noah's Ark proctor had been the unwitting agent. Rahel had a feeling she also knew which somebody's neck would be in the noose if fingers had to be pointed—and if she survived the crash. She wished she hadn't stowed all of her deceased terrier's dog toys in the pachyderm; she could have done with something to throw right now.

The route back to the cargo bay was short and unusually treacherous. Manufactured gravity kept her feet on the deck, but the jumpship's planetward acceleration tugged at her inner ear with images of weightlessness and falling. When she stumbled down the last ladder into the bay, she almost couldn't figure out which way would lead most directly to the pachyderm.

Then, catching sight of the suspension coffins, she veered off to take care of them first. Auto-salvage packs lined the cargo bay bulkhead, ready to be hauled down and strapped to anything smaller than a planetary aircraft. Slapping a salvage pack and a handful of signal tags onto each suspension unit, she ran for the pachyderm with the wail of atmosphere burn screaming in her ears.

Systems inside the pachyderm came up without complaint. Of course—she'd locked the pachyderm throughout most of the repairs, preventing the mechs from coming in and monkeying with anything. Besides, the silly bastards probably didn't think anyone would be stupid enough to pilot a low-atmosphere craft at higher than ten kilometers, imminent shipwreck or no. Showed how well they knew her.

"Better than nothing," she sighed, strapping into the pilot's chair and cold-starting the engines. "Pressure seal us." She hoped the AI could hear her above the growing roar from the outside hull. A sudden, gentle push against her eardrums was as good as an answer.

She patched into the cargo bay's system from the pachyderm and blew the bolts on the coffins, one by one. They'd survive the dumping, she assured herself—even human suspension units were, by definition, built to preserve their contents through almost anything short of a nuclear blast. Besides, so long as cell cultures could be harvested from the *eisborne*'s bodies, the species wouldn't truly die, so the lives of the individual animals were somewhat optional.

She didn't feel quite the same about herself, however.

I'm not going to be some stooge just so you can queer a business deal, she thought across the kilometers at Danoph.

The pachyderm shuddered as its last restraining bolt blew free. *Just see if you find these* eisborne *before I do.*

She jettisoned the contents of her bay without a single thought for her own safety. Beyond, of course, a half-formed hope that the pachyderm wouldn't shear apart under the stress and that she wouldn't end up falling to ground like the suspension coffins and their unknown, precious cargo.

Some hours later, knowing that she hadn't mated beyond recognition with the Reyson's ice sheet didn't afford Rahel quite the reassurance she'd hoped for. Maybe it was the monotonous crust of snow blurring the horizon no matter how far she walked or how high the sun climbed. Maybe it was the constant, random violence of the wind as it grabbed at her shoulders, jerked at her legs. Or maybe it was just simple exhaustion, burrowing past her stubborn resolve and finally making enough room for doubt and depression to fester. Whatever the reason, Rahel almost laughed when she reached the broken outline of the first shock ring and realized that something had gone wrong with the salvage pack. Apparently, her pachyderm hadn't made the most impressive crash landing after all.

Hopping gingerly from level to level, moving slowly forward and downward, Rahel felt as though she were following the stringer of some herculean stair. Christ—the impact site must look like a bull's-eye from orbit, the silver suspension coffin thumb-tacked all by its lonesome to the center of a dozen jagged, concentric circles. After walking all this way for the sake of retrieving her cargo, Rahel only hoped enough of the coffin had survived to yield up either data or physical samples. Or both.

She slid down the last few meters of break-up, faintly smelling a bitter mixture of burnt metal and ozone despite the i-suit's breath filter. The coffin waited half-buried in the ice, saved from having gone completely nose-down by the salvage pack still attached to one side. Rahel approached it cautiously, leery of having the atmosphere-scorched casing burn a hole in her suit. Something had skated alongside the coffin on at least part of its ride down; a palm-wide scar tore deeply into the casing, and one side of the salvage pack had been twisted loose and broken. It was a wonder the cargo hadn't vaporized on impact.

Sliding the rifle off her shoulder, she banged at the ice around the coffin with the butt. Cracks raced about the surface on her first blow, and it took only half a dozen more to loosen the coffin enough to rock it over onto its side. It landed with a less impressive crash than earlier, yet even that little more proved too much for the damaged salvage pack; it skittered off to smack against an ice spar and fall still.

Most of the coffin's control panel had shattered away, and the readout screen wouldn't waken no matter how she poked and pried at it. Plugging in her notebook helped a little. The coffin accepted the notebook as a download peripheral, but wouldn't let her override its systems through that keyboard to pop the tank. Rahel flicked her eyes across the images flashing from coffin to screen to memory, and beat back a twist of guilt. Nothing in the data stream gave any indication that the *eisborne* inside the unit had survived. She'd just have to hope the other three coffins had fared better.

Once the download was finished, she attached two different signal tags to the coffin's lid, then two more to opposing sides near the bottom to replace the ones burned off by the fall. The tags wouldn't transmit until blipped by an Ark query signal, but she'd at least be able to relocate the coffin whenever she wanted to come looking for it. Assuming she ever got off Reyson's in the first place, of course, or that the Ark ever let her return.

She worked the grav-dolly under the coffin and lifted it as gently as the rocking wind allowed. Frost snapped white splinters like demons' breath on any exposed metal surface; even the touch of her i-suited hands left shriveling dark fingerprints in the crystal patterns. She wished the pachyderm hadn't entombed itself so soon after touching ground. When it came to disposing of four suspension coffins scattered all over Reyson's arctic, even a grav-dolly wouldn't do much to relieve her from the walking and the weather and the somber, wailing white.

Her notebook map promised ocean a mere two hours' walk eastward, and, with it, the promise of sheltering water for the damaged suspension coffin. Rahel tried not to think about how far that would put her from the pachyderm while she towed the damaged coffin over gravel packs and frozen snow. She'd almost decided to just give up and bury the stupid thing in the snow, when the unmistakable stench of sea brine and guano crept through her breath mask to make her sinuses cringe.

She crested two more icy knolls before the coast itself came into view. At first she thought it completely rocky, volcanic-black boulders flecked in between with snow. Then a cry went up at her arrival, and the sea birds all rolled to their feet amid slapping wings and a sound like the rubbing of old, wet leather.

Chickens the size of ponies, Danoph had described them. Rahel paused at the edge of the hesper rookery and let the coffin bump her gently from behind. They'd make small ponies, Rahel decided, measuring only a little more than a meter and a half from head to tail, and barely able to stand on their giant, paddlelike feet. They bore the slick feathers and pinless wings of classic diving birds, and the water behind them proved it, boiling with the backwash of a hundred retreats. Good thing it wasn't clutching season, when uncounted poults would have given the hespers something to stick around and fight for.

Rahel picked her way among the few brave birds who'd stayed, guiding the grav-dolly and its coffin around old rock-and-down nests and the worst of the chalky feces. At the edge of the ice, she tipped the dolly away from her until the coffin broke loose of its own accord and plunged into the slushy black water.

"Sorry," she murmured as the bubbles sheened up in its wake, then broke and danced away. "It wasn't supposed to work out this way." As if human apologies and ill-spent intentions ever undid the damage done by human careless-ness and pride.

Out in the ocean, uncounted hesper heads bobbed on the seesaw waves, gossiping among themselves while she turned and trudged back the way she'd come.

Clashing colors enlivened the arctic horizon like crocuses braving a late-spring snow. Rahel counted nine stick-thin figures and four shivering desert cats before dropping belly-flat to the ice with her testing pack beneath her. Dammit. She'd hoped to have a chance at hiding her data before either the mazhet or Danoph arrived.

It looked like only mazhet so far—lots of flash and color, no one short enough to pass as human. Not even the little *dhaktu*. That meant the mazhet had probably savvied that Danoph wasn't exactly on their side. Rahel fingered the edges of her notebook with its contraband genetic data and wondered which side would leap to claim her if it came down to a debate.

She pumped up the magnification on her goggles and scanned the pachyderm's crash site, trying to decide how long the mazhet had been there. She'd left the site five hours ago herself, and would have been longer if the dimming sun hadn't conspired with lack of sleep to drive her back to the pachyderm and its promise of warmth and shelter. Even so, the mazhet didn't seem to have done much with the site beside land a sleek, gaudy in-atmosphere hop beyond the pachyderm's nose, and track footprints all over the refrozen landing scar.

Corkscrewing curtains of snow hissed across the tundra between them, blocking all but the clamor of alien fabric from Rahel's sight. Still, she could see enough through the blowing torrent to discern the pachyderm's blurry outline. The mazhet hadn't mistaken the chameleoned ship for an iceberg, though. They moved about it with ease, disappear-ing into its invisible image, absently stroking its camouflaged sides. It bothered her that they hadn't deactivated the chameleon. They must have recognized it for a device, and not some normal state for the airship. Humans found it distracting to try and navigate around a machine that continually tried to reflect its surroundings and hide itself—didn't the mazhet?

She waved one hand to chase the thoughts away like a pestering fly. The whole point of calling a race "alien" was so you wouldn't waste your time trying to figure out why they did things. No sense forgetting that now.

She crabbed backward to the last gravelly bank, slipped behind it to sink down on her heels. Mazhet at her homebase severely limited her options. She didn't want to wander back into Reyson's wilderness with nighttime threatening and no pachyderm to come back to. Still, she didn't want to hand herself over to the mazhet just yet, either. If they were anything like humans, they'd search her, take her notebook, and leave her right back where this whole thing started—with a useless jumpship, a couple of feuding businessoids, and a genotype facing extinction. Rahel was starting to feel like the proverbial wolf, willing to chew her own leg off just to escape what she'd stepped into.

First order of business, then: Hide the *eisborne* data. She squinted around at the cracked ground and dirty snow. Not really a lot of reasonable hiding places, especially if she wanted to find the notebook again after the mazhet dragged her back to the Colony and had her shipped far, far away. No, she had to keep the data on her. On her, and someplace the alien mazhet wouldn't know to look for it.

She pulled the pack between her knees and tugged it open. Hiding the whole notebook was damned unlikely. Hiding just the data, however, might have some promise. She popped the memory card from the notebook's back, catching the 2-cm wafer in her lap while she rummaged through the pack with her free hand. It was hard to feel tiny details through the i-suit gloves, but she recognized the hard squares of fresh memory cards when she found them in their customary pocket. A new card slipped into the notebook with a click, and she stuffed the notebook deep into her pack in an effort to make it look hastily hidden. What good was concealing information if you didn't drag a few red herrings across the trail?

But that still left the used memory card and its priceless *eisborne* data. Rahel turned the piece over in her fingers, thinking. Swallowing the card was too obvious. Besides, she wasn't sure what her stomach acid would do to the data, and she didn't want to find out what the card's sharp corners would do to her intestines. Best to skip that, then, unless she couldn't think of anything better.

A few other bodily orifices sprang immediately to mind, not that Rahel found them any more appealing. For all she knew, mazhet knowledge of human anatomy was too limited to allow a useful body search. She couldn't make herself believe it was smart to strip out of a one-piece i-suit and stuff contraband data anywhere around her pelvic girdle, though. Later, maybe, when she'd decided things were desperate enough to warrant courting frostbite.

Ducking her head, she scanned the length of her body. Nothing there offered inspiration. No pockets, no secret compartments, no jewelry—

She paused, angling a look at her right wrist and the narrow bracelet outlined beneath the i-suit skin. The bioscan.

Pinching the memory card between right thumb and forefinger, she fumbled with her left hand to peel back the long glove cuff. Arctic wind sliced unprotected skin with phantom razors, and she worked the bioscan loose as quickly as she could. Freed, it dropped straight into her lap before her wrist had done more than turn threateningly ruddy. She jerked the glove closed again, and renewed warmth crept over her skin in a flush of tiny prickles.

The Ark had designed the bioscan to warn of approaching life-forms, not to be field-stripped. Cursing the lack of fingernails on her i-suit gloves, Rahel finally snapped aside her breath filter to attack the backing with her teeth. Cold air tickled at her throat and lungs, billowing warm steam around her goggles and nipping her lips with numbness. No, this wasn't a good environment to get stranded in, even with an i-suit. She applauded her wisdom at keeping the outfit on. If Danoph or the mazhet didn't find her soon, she'd end up having to turn herself in—whether or not she hid the *eisborne* data—just to avoid freezing to death. Not a pleasant thought, no matter which outcome she imagined.

Spitting the bioscan's backing into her lap, she tipped the open compartment to catch the dimming light. There wasn't a lot of extra room in there—certainly not enough to tuck in a data card from some completely other piece of equipment. She took the card gently between her teeth and poked a finger at the bioscan's insides. Maybe she could make room, though.

The procedure, of course, required struggling completely out of her glove this time. Mindful of the data card, she resisted clenching her teeth against the cold. Her smallest fingernail fit under one of the bioscan's processor chips, and she managed to pop it out after only two attempts. It clattered out of sight amidst the ice-cracked gravel beneath her.

The data card fit a bit too snugly into the vacated slot, but fit it did. Which was just as well—the bioscan was probably useless now, and not worth keeping if it couldn't at least protect the *eisborne*. She smiled a little while snapping the cover back into place, barely able to squeeze the fingers of her bare, cold-whitened hand.

The bioscan felt chill against her wrist for a long time after she'd wriggled back into her glove and refitted her breath mask. She didn't know if that was thermodynamics or paranoia. She did know that she was tired, though, and stressed so thin she felt like a spider's web in a high wind. She didn't want to idly wait for the mazhet to tire of her pachyderm and abandon it, but she didn't know what else to do. Pulling her knees to her chest, she wrapped her arms

around them and sighed. If nothing else, it would be dark
soon. Certainly the mazhet would go back to their ships
then, leaving the pachyderm alone long enough for her to
get in and bounce a message back to the Ark. That was all
she needed—one message, and the time to send it.

I think I'm beginning to hate this place.

Bowing her forehead to her i-suited knees, she closed her
eyes and settled down to wait out the mazhet.

Rahel jerked awake to dark confusion, at first not realizing
that she'd just come up from sleep. A whistle of wind raised
knee-deep snow mist all around, and, above her, a sky so
clear it looked painted on splashed starlight down across the
tundra. She unwound herself onto all fours, muscle stiffness
and growing alertness hinting that she'd dozed longer than
just an hour or so. Chilled by inactivity rather than weather,
she held herself very still and listened, trying to determine
what had jolted her awake to begin with.

It came again, from the north—first as a bone-deep
thrumming in the ground, then as a rising howl that itched
to the roots of her hair. Thank God for albedo and
light-sensitive goggles: snow and ice glowed bright as day
against the rocky ground, and the hop that flashed across the
horizon blazed with running lights and reflection. A different hop than the mazhet's, though—broader, monochrome,
emblazoned with the Colony sigil. Danoph's people. Damn.
She'd been hoping for at least a little more time.

Rahel twisted to watch the hop roar out of sight behind
her. No search lights cut threads through the darkness,
which meant they were probably using IR. Gathering her
feet underneath her, she hoped the i-suit was as thermal-
tight to their equipment as it was to hers.

A crumbled *chuff* of sound billowed out of the silence left
by the hop's wild passage. Barely a disturbance, really—
just a rhythmic something that nearly evaporated when she
listened for it too hard. Tapping up her goggles' magnification, Rahel squinted across the ice field in search of some

color, some movement, some sign of either human or animal.

Nothing. Only permafrost, and gravel, and mound after mound of icy, dirty snow.

She started to turn toward the now-vanished hop, and a triangular flash of black bounced up from one snow mound, like a lazily tossed chunk of coal. She focused on it directly, squinting. Not until it changed trajectory mid-flight and swung to face her did she see the glitter of eyes, and recognize the black leather triangle as a nose.

The animal behind the face snapped into focus; Rahel's eyes were suddenly able to distinguish a square, quadrupedal form against the camouflaging snow, even at nearly a kilometer away. Nostrils fluttered the air in her direction, and almost-canine jaws continued to chew on a mouthful of broken ice.

Rahel climbed to her feet, dragging the snooze rifle up with her. She didn't want to shoot anything, but there was no sense being foolish. This was obviously a predator, with great, well-formed incisors and claws as long as her fingers all over its dinner-plate paws. Thick, snowy fur barely stirred in the wicked wind, but the animal swiveled around, tiny ears following every shift in Rahel's movements. It measured almost two meters at the shoulders, three meters from nose to rump, with hindquarter musculature that promised phenomenal endurance and power. Jesus. It massed 500 kilos if it massed a gram.

When it swung into motion, pacing parallel to her— watching, but not approaching—something tickled in the depths of her memory. Something that knew not to mistake this thing's lumbering amble for slowness, for sloth. Something that remembered six months spent tagging Terran *Ursus arctos* specimens several years after their reseeding on a wildpark planet named Cephes.

"You're Terran," she whispered. The same swinging gait, the same mighty shoulders, the same intelligent stare as this creature had characterized every one of those darker, shaggier cousins. Rahel couldn't believe evolution on Reyson's had so completely paralleled evolution on Terra. Not when she could vaguely recall static graphic overlays from research on that old apprentice project—not when another, more reasonable explanation waited only a suspension coffin away.

"You're Terran," she said again. "I don't know where they got you, or how they got you, but I've seen you before, and you're Terran." She rested the butt of the rifle by her foot and cupped her hands across the muzzle. "You're *Ursus maritimus*, and you've been extinct for almost two hundred years."

How the Colony's IR equipment missed the *eisborne*'s heat signature, Rahel couldn't begin to guess. Maybe they'd discounted it as some native animal, reasonably assuming Rahel herself would show up as a much smaller hot spot on their sensors. Bringing up the IR on her goggles, though, revealed she had more in common with the *eisborne*'s signature than she'd expected—the *eisborne* had none.

Rahel switched back to visual, and the *eisborne* reappeared. "Neat trick," she murmured. She'd have to remember to check Ark files for other animals impervious to IR. That was one nice bit of insulation, and without even the benefit of state-of-the-art thermals or long underwear.

Moving slowly around the edge of her sheltering ridge, she peered back toward the pachyderm to check on the mazhet. She saw no lights staining the snow or sky, even under full magnification, but the pachyderm's chameleon had been shut down. Nearby, the take-off burn from the mazhet's hop made twice-frozen ice gleam like glass. The mazhet could be anywhere, then. If they were smart—and Rahel had a feeling she could safely count on that—they'd left someone behind in case Rahel decided to return. Which meant she didn't dare walk down there with an *eisborne* so close by. Damn, but this was getting complicated. She liked things better when all she had to worry about was hiding a data card and three unsprung suspension coffins.

The Colony hop screamed by overhead again, and Rahel caught herself ducking into a couch as though that would conceal her. She shouldered her equipment pack as she straightened. Two fly-bys down, too many yet to go. Watching for the *eisborne* to take the bait and follow, she struck out southeastward across the open ground.

The *eisborne* scraped loose another chunk of snow with its paw, tiny black eyes tracking her as she moved clear of the ridge. Hungry, Rahel guessed. Who wouldn't be, after God-only-knew-how-long in a suspension coffin? She wondered if the *eisborne* possessed the patience to stalk her all the way to the seaside hesper colony. While losing it on the tundra might work almost as well, she preferred to disguise the *eisborne* amidst a great source of warmth and movement. IR should blur all to hell along the coastline, and the hespers themselves would form a sort of visual camouflage for the larger *eisborne*. On top of that, the predator would have a hiding place complete with buffet and wet bar for as long as it cared to stay. If only the damn thing would quit playing in the snow and follow.

Stopping, Rahel pivoted to face the *eisborne* squarely. "Come on, you stupid shit." Its great bulk shifted from foot to massive foot, and it drifted its head to one side as though squinting at her from the corner of its vision. "For crying out loud, I'm a tenth your size! What are you afraid of?"

As if alerted by her voice, the *eisborne* swung away to gallop out of sight in the opposite direction of the hespers. Rahel opened her mouth to swear in frustration, only to be silenced by the shush of padded footsteps behind her.

She turned, finger sliding to the snooze rifle's trigger, and impacted with some great force as if she'd met it at orbital speeds. The equipment pack over her shoulder absorbed enough of the blow to burst in all directions, but not enough to keep her from smashing to the ground in an explosion of shock and snapping bone.

Pain seared through rib cage, shoulder, arm, and she squeezed off a spray of rifle fire in primitive muscular reaction. An avalanche of snowy fur barrelled over her prostrate form, grinding bone against bone and pounding grey over her vision as it pinned her to the ice beneath weight enough to stop her breathing.

Then it sprawled to a halt on top of her, immobile.

Anguish stretched her on a tightrope between wakefulness and darkness. Trying to raise her head, trying to swallow a boil of nausea, Rahel could barely identify the mass of smelly white fur that buried her. She fell back flat again, almost laughing.

Bigger even than the first *eisborne*—more than twice her body length, and taller at the shoulder than she herself stood—it was snoozed for now, but would wake again too soon. She listened to the sound of hot liquid hissing over frozen ground by her ear, and knew she was hearing her own blood. Lots of it, no doubt. The *eisborne* only grunted in its sleep and sighed.

My fault for dismantling the bioscan, she told herself as her vision squeezed down to nothing.

Still, if she were really lucky, the *eisborne* would wake up before she did.

When consciousness finally drifted over her again, Rahel found herself warm, able to breathe, and in at least a little less pain than when she last remembered.

The L-shaped room was bright, and filled with mirrors. The sparkling scent of faint perfume curled over her, but no one stood nearby to murmur reassurances while she struggled to sit up. Her left arm had been strapped, elbow bent, to her side. Shoulder and ribs screamed shrewish complaints about the position, but Rahel thought it unwise to undo her savior's handiwork just yet. The "bed" on which she'd awakened was just the lounge in a women's restroom, after all—she didn't trust such medical care to hold together through much handling.

She'd been stripped out of her i-suit, dressed instead in an overlarge grey T-shirt and men's undershorts. Her hair fell loose across her cheeks and forehead when she rocked forward to catch her head in her hand. Inside the body of the shirt, the fingers of her pinned left arm twitched slightly, responding to some injury just beyond the realm of simple pain. They'd taken her gear, of course. Nothing that tied her to herself or the outside world had been left in view.

When a door somewhere behind her whisked open, she didn't even bother to raise her head.

"None of this had to happen, you know," Danoph said.

Just thinking about turning made her shoulder sing, so Rahel waited for the prelate to move around in front of her before looking up. "Bits and pieces of it, maybe. Overall, you underestimated the Ark if you thought this would be easy."

"Well, I certainly underestimated you." Danoph set a lumpy canvas bag on the floor next to a chair, then turned to seat herself as though ready to conduct a job interview. "How's your arm?"

Rahel touched her elbow beneath the loose shirt. "Hurts."

Danoph nodded with what looked like honest sympathy. "I'm not surprised. I've got a pilot with paramed training who set and patched whatever he could, but you'll still need a doctor to look at that. There's a lot of connective tissue damage in the rotor cuff."

Rahel snorted. "So you locked me in your ladies' room."

Danoph favored her with a tolerant grin, not even moving her hands from where they rested, neatly folded, in her lap. "You're not locked in."

"Isn't denial of medical care considered inhumane under the Second Convention?"

"Nothing's being denied you, Proctor. What kind of woman do you think I am? You'll get medical care as soon as we get back to the Colony."

"Which will happen," Rahel guessed, "just as soon as you get whatever you want out here."

Danoph's only response was to reach beside her chair and heft the pack in one hand. "It's been searched, of course, but nothing was taken." She leaned forward to swing it between them, letting it land with a *thump* at Rahel's feet. "It would have made things easier if you'd stuffed some piece of conspicuous evidence where I could find it, but I didn't really expect that."

Rahel fumbled one-handed with the pack's mouth, trying to keep both concern and too-pure neutrality out of her face. Notebook and bioscan both sat near the top, the first with both memory cards pulled, the latter with its backing askew. She used her thumb to pry the bioscan open without lifting the device. The hidden card was still in its slot, and nothing else in the device seemed disturbed.

"So?"

Danoph's voice made her heart jolt, but she finished latching the pack shut without hurrying. "So? What?"

"So where are the coffins?"

Rahel raised her head, surprised more by the thin slice of irritation in Danoph's voice than by her question. "You've got to be kidding. What do you care?" She pushed the pack off to one side with her foot. "Get new coffins from the mazhet."

Danoph's lips pressed into a frown. "That isn't funny."

"Nothing's funny." God, her arm hurt so bad she didn't know whether to throw up or cry. "You and the mazhet want to destroy an entire genotype just for the sake of a business monopoly, and you tricked me into helping you. Prelate, I'm laughing my head off."

"You? Helping?" Danoph rubbed at the bridge of her nose, a surprisingly guileless gesture for someone involved in this sordid business. "The mazhet would laugh to know how badly I bungled my working relationship with you." Such as it was. "Trust me, Proctor Tovin—with more help like yours, I'd be forced to retire."

For all it was nice to know she'd managed to inflict some damage where damage was due, Rahel couldn't imagine it was just the cost of search-time and fuel—or even four state-of-the-art suspension coffins—that had Danoph staging this negotiation. "You didn't get it." She couldn't help sounding amazed, any more than she could help laughing when Danoph flushed and glanced off to one side. "You didn't pick up the *eisborne*."

The prelate sighed and pushed to her feet, a certain amount of humor shining through her embarrassment, although not much. "We're in my private hop and the thing massed in at seven hundred kilos! Where the hell were we supposed to put it without a coffin? You're lucky we managed to get it off of you." She leaned back against one of the mirrors, arms crossed, and waited while Rahel bent to put her face in her lap, wishing it didn't hurt so much to laugh. "Did you know they didn't show up on IR when you took them?"

Rahel shook her head. That spiked enough additional discomfort to make her gasp, and finally stilled her laughter. But the little bubble of amusement inside her didn't go away. "I'll bet the mazhet did."

"So are you saying the mazhet let them out?"

"No." Rahel pushed against her knee with one hand to sit upright. "I'm saying they let themselves out."

Danoph snorted and started to pace again.

"Those coffins are designed to pop either when told to or when exposed to environmental conditions that favor their occupants. Since you made sure I didn't know anything about the *eisborne*, I couldn't very well have picked what environment to drop them in." She grinned again, enjoying Danoph's frustration. "I guess it's your fault for shutting down my drive over the arctic."

Danoph acknowledged that with a sigh. "All right, fine. But assigning blame doesn't get us back the *eisborne*."

Rahel shrugged her one good shoulder. "And neither do I."

Danoph paused behind her chair, hands on its back, brows crumpled with frowning. "It's to both our advantages. Four

animals won't make a viable population here—your genotype will still die out, and now there isn't even a modified
gene set for you to fall back on."

"I didn't have it to fall back on in the first place."

Danoph stared at her a long time, the muscles along her
jaw twitching faintly with her thoughts. Rahel stared back
with her own thoughts as well-hidden as she could make
them. It was easy to disguise almost anything underneath
enough pain.

"Are you going to make me get mean?" Danoph finally
asked.

Rahel nodded. "I guess so."

"All right, then." Moving around the chair, Danoph
settled herself again and wound her hands into a fist in her
lap. "You've attempted interplanetary grant theft—four
counts—with items either the mazhet or Reyson's could
legally prove we owned. You've succeeded in local grand
theft on at least an intercontinental scale. You've trespassed,
violated several intra-atmosphere safety regulations, and I
can probably pull out some old environmental laws to slap
you for leaving ship litter all over our arctic." She shrugged,
obviously not having to put too much thought into this list
of offenses. "That's not even taking into account your poor
attitude and repeated rudeness. I don't think even Noah's
Ark can double-talk you out of this one, honey. You've
broken so many local and interplanetary laws, I could make
a second career just out of keeping you and the Ark in
court."

Rahel tried to ignore the slow twisting in her stomach,
thinking through everything Danoph had said. "I hate
politics."

"I know you do." The prelate sounded amazingly sincere
in her sympathy. "That's why we're going to reach some
sort of equitable agreement before any of this has to get
ugly."

Rahel gusted a little laugh. "I don't know what you think

I have to barter with. The *eisborne* are loose—I can't fix that for you."

Danoph cocked her head, shrugging. "Maybe not. But I'm betting you can find the coffins." She fished into her jacket pocket to pull out an Ark signal tag between two fingers. "I found these among your gear."

Rahel glanced at the tag, looked back at Danoph. It hadn't occurred to her to count her tags when she checked through her returned equipment. She wasn't even sure how many there were. She'd had a good double handful before tagging the coffins in the cargo bay—all but twelve would still be in there, littered amongst all the rest of her gear. Danoph smiled in response to Rahel's unhappy scowl.

"If you really didn't know the coffins would pop," the prelate said, "you tagged them before you dumped them or you don't deserve your job. So I'm willing to let you walk just for pointing them out to me." She flicked the tag onto the lounge next to Rahel, returning her hand to her lap. "Surely you have some way to trigger these from outside your ship."

Rahel stared at the tag, a little uncertain what was being asked of her, and leery of walking into some trap. "You don't want me to do that."

"But you can?"

She looked up to find Danoph peering at her with intense interest. "Sure I can." She tested the offer again: "But I don't think you want me to."

The assertion seemed to strike Danoph as funny. She smiled and spread her hands in hopeless offering. "And I don't think you want to go to jail." Crossing her arms, she shifted to sit more erect in her chair. "Why don't you weigh both those options, then tell me where we're going."

Not where you think. Rahel bent to unstrap the canvas pack again, hoping this would be the last time for the sake of her injured arm. The notebook powered up at the touch of her thumb, and she blipped a widespread tag query for display against a Reyson's map.

Every Ark tag on the planet squealed back a silent signal. The notebook screen displayed each brilliant spot as a winking star, the collection of them at Rahel's feet coalescing into a glowing cluster.

Tracing the tag from the pachyderm would have been easier, of course, but Rahel could simplify the readout enough to suit Danoph's purposes. Blanking out every tag but the few still attached to suspension coffins, she turned the notebook toward Danoph to display the fresh, uncluttered screen.

The prelate rose from her seat with a smile. "You see?" She took the notebook in both hands. "Environmentalists can learn politics after all."

"What good is believing in evolution if you don't occasionally practice it?" Rahel moved one foot to scoot the equipment pack closer without actually looking down at it.

Danoph laughed with genuine delight as she moved toward the outside door. "I'm glad we could come to an agreement about things."

Rahel snorted. "Sure. So am I."

"You'll understand, of course, if I ask you to make yourself comfortable here until we've located the coffins. Would you like anything?"

"Food would be nice."

"Done. How about more painkiller?"

Her shoulder tightened its painful grip as if to encourage her agreement, but knowledge of the silent, shrieking tags beneath her seat overrode it. "No, thanks," she finally sighed with a wan, tired smile. "I think I'd just as soon stay clearheaded. For later."

"You are easily the most troublesome woman I have ever met."

Rahel stood, her pack already waiting at her right hand. "I take it the mazhet are here?"

"You know they are." Danoph shook her head in appreciation as she stepped aside to let Rahel through the doorway. "How did you do that?"

Rahel smiled and gripped her equipment bag. "Sorry— trade secret."

The hop was bigger than Rahel expected, maybe half the size of her jumpship with no huge chunks of volume eaten up by cargo bays. Danoph led her down a tight, very unship-like hallway toward a wood-paneled door that waited already ajar. Rahel noticed that the prelate was careful to match her own casual gait to Rahel's painful limp, but decided not to waste energy being grateful for this consideration until she saw where they were going.

The doorway opened onto a small conference room, complete with pedestal table and hand-tooled chairs. Warring colors filled the far end of the room in the form of three caparisoned mazhet and their little *dhaktu*. Rahel recognized Oro's magenta under-skirt and brilliant yellow headdress from their meeting back at the Colony. Another mazhet, swathed exclusively in pungent blues and orange, stood with both hands resting on the *dhaktu*'s narrow shoulders. Between those two, the vermilion and scarlet mazhet who had left the silent message on her comlink waited with such quiescence, even its masking screen of chains didn't jingle.

Rahel settled carefully into the chair Danoph offered her, not waiting to see if the mazhet would do the same. They didn't.

"Proctor Rahel Tovin, this is the *dohke* Pij." Danoph gestured slightly to the tall apparition in scarlet. "The *dohke* Pij owns the mazhet caravan parked on Reyson's, not to mention the *eisborne* you so recently attempted to steal."

Rahel raised her hand for a single wave. "Hi, there."

The chains on Pij's face veil chimed sweetly as it looked from Rahel to Danoph. Its liquid clicking almost vanished in the ringing.

"In what location is the merchandise?" the *dhaktu* translated from his place on Pij's left.

Danoph glanced unhappily down at Rahel, who only raised her eyebrows in lieu of having anything to say.

"Well . . ." the prelate admitted slowly, "we haven't exactly determined that yet."

Oil-slick eyes turned back to Rahel, and this time she felt the mazhet's attention fasten onto her like sunlight to a stone. One of the three traders started a thin, private ticking that the *dhaktu* made no move to translate. The other two added to the rattle until all voices braided into a single sound, then stopped again.

The *dhaktu* said into the silence, "You were aware, Proctor Tovin, of the arrangement between Prelate Danoph and the mazhet?"

Rahel nodded, trying to decide on which of the party she should be focusing her attention. She decided to stick with the *dohke* Pij, on the theory that anyone who owned an entire caravan was probably *de facto* in charge. "After you prove the *eisborne* can be downsized, Danoph pays you whatever she agreed to pay you, and you turn over the four full-sized specimens for her to have her way with."

The *dohke* Pij clicked and rang its reply. "Knowing so, for what reason did you relocate this merchandise?"

"I wanted to keep the deal from going down. But that's not why the theft occurred."

Three pairs of huge, whiteless eyes stared across at her, but none of the mazhet so much as jingled. Finally, the *dhaktu* whispered, "Confusion."

Rahel pretended not to notice the apprehensive frown Danoph flicked her way, scooting forward on her chair to keep eye contact with the mazhet. "Your business associate, Prelate Danoph, decided she'd like your deal better if she didn't have to pay you. So she pushed my buttons, got me all stupid and human, and I did the dirty work for her—I stole your *eisborne*."

"You have no proof I planned anything," Danoph interjected smoothly.

Rahel waved the protest aside. "This isn't a court of law.

I don't need proof, I just need them to believe me."
Although who could tell just by looking at them? "I think
you were supposed to go looking for me back at Noah's
Ark," she went on to the *dohke* Pij. "Either that, or you were
supposed to believe I'd gone down with my ship, and all the
eisborne with me. Whichever, Danoph was left with her
merchandise, and you guys . . ." She shrugged one shoulder and sat back in her seat. "You guys were skunked."

Pij blinked once, slowly. "But you did not succeed in
this."

Rahel shook her head. "No."

"And she did not succeed in this."

"No."

"And the *eisborne* are still alive on Reyson's Planet."

Most of them, anyway. Rahel nodded, not sure what all
this was leading up to. "Somewhere, yes."

Pij turned its onyx stare on Danoph. "Reyson's and the
mazhet must reach agreement on who will bear the cost of
recovering the merchandise."

"I'll accept the cost." Danoph tipped her head as though
conceding a well-made point. "My misjudgment incurred
it."

"This is equitable."

"Wait a minute!" Rahel stumbled to her feet, catching
herself against the table to glare across at the mazhet. "I just
told you that Danoph tried to queer your deal—and you're
still willing to do business with her?"

Pij's veils rang a glittering counterpoint to its speaking.
"An agreement was negotiated. Prelate Danoph's attempts
to circumvent that agreement do not negate it." It raised one
hand toward Danoph in a shower of bright sound. "She
knows her actions will impact all future dealings."

Rahel barked a bitter laugh without waiting to hear how
Danoph might respond. "You guys just don't have any ethics
at all, do you? Those *eisborne* are stolen property—!"

The *dhaktu* clapped his hands to underscore Pij's interruption. "The mazhet negotiated purchase of the *eisborne*

from their previous owner on the understanding that the merchandise was without connection to Noah's Ark."

Rahel dropped back into her chair, head pounding. "That's a lie."

The mazhet bent toward the floor until riots of fabric shrouded their faces. The *dhaktu* hovered behind them, hands making fists at his neckline. "Proctor Tovin," he offered in a tiny voice, "mazhet cannot lie."

"Then the poacher who sold them the *eisborne* did." She waited for all the mazhet to rise upright, but only Pij straightened to peer at her. "The *eisborne* is a Terran animal," she explained, trying to blank the accusation from her voice long enough to keep Pij's attention. "I know Terran DNA spins when I see them, and I know Terran body configurations when I see them. Since Noah's Ark owns the rights to all Terran DNA not currently tied up in humans, that means somebody stole those *eisborne* from us. I don't know where or how, but they have to have."

Pij coughed a single sound. The *dhaktu* said simply, "No."

Danoph moved to put her back to the mazhet, her scowl focused strictly on Rahel. "When did you have a chance to study *eisborne* DNA?"

"On the ship." The lie came surprisingly easily, with no hesitation at all. "After I stole the coffins, I dumped the data and 'linked it straight to the Ark."

Danoph drew back somewhat, eyes narrowed. "You didn't have time."

"Prove it. Make your deals with the mazhet and let me go home." She smiled and watched Danoph's veneer of pleas- antry falter. "You'll know in a year or so whether or not we can really bust your *eisborne* monopoly."

"What do you want from me, Tovin?"

Pij's brittle clicking caught their attention even before the *dhaktu* translated. "She wishes to barter."

Not so alien after all, these mazhet. Rahel grinned across at them, tapping the end of her nose.

Danoph waved aside the suggestion. "She hasn't got anything to barter." But she paced away from the table with her arms folded tight to her chest.

"I've got plenty to barter. The Ark has the power to completely wreck your plans for marketing the *eisborne*. We've got better cloning facilities, whole planets of breeding space. We could produce *eisborne* so cheaply, you couldn't even give yours away." Rahel made sure Danoph turned to find her smiling warmly, relaxing as best she could in her chair. "Of course, if we can come up with some equitable arrangement, none of this ugliness has to happen."

The mazhet abruptly broke formation, moving toward the door in a flurry of musical movement. Rahel felt her heart drop, unhappy with losing a barter chip so soon after orchestrating its arrival.

The *dhaktu* glanced at her on their way to the door. "You've initiated barter with the prelate," he said hurriedly as they passed. "It isn't allowed that they overhear your barter."

Rahel snapped her fingers, wishing she had two hands to leap up and grab the mazhet with. "Not so fast, *dohke*. This is a deal for you guys, too."

Uncomplementary colors swarmed together at the doorway, and three sets of liquid eyes fastened onto hers.

"Everybody ready?" When no one protested, she held up one finger and began. "First—the mazhet leave the *eisborne* loose on the arctic sheet, and Danoph considers that fair delivery of the merchandise." She quirked a wicked grin at the prelate. "She even pays you for them."

"Wait a minute—"

"In exchange, Noah's Ark will conduct a habitat evaluation of Reyson's Planet to determine the suitability of adding the *eisborne* to this environment. Free of charge."

"Uh-uh." Danoph stuffed hands into jacket pockets, auburn brows crumpled with displeasure. "The whole intent of our agreement was so my people would have unlimited access to *eisborne* genetic material for our program."

"You'll have it," Rahel assured her. "Sample the ones you have living out here, maybe twice a year per *eisborne*. Let us fix your spins when you pull them, and that way you'll keep your captive *eisborne* clean. Introduce artificially variegated specimens every now and then, and you'll have more unique genetic material than you know what to do with inside a few years. And all of it will belong to you."

She watched the prelate's eyes focus inward as though reading through layers of language no one else could see. "All right," she said finally, feeling the words with the edges of teeth and tongue. "I can agree to that."

Rahel threw a questioning glance at the mazhet, and Pij responded by sketching a meaningless gesture in the air. The *dhaktu* said, "This is equitable."

"You still haven't said anything about my marketing plans." Leave it to a politician to keep matters firmly focused on self-interest. "What assurance do we have that Noah's Ark won't undermine our monopoly the first chance it gets?"

Rahel sighed, regretting her earlier threat on Danoph's future marketing. It had seemed a good idea at the time. "So long as you keep up your side of the bargain, the Ark won't care two beans about your business."

"Not good enough. I want a fee."

"A what?"

"A fee," Danoph said. "A fine. Something to dissuade the Ark from dealing in household domestics, especially *eisborne*." She brought her hands out to lace them stubbornly across her chest. "If Noah's Ark ever produces or distributes *eisborne* of any size in any capacity outside the Ark's already established functions, Noah's Ark will pay to Reyson's Planet a fine equal to the then-current market price for Reyson's Planet and all its holdings."

It was scary how easily the snare of language spun out of her. "Are you *nuts*?"

Danoph grinned like a fox. "Not even slightly."

"A quarter your going price." She didn't even want to hear

what Saiah Innis would say when she tried to explain how all this related to what he'd asked her to do. "Maybe not even that much."

Danoph sighed and her arms fell to her sides. "My Colony's entire economy is riding on the future of our *eisborne* business. If that falls through, we lose everything, including the planet. You agree to full price, Proctor Tovin, or you agree to nothing. No deal."

Something in the area of Rahel's stomach started to chew itself into knots when she pictured the *eisborne*'s brilliant construction diluted to something the height of her knee. "Full price," she sighed. It wasn't like Noah's Ark would ever want to develop mini-*eisborne*, so what could be the danger? Besides telling Saiah about all this, of course. "We have a deal?"

Oro broke from the other two mazhet, the *dhaktu* scurrying to stand at its side. "The barter is not finished." It placed itself in front of the *dohke*, both hands splayed to its chest as though surprised by its own clattering words. "In exchange for mazhet compliance in all above-mentioned considerations"—the *dhaktu* blurted the words in an anxious, breathless rush—"Noah's Ark will deliver back to the mazhet all four stolen suspension devices, intact."

Rahel was surprised to feel embarrassment warm her face. "One of them's already wrecked."

"Then Noah's Ark will pay for damages to that unit."

That seemed only fair. "Okay."

Oro swept its robes close around it, and all the mazhet finery in the room seemed to catch the sound and sing it. "These dealings are acceptable to all parties involved?"

Rahel glanced at Danoph in search of some annoyance, but saw none. "Sure." The prelate only nodded.

Pij fanned elongated fingers across the crown of Oro's head. "This is equitable." Then it turned in a dervish of ribbon, silk, and golden chain, and whisked past the little *dhaktu* without pausing to bid them goodbye. The other mazhet followed as though beaded to their *dohke*'s skirts, leaving the *dhaktu* to murmur amenities as he closed the door behind him.

Rahel felt all her carefully hoarded adrenaline wash into her feet, and sat back in her chair with the shallowest sigh she could manage. It probably wasn't good to let Danoph see how relieved she was to have this over.

"Not bad for a first barter session with the mazhet. You do this evolution thing pretty well."

She opened one eye to squint up at the prelate. "When can I retrieve my pachyderm?"

Danoph laughed and offered her a hand in standing. Rahel accepted it without actually wanting to move. "You can have your pachyderm after you've been with a doctor, and I've been with a lawyer, and both of us have heard from Noah's Ark about their acceptance of our arrangement." She shouldered open the door and held it wide for Rahel. "Once the Ark has sent a ship and somebody to escort you home, you can have your pachyderm and whatever's inside it."

Rahel grunted something that was close to amusement, rubbing at her injured shoulder. "You make me sound almost dangerous. What do you expect me to do?"

Danoph left her to enter the ladies' room on her own. "I have no idea what to expect from you, my dear. That's entirely the problem."

Somehow, the tundra didn't seem so imposing in full daylight. Rahel tugged her parka tighter around her shoulders, wishing she'd been able to get her left arm down a sleeve but understanding that moving the injured limb wasn't a good plan just yet. Behind her, the pachyderm groaned and hissed as three of Reyson's spaceport mechs labored to cut it free from the ice. One of the *eisborne* had appeared at the edge of the horizon, nosing occasionally at the scent of warm bodies but not venturing any closer.

A new warmth appeared at her elbow. "That's a nice animal you've found there." Saiah Innis followed her distant gaze.

Rahel lifted one shoulder, not looking away from the *eisborne*. "The mazhet found it, but thanks anyway." The animal folded itself, slowly awkward, its hindquarters standing upright as it pushed chest-first across the dirty snow. "They really aren't in our database? Not anywhere?"

Saiah shook his head. "We've compared spins from all four specimens, but there's no Ark record of the *eisborne* anywhere. Widdier admits he recognizes the photos." His smile flashed white across his wind-burned face as the *eisborne* fell completely prostrate, legs in the air. "He says it's definitely genus *Ursus*, though, within a few million years of species *americanus*. That's all the closer he's willing to come to actually calling it *maritimus* for right now. Ask him again in a week."

The *eisborne* rolled lazily to all fours again, sniffed once more in their direction, then turned and lumbered away. Rahel tried to picture it among the vanishing ice fields of Earth—tried to imagine how it could have been rescued from there so many years before Noah's Ark was even born. "I wonder where it came from."

"I hope we can find out." Saiah turned away to glance at the pachyderm, uninterested now that the ursid's playful show was over. "Whoever relocated them—however they relocated them—have you ever imagined what other treasures someone like that might have saved?"

Rahel thought about a paper picture she'd once seen of tiger-striped wolves in the rock-and-steel confines of a big city zoo. She thought about descriptions in an ancient seaman's log of birds that stood as tall as humans, and about the soft wings of flying rodents that the night skies had taken for granted. She thought of all the damage she'd lived her life regretting mankind could never undo, and she nodded with a wistful smile.

"Yes," she said, "as a matter of fact, I have."

⚡Tide of Stars⚡

A stiff west wind punched at the balloon's gondola from below. Rahel grabbed reflexively for the basket's edge, forgetting for the moment that her intellect knew without doubt that the gondola couldn't tip. It was an easy thing to forget this high up, with the wind shoving at her like an ill-trained dog and the night-dark water stretching from horizon to horizon so far below.

She closed her eyes, blocking out the tactical display's glowing grid that jiggered in an effort to keep pace with her changing focus. Shutting out the unsteady display helped. Still, Rahel waited for the gondola to steady before opening her eyes to reestablish her bearings.

The Odarkan Sea pooled in the darkness below them like a sheet of still, black metal. Rahel couldn't even hear the lick and slap of gentle water movement, and the typically timid caress of this planet's breezes wasn't nearly enough to raise waves high enough to see from a couple hundred meters up. The only feature distinguishing this placid, land-bound sea from the sloughs around it was an ethereal thread of light stretching like sprinkles of stardust from the water's black center toward where the mother ocean waited in the west.

Rahel brought the optic fiber back into position, realigned the overlay grid with the realtime planet surface, then double-blinked to freeze-frame the image. "Sector twenty-three slash twenty-six," she said aloud. The computer picked out the individual jellyfish bodies among the long, glowing chain, and she counted them in rapid silence. "Medusae count: forty-two."

Behind her, the click-tapping of pen on notebook screen told her that Paval still stood with his back against the gondola's opposite rail, conscientiously keeping himself both out of her way, and out of the way of the pilot. "That brings our adult total to one hundred fifteen," he reported softly. Rahel heard him log the number along with all the others.

As long as it makes him feel useful. She'd argued bitterly when Saiah informed her she'd have to take an apprentice on this assignment. Whoever the kid was, she'd maintained, he'd just get in the way. He'd be useless for running tests, because Rahel would have to explain every little thing to him instead of just taking the fast route and doing it herself. And he'd be bored doing nothing more than watching her collect samples and count slow-moving jellyfish. And he certainly wouldn't learn anything, because Rahel didn't intend to talk to him.

Saiah had a habit of listening to the opinions of everyone and their mother, though, then doing whatever he wanted. It was part of why he'd survived mentoring Rahel all those years before. "You pay ahead," he'd told her simply. So on departure day she'd reported to the spaceport as usual, and found herself stuffed into a jumpship next to some young outworld colonist with eyes as round and brown as a puppy's and a graceful lilt to his accent that would probably tell her exactly where he'd been raised if she cared enough to pay attention. It would be a long time before she forgave Saiah Innis for this.

"Even on a generous estimate," Paval volunteered from behind her, "one hundred fifteen in our sample alone is a decline of nearly 62 per cent since the census last year."

Rahel didn't comment, instead flicking the optic fiber

away from her eye so that she could study the seascape below them without the computer grids interfering.

"That isn't enough, is it?"

And here she'd set him the useless task of writing down the numbers because she thought it would keep him too busy to ask stupid questions.

She pulled the phone from her field vest pocket and punched the contact button with her thumb. "Nils?" She heard the other proctor pick up, so didn't wait for him to acknowledge. "What's your total?"

"I've just completed my last sector." His voice over the com unit sounded flat and thin against the background hissing of wind across his own phone's mouthpiece. "I totaled in at two hundred and three."

"That brings us up to three hundred eighteen."

Rahel knew the number even before Paval dutifully reported it.

"That isn't enough to ensure genetic diversity." This time the apprentice wasn't asking her. And, no, it wasn't enough.

Rahel turned away from the depressingly empty waters and lifted the phone to her ear again. "Okay, bring it in," she told Nils. Across the gondola from her, she could see Paval quietly close up his notebook and slip his pen into its slot. "We'll pick up again in the morning, do another count tomorrow night."

"What? You're actually going to let us unpack and find our sleeping rooms?" Nils's voice danced with feigned surprise. "But, Rahel, we've only been onplanet six hours! You must be getting soft in your old age."

She closed the phone and thrust it back into her pocket.

"Turn us about, then, ma'am?"

"Yes, Jynn." She answered the pilot without really looking at him. He perched, comfortably casual, in the little swing seat halfway up the rigging. She could just make out the lighter patterns on his clothes in the weak moonlight, but couldn't see the features of his black-as-black face at all.

"I can't help but hear all this talk about the jellyfish,

ma'am." Jynn's ropes creaked and swung as he adjusted the balloon's engine to ease them back toward the resort. Rahel felt the balloon stutter faintly, but never heard the silent motor engage. "The jellies are going to be all right, aren't they? Mr. Sadena called for Noah's Ark in time, didn't he?"

Paval turned his pale face up toward Jynn and opened his mouth as if to answer. Rahel spoke before her apprentice had a chance to form his first word. "That's something we'll have to take up with Mr. Sadena, Jynn." She caught Paval's eyes when he jerked a look at her, pointedly not letting him go. "Like Proctor Oberjen says, we've only been here six hours. We've still got a lot of questions to answer."

Much to Rahel's surprise, Paval only nodded mutely and turned to look out over the water. She could tell by the strength with which he gripped his hands together when he leaned across the rail that he didn't agree with her decision to keep the details from the locals. But he'd listened to her, and done what she said without fighting. For a young man his age, that in itself was a miracle.

Maybe he wasn't so stupid after all.

Even at night, the shoreline of the Odarkan Sea was a riot of organic activity. Fist-sized moths, their wings flashing whitely in the dim illumination, bumbled from treetop to treetop, shore to shadow. Swamp lights licked brief, cold fire against knotted, moss-hung trunks while some slow, nocturnal herbivore splashed its way through the shallow waters. Two hundred meters higher up, Rahel wrinkled her nose against the sharply rotten smell that feathered up from the planteater's footsteps.

The bugs down there must be awful, she reflected, watching the balloon's shadow warp as it passed over the sleeping trees. She hoped they wouldn't have to spend much ground time along the Odarkan coast. Tromping around in outbacks and jungles was one thing; tromping around in fetid, bug-choked sloughs was something else. Rahel had always been sanguine about being killed and quickly devoured by just about any predator she'd ever met. It was the process of being eaten one tiny nibble at a time that wore on her patience.

"If the flying is still making you dizzy, try focusing on objects that are farther away. They parallax more slowly and don't disturb your eye."

Being eaten alive, and having an apprentice.

"Don't you have any background reading to do?" She wished she had some excuse to move over to the other side of the gondola.

"No, ma'am. I've already read everything pertinent to this safari that I could find." He barely stood taller than her shoulder, but massed about the same, with the lean, broad-shouldered build that came on young men who'd spent much of their lives in physical labor. "There wasn't much."

Rahel found herself wondering, much against her will, where exactly he had come from, and what had drawn him to Noah's Ark. "Well, call up some of my old stuff, then. It'll save me from having to lecture you."

"I did that before I came." Paval angled a polite but meaningful look up at her. "There wasn't much of that, either."

Rahel allowed the boy a thin smile. "Is that a coward's way of asking why I haven't published my research?"

She was surprised by the chase of color up his pale cheeks. "It was an observation."

"Well, damn fine observation." She clapped him smartly on the back and earned a startled jerk of his shoulders in response. "Keep up the good work." The next time Saiah Innis assigned her an apprentice, she was going to kill someone.

"Jynn—" Distracted briefly by the wall of darkness rising up from the approaching horizon, Rahel took one blind step backward before turning to face the balloon's pilot. "When we get back to the hotel, can you set us down near our pachyderm so we can offload our gear?"

She heard the shushing of the gondola's ropes more than

saw the pilot shake his head. "No, ma'am. I can set down on my assigned landing pad on top the hotel, but nowhere else. Them's the rules."

And, Rahel had to admit, Feles Sadena was laudably anal about enforcing his resort's many rules. It was the only thing that had impressed her about him so far.

"The staff will have transferred your things to your suites by now, anyway, ma'am," Jynn continued. A roar of flame and light suddenly painted his figure in shades of stark mahogany as he gassed the balloon upward a few more meters. Then he vanished again as mysteriously as he'd appeared. "With a full-season staff and no guests to look after, it's all any of us can do to keep busy. You'll probably be getting top-drawer service while you're here."

"We're here because the planet's suffering a marine die-off, Jynn. We won't be doing much relaxing."

"No, ma'am." He sounded subdued, and sadder than she expected. "I guess not."

A fragile thread of breeze met them at an angle, and Rahel turned to taste the salty freshness of its passage as Jynn tacked expertly across the wind's light current. The second balloon, with Nils's thin silhouette propped against the rail of its gondola like a leaned-over stick, slipped through the strait just ahead of theirs. Rahel watched it drift oceanward as silently as a dandelion puff, before a tiny jet of light nudged it ever so slightly about and pointed it back in toward shore.

The walls of the strait draped shadow over Rahel's swinging gondola when Jynn ducked them neatly between the coarsely wooded slopes. Clean, moving air replaced the stagnant bite of the margin sloughs, and the kiss of three dim, distant moons stitched trails of broken silver across the rippled surface of the open ocean. Rahel reminisced wistfully about the cries of diving ocean birds, the crash and sigh of tidal currents. The planet Uriel's tiny moons and greenhouse atmosphere had its disadvantages, as well as its pleasures—the people who came here paid for the temperate climates by giving up natural wildness and power. Which was perhaps just how they wanted it. Rahel found the end result charming, but rather dull.

The beach separating ocean from shore was narrow and mud-draped, as befitted a planet with no tropical storms or wave erosion to speak of. A long expanse of pale carbonate rock peeped out from a weep of gauzy fronds, following the shoreline as smoothly as a line drawn in the sand, while a glossy drizzle of seep water painted the outcrop's face in trickling crystal. It wasn't until Rahel glimpsed the un-shielded white of their pachyderm on a high, wide ledge that she recognized this rockface as the frontispiece of the Startide Hotel. Then a weird mixture of guilt and anger coiled together inside her, and she scowled against the unwelcome taste.

Just like all of Sadena's resorts, the Startide seemed to have grown out of the environment of its own volition. There were seven others just like it scattered all around Uriel's surface—among the hushing grasses of the great northern plains, suspended from the tree trunks in the equatorial woodlands, clinging to the slopes of youthful mountains so tall that the snow on their creased brows created its own mini-climates. Rahel remembered reading about Feles Sadena's brilliant plans for this place when he first bought the planet. How he was going to minimize impact. How people would be able to come and experience nature at its purest and best. How the planet's unique environment would itself be the attraction, and therefore more precious than any man-made commodity Sadena could introduce.

Rahel had thought the man a schlockmeister from the very beginning. She hated it that Sadena's only appreciation for what he had here was based on how much money it could bring him—hated it even more that no altruistic organization had ever succeeded in preserving an environment so thoroughly or so well. When Feles Sadena finally closed up his enterprise a hundred or so years from now, nothing on Uriel would be different for him having been here.

Well, almost nothing. Rahel thought about the stellar jellyfish, and couldn't silence a brusque, ironic sigh. It seemed both fitting and somehow hopelessly tragic that the first casualty of Sadena's hubris should be the very species of coelenterate that kept the Startide Hotel full of tourists.

Hot wind roared out their balloon's outgassing vent, and their gondola dropped with a barely perceptible lurch. Rahel clenched her hands, panic-tight, around the rail. It wasn't the height she hated so much about these balloons, she decided grumpily, it was the goddamned unsteady flight patterns. Maybe something resembling outdoor lighting on the roof of the hotel would prop up her confidence about landing, at least. She suspected nothing would alleviate the roiling in her stomach whenever a gust rocked the gondola and showed her ocean when she should have been looking at sky. If only because of the modes of transportation, this was going to be one very long safari.

"What the—?"

Jynn's startled shout was their only warning before a blast of light lashed and curled through the humid darkness around them. Rahel ducked away from the flame, throwing out one arm to corral Paval against the railing when he turned to do the same. Below them, movement seethed across the hotel's flat stone roof, an amorphous creature of shadows and angry voices. Then the gas driven upward by Jynn's flame swelled the sinking balloon and stopped its descent as surely as if the craft had hit the end of some invisible tether. Rahel pushed herself upright and leaned to look over the railing.

"They're all over my landing pad!" Jynn complained, fighting with the balloon's controls. His straps and harnesses squeaked and jangled.

Rahel blinked hard through the renewed darkness. Shapes refused to define themselves and be identified, but the braided stream of questions and netlink IDs sketched out clearly enough what was going on below. "Ah, shit . . ."

"What?" Paval appeared beside her, leaning so far out of the gondola that she had to quell an urge to grab him by the belt and haul him back in. Even from her more judicious position, Rahel saw the earnest frown that knotted his dark brows. "Who are they?"

As if Nils had heard them from the other balloon, the phone in Rahel's pocket chirped. She dug it out with an irritable sigh.

"Oh, please," Nils groaned the moment she opened the contact. "Please tell me those aren't what I think they are."

Rahel scowled down at the mass of shouting people. The first waspish whiz of remote antigravs joined the babbling voices. "Well, they aren't bellhops."

"They're reporters!" Paval, still folded nearly double over the gondola's rail, had to jerk himself upright to avoid colliding with one of the fist-sized minicams. It buzzed into position an arm's length from him and activated its seeker light.

"Reporters?" Jynn had finally succeeded in hovering them just a little farther above the crowd than stones could easily be thrown. He obviously hadn't counted on self-guided spybees.

"Either that or a Noah's Ark fan club." Paval swatted at two other whining remotes, to no avail. "How did they know we'd be here?"

Rahel barked a laugh, the phone resting against her shoulder. "Are you kidding? Reporters invented snitches. They can find out everywhere we go." Although why they'd chosen Uriel out of all the active Ark contracts was as much a mystery as anything the press did.

"Perhaps they're here to help us."

Rahel couldn't help laughing at the sincerity of her apprentice's suggestion. "You really are new to this, aren't you?" She picked up the phone again without waiting for

Paval to answer. "Nils, hit your lights. I want to get a good look at them."

Almost immediately, a fat finger of light dashed through the darkness to splash against the roof of the hotel. Rahel felt their gondola tip gently as Paval leaned over one section of railing to activate their own powerful lamps. The crowd on the roof recoiled from the light as though they'd been doused with water, then poured back across the open landing area the moment they realized there was no danger. Their swarm of little remote bees echoed their movement.

Rahel cocked a look at Jynn. "Take us down a little closer."

The pilot sighed unhappily, but outgassed the balloon with a barely perceptible hiss.

There weren't as many reporters on the pad as Rahel had first envisioned. A couple dozen, maybe, with that many again in hotel personnel trying to ring around them and keep them together—as if there were still guests in the resort who might be bothered by the shouting. The amoeboid gathering was the usual motel collection of suits, notepads, and budget-cloned faces. What did the netlinks do to get so many different representatives who all looked almost exactly alike? Rahel used to think they were all VR sims from the same length of flatscreen footage. She wasn't sure it was worth trading her enlightenment on that point for proof as graphic as what shouted at her from below.

Crossing her arms, Rahel leaned her elbows on the rail and peered down at the jostling reporters. "You know," she called, making a try at sounding amiable, "I could probably spit on you from here."

An impassioned plea for attention surged through the gathering, as if her words had been the sweetest encouragement to each and every one of them. Rahel caught a few fragmented questions and a confusion of overlapping accusations, but nothing that sounded like she wanted to answer it. When a voice finally sorted itself from the general tumult, it was from a tall, brown-skinned man at the very edges of the knot.

"Proctor! I'm Cek Lencel, Instant News Service!" He tried to push past the chain of hotel security, squinting up at the balloon with one hand over his eyes. "Why is Noah's Ark involving itself with a management problem on a planet owned by someone other than the Ark?"

Rahel opted not to dim the floods. "Why do you care?"

Lencel tipped his head in surprise. "The news netlinks care about everything."

Yeah, right.

That comment somehow invited another eruption of shouted questions, and Rahel had to straighten up off her elbows to bellow loud enough to be heard over the noise. "Yes, Feles Sadena owns this planet. But Ark policy doesn't limit us to trouble-shooting only in Ark habitats. If the private sector needs our engineering and research services to help manage *any* native environment, Noah's Ark doesn't think granting them that help is inappropriate."

"Nicely said," Nils purred approvingly across the open phone line. Just as well—it was the only piece of Noah's Ark PR she knew by rote.

"Valhanryn Esz, *Tomorrow Today*." This time it was a woman, too bunched up against the mass of hotel folk to be picked out of the chaos. "Does that mean Noah's Ark isn't accepting any financial compensation for your appearance here?"

"I guess it always comes down to that," Paval remarked, quietly enough to reach Rahel's ears but not the reporters'. He may have been an unasked for burden, but at least he caught on fast.

"That's what I hate about you netlink guys," Rahel answered the reporter. It took more control than she expected to keep from dropping things down onto their thick, news-gathering skulls. "No matter what I say, you're going to make it mean whatever you want it to."

Esz nodded blandly and buzzed her minicam closer. "So you are being paid."

"Rahel . . ." Nils's voice squeaked from the phone waiting down near her waist. "I think I should attack this subject."

But she'd already told them, "Yes," as flatly and non-combatively as she could. They all bent to their respective recording devices before she even started her second sentence. "Mr. Sadena is paying Noah's Ark a consulting fee commensurate with what we've been paid elsewhere for similar environmental impact studies."

"So it's not uncommon for Noah's Ark to produce planetary reports to the specifications of private buyers?" She couldn't even tell which bozo came up with that one.

Rahel smacked a hovering spybee away from her face. "Who told you that?"

"Well, you are accepting a great deal of money *from* Feles Sadena to produce a report *for* Feles Sadena, aren't you?"

"The company I work for is accepting the money." The act of sounding so gracious and patient made her teeth hurt.

"Oh, and that couldn't possibly have any effect on how you choose to interpret the data you collect?"

She clenched her hands around the open phone. "It never has before."

Nils groaned through the phone channel into her palm.

"Will you be working directly from Mr. Sadena's samples and records?"

"Who will you be reporting to?"

Rahel gave up trying to sort out the voices from the crowd. "We'll be conducting our own research—*privately*—and reporting back to both Mr. Sadena and the Ark as information becomes available."

"Then will Mr. Sadena be deciding in which locations you'll focus your search?"

She shrugged. "Why should he?"

"He has some pretty strong incentive to prove he *isn't* destroying Uriel's jellyfish, doesn't he?"

"Look . . ." Rahel slapped at another roving minicam, missed, then nodded a terse thanks to Paval when he used the offline notebook to whack it out of the air. "Whatever Feles Sadena's reasons for calling Noah's Ark to Uriel, they don't change the fact that *our* reason for being here is—"

"Monetary." Someone different—a woman with the raw, unpolished look of a professional believer—pushed forward from the outermost edges of the crowd.

Rahel bounced the flat of one hand against the railing. "It's not!" She already hated the young woman's coolly crossed arms and well-cut green suit.

The reporter's short-short hair flashed like polished silver when she shrugged. "You said Sadena's paying you."

"That isn't the point."

"That's entirely the point." She stalked to stand directly beneath the balloon, and Rahel suddenly realized from the ripple of attention that followed her that everyone else was eager to lap up whatever blood this young woman could draw. "As long as you're making a profit off your so-called scientific interests, Proctor, you've got no right to stand here and claim you're any different than this tourist trap. Both of you exploit some aspect of nature for your own purposes."

Rahel wished she were on the ground, face-to-face with this self-appointed moralist, or at least in range to grab and shake her pressed lapels. "What's your name?"

The reporter cocked her chin up with easy pride. "Eme Keim."

"From GreeNet," Rahel finished for her, and Keim's only answer was a twist of her mouth that didn't resolve into any particular expression. Rahel allowed herself a derisive snort. "Well, guess what, Eme Keim. Science takes money. Do you think Noah's Ark can just clone credit, the way we do the animals?"

"Rahel . . ." Nils's warning trickled up like smoke through the still-open communications line.

"If we had endowments from every planet in the goddamned sector, we *still* couldn't pay for the time—"

"Rahel!"

"—the food, the resources, the land—"

"Rahel!"

The bark of his voice leaping the distance between balloons caught her attention, and Rahel jerked an angry glare across the dark at Nils. He scowled back, just as fiercely, as though trying to mentally convey some message through the sheer force of his stare. Rahel clapped shut the phone in her hand in petulant dismissal.

If the gesture meant anything at all to Nils, he ignored it. Slipping his own phone into a pocket, he leaned over the edge of his gondola to address the reporters. "Excuse me, ladies and gentlemen." The group as a whole inclined heads to peer at him, and Nils smiled coolly. "I'm Proctor Nils Oberjen, Proctor Tovin's associate and counsel. I would be more than happy to explain the public particulars of Noah's Ark's contract with Mr. Sadena to you, but not from up here. I have travelled twenty-seven light-years, spent two days in a jumpship with my colleagues, and have neither bathed nor eaten since arriving on Uriel. If you'd like to have your curiosity satisfied, kindly let us set down and tend to our creature needs first. Perhaps we can talk in the morning."

"No."

Nils twitched upright as though he'd been poked in the ass. Rahel would have given anything to have a clearer view of his face just then. Maybe this would teach him to trot out his juristic bullshit for the media.

"You're not the only one to spend a lot of time and money getting here," Valhanryn Esz told him prissily. "We've been standing in the cold for four hours, waiting for you to get back from your sightseeing. Now, you're either going to answer a couple of questions, or you're not putting down." Her colleagues hooted and whistled their support, and she glanced around her with obvious pleasure. "That's the deal," she said at last to Nils. "And I'm afraid it's not negotiable."

Rahel snorted, and the reporters all glanced up at her as though they'd forgotten her presence. "I've done barter with

the mazhet," she told them, scowling. "Everything's negotiable." She nodded brusquely back at Jynn. "Set us down."

The pilot's eyes flashed white in the darkness. "Ma'am?"

"I said 'set us down.'" Rahel grinned maliciously over
the railing at the unsettled crowd below. "The only thing
netlink parasites care about more than their headline grabbing is themselves. They'll move."

Jynn reached uncertainly for the descent controls above
his shoulder. "And what if they don't?"

"They'll move."

The first blast of outrushing gas gained a haphazard
rumble of surly protest from below, then a more directed cry
of alarm when the first reporter realized the balloon was
descending rather than going away. People and spybees
scattered from beneath the gondola like pigeons. Rahel
heard Nils groaning something about "reckless endanger-
ment" and "litigious barbarians," but she had learned long
ago not to take his displays of anxiety too seriously. By the
time Rahel's gondola bumped to rest on the smooth pave-
ment, only Keim still stood close enough to clap her hands
on the rail and nod thoughtfully.

"Force." The GreeNet envoy very pointedly held her
ground while Rahel swung one leg over the railing and
started to climb down. "Very environmental. Very subtle."

"You've probably heard"—Rahel turned to accept the
pack of field equipment Paval passed down to her—
"subtlety isn't my strong suit." Her apprentice followed her
in silence, avoiding eye contact with the reporters in a way
that could have meant either great annoyance or embarrassment. Rahel couldn't tell which, but suspected both were as
likely.

"If I were you," Keim suggested, "I'd work on the
subtlety thing. You could have killed somebody here."

Rahel smiled and shouldered her pack with a shrug.
"You're not part of the native environment. Why should I
care?"

*   *   *

The Newborn robot who staffed the main lobby crouched behind the desk like a blue and silver crab. Rahel guessed it was an old construction mech, judging from the collection of arms and spare arm sockets bristling from its stumpy body. Probably a foreman or it never would have developed enough awareness to petition the courts for sentient status. Someone had done a bang-up job refitting its chassis to match the Startide's glass and aquamarine decor, even down to replacing the lenses in its optics with varying shades of blue and turquoise crystal. The hotel designers had even granted the Newborn a certain sense of freedom by hiding its necessary monofilament track in the sweeping kelp-frond pattern of the white-and-green tile floor.

There was obviously something for everyone at the Startide Hotel—whether you were human or not.

"Well . . ." Rahel stopped just inside the landing pad doorway and dropped her luggage with a sigh. "I guess no one can fault Sadena on accommodating nonhuman personnel."

Paval glanced up from setting down his own small roll of luggage, turning a look over one shoulder to note the Newborn at its slightly too-short registration desk. "I wonder how well he treats his human personnel." Then, seeming suddenly to realize how impolite that sounded, he pushed their field pack together with their gear and volunteered curtly, "I'll go get the keys," before Rahel could say anything to reprimand him.

Not that she'd intended to. She watched him cross the spacious lobby at a brisk trot, and wondered if Saiah had forced an apprentice on her because he thought it would be just like having another puppy. If only apprentices had such short childhoods and were so easily trained.

"Thank you so much for waiting to make sure the media didn't rend me limb from limb." Nils came up on her from behind, his footsteps characteristically unhurried even though he carried nothing but a pocket notebook and a single overnight valise. "Really—thank you."

Rahel glanced back to find him completely unscathed, his valise balanced neatly atop Rahel's equipment pack. "A lawyer as slick as you, Nils? I thought that was why the Ark sent you."

"And with your skills at client relations, Rahel, it's a wonder they even considered me."

Not in the mood for Nils's verbal sparring, Rahel leaned back against a nearby pillar and watched the fish in one of the self-sustaining tank colonies. They looked as confused and unhappy with their artificial surroundings as she.

"Anyone up for dinner in the Galaxy Ballroom?"

She looked up as Paval approached, and Nils lifted red-gold eyebrows with interest. "Are you paying?" the lawyer asked.

Smiling, Paval handed Rahel her flat plastic key-card with one hand, offering a similar card to Nils with his other. "I don't think anyone working for the Ark makes enough money to afford it." He fished in a front pocket of his field vest and withdrew a crumpled square of paper between two fingers. "Huan gave me this when I picked up the keys."

"Huan?" Rahel twitched the paper away from her apprentice just out from under Nils's reaching hand. Nils returned his hand to the top of his suitcase with quiet aplomb, too well-bred to bicker.

"The Newborn running the front desk." Paval retrieved his own bag and shrugged it over one shoulder. "He's our concierge and guest liaison while we're here."

Must be easy to lavish attention on hired researchers when the rest of your resort is shut down. Rahel spread the paper flat with one hand, and didn't even object when Nils leaned over her arm to look at it with her.

My apologies for the disturbance
upon your arrival this evening.
Please help yourself to any dinner on our menu

> *with my compliments. I will be honored to*
> *join you at my earliest convenience.*

> *F.S.*

"We've each been given a private suite, too," Paval went on when Rahel grunted and pushed the note aside to Nils. "Huan said if we need anything, all we have to do is let him know. This place has everything!"

Which Rahel suspected was rather the point.

"I think I need a swordfish steak and at least a half a bottle of good Terran wine." Nils picked up his valise and looked speculatively from side to side. "Not to mention a bellhop to take our things to our rooms so we don't have to be bothered."

Rahel stooped with a disgusted snort, sweeping up her bag and their field pack one in each hand. "I think you guys need to remember what we're here for." She glowered at both of them, but only Paval had the grace to look subdued. "Not only is Feles Sadena probably responsible for the very disaster we're trying to avert here, but running up expense tabs with big rooms and fancy food isn't why Noah's Ark hires out its services to private sectors. Or weren't you listening to all that yelling a minute ago?"

Nils made a face at her, waving Paval into silence when the apprentice opened his mouth as though to defend them. "The boy and I are quite aware that we aren't on Uriel to enjoy ourselves. But does that make it wrong to take a little pleasure when it's offered?"

"I'm sure that's what everybody who comes here says." Rahel turned away from them with a scowl and a dismissive shake of her head. "I just think maybe you ought to consider what made them have to call us here in the first place. That's all."

Rahel's suite took up half of the sixteenth floor. It smelled of sea-sand and hyacinth. She dropped her luggage, then danced a few steps forward when the door began to slide shut on her. The instant it hissed into its frame, she wished she could duck back outside again.

She didn't want to stay in a place like this, a place where live sea plants were confined to water-filled cylinders all for the sake of decoration. A place where Terran nudibranchs and *Aequorea* were depicted as often in the furniture carvings and artwork as any native Uriel species. What Sadena advertised throughout the galaxy as an homage to the natural world was a sham, constructed to look and sound and feel the way wealthy tourists expected it to, not the way nature really designed it. Just like the Startide's carefully downplayed frontispiece, and the spectacular robotic arthropod running the desk in the lobby.

Kicking her luggage to the foot of the bed, Rahel walked slowly across the opulent sleeping area, past the coffee table with its tangle of blooming plants, and tapped a hand against the floor-to-ceiling window that made up the suite's outside wall. Whether honestly or through some trickery of remote projection, she was rewarded with a stark, nighttime vista built all of ocean, starlight, and in-rolling clouds. Already the furthermost strip of sky looked like nothing but a blurry black smear where encroaching weather smothered the horizon line and smudged out the stars.

Held up against the manic complexity of Sadena's elaborate hotel, Uriel reminded Rahel of a chicken's egg subjected to comparison with its brighter, augmented Fabergé cousin. It didn't reassure her that the egg humans would pay millions of credits to preserve was not the one still containing all the subtle chemistries necessary to create life. Somehow, work done by human hands always impressed the masses more than anything done by nature, even when man was only copying what he'd already seen. That's why Uriel needed a series of resorts in the first place—to make sure the planet's natural splendors weren't "wasted" on her own nonsentient inhabitants.

And Saiah wonders why I hate these jobs.

No, come to think of it, he probably didn't.

The bathroom was dressed all in polished coral—taken from the oceans back home on Terra, no doubt, since Sadena found Uriel's environment far more valuable intact than it could ever be piecemeal—and the bed was a floppy monstrosity of water and pre-warmed silk. Sweeping off the shimmering turquoise comforter and stripping both pillows of their shams, Rahel carried the bundle to the sitting area and the big outside window.

One end of the window, captured behind a length of velvet sofa, slid open a crack, almost as wide as Rahel's hand—enough to let in a maddening whisper of ocean-fresh air, but not enough to let some heartbroken fool fling himself out onto the driveway. Just as well. It would have been awkward to explain how she ended up in the front of lawn planters if she happened to roll over in her sleep during the night.

Dropping the comforter and pillows onto the floor beside that crack, Rahel wrapped herself awkwardly in the shiny, slippery turquoise blob. The oceans on Uriel may have been quiet and shy, but at least she could fall asleep to their voiceless rhythms, not to the man-made silence of facile creature comforts and white, confining walls.

The next morning arrived in a haze of humid confusion. Rahel passed her flippers from one hand to the other in an attempt to get a grip on the equipment pack sliding off her shoulder, but still ended up trotting down the last of the Startide's front steps with the pack swinging heavily from her elbow. Behind her, curses and complaints ricocheted within the wall of reporters that hotel security none-too-gently pressed back toward the edge of the staircase. Rahel tossed the guards a mental thanks for their efforts, but didn't slow down to actually say anything. She didn't have time.

Rahel hated being late. There was nothing deep and psychological about it as far as she was concerned, just simple annoyance at the loss of wasted time mixed with some self-flagellation for being too stupid to pay attention to the time. The morning spent studying details of the stellar jellyfish life cycle of eggs, larvae, and breeding stalks had seemed like such a good idea when she'd sat down to it at dawn. Now—her mind sloshing about with data on spermatozoa, hydroids, and single-celled offspring—she wondered if she wouldn't have done better to sit down here on the docks to do her reading. At least then Paval would be the one feeling foolish as he hurried to join her, and not the other way around. She shrugged her pack up over her shoulder again, and resisted the urge to break into a trot when she reached the dock at the bottom of the stairs.

Paval jerked a look back at her when the vibration of her footsteps reached him, and Rahel was surprised by the eager hope that flashed in his nervous smile. Maybe the slim, bald pilot hovering at his side was getting too friendly for Paval's comfort. Rahel had no idea what kind of cultural taboos the boy labored under. Early morning crankiness made her toy with the idea of slowing her stride (just to see what would happen), but she resisted in favor of finding something more constructive to do with her mood. When Paval abruptly disengaged the pilot to hurry toward the skate at the end of the pier, Rahel was just as glad she hadn't dawdled—the face that turned to watch her approach didn't belong to a bald skate pilot after all, but, rather, to netlink ferret Eme Keim, with her androgynous clothing and too-short blond hair. The pilot, apparently, was the steel-and-Teflon robot bolted to the skate's navigation console. Rahel suddenly wasn't sure what to expect from this morning expedition, and that spurt of uncertainty made her stomach burn.

"Proctor Tovin." Keim said it half as greeting, half as identification as Rahel walked into easy speaking distance.

Rahel passed her by without slowing down. "Some reporter you are. What were you doing talking to him?" She waved at where Paval fidgeted, one leg already in the waiting skate. "He doesn't know shit."

"I'd assumed as much." Keim fell into step behind her, unperturbed. "Mostly, I was waiting for you."

"I don't know shit, either." Rahel tossed her pack at Paval. "Talk to me tomorrow."

"I don't know that I'll be able to get permission again tomorrow."

Rahel paused, one hand still on the dock piling, and turned slowly to cock a suspicious look at Keim. "Permission?" Behind her, Paval groaned.

"I know you won't believe it, but this wasn't even my idea." Coming a few leisurely steps closer, Keim presented a folded slip of paper. "The memo I got this morning said I should give you this if you made trouble."

Rahel plucked the note away without shifting her scowl from Keim's pert little smile. The faintest tickle of pleasant sweetness danced counterpoint to the smell of ocean when she spread the note open against her palm. The scent dissipated before she could identify what it was supposed to remind her of.

Feles Sadena's already-familiar script decorated the paper with hairlike grace.

Proctor Tovin—

Forgive my presumption in arranging this interview with Ms. Keim. I have paid generously for your presence on my planet, however, and so feel I have some liberty in interpreting the particulars of your duties here.

I would very much like to see at least one of the netlink services produce a truthful report of our efforts on behalf of the stellar jellyfish. With that in mind, Ms. Keim of GreeNet has been granted permission to accompany you on today's expedition. You do not, of course, have to answer everything she chooses to ask you, but I needn't remind you of the benefits of positive publicity.

Thank you for your cooperation in this.

F.S.

Cooperation. He obviously didn't know her very well.

"She showed me that, too."

Rahel hadn't even heard Paval move up behind her, and so shot him a sharper look than she'd really intended.

His attention, however, was focused on Keim. "Do we really have to bring her with us?" he asked quietly.

Rahel shrugged. "Did Sadena say anything about this during dinner last night?"

"He never even came to dinner last night." She couldn't tell if Paval's disgust was aimed at Sadena or the reporter.

"Well, then . . ." Rahel made no effort to keep her own voice down. "We could always push her off the pier."

"And she'd write all about it in her netlink upload tonight." Keim returned Rahel's glower with an angelic grin. *A Greenie,* Rahel reminded herself, *and a smartass.*

"Remember that skinny little redhead who came in with us?" Rahel rolled Sadena's note into a ball between both palms. "Well, we brought him along to talk to people just like you. Why don't you go bother him?"

"Because I'd rather talk to the people who are doing the real work," Keim told her, stepping down into the skate beside them. The boat listed drunkenly under her added ballast, and Paval scooted hurriedly to the other side to try and even them out. "Not to the people with the prepared answers who were sent to stonewall the people like me."

As much as Nils accused her of not understanding politics, Rahel knew enough to know that pissing off both the Ark's employer and a major netlink news correspondent in one fell swoop wasn't a very good idea. She just wished she could shake the feeling that Nils would have found some incredibly smooth way to convince Keim she'd rather count sea gulls from the docks. She jerked loose the closest tie-off, and turned away from the reporter with a growl.

"You got extra UV block?"

Paval looked up from strapping on his flippers with sharper, shorter motions than he needed to. "Me?"

"You?" Rahel parroted, not in the mood for anyone else's

ill temper but her own. "The man without a molecule of melanin in his dermis."

He pursed his lips and bent back to his equipment. "I'm already covered up." This despite the fact that his cheekbones and nose already looked pinkish above the bright yellow-and-black Ark skinsuit. Or maybe that was just a trick of the strong greenhouse sun.

"Not for you—" The skate's antigravs cut in with a kick, and their rise to a meter above the water made Rahel catch at Paval's shoulder as she leaned over him to jerk his pack out from under his seat. "For her." She found a tube of UV screen jammed under a clutter of sampling vials and a flimsy on skinsuit prep. "If she sunburns while she's out here, she'll probably blame that on Noah's Ark, too."

Rahel turned to find Keim sitting awkwardly on the floor of the skate. It soothed her irritation a little to see the faint startlement in the reporter's eyes as the skate crept silently up to speed. She held the UV block in front of Keim's face, then sighed when the reporter didn't immediately reach for it.

"You've got less than thirty minutes before me and my partner dive overboard and start getting down to that 'real' work you mentioned." Rahel caught at Keim's wrist and unceremoniously clapped her hand around the UV tube. "So if I were you, Ms. Keim, I'd start asking questions."

Sunlight, bright as fire on glass, exploded across the water around them as the skate slipped northward. Rahel squinted despite her sun visor, and heard Keim groan against the sudden intensity before Paval relinquished his own eye protection—for the sake of the Ark's reputation, no doubt. She wished that she'd thought to bring along extra visors, and couldn't help burning with renewed annoyance at the reporter. Then they passed out of the shallows, and the skate leapt into speed, leaving hotel, reporters, and frustrating hindsight doubts all behind.

Rahel hadn't expected the hush of the skate's low-friction

sprint. She gripped the edges of her seat even though the craft was streaking toward the Odarkan straits in a smooth, unnatural rush—no bobbing with the windy chop, no needle stings of water against her face or the exposed backs of her hands. The only wake behind them was a dotted trail of foam divots where wave crests were brave enough to brush at the stern of the boat as it raced by.

Rock clambered up from the water on either side, rising high and fast to build the ragged straits that marked the entrance to the Odarkan Sea. In the stately drift of a hot-air balloon, the throat of stone leading into the Odarkan had seemed long and wild and elegant. Now, it tore past too quickly to register as anything but a sketchy frame for the view of dawn-bleached mist and distant woodland. Then the fleeting sense of confinement whisked away, and the only thing Rahel could see besides the hectares of sun-splashed water was the smudge of border trees with their false rootwork of blurry swamp reflections.

"You've got to be making this up."

Rahel tore her gaze away from the slough's bleak grandeur, and sighed. Keim had actually been quiet for nearly two minutes now, paging back and forth through screen after screen of scribbled notes. Rahel had rather hoped the reporter's silence meant she couldn't think of any more annoying questions. So much for that.

"You think I have nothing better to do than make up stories for gullible netlink Greens?" Rahel asked her, turning forward in her seat. At the front of the skate, their boxoid pilot remained fixed and unmoving as it manipulated the boat's many controls in eerie machine silence. Paval, sitting one seat behind the pilot's position, swore that the steel-grey construct was a Newborn. Rahel hadn't bothered to crawl forward far enough to read the designation on its Robot Identification tag. "I can't believe your net sent you out to report on something you obviously know nothing about," she continued to Keim.

"I know enough," Keim said firmly, not looking up from

her notes, "to know that stellar jellyfish do not come from coral."

Rahel growled and tugged at her forelock while Paval stated in a slow, loud voice, "Nobody said they *did* come from coral."

"Stellar jellyfish make eggs." Rahel bent forward to lean her elbows on her knees, ticking off elements of the life cycle within a few centimeters of Keim's humorless scowl. "The eggs hatch into larvae, which swim around until they find some nice rock to latch onto. Once they attach, they grow into polyps—"

Keim flipped her notebook and stabbed at an entry. "Which is a type of coral!"

"Which is *like* coral!" Paval corrected, and Rahel grumped over him, "Sort of!" before Keim could take that as some kind of justification for whatever she'd written. "After the polyps have been around for a while, they start shedding single-celled ephyrae, which eventually grow into adult jellyfish. This is such an effective system that it's existed essentially unchanged for about six hundred million years both here *and* on Earth. It's partly because we've never had a chance to study such perfect parallel evolution in such a high-level organism that the Ark was interested in taking this job."

Keim flicked a look at her over the top of the notebook. "Jellyfish are a high-level organism?"

Rahel shrugged. "Compared to slime molds, they are."

"So does Mr. Sadena know that Noah's Ark has ulterior motives for being on Uriel?"

Rahel fought down a prickle of annoyance even as she saw Paval jerk his head up sharply in the seat behind Keim. "Everybody has ulterior motives. At least the Ark's are still related to keeping the jellyfish alive."

"So you acknowledge that the well-being of the stellar jellyfish population may not be Mr. Sadena's primary interest in engaging Noah's Ark."

This time it was clearly a statement. Rahel clenched her hands together into a fist.

"I can only tell you why *I'm* here, Ms. Keim," Rahel answered stiffly. "If you want to know what Mr. Sadena is thinking, you'd be better off taking it up with him." Nils would have been so proud.

"Oh, come *on*." Keim dropped her notebook against her knees with a *clack!* "Are you actually going to look me in the face and tell me you don't care why he really brought you in?"

What a stupid question. As if Rahel's caring could change one damn thing the man had done to this planet. As if Sadena's dissembling could change how much she cared even so. "I don't care," she told Keim simply. It wasn't exactly the first time she'd lied to the press.

Keim made some mark in her notebook, face calm but cheeks faintly red. "Don't care that Feles Sadena is using Noah's Ark to whitewash his poor management of this ecology?" she asked in studied sincerity. "Or don't care that even GreeNet doesn't believe you'll be allowed to tell the truth in your report, much less accomplish anything with it?"

Something about the way Keim waited with her stylus poised above the screen as though expecting some sort of straight answer made Rahel smile. "Let me tell you something," she said, pushing up from her knees to lean back in her seat again. "No amount of money can change the facts of a scientific investigation. Whatever Sadena *thinks* he's paying for, Noah's Ark is here to find out the truth about what's going on with this environment. Paval and I"—she waved at her apprentice over Keim's shoulder, but the reporter showed no inclination to glance at him—"are the first phase in what will probably end up being a very lengthy planetary study. But for right now, we'll check out the immediate complaint, produce a report based on what we find here, and suggest a course of action to both Mr. Sadena and the Ark. If Sadena decides he doesn't want to do any of the things we present to him, it's not like we can force him." She smiled thinly. "Any more than he can force us to lie about our findings."

"Is it Noah's Ark's position that a human arbitrarily granted with enough money to own a planet automatically has the right to destroy it, if they choose?"

Rahel snorted and tossed a look toward the sky. "Where do you get this crap?"

"I only ask what my readers would, if they were posing the questions."

Rahel nodded, unimpressed. "Then your readers are idiots."

"Her readers are here."

She and Keim twisted about together at Paval's growled remark. "What?"

Scowling off to his left, Paval threw the pack he'd been rummaging through to the floor of the boat. "There are laws against them congregating on private property, aren't there? Doesn't a privately owned planet count?"

Rahel rotated to follow the irritated wave of his arm, and glimpsed an uneven clot of green undulating with the waves where the sea met the sky. "Apparently not." She even flipped off her visor to make sure all the hoods and jackets really were in emerald, and not just distorted by colored lenses. "Shit."

The demonstration group was the usual motley collection of shouting and mismatched green. It was apparently traditional that members of a Green rally pull together whatever emerald, kelly, olive, or lime clothing they had lying around, swarming the point in question like leaves blown from a hundred different trees. They were the only officially organized group that managed to make the Ark's khaki-brown bush suits look like a Fascist uniform. Rahel supposed that impression was intentional, which only served to irritate her more.

"Did you tell them to show up here?" she asked, turning

back to Keim. "Something to make the interview a little more lively?"

"Are you kidding?" Keim didn't seem able to take her eyes off the renegade flotilla as she folded her notebook and slipped it into a pocket of her blouse. "The kind of Greens who come all this way just to cause trouble are fruitcakes."

Rahel snorted, and Keim shot a frown at her as though anticipating what she was planning to say. "That doesn't invalidate what they stand for," she asserted before Rahel could even consider a remark. "It just means not everyone in the Green is a good judge of how to best accomplish those goals."

Considering that hard-core Greens didn't believe humans should be allowed to set foot anywhere except their native Earth—and perhaps not even there—it was small wonder they didn't know how to react to the rest of their species' antagonism. "But they're here because of your uploads, yes?"

Keim pursed her lips and nodded, not taking her eyes from the rapidly growing green blot. "Probably."

"My God! Don't you even wait for facts before you—"

Rahel leaned across Keim to push Paval back into his seat before he could upset the skate's delicate balance. "Not now!" She dropped back into her own seat, facing Keim. "Any chance they'll listen if you tell them to back off?"

Keim looked at her as though surprised she'd even made the suggestion, then shrugged. "Most likely they'll think I'm only taking your side because we're in the same boat."

"And are you?" Rahel asked.

"Am I what?"

"Taking our side."

Keim made a face and turned back toward the Greens. "I haven't even said I'll talk to them yet."

The only difference between lawyers and reporters was a graduate degree. Rahel lifted her chin to call up toward the mechanical pilot, "I suppose it's too much to ask that they're nowhere near where we need to be."

The pilot extended a small remote mike in her direction from a panel low on its subjective back. "Query error." Its voice was finely tuned and masculine, but oddly devoid of character. Rahel wondered what it had been before it was Newborn. "Syntax not sufficient for specific data retrieval."

Paval twisted impatiently to face the bow of the skate. "Show us the coordinates of those other boats."

A brightly colored topo map grew into being above the skate's dash. The overlaid location of the Green flotilla made an almost visible dent in the trench near the middle of the hologram.

Rahel grumbled. "Of course. Shit."

The pilot remained singularly unaffected by her profanity. "Instruction: Please present activity modifications in command or query mode."

Paval, equally frustrated, gripped the edge of his seat with both hands. "Can't we just go around them?" The pilot apparently took that as a course change, and eased the skate into a parabola.

"Go around to where?" Rahel's shadow swept across the floor of the boat as they swung into a wide arc around the hub of waiting Greens. "They're sitting right on top of the jellyfish breeding site—there's no 'around' to go to."

"But *why*?" Paval rotated, his face directed toward the protestors no matter how wide a circle their own craft made. "Don't they understand we care about preserving this habitat as much as they do?"

A shout of recognition stuttered through the flock of Greens, and two boats—the only two fitted with outboard motors—awkwardly disengaged from the rest of the group to carve an interception course through the water. The mass of Greens was already close enough that Rahel could make out their individual faces. "Recognize any of them?" she asked Keim.

The reporter spared her only a single disgusted glance. "What? You think everybody in a conservation organization knows everybody else?"

"It was worth a try."

"No, I don't know them."

Rahel kept her eyes on the two approaching craft, trying to estimate whether or not they'd catch up to the skate before it finished its swing. "They're not inflatables," she commented aloud. "That means they've got their own aircraft, probably even their own jumpship in the system. God, I hope they didn't set down anywhere near here—the vibrations could kill the jellyfish."

Paval pulled off his skinsuit hood in one quick, angry motion. "What jellyfish those outboards don't chew up!"

She'd never seen him angry before now, and, for some reason, the sudden appearance of his temper made her smile. "The outboards don't reach deep enough. This time of day, the jellies are a good ten meters under to get away from the light." Climbing forward to slap the pilot's carapace, Rahel hoped it followed her gesture as she pointed toward the approaching Greens.

"So what are we going to do?" Keim asked, stylus poised above the screen of her notebook. "Run or stay?"

Rahel opened her mouth, but didn't even manage an intake of breath before Paval was at her side, dark eyes locked on the approaching boats. "This kind of stupidity should be illegal!" he shouted, more at them than at her, and apparently for their benefit. "Those hypocrites don't even understand what it is they're fighting for—!"

Rahel knotted one hand in her hair to keep from knocking her apprentice into the sea. "Will you just shut up?"

"Query error: Syntax—"

"Not you," Rahel cut the pilot off with another bang on its carapace. "This is a command: Pull away from the approaching boats, but not too far." She tried to ignore Paval's chain of foreign curses as she frowned across the bright water at the protestors. "I don't want them to think we're running away."

"Who cares what they think?" Rocking unsteadily as the skate purred into motion, Paval took two stumbling steps to his left to maintain eye contact with the closest raft full of Greens while their own boat edged forward. "They should be back at the resort, talking to all those reporters about why they think they're better able to save the stellar jellies than we are!" He shook Rahel's hand off his arm and shouted angrily across the water, "Ecologists are all supposed to be on the same side!"

That's when Rahel saw the spear gun.

Hooking her arm across his chest, she yanked Paval back with all her weight, tumbling them both to the floor of the narrow skate. Keim gave a short shriek; then a loud, hollow *thok!* echoed flatly through the space between the seats. Rahel felt a painful thrill of relief even before her rational brain realized the sound meant a spear striking boat sides, not a spear striking flesh. "Get down!" she shouted without looking behind. "They're not gonna wait to find out your credentials!"

Keim scrambled to the rear of the boat in a thumping clatter, and Rahel pushed herself up with one hand, shoving Paval back down to the deck with her other. She raised her head to look over the side just as the skate jerked and heeled over almost onto its side.

Then the craft righted again with a smack. Rahel gripped the wet rail with both hands. She was too stunned to see, but knew from the salty sting of wind on her face that they were moving—and not in a forward direction.

"What happened?" Paval's voice, so hoarse and quiet after his flash of anger, barely carried over the hum of the skate's laboring engine.

Water, chill from a long night of darkness, gushed past Rahel's leg and into Paval's lap. The spear had split a hole longer than the spread of Rahel's hand in the side of the skate, then filled most of it with the head and shaft of the weapon and a steady spatter of water. Her stomach clenched sickly at the image of one of them sitting with their back to that bulkhead. All the same, their skate probably wouldn't have been flooding so badly if the Greens hadn't attached the spear's unbreakable tether to the two outboards so they could drag the skate behind them in their own choppy wake.

Suddenly remembering the pilot, Rahel scrambled on her knees to the front of their craft. "Pull us loose!"

"Command noted." Despite its stoical monotone, the Newborn was doing a wonderful impression of panicked human flight as it slued the skate to make slack in the towline. "Data point: Designation of skate Number 6398240 is as a recreational vehicle, not as a high-performance water craft."

"Now he tells me." The cable snapped taut again with a *thrum,* and Rahel heard Paval thump into one of the seats with an angry curse.

Water sloshed wrist-high across the floor as Rahel crawled back toward the passenger seats. The space under her sitting place was empty, only a damp piece of torn fabric suggesting how her pack had gone overboard when the skate first tipped. She growled in frustration and grabbed at her seat for support. "Your phone!"

Keim, half-crammed under the farthest back seat, frowned at Rahel while she struggled to free herself.

"Find a goddamned phone!" If they couldn't get themselves out of this, they could at least call the Startide for reinforcements. The skate bucked, and Rahel slammed up hard against the opposite rail.

"Where are they taking us?" Keim shouted back at her. But she had one arm buried up to the elbow in Paval's field pack when she asked it, so Rahel didn't feel any immediate need to beat her for being distracted.

Not that she would have had the chance. Broken shadows flickered across the skate like tongues of cold, black flame, and the boat's own engine noise surrounded them in a cloud of bugs and bitter stench. A length of now-slack cable lashed a wake through the tree roots and swamp beneath the skate, then leapt with a crack of surprise when the skate sheered against some obstacle Rahel couldn't see, and overturned them all into the rancid mud.

* * *

"Data point: Mathematical models indicate that inversion of skate Number 6398240 is unlikely while antigravity repulsor units are still engaged."

Rahel gritted her teeth, shoving one shoulder against the side of the overturned skate and trying not to notice that the only movement she felt was her own feet sliding backward through the mud. A lurid belch of vapor curled up from the disturbed sediment, and she stumbled upright with a cough to escape the foul smell. "You could help me, you know!"

"Request noted." The pilot, its boxy body wedged above the water in a snarl of tree roots, was silent for nearly thirty seconds. "Data point: Reinforced appendages are prerequisite before external leverage adequate for independent motion can be achieved."

Rahel growled and dropped her head against the skate. Keim volunteered in a slow, helpful voice, "He doesn't have any legs."

It had been more a smart remark and less a real suggestion, anyway. "What about the antigravs?" Lifting up on her toes, Rahel stretched across the bow of the skate to rest her weary arms. Keim sat perched atop a knee of root to the pilot's left, lips pursed as she searched for dry patches on her clothing with which to clean her ruined notebook. Rahel couldn't help thinking how she would feel if it had been *her* data lost to the slough. "Any chance you can disengage the antigravs from there?" she asked the pilot.

"Request noted. Unable to comply. Data point: All ship's functions are referenced via hard-wired terminal junctures."

Which, of course, ceased to be hard-wired to the pilot right about the time the lower part of its casing tore away from the skate. She didn't even bother asking about the radio—it languished along with the antigrav controls under twenty-odd centimeters of mud, sinking deeper by the minute. Rahel kicked one of the boat's dented sides, but didn't even get a satisfying *boom!* for her effort.

The slosh and suck of shin-deep mud reached them just

ahead of Paval's disgusted groan. It was a sentiment Rahel could well appreciate right now. Every step, every movement in the brackish water broke the delicate layer of surface tension protecting their noses from the cesspool underneath. Bugs and little biting things not even big enough to see swarmed each upsurge of stench, changing their focus to breath-letting orifices and sweat-sticky skin as soon as their filthy bug brains recognized that higher life-forms were around. In general, Rahel tried to keep an open mind about the role various life-forms played in their environments—but if she had to snort out one more noseful of midges or spit another spider-legged intruder into her palm, she was going to storm through this slough and personally squash every flying thing she found.

Paval lumbered into view one long, awkward step at a time. He nearly lost his balance twice when his rear foot refused to peel out of the mire and his leading foot sank deeper than he expected, but he freed himself without glancing up for help, brow furrowed, mouth clamped resolutely shut against the cloud of fuzzy buzzing around him. His effort to wipe the mud from his face had only turned him into a more severe copy of himself—dark eyes smoldered inside a negative raccoon mask of cleanness, and his hair was plastered sloppily to his skull in five uneven, finger-width furrows. Mindful of what a mirror for her he probably made, Rahel scraped her own hands down both cheeks and flicked what mud she got back into the water.

"This was all I could find." Paval swung his arm up between them, dangling the soaked, twisted remnant of pack into Rahel's hands as he stumbled to a stop. Invisible midges and their more visible cousins jostled for position in his breath stream. "The rest must have gone under already."

The pack strap felt cold and slimy in her grip. Wrapping one arm under the bottom of the bag to steady it, Rahel dug her free hand inside to paw through the muddy contents. "No phone?"

Paval coughed, temporarily shattering the cloud of bugs,

and sat heavily among the roots on the other side of the pilot. "No phone."

"Damn."

"Not that it would matter." He aimed a sour look at the ruined notebook in Keim's lap. "Our phones weren't designed for swamp duty any more than her notebook was." Rahel watched him clap an uncounted number of bugs to death between his palms, and wondered if he was thinking about the Greens. "We're screwed."

"Any chance your groupies will follow us in here? Maybe try and do some more damage?"

Keim looked up from her labors, as though surprised that Rahel had asked her. "How should I know?"

"You write for them, don't you?" Rahel countered. "You must know something about the way they think."

"I know how the GreeNet editors think," Keim said. She finally gave up on her notebook and refolded it into her jacket pocket. "And they just happen to prefer a more radical shade of Green than I might personally wear."

Which answered at least one question.

Paval splashed one foot scornfully in the slime of mud below him. "Whatever color they are, their boats still need water. They could never make it back here through all this muck." Another million insects died with a sharp report. "And no one in his right mind would *walk* in this filth."

Grinning, Rahel yanked shut the zipper on their ruined equipment pack and turned to hang it on the bush behind her. "I guess that tells me where *we*'re gonna stand."

Paval made a sound of weary sarcasm. "Oh, great."

"What?" Bugs and noxious gas swelled up as if from nowhere as Keim slid down from her perch with a splash. "We *walk*? You can't be serious!"

Rahel shrugged. "You got any better ideas?"

"Yes! We wait right where we are."

Rahel snorted with laughter, and Paval rocked forward to hang his head between his knees. "We wait for what?" Rahel asked the reporter. "The hotel thinks we're out here collecting samples, and Nils knows me well enough not to expect any chitchat until we're done. It's not going to occur to anyone to come looking for us until well after dark. Which is about . . ." She made a show of squinting up at the sky through the ratty canopy of leaves. "Ten or eleven hours from now."

"We'll all be eaten to death before then." Paval swatted at some crawling thing on his hand, but not quickly enough to keep it from biting him.

"Well, then—" Rahel leaned over and pulled him groaning to his feet. "A little healthy exertion won't make things any worse, now, will it?"

"System request."

At first, the toneless voice surprised her. Then she looked over Paval's shoulder and remembered the disabled pilot, still propped among the tree roots and too heavy to carry.

"Data point: This unit massed five hundred twenty-three point six kilograms before truncation," it said, as if reading her thoughts in her expression. Maybe it could. "Data point: Central memory package masses less than point five kilograms. Data point: All but memory is hardware. Request: Transport memory package back to Startide homebase for installation in rebuilt chassis."

"Sure thing." She nodded Paval toward the Newborn, then turned to look a question at Keim. "How about you? You coming or staying?"

"Do I have any choice?" The reporter sighed as she watched Paval pry loose an access panel and pull the Newborn's memory free. "If only the trip could be so easy for all of us."

Rahel wondered how easy it was for the pilot to trust its brain to three strangers. "What are you complaining about?" She clapped an arm across Keim's sagging shoulders and turned her in a generally westward direction. "You and the Greens say you want to rescue this planet. Well, it's time you got up close and personal with what it is you want to save."

*   *   *

Seven hours, sixteen minutes, and one lost skinsuit shoe later, they mounted the steps of the Startide Hotel.

Rahel lifted her head to squint up the long stone stairs ahead of them, but could only summon enough energy to sigh. Beside her, Paval placed his foot on the first step and said wearily, "This is going to hurt."

As if she had a pain threshold left to worry about.

Bugs, stench, and cool suck-mud had leached out every micron of vitality she had in the last seven hours. Now, the very business of lifting her feet from one step to the next took more concentration than she usually expended on entire safaris, and sandy, mud-freckled footprints followed them up the stairs as they climbed. Rahel's eyes hurt from the endless glare off the Odarkan's surface, her throat hurt from coughing against the stink of rotten vegetation, and her legs hurt more than she could have imagined from high-stepping through the root-tangled mud. She'd been privately thrilled to have Keim struggling along with them—the reporter had given Rahel the excuse of occasionally calling a halt to let Keim catch up and catch her breath. Rahel had done this at first because she really didn't want Keim expiring of heat stroke fifty kilometers from nowhere. After a while, though, she stopped whenever her aching thighs couldn't stand pulling up against another step, and only said she was worried about the reporter. Neither Keim nor Paval questioned her, but she had a feeling she wasn't fooling anyone.

The last hour or so of their trek, at least, had been free of the slough. They'd made better time across the narrow strand of beach, but the unbroken sun and scorching sand did its own brand of damage. Paval's face looked swollen and shiny where the sun had singed his skin, and Rahel's shoeless foot didn't feel a whole lot better. Keim, damn her, was miraculously unburned. It seemed somehow unfair that the reporter would be the only one to come out of this adventure unscathed, especially since it was more than just slightly her fault that they'd ended up stranded in the first place.

Wind, roaring faintly with the echoes of surf against sand, rolled over them without actually stirring a breeze. Struck suddenly with that incongruity, Rahel stopped and looked upward for the source of the blurry sound. She recognized it for distant cheering right about the same time her brain identified the swarm of reporters and spybees pouring down the long staircase to meet them. She was surprised that she couldn't feel anything but dull annoyance at the prospect of confronting them, even with such a clear view of the jeering Greens discoloring the steps above them.

Her apprentice, however, hadn't yet reached such an impasse. Spitting some oath in a language Rahel couldn't identify, Paval scrambled toward the crowd of Greens at what would probably have been a run on any other day. Rahel watched him pound his way upward, his hands grabbing the steps ahead of him as if resorting to all fours could hurry him, and found herself faintly envious of his youthful vigor. Even if he was expending it on a stupid display of male ego. Reporters scattered to let him through without so much as interrupting their shouted questions.

"You probably oughta stop him," Keim commented dryly when she finally trudged up alongside Rahel. The reporter sat with a weary groan, obviously not planning to go any farther.

Up top, Paval dove into the knot of Greens amidst a crescendo of media enthusiasm, disappearing beneath the resultant tumble. A burst of irate shouting marked his arrival.

"Yeah," Rahel sighed, glancing back at Keim. "Probably." Then she started upward at the same pace as before, keeping tabs on the fight by the number and color of epithets raining down around her as she climbed.

Not surprisingly, hotel security beat her to the brawl. By the time Rahel reached the long plaza, a fashionably tailored contingent of turquoise-and-salmon suits had pushed themselves through the confusion of Greens and buzzing cameras, surrounding the lone spot of Noah's Ark yellow and pushing him grudgingly toward the entrance of the Startide while the Greens formed a protective clot around one of their own. Even without the shouting and turmoil, the conflict of colors—not to mention philosophies—was enough to make her head hurt.

"Rahel?"

Just the pleasure of walking on hard, level ground nearly buckled her knees. She pretended not to notice Nils squirming toward her through the press of bodies, and tried to keep her ears, if not her eyes, locked on her apprentice.

"Proctor Tovin! Do you have anything to say about your findings so far?" a reporter called out.

"Rahel, what is going on?" Nils appeared at her elbow, grabbing for her arm and looking her wildly up and down as though searching for some sign of damage. "My *God*!" He recoiled with a grimace when his hand made contact with her suit, then had to trot a few steps to catch up with her again. "You smell like a sewer! What happened?"

"Anoxic organic decomposition. I'll explain it to you someday."

"Proctor Tovin, is it true that you've requested Noah's Ark remove you from this safari?"

Ignoring the reporters, Rahel reached past the shoulders of two of the security guards to seize her apprentice's collar. "I've got him."

"Wait a minute, lady—"

"I said I've got him!" Elbowing the guard aside, she dragged Paval to her with a single imperative tug. The young man stumbled, pulled off balance by her hold on his collar, but didn't try to break her grip. Rahel couldn't tell if the scarlet in his cheeks was emotion or sunburn.

"Can you tell us if charges can be brought against Mr. Sadena?"

You can't sue somebody for pissing in his own bed, she

thought but didn't say, then pushed past that reporter just as she had all the others. "Hell of a job you're doing here, Nils." She spared the other proctor a sour scowl as she worked her way out of the knot of security guards. "Have you gotten past the wine and hors d'oeuvres stage yet?"

Nils blinked at her. "What?" He looked too sincere to even be worth yelling at.

"I wouldn't belittle Proctor Oberjen's work if I were you, Proctor Tovin." Valhanryn Esz, the stringer from *Tomorrow Today*, snapped fingers to redirect her minicam, and narrowed almond eyes at Rahel. "It's only because of his cooperation that the media hasn't characterized your behavior as a deliberate obstruction of free speech."

Paval stiffened next to her, and Rahel didn't even wait to see what brilliant rejoinder he might produce. Clapping her hand over his mouth, she matched stares with Esz over Nils's shoulder. "Obstruction?" If she'd had the strength for humor, she might have found the idea laughable. "Guess what, boys and girls," she called, loudly enough that Nils winced and reporters half a staircase down pricked their ears. "Noah's Ark isn't on Uriel just to supply fodder for your netlink uploads. We've actually got a job to do—a very serious job." She scowled at the Greens cordoned behind hotel security. "These assholes aren't helping." When Paval reached up to grip her wrist in both hands, she tightened her fingers on his jaw as a silent warning not to piss her off any further. He let his hands drop back to his sides.

"The Greens?" Nils twisted a look over his shoulder at the activists, frowned at the reporters, then turned a hopeless shrug on Rahel. "What have they got to do with this?" he asked blankly. "Where did they come from?"

"Out of her uploads to GreeNet." Rahel jerked a nod down at Keim, still watching from the foot of the long staircase. "Whatever 'free speech' she's been dumping on them, it just convinced *them* to dump us in the slough along with Sadena's million-credit skate and a busted-up New-born."

"Oh, my God . . ."

She almost enjoyed the look of pale horror on the other proctor's face as she dropped the half-kilo memory pack into his hand. "Tell Sadena he can avoid future equipment loss by using some of his influence to keep Greens and reporters out of our hair instead of kissing up to them. And we're going to need some pretty basic sampling equipment replaced, not to mention a little extra time built into the project."

"Does that mean you're not prepared to make a statement about the cause of Uriel's ecological crisis?" a reporter shouted.

Scraping her hand up the front of Paval's skinsuit, Rahel collected a handful of stinking mud and slapped it onto the reporter's notebook. "That's right—I'm not."

"Rahel!"

Cameras and notepads flew into excited activity even as Nils hurried to interpose himself between the reporters and his colleagues. Crooking her arm around Paval's neck, Rahel turned her back on the crowd and limped toward the hotel entrance with Paval firmly at her side, leaving Nils to sputter whatever apologies or explanations struck his fancy.

The next day, two plastically handsome young men in turquoise-and-salmon suits met Rahel at the door of her suite to escort her up to the roof of the Startide. They tried hard to make the detour chatty and inoffensive. Their smooth and well-practiced behavior, however, only convinced Rahel even more that Sadena was beginning to consider the Greens a greater risk than the feeding frenzy of reporters. By the time they joined Paval and his own escort beneath the wings of an elegantly sculpted short-range hop, Rahel could hear the Green chant of "You stay, you pay!" battling against a babble of reporter questions below. Nils, poor thing, was probably down there already, wading through the morass of human stupidity and earning his keep.

"I don't know what's worse," Rahel commented aloud as she mounted the stairs into the open hatch. "A day penned up with those reporters, or another hike through the margin sloughs."

Paval followed with a new equipment pack slung across one shoulder. "At least the reporters don't stink or bite."

He obviously hadn't dealt with the press for very long.

In contrast to their two previous sojourns into the Odarkan, the hop lifted them away from the Startide's landing field in whisper silence, with no real sense of acceleration to betray the moment when they took off. There weren't even windows or viewscreens in the passenger cabin. No scenery to watch, no reporters to piss at, no fresh air to breathe. Rahel sat heavily on the silk brocade settee and watched Paval experiment with opening and closing the bar with one flipper.

"This place is nicer than our hotel rooms," he said at last. Apparently, the tri-D VR cabaret impressed him.

Rahel was more worried about the immediate reality before them. "You ever done an ocean dive before?" It was something they should have talked about yesterday, but Keim's presence had sidetracked things somewhat.

Paval glanced at her over his shoulder, then shrugged and went back to playing with the entertainment automation. "Recreational scuba, but not with these kinds of skinsuits. I've done a lot of EV work, though. I figure these suits can't be very different."

Not that Rahel would know. She tended to avoid EVA at least as much as she avoided underwater time. "No rebreathers," she told him, snapping her own flippers onto her feet. "The skinsuit extracts dissolved gases from the surrounding water to supply you with breathable atmosphere, then uses the waste gases to keep you warm, keep you buoyant, and whatever else you need to stay happy underwater." She'd passed Ark certification in these skinsuits only a few months before, so still had a lot of the junk information memorized. That had been in an aqua tank back home, though, with less than four meters of water over her head. "Skinsuits won't process as fast as a tank system, so you can't get too wildly active. These things were designed so we could bob around watching animals without coming up for air, not so we could tango underwater."

Paval nodded, then turned away from Sadena's techno gadgets as though just realizing that Rahel was ready to get down to business. "That's why sport divers don't use them," he said as he sat on an ottoman directly in front of her. "But I watched somebody in a full skinsuit once, and I've always wanted to try one."

"Well, now's your chance." Rahel leaned forward to grab the ottoman's skirt, dragging it and her apprentice to within touching range. "The buoyancy control device is built in, just like usual. You vent it"—she pulled Paval's mask down over his face and tapped the upper left-hand corner— "here. Blink twice to vent, three times to fill. One long blink stops it, either way."

Paval raised both hands to touch the sides of his mask, then had to reach quickly to his right when the hop banked abruptly and started its descent. "Two, three, one. Got it." The full-face visor kept Rahel from seeing his expression, but he sounded grim enough to sink a boat. A young man's way of paying attention.

"Your BCD pressure valve is still back here." She slapped the vent at the back of his neck, and he nodded understanding while gathering up the bandolier with his slides and sample bottles. "Be careful—the blink toggle is a lot touchier than the tongue release. You'll lose buoyancy faster than you expect. Play around with it while you're still up top, and don't dive till you're sure you've got the feel."

And that was all they had time for. A resort employee in a fashionable short-sleeved halter cat-footed out to them from the cockpit and hurried them politely toward a cargo door in the rearmost compartment. From there, a wide-open loading platform lowered them through the floor and into the bright, heady spangle of full sunlight above the rucked-up sea. The skate waiting below looked nearly shattered by the force of the hop's repulsors.

"I think I liked the balloons better," Rahel commented as the skate pilot ran out to meet them. Paval only grunted. She assumed that meant he was no more crazy about trying to jump from one craft to the other than she was.

"Slide down on your bottom!" the pilot shouted above the hop's wind pollution. Rahel recognized his iron-dark features and patterned shirt from their first night counting jellies from the air. "I'll take your gear, ma'am! You just slide on down!"

Gripping a corner cable with one hand, she eased herself awkwardly over the edge of the platform and dangled her pack into Jynn's waiting arms. He placed it quickly but gently to one side, then positioned himself underneath her to offer support while she slid down.

"Is this thing gonna be here the whole time we're under?" she asked as Jynn guided Paval down in turn. She didn't like trying to imagine the noise and turbulence the aircraft's constant presence might cause.

"Oh no, ma'am." The pilot darted a smile at her over his shoulder before turning back to wave off the waiting hop. "We'll be going another few kilometers north and east of here yet. Mr. Sadena arranged it specially so we wouldn't put you down right on top of the jellyfish site."

Instinct made Rahel grab the edge of the skate when the hop's retreating pressure swell shoved it down into the water, then roughly released it again. "Apparently, fuel and time are not an issue as far as Mr. Sadena is concerned." She scowled at Paval when he stumbled against her, but didn't shake him off when he ended up clinging to her shoulder to steady himself.

"Mr. Sadena's not the sort of man who cares too much what it costs to get his druthers," Jynn remarked as he picked his way across the heaving deck toward the pilot's station. He flashed Rahel a wry smile as he squeezed past her. "But, then, I figure you noticed that already."

Samples, Cells, and Stiffs. That was the litany Rahel had created to remind Paval—and herself—of their goals for this dive. As a mnemonic, it wasn't the most brilliant creation, but it seemed to serve its purpose. When she asked Paval what he was going down for while Jynn piloted them the last hundred meters to their dive site, her apprentice held up his hand and ticked off three fingers without even pausing to think.

"Water samples to screen for contaminants. Cell samples from both breeding polyps and new medusae, but no eggs, no live larvae, and no live medusae. Any dead jellies—larvae or medusae—I might find floating around." He grinned at her then, in that irritatingly youthful way that made him look ten years younger than he probably was. "At least I'll be able to fit my corpses into a specimen jar."

Rahel pulled her mask down to cover her unamused scowl. "That falls into the category of 'something I'll deal with when I get to it.'"

Dropping their speed, Jynn mated the boat so gently with the water that their sudden entrance into the rhythms of the Odarkan seemed almost magical to Rahel. She hadn't realized how much she missed the heavy swaying of a boat on the breast of the water, how separated Sadena's code of zero impact required each person to be from the living world surrounding them.

On the wake of that thought, a fierce specter of dilemma swelled inside her. Could humans learn to love a world they weren't allowed to touch? Could humans touch a world and not disrupt the thing they claimed to cherish? Rahel had a feeling the answer lay somewhere between the Greens' radical separatism, Noah's Ark's respectful intervention, and Feles Sadena's sanitized exploitation. Yet still outside the reach of the everyday human. It wasn't a happy thought just before this kind of sampling dive.

"Okay, Junior, let's go."

Leaving Paval to settle his mask and pick up his gear, Rahel slipped over the side into water warmer than she'd expected. A pleased but startled shiver rippled just beneath the surface of her diving suit. The sea closed its gentle grip around her as if to soothe her fears, and suddenly her horizon became a disc of glass from elbow to elbow, a steady platter with her in the middle and the sky all around bobbing and dipping in every direction. She blinked on the BCD control in the upper corner of her mask, and melted below the surface on the drag of her equipment belt and body weights.

As usual, Rahel's first underwater breath took a touch of bravery and a lot of faith. It was one thing to know that diving gear would keep you safe in an ocean environment, another thing to truly believe it. Her first breath hitched up short, and she had to forcefully clear her lungs and make herself breathe more deeply the second time around. It only partly worked. She felt the dissatisfied tightness in her lungs that said she still hadn't filled them completely, and had to adjust her perceptions yet again to breathe what felt like a huge, languid sigh against her mask. This time her body relaxed a little with the flush of oxygenated air. Rahel tried to set a flag in her brain to remind her that even breathing couldn't be taken for granted down here in the stellar jellies' realm. Even that much thought threw her off rhythm, though, and forced her to pattern her breathing again.

Sunlight glanced brightly off the surface far above her. It bleached the sky grey-white, and blurred all sign of Jynn's skate except for a dark, broken outline where the resting craft met the water. Below, beetle-green stretched as deep as the brightness would allow; then a silent, shifting mat of shadow formed a floor on which the sunlight pooled. The first ripple of light across that surface brought a smile to Rahel's face: Movement. She blinked again on her BCD, and let its functions draw her slowly downward.

"This is incredible . . . !"

The sound of Paval's voice in her left ear made her glance unconsciously over that shoulder. A shimmer of reflective flatworms exploded silently away from her sudden movement. Rahel relaxed to face her own subjective forward again, reminding herself with a sting of annoyance that hearing her apprentice through a suit com told her nothing about where he was in relation to her.

"Be careful." That seemed a safe admonition, regardless of what he was doing. A jellyfish—half-unseen amongst the rest of the translucent mass below her—brushed languidly against her flipper, then furled away into the jumble of others. She pulled her knees up to give it more room.

"Don't worry—you're clear." Paval could apparently see her. He laughed as the jellies tumbled in a slow-motion tangle, swelling and shrinking on dreamy puffs of motion. "Besides, their nematocysts can't penetrate most human skin. With these suits on, there's almost no chance they'll sting either of us."

"It's not us I'm worried about." Rahel sculled in a circle until she found her apprentice hovering far ahead on her right, his hands barely stirring the water above pearlescent bells wider across than he stood tall. The jellies rippled like a second surface in response to his soft movements. "I don't want you tearing any tentacles or floats on your way down. Push through them *gently*."

Paval nodded, his expression unreadable through his mask at such a distance. "I'll be careful." He sounded a tiny bit chastened, though. "I'll be another twenty straight down. Call me if you need me." And he melted into the mat of jellies before she could comment further on his handling.

Samples, Cells, and Stiffs, she reminded herself. There was still a lot of work to do. Tucking her knees against her chest, she wrapped her arms around her legs and blinked the BCD to take her lower.

Jellyfish membrane oozed across her feet, her back, her shoulders. They were warm, like the water, and nearly as fluid, flowing away from her slow passage the way bubbles slip around a falling stone. Flashes of silent, cold-bright lightning formed their only response to Rahel's brushes with their bodies. In their gentle liquid world, she thought, this must be the same as startled cries. She felt obscurely guilty for disturbing them. Even acknowledging that they hadn't enough nervous system to truly notice or care didn't make her feel any better.

The kiss of their fragile bodies lifted, drifted upward, and Rahel was suddenly beneath them. Tentacles drifted around her in tangles and clouds. A long, lacelike ruffle marked the center of each delicate creature, and ghostly colors flickered up the crinkled edges almost in time with her breathing. The net of sparks that laced their bells whenever they jostled against each other made it easy to understand why tourists paid so much to watch them rise and feed every night. Absently watching little swarms of aquatic insects dart from ruffle to ruffle, Rahel wondered how many tourists had ever tried to imagine the subtlety of organisms with skin but one cell thick, much less what that said about the complexity of the rest of their world. Feles Sadena probably offered gratis dinners to anyone who found the concept of Darwinian hierarchy too stressful.

Sunlight filtered past the gossamer flotilla, mottling abstract patterns across the yellow-and-black panels of Rahel's skinsuit. Jellyfish thoughts, reflected. There couldn't have been more than thirty of the creatures, drifting with their aimless jellyfish whims, yet they made a raft nearly forty meters at its widest. Uncounted ruffles and threads of tissue sifted through the darkness below them. Tipping herself horizontal, Rahel flashed the beam of her handlamp through the water below as she worked a string of water sample bottles off her equipment belt.

"I'm not seeing much in the way of juveniles," she commented aloud. "The smallest one I've got up here"— she rolled a look over each shoulder—"is still about two and a half meters across. That's almost big enough to head for open water within the next few weeks." She was guessing a little on that time frame—she knew it took a good three Uriel months for stellar jellies to reach migrating size, but didn't have the slightest idea about their growth curve. "Maybe something's inhibiting breeding before they head out."

"Then they should be dropping larvae in the main ocean, with a corresponding rise in the stellar jelly population out there."

And so far no one on Uriel had reported finding another stellar jellyfish breeding population. Rahel shrugged, capping her water samples and threading them back onto her belt. "We can check the water here for larvae and ephyrae, and I'll do a head count on the ovigerous adults to see how many are carrying egg clusters."

Paval's breath snorted against his pickup wherever he floated far beneath her. "I can't speak for this year's crop, but they seem to have done all right the last few years. We've got what looks like a good carpet of polyps, and—" He cut himself off with some noncommittal curious noise. "Oh, now *that's* weird."

"What?" Rahel made an impatient face in his general direction. "Talk up, Junior, or I'm leaving you here."

He took a breath, as though planning to say something else, and instead only coughed once, shortly.

For an instant, Rahel thought Paval meant this sound as his reply. Some private ritual of disgust—at the jellyfish for doing something unexpected, or himself for fumbling his sampling gear, or even Rahel for the tireless lash of sarcasm that had finally exhausted his patience. But the next bark of sound across her skinsuit's com was unmistakably choked with panic, and the pain behind his strangling was impossible to ignore.

"Paval?" She tried to keep her voice calm, flailing herself into an awkward spin in search of she didn't know what, trying to remember exactly where he went down. "Paval, where are you?"

The ocean's heavy presence crowded her senses with

blobs of blurred data. Sounds as thick and clumsy as slough mud stuffed her ears while sights made up of nothing but bubbles sheeted everything else from view. A smoky tangle of jellyfish tendrils curled and flattened against her face. "Dammit, apprentice, answer me!"

His sobs over the com channel were no help. No matter where she twisted, his voice hung eternally over her left shoulder, distorting her perspective when his coughing broke down into whistling gasps. Rahel dumped her BCD with two frantic blinks, then kicked downward as hard as she was able.

"Ma'am, what's the matter?" A new voice sliced across the channel, quick and high with alarm. "Can I do something?" Jynn asked frantically. "Can I help? What happened?"

Like a smear of smoke against cracked glass, a wash of body and bubbles rocketed surfaceward an unreachable distance ahead of her.

"Careful!" Rahel tried to bring her flippers down under her, pushing against the water until she could slue to a stop and struggle her way in his direction. "Paval, don't surface too fast!" It didn't matter—he disappeared into the glistening curtain of jellies that blotched out the sun. "Jynn, we're coming up! Don't let him hurt himself!"

Thirty meters in less than thirty seconds. God. Rahel kick-started her own ascent, resisting the urge to race her bubbles to the surface, worrying that Paval had made things even worse by giving himself decompression illness in his panic. *How could things be worse?* She didn't even know what had happened yet. Maybe he hadn't been down long enough. The deepest of the jellyfish tendrils wafted against her faceplate, then twitched dreamily away again in rhythm to their pulsing bells far above. Rahel stretched her arms over her head to reeve a gentle passage through the gossamer forest.

She broke surface with more momentum than she planned. Air crashed around her in place of water, and the kick and bob of wind-driven waves replaced the stillness of only a few meters below. Rahel caught herself, arms spread wide across the water, when she would have splashed back under again, fighting to equalize her BCD to keep her buoyant. The skate floated less than a dozen meters away. Only the back of Jynn's lavender crew shirt showed where the pilot knelt on the bottom of the boat, bending over something that Rahel couldn't see. She kicked off as powerfully as she could, at the same time chinning her com and shouting, "I'm coming! Tell him I'm coming!" She didn't even know if Jynn was still monitoring the line.

Jynn met her at the side of the skate, though, and grabbed her at belt and shoulder to haul her over the side. She splashed to the deck in a slosh of excess water. "What happened?" the pilot asked, pulling her into a sitting position. "Ma'am, what happened to him?"

"I don't know!" Rahel struggled to her knees almost on top of Paval. He was clenched into a fetal position; a froth of vomit pooled along the curve of his face mask as he jerked dully, weakly. She grabbed Jynn with one hand and pushed him toward the front of the skate. "Get us to shore!" Her fingers felt numb and stupid as she fumbled to unlatch her apprentice's visor.

Water splashed across her knees, against the curve of Paval's back when Jynn jump-started the antigravs without first priming the engines. Rahel slipped one hand under the boy's cheek to lift his mouth clear of the rolling lake in the bottom of the boat, then snapped aside his faceplate to dump the accumulated vomit.

And recoiled from the puff of bitter stench that escaped his mask beneath her fingers.

"Oh, no . . ."

Rahel couldn't hear his gasping above the rush of wind and sea, but she could see the frantic working of his jaw as he sucked down every breath, feel the rigid quiver of every fighting muscle. His eyes, pupils dilated to unseeing black coins, glistened pinkly, and a thin stream of mucous ran from his nose. When she bent to sniff his open lips, the biting stink of rotten eggs stung tears into her eyes.

"*Jynn!*"

She found the control for her oxygen mix in one of the skinsuit's submenus while she pushed Paval onto his back and threw his mask apparatus aside. Her brain remembered from somewhere that a medic would have given Paval oxygen right now, and his own suit was certainly no longer a trustworthy source of that gas. Unfortunately, she could only push her O_2 mix as high as 36 per cent. She didn't know if 15 per cent higher than normal would be enough to matter.

"Get that hop back here!" she shouted at the pilot as she dragged her mask down below her chin and flipped it to give the air to Paval. If only there was enough water in the boat to supply oxygen for more than a few seconds. "We've got to get him to shore *now!*"

Jynn only half-turned away from his controls. The spray thrown up by their velocity had seeded bright droplets through his tightly curled black hair. "Ma'am, we can't use the flyer!"

"The hell we can't!" She couldn't even mate much of her suit to the standing water—not and still keep good contact with her mask. She stretched out both legs and went down awkwardly on one elbow. "Dammit, we don't have time to argue!"

"No, ma'am." Jynn shook his head insistently. "I mean we *can't* use it. He can't go up, not so soon after being under. The bends could kill him!"

If the Greens hadn't killed him already. Rahel reached blindly for the pack under the seat ahead of them and tried not to let the skate's maneuvering shift too much of her weight across Paval's torso while she rummaged.

The phone fell out into the water with a plop. She snatched it out of the brine before it even hit the bottom and shook it open. Beneath her, Paval shuddered weakly.

The line opened after only half a ring.

"Rahel . . ." Nils's sigh blended neatly with the surrounding roar. "I don't know how you can expect me—"

"Nils, shut up! We've got an emergency."

He cut himself off, and the skate passed between the straits and into a wall of shadow, slicing Rahel through with chill. "Paval?" Nils asked in a more contrite tone. He could at least put two and two together.

"Hydrogen sulfide." Rahel thought she still felt the rotten sting at the back of her nose, but knew that must be her imagination. "I don't know how bad it is—he's still breathing." *Barely*. She shifted position on top of him and forced that thought aside. "I promise you the hotel medic can't take care of this."

Nils's voice seemed to rise in pitch even as it blurred beyond understanding. He must have lowered the phone away from his mouth, cradling it against his shoulder, or his lap, or his chest while he shouted to someone farther away. The skate etched a neat pivot just beyond the mouth of the strait, ejecting them from shadow into blinding sun, and bucking Rahel off Paval into the swamped skate bottom. She twisted to keep the mask still on him and still connected to her own suit. Water made suits and deck slippery, and the sidelong glimpses of shoreline flashing by on their left made Rahel's head ache. Picking the phone up out of the water was barely an afterthought.

"All right . . ." Nils, of course, had no idea they'd been interrupted. "I've talked to Huan. He says he can 'link the continent directly and have someone fly out for pickup. It shouldn't take more than twenty minutes."

From time of contact or time of launch? The answer wouldn't change things, so Rahel didn't ask.

"What happened, Rahel? *Hydrogen sulfide?* How on earth did he get exposed to that?"

Spatters of green broke up the hurried movement of hotel turquoise down to the Startide docks. Rahel watched both Greens and reporters gather morbidly at the back of the waiting medic team, and hatred and rage burned a hole straight through her. "How do you think?"

She didn't really care to hear Nils's answer.

Jynn killed their velocity with a stomach-dropping growl; the skate thudded the dock so loudly, a dim echo lapped back at them from off the hotel's façade. Hands grabbed her, grabbed Paval, rocked the skate and shivered the planking as they helped Rahel to the dock as much as they hindered her. When she stumbled beneath the pressure of tangled bodies, a strange, cool openness whispered across her front, and Rahel realized that Paval's body had slipped away from hers. A shock of panic jerked her to her knees. "Wait! My mask—!"

—was connected to her skinsuit, which was no longer in the water it needed to extract oxygen. She let the mask dangle underneath her chin, both hands still gripping the wet edges. The medics swung Paval onto their litter without pausing to acknowledge her cry.

Security closed in behind them like cells reknitting a wound. Only then did Rahel remember Paval's bandolier of sample flasks, and the potentially lifesaving water trapped inside them. She jumped to her feet and glimpsed a flash of pale, glistening skin, heard the ghost of a sobbing gasp, before litter, team, and apprentice all melted beyond her sight. It didn't matter—Paval's skinsuited chest was missing his bandolier, lost somewhere between the jellyfish breeding grounds and home. Rahel hadn't even noticed it was gone before now. The dock beneath her feet seemed very hard, the sun beating down on her shoulders bright and cruelly hot.

How was she going to tell Saiah?

"Proctor Tovin, I'm sorry but . . ."

She turned a look behind her, almost expecting to find Huan the Robotic Bellhop. Certainly no human being would dare approach her now with such an empty, idiotic palliative.

The dark-haired reporter behind her swept a minicam in

front of her face and asked placidly, "Is this the first apprentice you've had die while you were on safari?"

Rahel hit him.

First with her elbow as she finished her turn, then with her fists, and her knee, and anything else she could reach him with as he scrambled away from her with the minicam constantly circling them and his arms laced over his head.

But it was the green-clad arm that reached out to block her from the reporter that focused her anger with the strength of a well-aimed laser. "You bastard." The cold lucidity of her own voice made her even angrier, so she grabbed the interfering Green by the front of his emerald jerkin and shoved him to the ground. "You son of a bitch! How could you *do* something like this? How could *any* of you?"

"Rahel!" Nils, suddenly beside her, fumbled for a hold on her arm. He wasn't serious enough, though, and she pushed him away without even turning.

"What did he ever do to you? Did he ask Sadena to set up shop here? Did *he* decide to make the stellar jellies die?" She kicked the downed Green once, maybe twice; then other, more determined arms snaked around her and dragged her backward down the dock. Her feet skipped between puddles and dry spots as she scrabbled for footing on the Terran-imported boards. "He was just a kid, goddamn you! Just a stupid kid!"

"Proctor Tovin, *stop* it!" Keim forced her way between two of the hotel security personnel, taking hold of Rahel's diving belt while she shoved the rest of the restrainers away. As if her grip and earnest scowl could hold Rahel more securely than physical prowess.

Rahel knocked Keim's hand aside and stepped back before she could grab her again. "Keep out of this, hypocrite. You and your netlink headlines have done enough harm already."

Keim pulled her chin up in surprise, and hurt glinted briefly in her eyes. In a way, it both relieved and disgusted

Rahel to know she could still inflict damage with just the sound of her voice. It seemed the only power left her right now, and even that was pathetic and small. It couldn't have stopped anything that happened today.

She stooped to fling first one, then the other flipper in no particular direction, and jumped off the dock's shore side into sand barely deep enough to take her landing. The pain that jolted up her back seemed appropriate somehow. On her left, a breeze that couldn't cut the heavy warmth of the sun feathered in from over the ocean, and timid waves licked the farthest fringes of shore, afraid to slide even as high as her shoes.

A dead jellyfish rode in and out on the tideless water, and, somehow, that seemed appropriate, too.

No one came looking for her, and for that Rahel was obscurely glad. She slipped into the ocean between glossy, muddy boulders that had rolled into the water years before from a cliff face high above, and let the slow, silent lives of plankton and *pelagia* float her anger away. Some numbed, removed part of her realized that it took an uncounted number of hours; a haline spider had furred nearly half her left shoe with uprooted hydroids before the angle of sunlight squeezed down too low to stimulate the little arachnid, then abandoned her to curl into its rock igloo and wait for morning. Loath to destroy an entire day of spider work, Rahel eased her foot out of the flexible slipper and left the shoe behind.

The evening air felt deceptively chill on her face, the rough sand inappropriately warm between her bare toes. Moisture-rich clouds smeared the sun the color of ferrous clay. Even greenhouse planets breathed and cooled during the long, dark nights, Rahel told herself. And even Noah's Ark proctors could succumb to hypothermia. Peeling off the skinsuit mask with a sigh, she wiped salt water from her cheeks and turned to look back toward the indiscernible hotel. *Out of sight, out of mind.* If only that were true. The

Startide and what she'd left there were all she'd been able to think about since retreating into the ocean. It had more to do with her returning than any true thoughts for her own safety.

That first step southward was so hard, she almost couldn't take the second.

But inertia was a wonderful thing. Once her body was in motion, it was willing to stay in motion, and walking soon became no harder than floating at the bottom of the inlet had been. As long as she didn't think too much about her destination. Not for the first time, she wished for the growl and sigh of sea waves for distraction.

"Oh, thank God."

The Startide had only just begun to take shape among the limestone and granite of the coastal cliff face, with the stairs to the primary dock still another kilometer or more down the beach. Rahel stopped, wondering how likely it was that a reporter would be missed so far from the main hotel, and whether there was any chance some maintenance robot would find the body before she left the planet.

"I am *so* glad you can't hold your water as long as you can hold a grudge. Otherwise you might never have come home." Nils shifted his seat on one of the drier rocks at the foot of the bluff, pulling his light daytime jacket more tightly closed beneath his chin. "Are you all right?"

Just because he was a lawyer didn't mean he couldn't ask stupid questions. "What do you think?" Rahel moved slowly up the beach to stand in front of him, not wanting any unwelcome listeners to pick up on their voices. "How long have you been out here?"

Nils twitched a shoulder in a half-shrug, half-shiver, glancing around at the now-dark scenery as though surveying a gathering of old friends. "Oh, not that long," he sighed with dramatic nonchalance. "Five, maybe six hours." He looked up at her and smiled. Even his friendly smiles always managed to look priggish and thin. "Huan showed me a service tunnel just up the hill from here. It beats the hell out

REGENESIS   169

of going through the reporters, and I thought you might enjoy the detour."

Because the nets want to ask me some horrible questions, and I don't want to give the answers, I don't want to have to know the answers. She didn't even want to have to ask Nils, and he'd been sitting out here half the day waiting to tell her. She made herself look him straight in the face, but then could only squeeze her hands into fists when she knew she ought to be speaking.

Nils saved her with a nod. "Paval's alive," he said, very serious now despite his gentle tone. "The medical team got here just a little while after you left—" A slight smile broke through and he cocked his head in dry comment. "A record, Huan says. They brought a mobile ER unit with them, and took Paval into their ship for treatment the minute they got here. It was good you gave him oxygen so soon after his exposure, they said. You probably saved his life."

Yes, but she shouldn't have had to. "Where are the Greens?"

"Kicked offplanet." Nils slid to his feet with a tiny sound of discomfort, then scrubbed at his arms as he started up the beach toward the hotel. "They're talking about suing, you know."

Rahel blinked into the darkness as she followed him, glad for his pale complexion and ivory jacket. Until the moons rose, those were the only parts of Nils that she could reliably see. "Well, good for the Greens. Maybe it'll give them something more constructive to do than attack apprentice proctors."

"How nice that you can be so cavalier."

"Sadena owns the planet," Rahel pointed out. Rocks bit and pinched beneath her feet, and the occasional little something scrabbled away out of sight across the sand. She missed the taste of sea spray against her nose and tongue. "As long as he doesn't violate Interplanetary law, he can throw anybody off Uriel he wants to. Even us, if we're so lucky."

Nils stopped abruptly and turned about to stare. She nearly tripped over him in the darkness. "Not Sadena, Rahel," Nils said in a slow, understanding voice. She wanted to hit him. "You. The Greens want to sue you for slander." He caught hold of her elbow and kept her beside him as he started walking up the beach again. "This is exactly the sort of thing I'm supposed to be here to avoid."

Rahel snorted and pulled her arm out of his grasp. "Hell, if I'd known they were going to sue me, I'd have said a whole lot more of what I had on my mind."

Nils rubbed at his eyes and sighed. "No, you will not." He bit off each word with long-suffering precision. "Right now, the Greens are just posturing for the media. You haven't really said anything destructive—nothing they can build a case on, anyway. And if you stick to your work from now on"—he angled a warning glare up at her—"preferably by staying underwater, we can probably finish out this contract without landing half of Noah's Ark in court."

"Would we, anyway? I mean, is it slander if it's true?"

Nils shook his head, but obviously not in direct response to her question. "That isn't pertinent unless you can *prove* it's true."

How come she had to prove her insults, and GreeNet got to print anything about the Ark it wanted? Deciding she wasn't really in the mood for the answer, Rahel continued her trudge up the beach without asking.

A bevy of shivering bellhops clustered around the entrance to the service tunnel, more than happy to converge on the proctors and usher them into the hotel. Rahel waved off Nils's offer to see about sending dinner up to her suite, and abandoned him with the bellhops at the service lift. That he held up a hand to stop anyone from following her surprised Rahel even more than his own willingness to stay behind.

The elevator glided with the same silent perfection as everything else in Sadena's hotel. For a change, it was nice to close her eyes and let the machinery do all the moving for her, nicer still to strip open her sandy skinsuit and drop it wherever she wanted as soon as she stepped through her suite's sliding door. Her hair felt gluey and crusted with salt, but she stopped just shy of the bathroom to stare in shock at the living area with one hand still splayed on top her head.

Flowers. The largest, most elaborate, most delicate bouquet she'd ever seen replaced the oval coffee table. A half-dozen iridescent insects floated from blossom to blossom like fairy gems in search of nectar. Rahel crept up on the construction as though it were a tiger, and used two fingers to slip a platinum card from between two glowing Lunar orchids.

> *My sincerest sympathies for*
> *the attack on your apprentice.*
> *Please let me know*
> *if there is anything I can do.*
>
> *F.S.*

Rahel decided not to bother with a shower that night. She took only long enough to put on clean clothes and throw the flowers into the hall outside her door, then collected her water samples from that morning and carried them up to the pachyderm. A night in the pachyderm's bunk would feel good after the stuffy hotel, and, if she was lucky, the testing station AI could have all of the samples run before dawn.

The persistent beep of the pachyderm's intership com irritated Rahel out of sleep. It seemed like only minutes since she'd closed her eyes. In reality, the chronometer at the pilot's station read 0816 when she finally stumbled over to slap the damn thing off, so she had to accept that it was well past sunrise and time to crawl back into the world of conspicuous consumption in search of answers. Leaning both elbows on the edge of the console, she keyed in the com answer sequence with a yawn.

A text-only message scrolled up the little screen in a

swarm of turquoise letters that were disgustingly hard to take so soon after being asleep.

Mr. Kuvasc is doing well, although he still isn't able to handle visitors. He sends his greetings to you, and his thanks. You handled the emergency superbly—the medics seem confident he'll make an adequate recovery.

I was able to negotiate for custody of Mr. Kuvasc's skinsuit. It is currently being held at a research facility on the mainland, and should be ready for your retrieval when you finally return to Noah's Ark. Simply let me know. Preliminary tests reveal traces of H_2S all throughout the suit's primary gas extraction system. So far, no one is willing to speculate as to how the H_2S was delivered, or whether the suit can ever be made user-safe again. I shall keep you apprised of any further developments.

I'm glad you were able to find some use for the flowers.

F.S.

Sadena may have been a bastard, but at least he could be a helpful bastard. Rahel deleted the message without sending a reply.

"Anything worth mentioning in last night's samples?" she asked the AI as she pulled on her shoes and dug a handful of breakfast packs out of the galley.

"No statistically significant evidence of contamination or disease," it told her. "Salinity displays an apparent tendency to increase in direct proportion to ocean depth, but I don't have enough samples to flag this trend as significant. The presence of shed cells and larvae does not deviate significantly from the predicted model for this time of year. Insufficient evidence exists to determine ephyrae population at this time."

Oh, well. It never hurt to hope for a miracle as long as you weren't really counting on one. "Log it as Uriel:

Odarkan Sea, Sample Series Number 1. I'll bring some
more to compile with it tonight."

"Okay."

Sunlight bright enough to burn the fog off her brain met
Rahel outside the pachyderm's hatch. Taking one of the
pseudo-food bars between her teeth, she squinted so hard
she could barely see to lock down the ship before leaving it.
By the time she'd finished and turned to find her place on
the rooftop landing field, Nils and a nosegay of pastel
security were halfway between the pachyderm and the hop
Rahel and Paval had taken to the Odarkan yesterday. She
took another bite of her breakfast and waited for them to get
closer than shouting distance.

Nils marked the transition for her. "Where the hell have
you been all morning?"

Rahel glanced behind her as though to make sure the
pachyderm were still there, and peeled another breakfast
bar. "In the casino, Nils. I just decided to teleport up here for
breakfast." She scowled at him, dropping the ornamental
innocence from her tone. "Where do you think I've been?
Running yesterday's samples through the AI. I camped out
in the pachyderm in case I needed to clarify something."
That last part was a lie, but her reasons weren't really the
issue right now.

"You should have told me you were going," Nils persisted, a little of the fire leaving his voice now that he had
her in sight and undamaged. "When you weren't in your
suite this morning, I thought the Greens had somehow got
back onplanet and taken you! I had security search the hotel
from top to bottom—no one had the faintest idea where to
find you!"

Well, *someone* had. Rahel wondered if Nils or the
security personnel had thought to ask Sadena, and what
reasons Sadena would have for lying to them if they had.
Curious guy, that Sadena. His rationale for doing anything
probably didn't mean very much to the average person.

Rahel offered Nils a breakfast bar in lieu of an apology.

"Did you get my skinsuit?" she asked so they wouldn't have to linger on a subject she wasn't sure she wanted to pursue.

Making a face to prove he wasn't mollified by her sacrifice, Nils plucked the bar from Rahal's fingers and sighed. "I took it from where you left it folded on your dresser."

Not where *she'd* left it. When Rahel last looked, the skinsuit lay in her room in a puddle of sand, the flowers and pottery scattered in shards all over the hallway floor outside. She nodded, though, a little amused by the discrepancy. "Helpful little bastard, isn't he?"

Nils raised his eyebrows in what looked like mixed question and concern. "Excuse me?"

"Never mind. Come on . . ." Rahel clapped her arm across his shoulders to turn him toward the waiting hop, security swarming around them to follow in their footsteps. "We've got lots of work to catch up on yet."

She'd just feel a whole lot better about the project if Sadena wasn't putting so much charm and effort into trying to curry her favor. The more he tried to convince her that her opinion really mattered to him, the less, Rahel knew, he was actually looking forward to hearing it.

The water didn't feel as warm and welcoming today. Bracing her knees against the keel of the skate, Rahel gripped the boarding ladder with one hand while she accepted a spare bandolier of sample jars from Nils with the other. He looked surprisingly businesslike and sturdy out here under the open sun, not at all like some stuffy lawyer who wore gloves to prevent calluses and had to clip his nails to keep them short.

Rahel pushed away from the boat and slipped one bandolier crosswise over the other. The two together were barely heavy enough to register on her BCD control. "I'll keep the com line open," she said, drifting back from the skate in preparation to go under. "Make sure you acknowledge my transmissions, or I'll think you've fallen asleep up here."

Nils nodded, brow wrinkled somewhat unhappily. "What should I do if I lose contact with you?"

"Sue somebody." She smiled at his annoyed grimace, and dropped down under the water. "I'd suggest Sadena. He's probably good for a higher out-of-court settlement than the Greens."

Nils answered her comment with a patient sigh.

Dumping her BCD, she floated smoothly down toward the carpet of jellies with a sheen of bubbles glistening the water above her. The drift into darkness wasn't nearly as pleasant today. Darting shadows snagged at her attention with little stabs of adrenaline even though she couldn't have told herself what she was looking for. The taste of each breath registered consciously on her brain, and every minor adjustment in the skinsuit's gas extraction system made her lungs freeze up for a heartbeat while they waited for disaster. Even checking, checking, and rechecking her O_2 levels accomplished nothing except to leach all satisfaction from this temporary privacy. She didn't even realize she'd reached the jellyfish swarm until the first gauzy body pulsed beneath her hand.

"Okay . . . I'm at the jellyfish interface."

"I know," Nils's voice said, sounding closer, even, than it had when she'd talked to him on the surface. "I can see your reflection on the remote sensor." Rahel hadn't expected him to be clever enough to use something like the skate's mapping system to keep track of her. "Gee, I had no idea jellyfish would look so . . . squishy from a distance."

Rahel smiled and felt for a path between the bodies. "Well, squishy is what jellyfish do. I'm going to pull a whole set of samples to augment what I brought in yesterday, then drop lower to cover Paval's sector." She pulled her knees against herself so tightly that the sample jars on her belts pressed into her stomach. "Try to make yourself useful while I'm gone."

"Be careful."

The honest concern in his words surprised her. "I'll try," she said seriously. Then she sank into the tendrils and let the milk-white world of the jellies lull the surface world from her mind.

Their silent, graceful peace crept over her more readily than she expected, but couldn't find sufficient purchase in the jumbled texture of her worries. She meticulously collected samples from various depths and various locations, making sure to catch any particulate matter or jelly sloughings that might prove significant. Wending her way delicately in between ruffles and frills, she even went to the effort of siphoning water from within the bells of both egg-heavy and empty adults without disturbing their reproductive systems. This, then, led to an idle thought regarding how many ovigerous medusae were actually floating with this swarm, and that in turn led to an impromptu census of egg clusters glued to the bellies of the adults.

Rahel felt a little funny, swimming from jellyfish to jellyfish and lifting up their skirts to see who was pregnant. Considering stellar jellies weren't sexed in any Terran sense, any of the adults could have—and should have—been able to carry eggs as long as they'd had enough genetic exchange to ensure a viable clutch. The fact that barely one in ten appeared to be carrying seemed unreasonable. Rahel paused, letting the jellies swell and throb away from her as she chewed the inside of her jaw.

Season? she wondered. Food? Hell, maybe the population was too inbred, and something in the stellar jelly's genetics could recognize when it had a bum deal going. She pushed herself down below the lowest tendrils and blew a frustrated sigh. It could be anything from lighting to water temperature to a drop in ambient salinity, and she wasn't going to figure out which while floating around under here. It might have helped, of course, if Sadena had ever allowed a full-scale study of the jellyfish before now. But no—he hadn't wanted to disturb his resort's primary source of tourist trade, even for the sake of science. And now both his resort and the stellar jellyfish might have to pay for that selfishness.

"I don't know if it makes any difference, but I'm roasting up here."

Rahel glanced skyward at the sound of Nils's voice, grinning a little despite herself. Somehow, he managed to make everything sound like some kind of personal attack. It must be a lawyer skill. "All right, I hear you." She slipped the bandolier of completed samples off her shoulder while she wriggled up through the milling jellies. "You still got me on your sensor screen?"

"You're a lot more solid than the jellyfish—you're hard to miss."

"You've got a sample pack coming up directly above my position." She extended her arm up over her head and pressed the sample belt's thumb tab. A brilliant yellow balloon blossomed at the shoulder seam, tugging the bandolier out of her hand and upward as if pulled by a string. She watched it disappear into a blur against the surface light. "Log those as Uriel: Odarkan Sea, Sample Series Number 2. Then put them in my equipment pack and *don't touch them again*. Got it?"

"And here I was planning to line them all up on the seats and play scientist with them until you got back."

Rahel eased back down past the jellyfish barrier again. "Don't get smart with me, Oberjen."

"I can't help it," he replied dryly. "I'm a lawyer—it's my job to be smart." He went on more seriously before she could contradict him. "We've got your samples. Are you sure you don't want to come up for a suit check before you start the next series?"

No, she wasn't sure. The whole thought of doing work in Paval's sector felt like walking on someone's grave. "What good would surfacing do?" she asked aloud. "I checked the suit six times on the hop coming out here, and we don't know what we're looking for anyway. My O_2's good"—she sneaked a look at the reading, just to make sure—"and I know to expect trouble." She tossed hands up in a shrug even though there was no one in sight to appreciate it. "I think we're as safe as we get." And wasn't that a depressing thought? "Just make sure you take care of those samples."

"You take care of yours."

She nodded, the way she always did when Saiah bothered to tell her the obvious. "Yes, Mother." Then she pushed off against the water behind her, and started her first swim-by of the sector.

She worked her way slowly back and forth across the levels, the lantern at her waist carving a fat tube through the dim waters ahead of her. Flashes like flitting coins winked on and off in the slashing light, little fish-things stealing glances at the new intruder; diaphanous ripples of jellyfish tissue danced in slow blindness away from disturbances they could barely sense with their primitive nerves. As Rahel bottled sample after sample on her way toward the sea floor, the O_2 monitor at the edge of her mask seemed to swell in size and importance. She found her attention caught by it every time she looked up from capping a flask, and her breath stopped with each glance—it *must* be some anomaly in the levels that made her look so suddenly.

Of course, the gauge sat placidly at the 21 per cent she'd originally set it for. The only thing fluctuating here was her blood pressure. And her attention to the job at hand. Jamming the latest bottle back into its holster loop, she aimed herself downward with a disgusted sigh.

What looked like gnarled, scattered fragments of crab shell misted into being below her, impossibly huge, as big and broken as boulders, with edges blurred by time and moss. Rahel widened the beam on her lantern, and the fur of pearly velvet on each rock ruffled in response to her movements through the water. She pulled herself to a clumsy stop.

"Oh . . ."

"What?" Nils's voice cracked nervously in her ear. She could almost picture him scrabbling to peer over the edge of the skate as if that would somehow help him. "Rahel, what is it? What?"

"Nothing, Nils! Calm down." She drifted off to one side of the rocky heap, shining her light all down its length, kicking gently to verify its width and height. "It's just . . ." Amazingly tiny little creatures reached up from the rocks to stroke the water with pink feather dusters, as unlike the huge, graceful adults as a zygote was to a human. Rahel lowered her mask to within bare centimeters of the polyp mat, and still she could only just make out the individual branches of their bodies. Occasional one-celled ephyrae twitched away from the budding stalks like specks of dust on independent breezes.

"I just came across the polyps," she finally remembered to say. She uncapped a sample flask while she talked, trying hard not to catch many newly shed ephyrae. "The Odarkan's coastal shelf drops off here, and most of the polyps have set up shop on a broken spur of rock about . . ." Her light searched for an end out in front of her. "I don't know. Maybe a hundred meters long. I can't see where it lets off."

"According to Jynn's topo map, the actual lip only goes another fifty-seven meters before meeting up with the shoreline again." There was a pause marked by a terse, muffled exchange while Nils checked something with Jynn. "A lot of that fifty-seven is deeper than your current position, too. The Odarkan apparently doesn't have much in the way of shallows."

Rahel twisted to turn her light over the edge of the lip. "Yeah, it drops off pretty steeply here. I can't tell how—" She froze with the lantern aimed between her feet. "What the hell . . . ?"

"Rahel, don't do this to me."

The rock a dozen meters below looked as though it had been shaved. Remnant podetiams clung to the surface like gooey white blisters, but no carpet of stalks combed the water for microbes, no flecks of bright color revealed budding polyps crowned with umbrella platters of ephyrae.

Above the line of destruction, another handspan worth of polyps dangled limply, still attached to their gripping feet, but obviously not still alive. "Something's the matter down here."

"With you?" Nils asked testily. "Or with the jellyfish?"

Rahel wasn't sure if she appreciated his concern, or was just annoyed by it. "The jellyfish," she said as she lowered herself over the drop-off and started downward. "The polyps, at least. About ten meters below my current position, we've got a massive die-off. I'm not going down that far," she was quick to add. "But I want to get a better look at the environment while I pull some water samples from that depth. I've got a reach-stick that'll go three meters."

"If it's some kind of free-floating toxin, are you sure that'll be far enough away?"

Irritation jabbed at her, colored with embarrassment when Nils's worry only made her glance again at the oxygen gauge near the edge of her mask. She cut off whatever sharp reply she'd meant to make when the oxygen level dropped from 18 to 11 per cent in the moment that she watched.

An instant later, she'd rocketed five meters back to the top of the polyp bed.

"Well?"

She clapped hands to both sides of her mask and frantically sought out the oxygen gauge while her lungs begged her to take another breath. But not yet, not yet—not until she knew what they'd done to her. She wanted to die knowing what the bastards had done.

The O_2 gauge glowed a helpful green, telling Rahel that levels were considered optimal even before she specifically identified the reading of 21 per cent. Her breath gusted out of her as though she'd been punched.

"Okay." She was surprised at how thoughtful and calm her own voice sounded in her ears. "No, Nils." She glanced back down through the darkness, toward the drop-off and the carpet of dying cells. "I don't think three meters will be far enough."

"Oh?" The lawyer sounded disgustingly eager. "Did you find something?"

Rahel pushed herself to lie even with the ledge through sheer force of will, digging her fingers into the muddy floor as if that would somehow keep her from toppling over into oblivion. "I've at least found the hint of something. Sadena's got a problem with his water."

"His water?"

She pointed, then remembered that Nils couldn't see her and pulled her arm back to her side. "Down where the die-off occurred, my gas exchange system registered a drop in available oxygen. I thought there was something the matter with my suit, but when I got back up here, my oxygen level was back to normal."

"Meaning what?" Nils asked, his voice sounding almost annoyed with confusion. "That there isn't oxygen for the suit to process in the water ten meters below you?" Something that his tone said he found distinctly unlikely.

"Very good, counselor." She rolled onto her back and sat up. "Would you like to go for double or nothing?"

"But I don't understand." Nils was obviously too disconcerted for recreational betting. "I thought water was always one-third oxygen—H_2O. How can you not have oxygen when you're in the middle of an ocean full of water?"

Rahel sighed and looked up toward the surface, wondering how easy this would be to explain with forty meters of sea between them instead of a half-full bucket of water and two bell jars. "Because that's not the type of oxygen I'm talking about. The oxygen in H_2O is busy being water, and you can't get it to *stop* being water without running an electric current through it." She peeked at the O_2 gauge in her mask to ward off a sudden shortness of breath. "What I'm talking about is dissolved oxygen—little bits of oxygen that aren't hooked up to hydrogen being water. When there isn't any of that in the water, the suit can't extract it out. That's why skinsuits don't work for long in a closed system like an aquarium, or why they're not useful in swamp studies. . . ." Whatever point she'd meant to make evaporated from her brain, burned away by the sudden brightness of her understanding.

"That still doesn't tell me why this water's lacking oxygen."

"Because of the swamp," Rahel said excitedly. She pushed up to her knees so quickly that she nearly lifted herself into a tumble. "Uriel's swamp water is anoxic—it doesn't have enough dissolved oxygen in it. That's why it's stagnant, why not much can live in it, why it smells bad—*Nils!*" She clapped a hand to the top of her head. "That's where the hydrogen sulfide came from! Paval's suit extracted it out of the standing swamp water!"

Goddamn. The Greens had a slander case against her after all.

"Wait a minute." Nils cut across her, ranting impatiently. "Are you telling me you think swamp water is leaking into the Odarkan and killing the stellar jellyfish? How?"

Rahel shook her head and felt around the back of her belt for the reach-stick. "Dunno." She looked around as though that might enlighten her, while paying the stick out to its full three-meter length. "Maybe by flowing along a rift in the shelf platform. Or maybe Sadena's pumping someplace and didn't feel the need to tell us. However it's getting here, though, it's coming through in pretty large quantities."

"And you're *sure* the water's coming from the margin sloughs?"

"Not one hundred per cent sure." Rahel had to be honest about that or scientific methodology wasn't worth a damn. She clipped a sample flask to the reach-stick, then tied a cable to the other end before lowering it over the edge into the anoxic darkness. "But there's one real quick way to find out."

The churlish, rotten stench of hydrogen sulfide belched up at Rahel when her reach-stick broke the surface of the margin slough's morass. She turned her face away with a little cough, and signalled the stick to pop caps on all the specimen jars arrayed along its length. Even a cloth filter mask didn't do much to keep out the smell, and nothing did much against the insects. Since returning to the slough after her ocean dive thirty minutes before, Rahel had spent half her time batting noseeums away from her eyes, the other half trying to get the lids back on sample jars so she could retreat inside the pachyderm. She'd never been more grateful for watertight surgical gloves and hip-deep waders.

"Is nature always this smelly?"

She glanced back toward Nils and the pachyderm as she withdrew the reach-stick from the filthy water. With one hand braced against the pachyderm's open hatchway and the other holding a filter mask against his mouth, he looked like an unwilling attendant at an autopsy. Rahel doubted she could have convinced him to step down into the swamp water even if she needed him to.

"This is about as bad as it gets," she admitted, wading back to join him. "Methane from large ungulate farts is pretty nasty, too. But it explodes, so at least you can have fun with it."

Nils stumbled aside to let her climb past him into the pachyderm, then keyed the door shut once she was inside. "You've got to be joking."

Rahel didn't see the point in enlightening him.

Jynn looked up from the pilot's station when she entered, but didn't stand or say anything, only offering a nervous wave in greeting. Rahel acknowledged him with a nod. He'd insisted on piloting the pachyderm from the Startide to the sloughs because neither Rahel nor Nils was cleared by Feles Sadena to fly within Uriel's atmosphere. "Mr. Sadena wouldn't want me to start ignoring his own rules now, ma'am." The fact that Rahel's mobile laboratory was even more rigorously nonimpact than any of Sadena's aircraft wasn't part of the equation. "Either I'm responsible for what flies outta here and where, ma'am, or we go to Mr. Sadena and you explain to him what you want to do. It's not my place to make the rules."

In the end, Rahel was just as glad to have Jynn along. He proved remarkably adept at keeping the pachyderm no higher than the skin of the water—"You been down underwater, ma'am. We can't take you no higher in the air than this"—and having him to pilot let her pull her gear together before they arrived at the sloughs. Unlike Nils, Jynn also seemed to feel no need to understand every little step of what she did along the way.

"Computer." Rahel stopped in front of the pachyderm's testing station and starting unclipping sample jars one at a time. The inside of the ship already stank from her wet footsteps, and she despaired for a moment of ever removing the smell. "Get ready for another collection set. Log this one as Uriel: Southeastern Margin Slough, Sample Series Number 1." She telescoped the reach-stick, tossing it into a basin for later cleaning, then stripped off her gloves and dropped them carefully into the disposal. "I'll want a full work-up on resident chemosynthetic bacteria using the same criteria you applied to Odarkan Sea Series Number 3. Run a split-screen comparison of the two series, and alert me as soon as you're done."

She wiped the bottles while waiting for a reply, but still had three to go when the AI reported, "I can have general population figures on both series in six minutes sixteen seconds."

"Great." It took almost that long to pipet out the samples and slide them into the machine. "Have a good time."

The AI clicked as it received them. "Okay."

Nils moved around in front of her as she bent to unstrap her hip boots. "What exactly will this run of tests tell us?"

"It'll tell us whether or not the margin sloughs and the Odarkan Sea share the same bottom water. If they've got the same bacteria in the same populations, it's a pretty safe bet the water's all coming from the same place."

"Wait a minute . . ." Nils offered his elbow as a brace

when she stepped one boot on the toe of the other for leverage. "I thought you said nothing could live in anoxic water."

Rahel accepted his outstretched arm. "Nothing *you'd* ever notice can live in anoxic water," she amended, jerking one foot loose with a hopping stumble. "But there are various one-celled organisms that get their energy from compounds other than oxygen, so they don't care how stagnant the water is. They live in the water in different percentages at different depths, depending on how much oxygen has already been eaten up, and what compounds are still left to munch on." She freed her second foot, then padded barefoot away from the puddle that had gathered under the waders. "Those are the bacteria we're looking for."

Picking up the boots one in each hand, she slipped sideways past Nils to carry them hastily into the bathroom. She could always rinse them off later. Or—better yet—get one of Sadena's ever-helpful hotel staff to come clean the whole inside of the pachyderm as though it were a guest room. Nils handed her the basin with the reach-stick and used glassware, and she slid it into the bottom of the shower stall with the boots.

"Ma'am?"

Rahel paused in hauling mop rags out of the cleaning supplies. At the front of the pachyderm, Jynn stood poised on the step between the pilot's area and the rest of the ship, his dark face painted with concern. He came down to take a rag from her when she moved out to join him.

"Ma'am, I didn't mean to be listening, but I couldn't help but overhear." He dropped the rag across the biggest puddle and moved it around with his foot. "Am I understanding right? If you find the same bacteria in both the jellyfish water and the swamp water, that'll mean you're right—that water leaking out of the swamps is what's causing the jellyfish to die?"

Rahel nodded, kneeling to sop up the trail of footprints

leading from the testing station to the door. "That's right, Jynn."

The pilot nodded slowly. "Ma'am, is this something Mr. Sadena can fix?"

She rocked back on her heels and looked up at him. Nils, sitting in the chair at the testing station, looked back at her without offering any frowns or eyebrow lifts to try and tell her what she should say. When even the lawyers are quiet, you know you're in trouble.

"There's a good chance," she finally admitted. "First we'd have to locate where the anoxic water's draining from. If it's a point source—like an old estuary, or a fissure in the bedrock—we should be able to divert the water and aerate it before it hits the Odarkan. Add oxygen and bingo! No anoxia."

Jynn nodded. "But if it isn't a point source?"

"Well, that's a little harder." Rahel planted her hands on her legs with a sigh. "If it's coming off the entire slough shoreline, it'll take a lot more engineering to aerate it all. You could still *do* it, but Sadena's gonna need a geological investigation before he can even think about it, not to mention some estimate of the environmental impact that kind of intervention would have on the sloughs." She shook her head. "That size project would take a hell of a lot of money."

Jynn lowered onyx eyes as though in thought, but a polite chime from the testing station postponed any other questions he might have asked. "I have the preliminary sample results for Odarkan Series Number 3 and Southeastern Margin Slough Series Number 1."

Rahel climbed to her feet and waved Nils out of the testing station chair. "Put it on screen."

"Okay."

Neatly carved wedges of statistical data grew up on either side of the screen, snake lines of blue, yellow, red, and green chasing after bits of information in an effort to pin down primary indicators. Rahel slipped into the seat, searching out the few specific microbes who would most readily tattle on their wandering brethren. Her hand stopped with its index finger pinning the Odarkan Sea's iron reducers, her pinkie angled down to find the margin slough's sulfates. "This can't be right."

Nils jerked beside her. "What?"

"Chemosynthetic bacterial concentrations are correct within 0.0015 per cent."

Rahel hit the side of the machine with her hand. "Not you."

"Rahel, what is it?" Nils squirmed unwillingly aside as Jynn pushed in beside him. "Isn't this what you were looking for?"

"Ma'am, does this mean we have a problem?"

Rahel snorted and tapped the top of the screen. "Hell, Jynn, we already had a problem. But see this?"

Both men leaned forward to glance at where she pointed. Jynn only nodded, but Nils asked, "What of it?"

"Basically, everything up here at the top of the display is from the highest water, water that still has some oxygen in it." Rahel moved her hand to the lower part of the display. "Everything down here is from the bottommost water that doesn't have any oxygen left at all. Anything that can live up here"—a single tap above—"can't live down here." She rested her hand on the bottom of the screen again. "And vice versa."

"Ma'am . . ." Jynn touched the display alongside her, as though feeling out the printed pages of a book. "These numbers don't look like they match."

Rahel sat back in her seat with a sigh. "That's because they don't." Nils groaned softly behind her. "Look at the percentages of methanogens here at the bottom. These guys can only live in *the most* stagnant water—oxygen can't even *think* about sharing the same water space. If I took a cupful of that swamp water out there and poured it into a glass of tap water, the oxygen in the tap water would wipe out the methanogens in a matter of seconds."

"But . . ." Nils reached over her shoulder, tracing a line from one side of the screen to the other. "There's 77.65 per cent methanogens in the Odarkan water, and only 3.37 per cent in the slough water." He angled a look down at her, and Rahel could see the question in his frown that he wasn't sure he was supposed to ask.

"The biggest bacterial population in the slough water is sulfur reducers"—Rahel pointed to the wedge of microbes that gifted the sloughs with their lovely aroma—"at 69.89 per cent. But the Odarkan water only carries 15.02 per cent sulfur reducers, and they're *both* low on iron and nitrogen reducers."

"Ma'am, it sounds like you're saying the Odarkan Sea has even less oxygen in it than these margin swamps."

"Nonsense." But Nils sounded more brusque than usual, and leaned down to half look at Rahel as he talked, as though quietly requesting her approval. "It ought to be like with the glass of water—*more* oxygen after the slough water mixes with the Odarkan, not less."

Yes, it should have been. A horrible trickle of thought wormed its way into Rahel's brain—so terrible, so hopeless that she wouldn't even let her mind give it words. Picking out a random selection from both series of samples of something that looked vaguely like Terran *desulfo vibriens*, she said, very calmly, "Computer. I want a genetic blow-up and comparison on these two populations."

For a gene spin, it took almost no time at all. Eleven minutes. Maybe twelve. When the spin finally popped up to supersede the population statistics on the testing station's screen, it proved a wonderfully complex weave of structure and purpose for such a tiny, straightforward organism. Rahel walked quickly through the ladders of their chromosomes, not even taking time to marvel at their design. Her stomach tightened and her mouth grew sour with each inconsistency that passed beneath her hands.

"These bacteria aren't related," she finally admitted.

Nils shook his head at her, then at the genetic display. "At all?"

"Not for a couple billion generations." Rahel wanted to look at him, wanted to make sure Jynn understood what they were talking about here. But she couldn't pull her eyes away from the screen, with its damning statistics and mismatching bacteria. "Nils, I was wrong. The Odarkan bottom water can't be coming from the margin sloughs."

Nils sighed with the frustration of a man already left several steps behind in the conversation. "Then where *is* it coming from?"

Rahel turned her chair to face him, including Jynn by the sheer fact of his proximity. "Remember when I said someday I'd explain anoxic organic decomposition to you?" she asked the lawyer. When Nils only nodded, she waved him toward the floor. "Sit down . . ."

They didn't head back to the Startide Hotel until dusk. By then, Rahel had guided Jynn all over the landlocked Odarkan before having him skim the pachyderm to a dozen different locations across Uriel's ocean surface. It had been a long and silent day. They ran out of sample flasks while there were still places Rahel wanted to visit, Nils gave up trying to separate slides when they ran out of table space to stack them, and Rahel's limbs felt weak and rubbery from too many hours underwater. She let Jynn turn back for lack of anything more productive to do. At least they had data enough to support whatever report Noah's Ark finally decided to deliver, not to mention enough methanogenic bacteria to open a sizable zoo.

Jynn left them at the foot of the Startide's great front steps. "I don't want to take you up to the roof while I park this, ma'am. You understand."

To a certain extent, she did. Another part of her would rather have courted the bends than have to trudge up a two-hundred-meter flight of stairs dogged by every breed of reporter known to man. She groaned and stepped awkwardly down from the pachyderm's hatch, obscurely glad when Nils hopped out beside her. Maybe he could distract the godless hoards with legalspeak while she made a slow-motion getaway. The appearance of the first reporters made such a reprieve unlikely.

"Proctor Tovin, the Green has officially announced its intention to take legal action against Noah's Ark. Do you have any comments in your own defense—?"

"Are there any new findings today regarding allegations that Mr. Sadena—?"

"Proctor Tovin, on whose authority—?"

"Have you heard anything about Paval?"

That last came with a hard grip on her elbow and the sudden heat of a body very close by. Rahel wheeled, jerking her arm back with a snarl, but stopped herself just before letting the hateful words boil over. Keim pulled her hand to her side as though only just realizing how intrusive she'd been.

"I just wanted you to know—I'm really sorry about what happened." Somehow, the respectful intimacy of Keim's voice carried over the tumult more clearly than simple shouting. "What they did has nothing to do with conservation or love of nature, and you and I both know it. I hate that they're a part of what I stand for."

Rahel sighed and ran a hand through salt-encrusted hair. Five steps lower down, Nils was insisting on courtesy before he'd acknowledge any netlink questions. "I'll give you a scoop." She was impressed when Keim didn't dive immediately for her notebook. "What happened to Paval— your Greens didn't do it."

The reporter's eyes widened, and one hand splayed wide as though longing to type. "You're sure of this?"

Rahel nodded. It seemed only fair to give GreeNet first shot at the story, since they were suing her and all. It was the closest she could come to an apology. "You'll hear the details when I know them. But tell your bosses I was wrong."

That was a phrase she expected to repeat often over the next few days.

The Startide's lobby somehow looked even larger and more empty than on the day they arrived. Rahel shivered a little when a bellhop finally sealed the door behind her and Nils, and let silence clap shut around them like a vacuum. Here they were, she realized, encased inside a replica of nature that had no idea the full power of what it tried to represent. Caught between the destructive nature of the mild, patient ocean outside and the conspicuous hubris of display in here, Rahel's concerns suddenly felt very ridiculous and small.

"Don't look now."

She looked where Nils pointed, then couldn't even reach out to take the note when Huan glided to a stop in front of them with waldo outstretched. "The guy's good," she allowed as Nils accepted the piece of paper and unfolded it into a square. She guessed what it said even before Nils scoffed with disgust and held it out to her.

Please do me the honor
of stopping by my suite before you retire.

F.S.

Rahel took the note and crushed it between her palms.

"What are you going to tell him?" Nils asked.

She sighed and followed Huan when the Newborn pivoted to retrace its winding path across the lobby. "The truth."

"Proctor Tovin, Proctor Oberjen. Thank you for coming by." Feles Sadena smiled politely, lacing long cinnamon fingers over one knee and sitting back in his tastefully polished coral chair as though pleased with himself for having greeted them so well. Behind him, Jynn stood with hands behind his back, dark eyes slightly averted. "I know

you must be tired after such a long day in the sun." Without
any overt signal from Sadena, a service drone glided in with
a tray of steaming coffee.

Rahel neither smiled nor glanced at the tray. "Do you
know anything new about Paval?"

"Yes . . ." Sadena pursed thin lips in gracious concern,
reaching for one of the tiny cups. "Yes, of course. Mr.
Kuvasc is doing extremely well." The coffee was apparently
already brewed and sweetened to his tastes—he took a sip
without adding sugar or waiting for the contents to cool.
"He's been asking for you."

Rahel's stomach squeezed with unexpected guilt, only to
burn a moment later when anger flashed up to replace it. "I
was finishing our work. Mr. Kuvasc understands." And
damn Sadena for trying to unbalance her with such a
heartless ploy.

"Speaking of your work . . ." Sadena siphoned off
another decorous sip. "I'm told you've located the cause of
all my jellyfish problems."

Rahel flicked a look at Jynn over Sadena's shoulder, but
the pilot dropped his gaze without meeting her eyes. "If
your man told you about the problem," she said, not caring
that her tone made Jynn flinch as though she'd pricked him,
"then maybe he also told you there's nothing anyone can do
about it."

Sadena replaced his cup on the tray, managing to glance
back at Jynn and disregard him all with a single gesture.
"Proctor Tovin, Jynn is merely an informant. If he didn't
believe in impossibility, he might have some more meaningful job. I, on the other hand, am a man with a great deal
of money. I have found that, in the main, impossibility is
highly overrated." He sat back again in his chair and fixed
her with unfeeling eyes the color of iron. "I would like you
to tell me yourself how you see the situation."

"Your ocean ecology is screwed and there's nothing
anybody can do about it."

Nils stirred beside her, shooting her a sharp, reproving

glance. "Uriel's oceans are becoming stagnant, Mr. Sadena," he said, ignoring Rahel's returning scowl. "It's part of the planet's natural global cycle, and right now it's smothering the stellar jellyfish. Eventually, though, it will smother almost everything else in the water. I'm sorry."

Sadena studied Nils with the very faintest of frowns wrinkling his high forehead. Then he tipped his head toward Rahel and asked the question with his eyes.

She thought about pacing to conceal her distaste of his attention, but made herself match his stare without flinching. It felt like sharing handclasps with a corpse. "Uriel's a greenhouse planet," she told him in her most businesslike tone. "That means you've got no polar caps, which means you've got no deep thermohaline currents. You've also got three puny natural satellites—that means no significant gravitational stresses, and that means no tides. So basically put, Mr. Sadena, Uriel's ocean water doesn't move around. You get a little bit of chop at the surface due to wind movement, but that only oxygenates the upper level. The rest of the ocean has to collect oxygen through diffusion. That isn't very fast, and a lot of things can screw it up. Like when crap falls down from above—"

"Crap?" Sadena interrupted delicately.

Rahel waved her hands in ill-tempered impatience. She wasn't interested in playing to his sensibilities. "Dead algae, dead fish, dead birds—anything organic that sinks from the ocean surface to the bottom. Once organic stuff gets down there, it rots. Rotting uses up oxygen. If you've got more organic stuff floating down than you have oxygen diffusing—which in Uriel's environment isn't too hard—your organic rot uses up all the oxygen. Without oxygen, the organic waste can't rot, so it starts to build up. Once it builds up high enough to touch oxygenated water, it starts rotting again. After a while, it uses up all that oxygen, too, and so on, and so on."

Sadena nodded once, a cordial acknowledgment that he

was paying attention. "And you say this is happening all over the planet?"

"As near as we can tell. You noticed it in the Odarkan Sea first because that's a much smaller body of water than the ocean, and because you pay special attention to the wildlife there. Who knows how many deepwater species in the main ocean you've lost without anybody noticing?" She could tell from Sadena's dismissive shrug that the thought disturbed her more than it did him. "You'll need a Geological Survey ship if you really want details on a planetary scale," she went on, making no effort to hide her dislike of him. "But I can tell you that every bottom-water sample I pulled today indicates the development of a major anoxic event."

Glints of dispassionate thought moved in Sadena's dark eyes as he steepled fingers beneath his chin. "But the presence of my resort," he asked carefully, "of *any* of my resorts, has nothing to do with this development?"

Rahel snorted. "Even you couldn't produce enough garbage to turn an entire ocean stagnant."

"But at some point—" Nils moved to sit on the sofa directly across from Sadena, his hands clenched into a bundle of worried energy in his lap. "At some point, all the methane gas, and garbage, and hydrogen sulfide that's building up at the bottom of the ocean—" He glanced at Rahel for verification, then continued talking without actually waiting for her response. "If that ever needs to escape, Mr. Sadena, it has nowhere to go but up. The rotten bottom water is going to rise to the surface, and all the surface water will sink down below, and Uriel's oceans will put out a cloud of gas so poisonous you'll have nothing left alive within three kilometers of your beaches."

Ever since she'd explained the result of anoxic turnover to Nils, he'd been obsessed with making sure Sadena understood the details. Rahel, on the other hand, knew Sadena only needed to understand one thing. "Your ocean ecology is screwed."

"How soon can I expect the planetwide repercussions Proctor Oberjen describes?"

"Like I said, you need to talk to geologists about that." Rahel tossed a shrug and guessed anyway. "Five thousand years? Five million?" In the lifetime of a planet, both were equally imminent, barely a heartbeat away.

Sadena's little chuckle of amused relief disagreed. "Thank you for your report, Proctor Tovin. In the meantime . . ." He waved away the service drone, causing Jynn to dance back several steps to keep from being run over. "I believe our business here is done. Noah's Ark's services are no longer required on Uriel. You may, of course, make yourselves comfortable at my expense until Mr. Kuvasc is ready to travel, but you needn't trouble yourselves with any additional—"

"But . . ." Jynn looked startled with himself, as though he hadn't expected to hear himself speak. "But what about the jellyfish?" he asked in a little-boy voice.

Sadena's hand curled about the arm of his chair, and he sighed, very softly. It was the first honest sign of emotion Rahel had seen in the man. "Jynn, I'm sorry to have kept you from your duties. You may consider yourself excused."

"No, sir—" Jynn rounded Sadena's chair in a few uncertain steps, darting his attention between Rahel and his employer as though unsure to which one he should appeal. "Are you just going to talk about it and call it done?" He finally settled his gaze on Rahel. "Ma'am, what about the jellyfish?"

"Jynn . . ." Her back hurt, her lips tasted like tears, and the skin on her face and hands felt dry enough to peel. Even if she'd known how to say what the pilot wanted, Rahel hadn't the strength for it right now. "I'm sorry."

"But you got brought here to do *something*," he insisted. Big hands implored Rahel for help as they reached out to her. "Can't you take them back with you? Just some of them. Keep them, and breed them the way you do the other

animals. That way there'll still be some left to bring back
when the oceans get right again."

Rahel gently shook her head. "Noah's Ark doesn't work
that way. We aim our reproduction efforts at animals who
were pushed to extinction by unnatural forces—people,
usually," she added, glaring once at Sadena. He returned her
stare with impassive disinterest. "But when things die in
nature . . ." She wished Jynn would blink and clear the
tears that had gathered in his eyes. "Whole species die and
get replaced all the time. They always have. If it isn't right
for humans to wipe out an animal that Nature intended for
survival, then it isn't right for us to save an animal that
Nature meant to destroy." When Jynn didn't say anything
for what seemed a very long time, Rahel asked softly, "Do
you understand?"

In answer, he jerked to face Sadena. "You could hire
Noah's Ark to do it, couldn't you, sir? You're always saying
you can do anything with the jellyfish you want to—"

"And, indeed, I can." Sadena cut the pilot off impatiently.
He reached around Jynn for another cup of coffee, and his
face darkened slightly when he realized the serving robot
was no longer by his chair. "However, I am not interested in
entering into any such arrangement with Noah's Ark at this
time."

Jynn shook his head slowly. "But *why?*"

"Because . . ." Rahel caught Sadena's eyes with her
own when he glanced at her. "Mr. Sadena isn't actually
interested in preserving Uriel's jellyfish. He never has
been."

The languid composure with which Sadena shifted to
drape one knee over the other made anger rise up into
Rahel's throat so hot, it was all she could do not to bite him.
She suddenly understood why Paval hadn't been able to
restrain himself from beating the righteous superiority off
those Green faces.

"Let me tell you something, Proctor Tovin," Sadena
offered, the voice of a man with a great wisdom to impart.

"I own Uriel. I did not buy it to preserve it, I bought it to exploit it. I preserve the planet as aggressively as I do because I cannot exploit what I do not have, and because it is just bad business to let consumers believe I shit where I expect them to vacation." Whatever passed for sensitivity drained from his face, and the cold impatience of a businessman darkened his eyes. "My interest in Noah's Ark was never about jellyfish, Proctor Tovin. It was about publicity, and reputation, and considered self-interest. But it was *never* about jellyfish."

Jynn left, very quietly, through the same door the service drone had used to come and go. For just a moment, Rahel wasn't sure if Sadena's show of disdain had really been aimed at her, or at his insubordinate employee. It probably didn't matter—she doubted Sadena would see either of them again.

The sofa creaked softly as Nils leaned forward in preparation to stand. "I think that's all we need to cover right now, Mr. Sadena," the lawyer said politely. "I'll be in touch with your financial division—"

Rahel cut him off. "Don't bother."

Nils twitched a panicked look at her, but Rahel refused to take her eyes from Sadena. "I beg your pardon?" Sadena inquired.

"Noah's Ark won't be accepting a fee for this safari."

"*Ra*-hel!" Nils scurried around the end of the sofa as if to protect her from herself, all his lawyerly instincts no doubt soaring with his blood pressure. "You can't just renegotiate the agreement at this late a date!"

Rahel stepped to one side so she could keep eye contact with Sadena without leaning over Nils's shoulder. "Read your Ark contract," she told the lawyer. "While we're out on safari, *I'm* your boss—that means I can do anything I think necessary." She pushed Nils back into his seat with a glare. "And I'm telling you to shut up."

Nils sank onto the cushions with his forehead in his hand.

"I'm good for the contracted amount," Sadena assured them. He didn't sound particularly offended, though.

Rahel almost grimaced with disgust. "I'm sure you are. But if the Ark accepts payment from you, we're bound by all the provisions of your contract—including the gag clause that says we can't go public with the details of our relationship with you." She shook her head grimly. "I won't have GreeNet posting that Noah's Ark will tailor its data to suit high-paying customers, and I *won't* have you implying that we knowingly came here to whitewash your operation. You'll pay for our expenses—including Paval's medical care and our upkeep while we wait for him—but you won't pay the usual consulting fees, and you won't interfere if we choose to make our investigation here public."

"Considering your data reveals no misconduct on my part—" Sadena spread his hands with a pleased little laugh. "In fact, you prove I'm completely justified in not spending a credit to rescue Uriel's environment. I'm more than happy to let you spread the word as far as you'd like. It won't affect my business over the next five thousand years."

"And you'll give us all this in writing?" Nils still hadn't looked up from his lap.

"I'll see to it immediately." Sadena came brightly to his feet, bringing his hands together with a clap. He held them that way in front of him, as though proud of having snatched something out of the air before the rest of them. "Proctor Tovin, Proctor Oberjen—" He dipped a brisk nod toward the still despondent Nils. "Thank you very much for your services. It's been a pleasure doing business with you."

Rahel waited until the man had left the room before kicking a nearby end table into the closest wall, chipping off a corner.

Nils jerked his head up with a scowl. "What did you do that for?" The accusation sounded more betrayed than Rahel had expected. "You got what you wanted, didn't you?"

She righted the end table, swallowing a little twist of disappointment when it turned out to be too broken to stand where it belonged. "If you think I got anything out of this safari I wanted," she said as she eased the ruined furniture back down to the floor, "then you don't have the faintest idea what I came here expecting to gain."

Rahel left the hotel that evening by way of the lone service entrance. All three moons dotted a broken line from horizon to apex, and the ever-present rime of clouds stained the sky dull white instead of a more appropriate black or grey. Beach mud slipped under her feet, devoid of shells or bones to crunch. A clement breeze from the west lifted her hair away from her eyes, shushing like a maiden aunt who longed to assure her that everything would be all right.

No spybees buzzed for her attention this time, no reporters climbed over each other's shoulders for a chance to bark their hateful questions. Nils had held court with the netlinks for nearly two hours after leaving Sadena's private chambers. No one stayed on to the end except Keim, a small public access science service, and a token representative from one of the major nets. Natural disasters just weren't news unless there were people involved.

Rahel had left before Nils got done explaining that there wasn't even going to be a scandal. She could imagine the disappointment for netlink executives the galaxy over.

Darkness softened the walk to the Odarkan straits, blurring the landscape, muting the sounds. Even the tongue of rock at the top of the ridge seemed to reach out with no transition between it and the dark water it overhung. Rahel eased herself up to the very thinnest finger of that stone, then used hands and feet to feel her way down to her knees, and finally her stomach, letting her chin hang over the edge so that the view below her stretched on forever, wild and endless.

Water as still as satin, as perfect as black glass. Faintly— first in the deep waters far off to her right, then drifting slowly toward her in swirls of diamond spray—an angel's kiss of light stitched itself beneath the Odarkan's surface.

Twinkles of simple jellyfish thoughts passed silently from bell to lash to ruffle. Knowing the patterns for moonslight dancing off the jellies' crystalline cilia didn't soften the throb of wonder Rahel felt at seeing them move.

How long was a year for a jellyfish? Long enough to do everything important in their quiet, jellyfish lives? Long enough that five thousand or five million or five hundred of them would support enough jellyfish memories to take the sting out of dying unfairly? And what if their remaining years numbered less than five? Was that long enough for anything at all?

"You're better off than we are," she whispered, letting the voiceless wind carry her words to the starlight ripples down below. "We know when your dance is over, but you get to think you live forever."

Right up to the moment when the last glimmer of jellyfish thinking flickered down into the darkness of extinction.

⚡The Human Animal⚡

"I'm sorry, but animals are not allowed on board the Interface."

Rahel Tovin looked at the cluster of robots blocking her path, wondering how many were programmed nobodies and how many were the sentient Newborns who ran Interface Station. At least one sported a glossy brass plate riveted over its old Robot Identification Number: MECHANIC. Rahel couldn't help feeling that if she'd had to fight in court to obtain even the most basic "human" rights, she would have picked a better name than her previous job.

"Interesting house rule." On the ground beside Rahel, Toad hit the end of her lead and snuffled all over Mechanic's treadmill, pretending not to be leash-broken. "Sounds kind of like an anticarbon bias to me."

"On the contrary." Mechanic rolled straight back and stranded Toad at the end of her line. The drones to either side didn't move, but Toad still cocked her head attentively from side to side, as though sure they were about to do something fascinating. "The regulation was established at the request of several carbon-based life forms who frequently ply their trades on the Interface."

"Animals restricting animals?" Rahel tucked one foot under Toad's broad, brindled rib cage, and used it to slide the puppy back toward her. "That's pretty funny."

"Sentients restricting animals," Mechanic countered smoothly.

A yellow playback light blinked into life on the shoulder of one of the drones, and a flat, overloud voice reeled forth from its chest speaker. "Any self-motivating life form judged incapable of making informed decisions regarding its own safety or the safety of others shall be defined an animal and restrained accordingly."

Mechanic extended a manipulator arm, and Toad's ears flicked forward with interest. "Visual reference identifies this as *Canis familiaris*, breed unknown, age approximately four and one half Standard months. You lead it about on a leash, indicating you fear its behavior should it pass outside your influence—"

"I fear she'll piddle all over your space station, that's what I fear."

"It is the opinion of the Interface that the life form in your possession is an animal. We must ask that you remove it from the Interface, or it will be impounded."

"The opinion of the Interface, or the opinion of your sentience bigots?" Rahel didn't really expect an answer, and Mechanic didn't offer one. Its optics clicked into focus between Rahel, the puppy, its drones, while the drones themselves waited with programmed patience for something decisive to happen.

Ten meters down the corridor, a tall, grey-brown creature sidled into sight from behind a structural support. Combing rear legs over its velvet-furred abdomen, it chewed at its uppermost appendages while the eyes in its thorax glittered attentively. It looked like a melding of centaur and mantis, minus the exoskeleton, plus an additional set of pincer arms around the area of its waist. When it saw Rahel studying it across the distance, a shiver of distress trembled through its multijointed limbs and it scurried forward to crouch behind the line of robots, weaving nervously.

"Worry. Pungent. Breathing. Worry." The clean, Standard words—so expressionless and mechanical—obviously stuttered forth from the knobbed and fluted cylinder the spindly creature scraped erratically across its underside. Whatever concepts were supposed to be transmitted by the words were just as obviously alien in origin. "Animal. Yes? Animal. No?"

"This is a puppy," Rahel said clearly, hoping the alien's translator device had some means of sending language the other way. "A dog, domesticated by humans almost since day one." Toad stretched her neck out as far as thick terrier muscles would allow, groaning at the prospect of never exploring those thorny alien legs. "You wouldn't recognize her breed even if I told you what it was—it was extinct up until six months ago."

A flutter of movement marked the passing of translator rod through two sets of appendages to some orifice at the top of the creature's thorax, then back down to its belly again. "Inside-in-food-protect-living no. Answer. No."

Mechanic translated simply, "Domestication is not an issue."

Rahel scowled up at the alien and it skittered backward in apparent alarm. "What? You don't domesticate animals?"

"Breathing. Not-think. Smelling frighten. Abomination."

This time, Mechanic didn't offer a clarification.

"Look," Rahel sighed to the Newborn, "you guys set up this space station so various species could negotiate trade agreements, right? Well, I'm here to talk to some people about trade, just like you want." Rahel gathered up a fistful of leash and pulled the puppy a few sliding steps closer when Toad cocked her head as though contemplating another approach on the alien. "She's free of parasites and diseases, and I won't let her off the leash. I'll even put a diaper on her, if that'll make you happy." Toad would just love that. Still, the brass at Noah's Ark would kill Rahel if she got kicked offstation all because of a puppy and some touchy alien.

If Mechanic could have shaken its head, it probably would have. Instead, it snaked out an arm and pinched

Toad's leash between two fingers. Rahel tightened her own grip on the bundle when drones closed in on either side, and Toad leapt to her feet, whiplike tail slicing the air into shreds of doggy delight at the very suggestion of play. The alien minced a half-meter closer to chew on its own hands.

"To avoid seizure of this animal, you must leave it on your transport," Mechanic instructed Rahel. "Your transport must then remain disconnected from the Interface and parked no less than fifteen thousand kilometers away."

"You've got to be kidding." Rahel avoided picking up Toad as a rule—she'd be a 13-kilo terrier when she was full grown, and shouldn't get used to being carried around—but she stooped now to tuck the puppy protectively under one arm. "There's nobody to pilot my jump if I'm not there. I travel alone."

"Perhaps that's something you should rectify before you revisit the Interface."

"Look . . ." She reached to twitch the leash out of Mechanic's grip, but the alien behind the Newborn was faster. Pinching a roll of white-and-brindle skin in the longest of its thorax pincers, it dragged Toad forward by one jowl and one ear, producing a piercing scream from the puppy. Rahel's heart lunged for her throat. She hugged Toad like a mother bear and twisted her shoulder to the creature, striking out at the same time to grab the alien hand and thrust her thumb into the hinge of its largest joint. It felt like grabbing the mummified remains of a snake. But like a stubborn horse's jaw, the grip popped almost reflexively open, and Rahel scrambled two long steps backward before either alien or robots could reach toward her again.

The creature's legs bent into sharp peaks, and it sank almost supine behind the line of robots, its thorax curled down across its back. The translator beneath its belly groaned and stuttered, but didn't offer any words. Just as well. Rahel wasn't in the mood for its explanations, anyway.

"I came a couple hundred light-years to do business at your station," she told Mechanic, still hugging Toad. The puppy had burrowed her head into Rahel's armpit, her tail sleeked between her hind legs. "I'm willing to leave the dog on my ship if that's what the Interface wants me to do, but if you think I'm going to let some chickenshit extra-terrestrial—"

"If you behave violently toward any other denizen of this station," Mechanic said in a voice too artificially calm to ignore, "we will deport you and forbid your return for up to one hundred Standard years."

Rahel wondered fleetingly if the Newborn meant her personally, or humans in general. She would no doubt become very unpopular if she got her entire species banned from one of the galaxy's main mercantile stations. It wouldn't do much toward helping her locate her poachers, either, since Noah's Ark hadn't been able to verify Terran animals being sold on the black market anywhere but at the Newborns' Interface. Curling the fingers of her right hand, she tried to hide the frustrated gesture by gathering up the rest of Toad's leash in that fist.

"I'm sorry if I behaved violently." Rahel aimed for that air of civility that made her teeth grate when she heard other people use it. Having to force the words out almost made her want to kick the cowering alien. "I was only trying to safeguard my property against what I thought was violence from . . ." She wasn't sure if either "him" or "her" was applicable, so settled for, ". . . your companion. It hardly seemed reasonable to attack me that way, since I know for a fact that mine isn't the only ship docked at the Interface with animals on board."

The moaning hiss from the alien's translator fell silent.

A 'link light flashed beneath Mechanic's faceboard, then went dark again. "That information is incorrect."

"Like hell it is." Or maybe that would be considered violent again. It was so hard to tell with inorganics. Rising up on tiptoe, Rahel scowled left and right across the river of Newborns and extraterrestrials pouring down the hallway to either side. She'd seen the string of elaborately decorated

jumpships while she was parking her own ship, so she knew
a mazhet caravan was onstation—it was just a matter of
finding the scream of eye-aching color in the swarm of
businessfolk around her.

As it was, Rahel heard the rhythmic *jing-jing-jing-jing* of
a quadruped scratching a ring-spangled ear before she
actually turned and caught sight of the alien felid. She aimed
Mechanic's attention at the duac who now sat, languidly
pulling at the nails on its hind toes. "What do you call that?"

The alien lifted itself to full height again, and Mechanic's
primary optic extended to adjust its focus. "That is a duac,"
the Newborn said.

As though recognizing the word, Toad squirmed in
Rahel's grip and sneaked a timid look. Just what Rahel
needed—her puppy slobbering all over the mazhet's dun
cats, chewing on their tall, upswept ears and barking at their
profusion of nose, toe, and ear rings. She tightened her
elbow until the little dog grumbled with renewed disappointment. "That duac is here with the mazhet—not even
on a leash, I might add, or at its mazhet's side." In fact, the
mazhet in question was nearly out of sight beyond the door
of some small, overlit curio shop. Only the occasional flash
of puce, violet, and vermilion robes—overspread with
meters and meters of gold chain—betrayed the mazhet's
position when it gestured. "How come the mazhet get to let
their duacs wander free while you and your cringing
arachnid give me grief about one domestic puppy on a
leash?"

Mechanic turned its optics away from the duac in a
dismissive manner that was clear even without expression
or tone of voice. "The mazhet have a special arrangement
with the Interface."

Of course they did. The mazhet had a special arrangement
with everybody.

Rahel rubbed at her eyes. "Then what about Comtes
Nadder?"

"Interface registration lists Comtes Nadder's ship *Medve*

as a specialized class-three transport." Mechanic consulted
the station's database for another few blinks of its light. As
though encouraged by Mechanic's control of the situation,
the alien behind the robots rose creakily to full height again.
"Comtes Nadder is a licensed dealer in exotic goods."

That much Rahel knew—she was supposed to have been
at Nadder's berth fifteen minutes ago to discuss a transfer of
livestock.

"Exotic dealers are encouraged on the Interface, as they
stimulate trade and interspecies goodwill." Whatever moved
Newborns to *care* about interspecies goodwill was a mystery to Rahel, not to mention the rest of the galaxy. Maybe
the Newborns reacted to some sort of perceived social
inequality that non-chip-driven sentients weren't sensitive
to. Or maybe goodwill just promoted good trade, thus
guaranteeing the Newborns enough money to buy the parts,
programs, and power they needed to stay running without
selling themselves into slavery. Rahel didn't care which.

"Nadder's 'exotic goods' are animals," Rahel pointed out
to the Newborn and its alien eavesdropper. "She's docked
with this station in a ship twice as large as mine, and her
whole cargo bay is stuffed full of live animals. Goodwill or
not, you just told *me* that's illegal."

The alien rubbed at its eyes with all four arms, and
its translator squealed. Mechanic was not so nonplussed.
"*Medve*'s cargo is not prohibited under Interface regulation
4731 Section 2 Paragraph 7. As specified in this free trade
statute, *Medve*'s cargo qualifies as merchandise, not animals."

Rahel stared at the Newborn for almost half a minute.
Behind it, the alien bobbed twice, silently. "You mean if I
were here to sell this dog, then it would be okay for me to
have her onstation?"

"This animal would then be classified as legal merchandise under the Interface statute referenced above."

"Well, what do you know?" Rahel snorted a laugh, then

brought her face under control. "It just so happens that I came here planning to sell her."

The alien shuddered as though struck with a cold breeze, and one of the drones rolled away. Mechanic asked, "Do you have papers attesting to these plans?"

Rahel scowled, squatting to let Toad wriggle loose and hop back down to the floor. The puppy oozed behind her to get out of the alien's sight. "Not everybody needs papers to prove they do fair trade." Rahel bobbed up on tiptoe to search the crowd around the mazhet's multihued skirts. "I can give you references better than any set of papers," she said, assuming mazhet memory worked at all the way rumor suggested it did.

Rahel found the *dhaktu* right where she'd expected— stone-still to the mazhet's left, hands laced passively behind his back while he waited to translate the mazhet's alien clicks and rattles. The shaven head and simple rose-orange-lavender tunic marked him as a mazhet employee; the remnants of an ash-blond topknot marked him as human, and still young enough to not have grey in his hair. Whatever discussion the mazhet conducted inside the little ship, the human didn't seem to be involved, or even very interested. When the duac threaded its lazy way between patrons to rejoin the mazhet, the human *dhaktu* didn't so much as glance at the cat. Rahel wondered how long *dhaktu* had to practice before perfecting the details of their self-imposed invisibility.

"Hey!" she whistled shrilly. The duac turned to swivel its ears in Rahel's direction and Toad barked a greeting, but neither human nor mazhet moved. "Invisible Voice!" This time, the *dhaktu*'s spine jerked even more stiffly straight than before. "I need to talk to your boss. It's kind of important."

"Ms. Tovin—" Mechanic poked at her kneecap with the end of one retractor arm. "Such shouting is considered socially unacceptable in many sentient cultures, including your own." Toad stretched up to lick the Newborn's gripper.

"Well, if we're lucky, I won't have to do it again." Rahel gathered up the slack in Toad's leash when she saw the *dhaktu*'s hand creep forward to pluck the webwork of chains hanging from his mazhet's sleeve. Although nothing physical seemed to change in the alien's stance or attitude, Rahel felt the mazhet's shift in attention almost as clearly as the *dhaktu* must have. Tipping forward as though pushed delicately from behind, the *dhaktu* whispered into the back of his mazhet's shoulder—as close as he could come to the tall alien's head. Then they both turned in a neatly executed whirl of ribbons, bells, and clashing fabric, and the mazhet glided out into full view for the first time.

Except for the colors and patterns in their obstreperous robing, the mazhet seemed truly indistinguishable from each other as far as Rahel could tell. They stood a nearly uniform two and a half meters in height, their huge eyes an identical, whiteless ebony, their skin the same shade of luscious burnt mahogany. If their humanoid faces had been constructed with a breath more subtlety, they wouldn't have had faces at all; if their skin had kissed their bones more closely, they'd be nothing but a collection of brittle sticks, artfully arranged to resemble a man. And if any mazhet anywhere had ever displayed something reminiscent of a human emotion, Rahel had yet to hear about it.

She tucked Toad between her ankles, holding the puppy with the gentle pressure of her legs as the mazhet approached.

"Ayr." Mechanic spoke the single word as a name, pivoting on its treadmill to face the mazhet. The mazhet inclined its head toward one shoulder with a faint jingle of jewelry, but gave no other sign of greeting. It offered no acknowledgment at all to the shivering mantis-alien. "This woman wishes to bring an animal on board the Interface for purposes of barter. She claims you can serve as her reference."

Rahel waited until Ayr turned its face toward her, then

clenched her fist apprehensively in the tangle of leash. "Do you know who I am?"

Ayr blinked slowly, and the duac stretched itself into a C around Rahel's legs to snuffle at Toad's backside. If the mazhet even flicked a glance down at the felid, Rahel couldn't tell—she hadn't yet figured out how to judge when mazhet focus moved.

A short, startling burst of clicking prompted the *dhaktu* to take a step forward. "This human is known to the mazhet." The *dhaktu* spoke as if the words were wholly his, but he never moved closer than his mazhet's left elbow, and he never made eye contact with anyone. Even the mantis seemed to keep its attention locked intently on the mazhet.

Rahel forced herself to stare directly at Ayr. The alien's intricate bodice reflected like wine in its eyes. "Did I barter with the mazhet on Reyson's Planet for the exchange of exotic animals?"

Although she had never seen or heard of Ayr until a few moments ago, its barrage of hissing clicks passed on through the *dhaktu*'s mouth as, "Such barter with this human did occur."

Mechanic watched the duac circle Rahel slowly, stubby white tail flicking in time to the tap of its toe rings against the floor. "Do the mazhet accept this woman as competent and capable of managing the animal in her possession?"

The duac finally snorted with boredom and wandered away. The mantis-alien jittered out of its way before the cat came close enough to touch it.

Toad craned her neck to watch the duac leave, although neither Ayr nor the *dhaktu* seemed particularly concerned about the big cat's departure. "This is accepted by the mazhet."

"Very well." Mechanic squawked a blat of machine language, and its entourage of drones rolled off in separate directions, mindlessly intent on new places and new things. The mantis turned in a circle, watching them go. "The Interface hereby issues this temporary livestock merchandise transporting permit, valid until eighty hours from moment of issue." A scrap of flimsy curled out of a slot on its stomach. The Newborn rolled a half-meter forward, apparently offering the printout to Rahel. She tightened her grip on Toad before bending to take it.

"You must carry this permit with you at all times while on board the Interface with this animal. If at any time you cannot produce this permit on demand, the animal in question will be confiscated. Say 'yes' if you understand."

Rahel nodded and tucked the flimsy into her trouser pocket. "Yes." She flicked a look at the alien still twirling in distress from behind the remaining Newborn. It muttered into its translator without looking at her.

Mechanic's 'link indicator twinkled briefly. "So logged. Enjoy your stay at the Interface." It rotated and trundled off around the corner before it had even finished speaking to her. Rahel couldn't help wondering if Comtes Nadder and her shipload of illegal animals had gotten as much hassle the first time *Medve* tried to set up shop on the station.

"Proctor Tovin . . ."

Rahel nearly collided with Ayr when she turned, finding herself for the first time close enough to a mazhet to smell the dusty perfume of its robes when it moved. Ayr angled its head to blink down at her, and Rahel took two unconscious steps backward under the pressure of those pupilless black eyes.

"Always has your employer censured mazhet trade in obsolete genotypes." Rahel wasn't sure how much of the innocent curiosity in the words came directly from Ayr, and how much was supplied by its *dhaktu*. "Does Noah's Ark seek now to busy itself in the barter of such exotic animals?"

Rahel slid Toad down to the floor. The puppy immediately busied herself snuffling the mazhet's feet, ringing the alien's adornments with her tail. "I'm not here in my capacity as a Noah's Ark proctor. This is more like a private business matter that I'd rather not discuss." She twisted to

point, but the insectoid alien had already backed halfway
down the long corridor, its hands back in its mouth. "Do the
mazhet know what that is?"

"That is Larry."

If the mazhet weren't naturally constructed to be so
deadpan, Rahel might have taken that as a joke. "Larry?"

"He is tlict, and deals not often with human beings." Ayr
raised its head to make contact with the departing creature,
closing both fists in front of its mouth in some sort of
gesture of greeting or farewell. "Tlict identifications cannot
be rendered audibly. All male tlict, therefore, respond in the
human language to the identification 'Larry.'"

Rahel watched the tlict pick its way gingerly through the
deepening crowd. "Then what am I supposed to call the
females?"

The *dhaktu* laughed. Or maybe it was the mazhet after all.
Who knew what they used as a natural expression of
humor? "You will not ever see a female tlict," the mazhet
told her with a graceful wave of its hands. "And if you do,
Proctor Tovin, you will not see a human again to talk about
it, so what you do or do not call her hardly matters."

Comtes Nadder's docking berth smelled of ammonia and
gamey animal breathing. Rahel assumed this was on purpose. After all, *Medve* itself must be as airtight as any other
ship in the void, and Nadder certainly hadn't allowed her
stock to wander out of the cargo bay where prospective
buyers might catch a premature glimpse of the offerings.
The black-marketeer no doubt wanted customers to be
confident that her livestock ate, breathed, and shat just as
much as the most legal reproductions. Conversely, Nadder
probably would have had the berth smelling as pure as a
Newborn's bottom if she'd known Rahel was a Noah's Ark
proctor. So maybe the godawful stench was in truth a good
sign after all.

Rahel stopped outside *Medve*'s airlock and palmed the
signal. Toad made bored circles around her ankles, sighing

at her predicament when the leash finally cinched too tight
for her to move. "It's called aversion therapy," Rahel
commented aloud.

As if in response to her voice, *Medve*'s hatch whisked
open. "You're late."

Rahel had expected the accusation, but not the whippet-
sparse figure who delivered it. Her hand braced impatiently
against the airlock hatchway, Comtes Nadder looked older
and more sallow than Rahel had imagined in their comlink
talks. The deep, rust-edged voice was the same, though, and
the black leather jumpsuit and red headband seemed at least
as carefully chosen as the smuggler's waist-length black
hair and garnet eyes. Not necessarily a flattering combina-
tion, but effective enough, considering Nadder's occupa-
tion. Rahel suspected the other woman wasn't much of a
slave to current fashions.

Trying on an arrogant scowl, Rahel stepped free of Toad's
leash with the ease of much recent practice. "I tried to get
here sooner, but the Newborns caught me coming onstation
with the dog and gave me some 'no animals' song and
dance. It took a while to get past them."

"Yeah, I hear you." Nadder flashed a smile as thin as her
face, and stepped away from the hatch to let Rahel past. The
inside of *Medve* didn't even smell like people, much less
like wild-animal feces. One more illusion shattered.

"Next time," Nadder said, closing the lock behind them
and leading the way into the rest of the ship, "tell the
Newbies she's cargo. They don't care what you're really
carrying, so long as you give 'em the papers they want."

As if that much weren't apparent simply by Nadder's
presence here. "I told them she was merchandise." Rahel
tried very hard to sound cursory about the falsehood.
Knowing the extent to which Nadder abused the same
loophole in Newborn regulations, though, made her words
come out disdainful and angry.

Which seemed to work just as well. "So is she?" Nadder

brushed an intent glance across the puppy, shouldering open another door.

Rahel tightened her grip on Toad's lead. "Is she what?"

"Merchandise. Did you bring her here to sell her?"

Cold day in hell before I let any animal go with you. "No. She's kind of a project of mine—I only just got her myself."

"Too bad." Nadder paused outside the great double hatch of *Medve*'s cargo bay, punching some lengthy code into the lock while her body kept Rahel from seeing anything interesting. "I'd love to have a shot at her chromosomes. There's not a lot of choice in extinct dogs on the open market, and she looks about as Terran as they come. Oh, well." She pushed open the door with another nanosecond smile. "We can talk again after you see what I've got. Maybe we can cut us a deal."

Or maybe not. Rahel followed her into the cargo bay, pausing only long enough to bounce Toad up into her arms.

Rows and stacks and walls of crates stretched a startling distance in all directions. No distinctive markings to separate one steel container from the other, though. Not even a manifest pad left hanging near an inventory port that Rahel could steal a peek at. Just a loader drone backed into its parking station, and whatever webbing and antigravs were necessary for holding the cargo in place. She swallowed a curl of annoyance. For all Rahel knew, Nadder's boxes could be filled with party condoms, on their way to the mazhet embassy.

"I thought you said you had animals."

"Oh, I've got animals." Nadder waved her toward a comp station along the starboard bulkhead. "I've got whatever animals you want. Sit down."

Rahel sank into the station's only chair, lacing her arms across Toad's back to encourage the puppy to lie down. What she'd taken from the doorway to be a smart loading system revealed itself instead as a gangling collection of I/O interfaces, headbands, and gloves. Rahel picked up the closest optic projector and let it dangle from her index finger. "I had something a little more concrete in mind."

Nadder shrugged as she dug another set of VR equipment out of a drawer. "While you're on my ship, you do my business, my way." She wiggled her hand into one of the gloves. "I've been doing this longer than you've been around, honey. Don't try to teach me new tricks."

Nadder's VR simscape was built on cheap stock background coding. Nondescript trees of a deciduous nature rustled without moving, birds from various climates and planets twittered and sang without deigning to make an appearance. Rahel's feet and hands and torso appeared as little more than an idealized mannequin, and the VR channeled nothing back by way of sensory input except for the occasional sound. Just as well. Captured by the VR's manufactured visual frame of reference, Rahel already felt refracted from her physical body—she didn't need the rest of her senses lying to her, as well.

"So what happens here?" Rahel felt Toad walk a circle in her lap. The weird division of her attention made her dizzy.

"Here, you get to look at anything available that strikes your fancy. For as long as you want, and as close as you want." Another featureless mannequin appeared against the simscape. Rahel thought the effect a lot more gruesome now that she was confronted with the golem in its entirety. "What are you interested in?" Nadder asked through a lipless mouth.

Rahel shrugged, then realized such a subtle gesture wouldn't be picked up by her simulacrum. "What have you got?"

"They're listed by family down below."

Sure enough, a multilayered tap menu floated in an arc at her waist level. Rahel hesitated with her hand spread above the choices, like an uncertain god. The number of species represented in that color-coded strip would have filled the Breeding Compounds back at Noah's Ark for generations. From there, they would go on to freedom on new homes throughout the galaxy, new histories for their young. What kind of life did they have to look forward to from here? Illegal purchase by the galaxy's filthy rich, and a decidedly substandard existence in some private exhibition where they would never know the dignity of self-sufficiency, never know the company of their own kind.

Rahel tapped out a family at random, found only one genus underneath it, and only one species under that. She called up the choice without reading it. Whatever it was didn't matter—it was the fact that Nadder had a copy of it when it no longer existed that made it significant.

The bad stock simscape flashed away, replaced by a more detailed reconstruction on an up-close-and-personal scale. Dark, serrated leaves dropped over a slip of muddied rock, and a transparent grey mass crept across at Rahel's eye level, its creamy rust-and-white shell balanced as delicately as a teacup on its nonexistent shoulders.

"*Partula exigua.*" Nadder sounded very close, but didn't appear in Rahel's view of the scene. "Interesting choice. Go ahead—pick it up."

Rahel lifted the chip of stone across which the little snail labored. It continued crawling with no knowledge of its relocation. *That's because it isn't real,* Rahel told herself. *It's just a little computer worm that's supposed to look good and rake in buyers.* She couldn't feel the cool kiss of its flesh when it oozed onto her fingers, couldn't feel the chalky smoothness of its shell when she traced its dextral swirl. She'd never before held an extinct animal in her hands and believed so keenly in its absence—like weaving with shadows, or fondling air.

"Partulas are a nice choice if you've got space limitations," Nadder was saying, her voice moving around the sim even though she didn't materialize. "They move maybe thirty centimeters a year—a half-meter, tops—and they even eat their own crap, so you don't have to clean up after them. Feeding this guy's your biggest problem. He's strictly carnivorous, and won't eat anything except a particular

family of snails that are about as easy to find as he is."
Nadder's hand appeared for the first time, there only long
enough to pluck the partulid from Rahel's fingers, turn it,
and replace it on her palm headed in the opposite direction.
"He'll live off a specialized protein gel for a while, but
partulas have a tendency to starve to death before they'll eat
anything new." The spiel sounded well-rehearsed, Nadder's
voice slightly distracted as she recited it. "Your best bet
would be to work out some kind of supply deal with me. I
can send the same kind of snails he's been eating here
whenever you say you need 'em—in a nonbreeding variety,
of course."

Of course. Rahel carefully tickled the snail off her palm
and back onto the virtual mud. It bounced onto its side when
it met the ground, cringing back into its shell until only the
tips of its slow antennae floated ahead to feel for danger.

Rahel righted it gently with the side of her thumb. Even
knowing it was virtual didn't save her from feeling guilty
for having startled the little snail. She couldn't force herself
to be cavalier about any creature's welfare, even when she
knew the creature was only make-believe. This particular
virtual specimen, at least, presumably represented some
live individual, hidden amongst Nadder's extensive cargo.
Keeping that in mind, Rahel tapped the snail's spiral shell to
see if that would give her additional information on the
species.

A submenu exploded upward from the partulid's location.
A bright yellow rectangle, outlined in red, hung in front of
her face long enough to blink ACCESS RESTRICTED four
times, then diminished into a point again and vanished.
Rahel twisted her mouth into a frustrated scowl, but resisted
actually swearing out loud.

"What the hell was that for?"

She glanced up for Nadder's simulacrum before remembering she was in this VR 'scape alone. "Just browsing. I
was curious about things like the snail's original climate,
altitude, mineral requirements—"

"DNA spins?"

Rahel called up a sample of *Alytes obstetricans* in an effort to hide her surprise. "Whatever you might have had on tap," she said with feigned nonchalance.

Light shattered across the simscape, dashing apart the pieces of unreality and leaving Rahel blinking at the sudden solidity of the cargo bay around her. Nadder pitched Rahel's optic set at the VR station, then didn't bother bending to catch it when it slid off the panel and onto the floor. She left that to the silent, white-skinned, pink-eyed man behind her.

"Chat over." Nadder tugged the headset from the albino's hands and threw it back onto the station. This time it stayed. "Vacate the ship like a good girl, Proctor, and we'll call this barter even."

Rahel stood slowly, Toad kicking unhappily in her arms until she settled her in a more stable position. "I didn't even get to see what I was looking for."

"You've seen enough."

Not nearly.

"Don't you guys have better things to do?" Nadder asked as she gestured oh-so-politely toward the door they'd come in by. "I'd think you'd have enough problems with the animals you've already got." The albino circled around to Rahel's other elbow, just in case she entertained some silly plan to resist.

She didn't. "Well, we're funny that way." Rahel fell into step between them without bothering to put Toad on the floor. "People who sell genotypes that we own all the legal rights to have a tendency to tick us off."

"Moral superiority has a tendency to tick me off." Nadder levered open the cargo door and ushered Rahel through. "You guys think your kind of purist conservation shit is the only right way to keep four-legs. Even if I *was* selling your genomes"—she slammed the door behind them—"which I'm not, what makes it so wrong to give people a taste of what they can't get anywhere else?"

"Don't try to tell me you're not selling Terran genotypes."

Rahel opted to stay with the strictly legal end of their discussion—the black-marketeer's profession made the larger ethical question seem hardly worth pursuing. "You think I don't know authentic gross structures when I see them?"

Nadder shrugged. "I'm glad you think so. But it's not like you actually looked at any *animals* today."

Rahel stopped just inside the final hatchway, bumping her elbow back against the albino when he would have shoved her forward to keep her moving. "What are you talking about? I saw the partulid and—"

"You saw a partulid *simulacrum*," Nadder corrected her. The marketeer's smile was as slick and artificial as her hair when she took Rahel's arm and accompanied her the last few steps onto the dock. "That's what I sell, after all—VR tours of an extinct zoo. If you came here thinking otherwise, Proctor, I'm afraid you were misinformed."

Noah's Ark had spent nine months and a small jumpship's worth of money tracing leads and rumors beyond the edge of human space to the Newborns' Interface. What had started as a search for the origins of a single bootleg Terran cargo had grown into one of the Ark's primary projects. It was the strength of that history and her own long hours of clue-sniffing and travel that let Rahel scowl down into Nadder's face and say with grim certainty, "Bullshit."

The marketeer's smile became even more irritatingly serene. "I guess you'll have to prove that." She slapped the control that closed *Medve*'s airlock door.

"Wait a minute!" Dancing forward a step, Rahel caught the edge of the door with her palm to halt it in its track. "Aren't you at least going to tell me how you found out where I was from?"

Nadder tipped her head as though considering, then smiled in what looked like honest amusement when Toad echoed her gestured with one brindled ear cocked higher than the other. Behind her shoulder, the albino actually laughed.

"Staffordshire bull terrier," Nadder said suddenly. She

wiggled her fingers at Toad, then turned her eyes more directly on Rahel while the puppy fidgeted delightedly at the attention. "Holds the domestic record for going from endangered to extinct in less than ten years back in the early twenty-first century—one of many victims of the pre-Reform urban paranoia. I've never heard of anybody offering that kind of blueprint for open sale." She hooked a thumb back toward the albino. "Took Styen nearly fifteen minutes just to match a visual to our records. That left only one place that little dog could've come from."

Rahel nodded, already blushing with self-anger at her own shortsightedness. "Noah's Ark."

Smiling, Nadder tapped the end of her downturned nose and poked at the door controls again. Rahel stepped grudgingly back to let the airlock hatch slide closed. Nine months and uncounted millions of credits, just so Rahel could put them right back where they'd started less than two hours after setting foot on the station.

She kicked at the now impassable airlock door. "Dammit."

"I can't believe I blew it!"

"Does that mean it's too late for me to suggest you leave the dog behind next time you go onstation?"

Rahel aimed a withering glare at the comlink over her shoulder, and Paval's on-screen image returned her scowl with eyebrows raised in his traditional expression of innocent query. She still hadn't decided how much of her apprentice's little-boy sincerity was for real, and how much he affected just for the sake of annoying her.

"Your next lesson when I get home will be all about giving advice *before* it's needed, not after." She pitched Toad's ball over the puppy's head, sending both ball and dog bouncing madly down the jumpship's center aisle.

"Well, then here's some advice for your next course of action: See what you can find out about Nadder around the rest of the station. Who knows what we'll find useful next time—"

"There's not going to *be* a next time." Rahel sighed in frustration as Toad cavorted back to shove the warm, spit-slimed ball into her palm. "By tomorrow morning, Nadder's going to have memorized the name, face, and description of every proctor in Noah's Ark." She threw the ball again, wiping her hand on the leg of her pants. "Face it, Junior—we're screwed."

"We're not screwed." Ah, the certainty of youth. If she hadn't been so angry with herself, Rahel might have laughed at his grim earnestness. "Nadder won't bother arming herself against us, Proctor Tovin. It's not like we're some sort of legal authority—we're a private corporation that's taken on an investigative task because nobody else cares about it. Even if you'd gotten past the contact today, we would still have had to prove wrongdoing on Nadder's part before the legal net would make a move."

But now they couldn't even do that. "She's never going to let an Ark proctor on the same station with her again." Rahel tugged the ball from between Toad's teeth and slung it down the aisle somewhat harder than before.

"Then we'll just send somebody else."

The apprentice's words poked her like an electric shock. Ignoring Toad's happy snarlings when the dog returned with her fresh-killed ball, Rahel swung to face the comlink and Paval's startled blink. "What did you say?"

He shrugged uncertainly, as though not trusting whatever verbal trap he'd unwittingly stumbled into. "Noah's Ark has money. Surely we can hire someone not affiliated with the Ark to go in and make the purchase for us. Once we've got the merchandise and the manifest, we can press the cops to at least open up an investigation." He brought one hand up to touch the edge of his screen when Rahel jumped to her feet and Toad began barking with excitement. "This is a setback, Proctor Tovin, not the end of the world."

Not even much of a setback, if she made good use of her

options. She kicked Toad's ball farther down the aisle, then snatched up a blue-and-green print jacket to shrug on over her khaki Noah's Ark bush shirt. "I should have thought of this from the beginning!"

"Proctor Tovin?" Paval's voice echoed slightly in the empty cockpit behind her. "You're off visual. Are you going somewhere?"

She jumped back up the stairs to lean over the comlink and smile down into his anxious face. "Junior, I'm going out to buy some Terran animals." She chuckled wickedly before punching off the channel. "I'll give you a call when the setback's over."

"I want something Terran," she told them. "Something *big* and Terran. Price is no object, and size isn't a problem. Just get me something living, and *make sure* it's authentic."

That was part of the brilliance of her plan. By sending her agents off with such a specific—yet broad—requisition, Rahel could almost certify they'd return with one of the high-demand "glamour animals"—a lion, or an orca, or maybe even a gorilla. Something of the romantic, frightening nature that appealed to people who fancied they could "own" animals, rather than just live with them. Nadder was certain to have a wide selection of such genomes available. Rahel, meanwhile, would be able to tell with a look if what she'd purchased was Terran without having to wade through the snails and toads and spiders who weren't in her area of expertise.

"Arrange for payment through whatever third party makes you happy—I don't want the Ark's name showing up *anywhere*. And no matter what else happens, no matter who asks, don't say anything to anyone about the details of this transaction. This has to be completely private. Do you understand?"

They'd just stared at her in unreadable silence, then turned and ghosted off toward center station in a cloud of brilliant ringing.

She'd expected them back within the hour.

Instead, morning crept into afternoon, she turned down two 'link calls from Noah's Ark, and Toad went to the bathroom in the airlock. After that, Rahel took the puppy outside to chase her ball up and down among the maintenance sleds, then sat under the jumpship's landing gear until Toad found gnawing on her ball too much effort to maintain. Groaning with contentment, the puppy fell asleep with her head hanging over Rahel's knee and her tongue peeking out of her mouth.

Rahel followed Toad into sleep less than three hours later. She'd been sitting up in her bunk with half-read downloads strewn across her lap and Toad draped over her ankles, when she noticed that a simple figure reference made absolutely no sense to her conscious mind. So she sighed, closed her eyes, and tipped her head back against the bulkhead for just a moment's respite.

Something jerked her back into wakefulness, seemingly only an instant later. "What?" She bolted upright in the bed, scattering downloads everywhere. "What is it?" Toad stretched with a grumble, but didn't awaken.

"There are seven beings requesting entry at the main airlock," the ship informed her. Rahel liked this jumpship's voice—helpfully female without being obsequious. "Shall I admit them, or do you wish to escort them manually?"

Seven? Good God, please don't let them have bought her an elephant! She squirmed hurriedly out from under Toad and the rest of the downloads. "Do they have any cargo with them?"

"They have a livestock shipping crate. I cannot see inside it."

Good enough—and better than she thought she'd get after leaving Nadder's berth this morning. Padding stocking-footed through the ship's empty corridor, Rahel called up the lights as she went. She skidded to a stop at the airlock and slid aside first one, then the other hatch to face the small crowd and their shiny, steel-sided shipping crate.

One of the duacs sneezed and leaned over to lick its neighbor's ear.

For some reason, when the ship reported seven beings waiting outside her jumpship airlock, Rahel hadn't expected four of them to be duacs. And she'd rather hoped at least one of them would be *dhaktu*. Glancing at the three mazhet ringing the crate, she raised her eyebrows at the puce and violet figure she assumed to be Ayr. The mazhet looked back at her with emotionless patience.

"You got the Terran animal I commissioned?" Rahel nodded toward the crate without taking her eyes off the aliens. The crate didn't seem as large as she'd hoped for—only about three meters deep, and not even as tall as her shoulder.

Ayr dipped its chin to touch its chest once, quite deliberately.

"And I don't suppose any of you has a *dhaktu* up his sleeve?"

This time the three mazhet only stared at her, and Rahel had to scrub at her eyes to keep from laughing with weary frustration. "No, of course not. All right . . ." She stepped aside and waved them through the airlock. "Bring it in here."

The green and aqua mazhet on the left flicked one spidery hand across the top of the crate; then Ayr and the mazhet in yellow, salmon, and pink applied gentle pressure along both sides to glide the metal box forward. Rahel couldn't see that it rose above the decking, but it slid forward as easily as hot oil on ice, even clearing the hatchway without appearing to lift up over the edge. The duacs stirred themselves in no discernible order and followed the mazhet inside.

Toad sat blearily in the middle of the main compartment, watching Rahel and the mazhet maneuver the crate through the open hatchway. Even when the duacs clustered around the puppy to nudge at her with their blunt noses, all Toad did was lean against the nearest one and sigh sleepily. That duac twitched one ear flat to its skull and glared at the puppy. Its three companions sank to their haunches a respectful distance away.

"I want to have a look at this thing before we finalize our transaction." Rahel trotted away from the mazhet long enough to retrieve the snooze pistol she'd left lying on the flight panel. "It's not that I don't trust you—it's Nadder I expect to play some tricks. Now, if you'll let me—"

Ayr stepped in front of her before she could approach the box. It closed long, dry fingers around her wrist, pushing the snooze pistol off to one side as it clicked and ticked and rattled in the longest run of untranslated mazhet Rahel had ever heard. She shook her head slowly, not sure if she should be watching the mazhet's face or the quick, elaborate hand gestures it rang and sparkled in front of her.

"I'm not going to hurt it." She tried to bring the pistol up between them again, wanting to explain how gentle and harmless it was. Ayr only persisted in pushing the weapon aside. "This gun will only put it to sleep for a little while—just long enough for me to run a few tests, that's all."

Ayr patted Rahel's chest, hands fluttering like bird's wings, then pressed a corpse-cool palm to her forehead.

"I don't understand what you want from me." Rahel ducked a look at the mazhet still waiting by the unopened crate. "Do you have a *dhaktu* you could send for? Anyone you could bring?"

They might have been deaf for all the reaction they gave her. Ayr pushed at her forehead again, touched her chest, and Rahel caught its hands between hers to keep the mazhet from flustering through the senseless pattern again. Its hands felt as though she could shatter them with a single intemperate squeeze.

"Just let me have a look at it." She locked eyes with the mazhet's fathomless black ones, not at all sure if that gesture was socially correct. "I won't hurt it, I won't let it out. But I need to see what you've brought me before we can go any further." The gentlest of pressure backed Ayr into its former position alongside the others. "You know, you could have brought one of your 'invisible voices,' and we wouldn't be having this problem."

The mazhet all rustled with the same ringing of bangles, but they said nothing to her or each other.

Rahel repositioned herself in front of the crate, and checked the charge on her snooze pistol. More than enough to lay low anything that could fit inside a container this size. "Okay, then . . ." She nodded tightly to the green and aqua mazhet. "Open her up."

A chime and brush of movement, and the mouth of the crate hissed open. Rahel crouched, steeling herself for an explosion of movement, a scream of animal anger, a howl of animal pain. Instead, still silence puffed out on the stench of sweat and feces, and the tiny, rapid sound of breathing echoed through the empty crate like thunder. Frowning, she knelt very slowly.

"Oh, good God . . ." She thumped down onto her bottom without meaning to, and the snooze pistol fell, unfired, across her lap. Hand tangled halfway through her sleep tousled hair, she stared into the long, darkened crate without even being able to marshal enough thought to disbelieve.

From the back of the crate, the brown, frightened eyes of a very human boy stared back at her in silence.

"It's all right, nobody's gonna hurt you . . . Do you have a name? Do you know what I'm saying?"

No, of course he didn't. Rahel could tell by his eyes—those quick, intelligent eyes that followed her every gesture, her every shift in weight with the desperate intensity of a wild animal. She'd seen Toad look at her with more understanding whenever she said the words "out" or "play" or "good dog." All this boy's reactions proved was that he wasn't deaf—and that he was nearly mindless with fright.

"You poor thing . . ." Rahel eased into the mouth of the crate and sat back on her heels. "I wish I knew where the hell she got you." The boy only stared at her and hugged his knees even tighter to his chest.

Naked and unwashed, he wasn't recognizably from any particular culture, and his small, Caucasian features placed him squarely in the least remarkable genotype. Even his filthy hair and build proved little help in guessing his origins; Rahel thought the matted snarl might be yellow (but wouldn't put money on it until she had him washed), and his 150-centimeter height could be indicative of either a normal child or a smallish adult. His face and chest were hairless. The muscles of his legs and shoulders, though, were those of a post-pubescent who'd reached the wiry spareness of maturity. Yet he'd defecated in the opposite corner of his crate, which was something even a dog wouldn't do.

She leaned back into the open and met Ayr's eyes across the top of the box. "Has anyone got the control for the collar?" From a crate-length away she could see how the boy's collarbones were bruised and raw from the restraining band Nadder had bolted around his neck. She wondered how many times the black-marketeer had found it necessary to sting the boy with the restrainer's neural pulse, and how many times she had jolted him completely unconscious. Getting rid of the damnable "training device" moved up to Rahel's first priority.

"The collar," she said again, a little louder and more slowly as she traced an arc on the front of her neck with one finger. "Did Nadder give you the control for the restraining collar?"

The mazhet stood as though unhearing. Rahel groaned and turned away from them with an angry wave. "Why do I bother to ask you anything?" It hadn't occurred to her she'd need to insist the mazhet retrieve all the hardware associated with Nadder's merchandise. But, then, it hadn't occurred to her the merchandise would be human, either.

A melodic chime fell from the AI's shipboard speakers. "There are two beings requesting entry at the main airlock," the ship informed her.

Rahel craned a hopeful look toward the ceiling. "Is either of them human, by any chance?"

"One of them is human."

"Hallelujah." She shimmied the rest of the way out of the crate, then stood and placed her body in front of the exit with both hands on either corner of the roof to feel for any movement from inside. "Let them in."

The *dhaktu* scurried through before the airlock door finished sliding open. True to his job description, he slipped among the mazhet in timid silence, not sparing Rahel so much as a smile. Maybe he was afraid she'd humiliate him by offering a greeting. Rahel made an effort to contain herself. It wasn't until Toad scrambled to her feet with a growl of distress that it occurred to Rahel to look and see who followed the *dhaktu* inside.

The larry tlict cringed away from Toad's frantic barking, upper appendages flaring wide in what had to be a threatening display, medial appendages pulling close to cover its eyes. Remembering the barely controlled violence of the first tlict she had seen, Rahel dove to grab the puppy out of this one's way. Toad's only movement was to back away from the tlict in panicked hops as she barked. The puppy wheeled with a startled shriek when Rahel's hand closed on her collar, then hunched into a crouch and squirmed up into Rahel's arms. From that position of safety, she took up her barking again while Rahel trotted down the corridor to lock her in the bedroom. She'd never felt the little dog tremble so violently.

By the time Rahel made it back to the central compartment, the tlict had crabbed its way halfway around the room so as not to lose sight of the dog. "Private abode. Restrictions. Restrained. Yes? Yes?" The translator pressed against the tlict's abdomen muttered and hummed with untranslatable pheromones.

Rahel ducked a peek into the unattended shipping crate. Eyes bright like polished walnut glinted back at her through the darkness. At least they hadn't lost the boy.

"This ship is my private property," she told the tlict, turning back to face it. Limbs wove between each other to pass the translator up to the alien's tiny mouth. "My animal has the right to run free in here, and the Newborns promised me this."

"Yes. Yes."

"She'll stay in another part of my ship now, so that she won't bother you or the others."

"Yes. Yes. Good air. Good breathing."

Whatever the hell that meant. "Now will somebody please tell me why I have this larry on my ship?"

Ayr drew her attention with a gentle ringing of golden chain. "The merchandise did not appear in a healthy state." The *dhaktu* stood as still and servile as ever behind the row of mazhet, but Rahel had never heard an invisible voice sound sweeter. "It was determined a physical caretaker should be consulted as to its viability."

Rahel nodded, then realized what exactly they'd just told her. "A *doctor*?" She jerked a startled look at the larry. It stroked its eyes in nervous repetition. "The tlict have a *doctor* who can treat human beings?"

"Tlict. Not-tlict." It shifted uneasily onto its hindmost limbs. "Medicine treatment of not-tlict."

She shook her head in slow confusion. "I don't understand."

"This tlict is a veterinarian," the *dhaktu* volunteered without benefit of a mazhet's initiative.

A veterinarian? When its species apparently had no tolerance of animals, and very likely kept none as pets? "Well, I suppose that's appropriate, at least." She retreated an uncertain step, not sure if she should drive the tlict out or thank it for coming. Finally, she settled for sinking to her knees at the mouth of the crate and sighing at the boy still huddled at its rear. "Let me see if I can get him out for you." She went down on all fours, slipping the fallen snooze pistol into her pocket as an afterthought.

The floor of the crate felt clammy and damp beneath her

hands. Sour with human sweat, humid from urine and the boy's labored breathing, the air in the crate nearly gagged her. She bit down hard against a cough, then stopped halfway down the box's length to sink back on her heels and make eye contact with the boy. He pressed himself deeper into the corner he'd claimed as his own.

Rahel's stomach tightened with regret. "I'm not gonna hurt you," she whispered, just like she murmured to all the coyotes she'd tagged and sampled back home. "I know you're scared, but it's okay, everything's gonna be okay."

Just like the coyotes, his eyes reflected back a ghostly red that showed no signs of understanding.

"But you're not a coyote, are you? You're a boy. Which means there's something besides instinct going on in that oversized skull of yours." Deliberately keeping her voice gentle and soothing, her face serene despite her words, Rahel eased forward on hands and knees. The boy's eyes flicked to follow her movements. "You know I'm a human, too. You know from the way I'm talking and moving that I'm not coming in here to rough you around, don't you? We're just gonna get a look at you and make sure everything's okay." She placed one hand feather-light against the side of his leg. His skin twitched away from her touch like a horse's skin away from a fly.

She didn't pull her hand back. "There's no place else for you to go," she said, sliding up his leg to where his arms were locked around his updrawn knees. "You're just gonna have to come out here with me." And she closed her fingers around his wrist with a carefully calculated amalgam of tenderness and strength.

The boy exploded with a howl of rage. Rahel found herself jerked violently forward while he twisted and kicked and clawed to be rid of her. One wall of the crate banged into her shoulder; the boy's back shoved awkwardly against her armpit as he planted bare feet on the opposite wall and clenched every muscle in his scrawny little frame to break away.

"Oh, no, you don't!" Still fiercely gripping his wrist, Rahel snaked her free arm across the boy's chest to wedge him against her and break his leverage. He gave in to her pulling immediately, and they crashed sideways onto the bottom of the crate. Rahel was willing to count that as a preliminary victory right up to the moment he wrenched his captive hand up in front of his face and bit into her forearm with a gristly crunch.

"Ah, god*damn*it!" Anger took the short route straight into her bloodstream. She swung one leg over the boy and pinned him in retaliation. "You little—!"

"Proctor Tovin?"

The boy squirmed frantically beneath her, jabbing his elbow at her thigh, and bit down harder when she tried to use her free hand to grab his flailing arm. She shouted again in pain, and suddenly understood what it felt like to want to beat another human being senseless with your bare hands. Jamming her forearm more firmly into the little beast's mouth, she rolled onto one hip and dug across her front for the snooze pistol in her opposite pocket. It jutted against the fabric of her trousers like some dissatisfied animal who wanted to escape.

"Proctor Tovin?" the *dhaktu* called again. "Is some assistance required?"

Surely some mazhet had initiated the request, but Rahel would be damned if she could guess which one. "No!" She squeezed the pistol's trigger without bothering to work it free of her pocket. The boy jerked with a yelp, then collapsed into a loose sprawl beside her. If anything, the pain in her arm redoubled with a throb when the boy's bite pressure lifted.

"Doings between you sound most violent," the *dhaktu* pointed out in sync with someone's rapid clicking. "The mazhet remain available to assist in the unpacking of this merchandise."

"All right, then." Trying to ignore the progressively sticky feel of her shirt sleeve, Rahel untangled herself from the boy and rolled him over. "Get me the medikit from under the pilot's console in the cockpit." He seemed so light and tiny, now that she could drag him from the crate without fighting. It was almost like handling a toy.

The yellow and salmon mazhet shadowed her, medikit balanced on one hand, as she backed out of the crate with the boy in tow. "Spread the blanket there." Rahel jerked her chin toward the floor to her left, then waited somewhat impatiently while Ayr helped the first mazhet unfurl the blanket from the lid of the kit. Blood gathered in the elbow of her sleeve, hitting the floor one fat drop at a time with a brittle *tick, tick, tick*. Behind her, the tlict echoed the sound with its toenails in apparently unconscious mimicry.

The mazhet laid out the blanket at a angle to her, one corner near her ankle, the opposing corner pointed across the deck toward the cockpit door. She lowered the boy onto the square without commenting on its odd positioning. Tugging her sleeve into a lumpy wad near her elbow, she backed away from both mazhet and boy to give the tlict whatever room it thought necessary. "Get to work, Larry. He's not gonna be snoozed-out forever."

The tlict scrubbed fretful arms across its eyes, then scuttled forward to straddle the boy's body and probe him with some abdominal appendage. Rahel hoped to hell the kid didn't wake up to that view.

She accepted the sterile wipe yellow-and-salmon handed her, then hissed through her teeth half in pain, half in dread as she daubed away the blood obscuring the wound. More welled up to replace it, but not before she could see the ragged half-moons of actual damage. He may not have had well-developed canines, but the little bastard had certainly got her good.

Yellow-and-salmon pressed another clean wipe into her hand, and Rahel cocked a glance at the alien as she took it. The mazhet had turned the rest of the medikit to face her, obviously expecting her to select whatever medicaments she needed from the array in the bottom of the box. Rahel plucked out a largish handful of dry gauze to pack against the wound.

"Now that I've got your undivided attention . . ." She aimed the comment at the other two mazhet as much as the one by her side. "Can one of you tell me who's got the control for the merchandise's restraining collar?"

Yellow-and-salmon's huge black eyes studied the treatment of her wound without blinking. Ayr and its companion only stood complacently, as though she'd never spoken.

Rahel wasn't surprised to discover she was in no mood for mazhet weirdness. "What?" She looked irritably among the three of them. "Is there some mazhet rule against answering simple questions?"

The boy's rapid breathing and the creaking of tlict limbs were the only sounds in the central compartment. The duacs had wandered off to sniff at Toad's door and annoy her.

"The rules of the barter." The *dhaktu* said it suddenly, without any mazhet's urging and as though he surprised himself with the sound of his own voice.

Rahel aimed a frown at him. "What barter? Ours?"

The *dhaktu* dipped a stilted nod, wringing his hands in the folds of his orange robe and speaking in a quick, breathless voice completely unlike the competent tones he used as a translator. "They're bound by the conditions of your agreement, Proctor. You instructed them never to speak of the transaction with anyone."

She dropped her arm to her side in shock, and was rewarded with a thick pulse of pain. "I didn't mean me!"

The *dhaktu* winced a shrug. "You said anyone."

The concept of banging her head against a bulkhead suddenly seemed very appealing.

"Healthy scenting. Tasting strong."

The tlict stepped over and away from the boy with the delicacy of a four-legged dancer. Rahel brought her arm back up to her chest with a sigh, just as glad to turn her attention to the larry and away from her own stupid barter technique.

"Yes. Yes," the larry's translator stated solemnly. Its smallest arms danced here and there across its thorax as though searching nonexistent pockets for something. "Small food. Dark air. Non-tlict merchandise. Large food. Wise air."

Rahel nodded slowly. "The boy needs food and a better environment." She was guessing at the tlict's full meaning, and wondered if repeating what she thought it meant would just get her words translated back into the same near-nonsense the tlict had said before.

Whatever happened when her voice crossed the language barrier, the tlict's tiny mouthparts played across its translator and it waved its lower arms enthusiastically. "Large food. Wise air. Yes. Yes."

Well, at least that kind of help wouldn't be too hard to administer. Just about anything would be better than what this poor kid had already been treated to. "Thank you." She touched her fists to her mouth the way she'd seen Ayr do with the first tlict this morning, hoping it was remotely appropriate to the situation. "Is there something I owe you for doing me this service?"

"Worry. Answer." The tlict bobbed twice on its multi-jointed legs. "Answer. Worry."

Rahel took another blind stab at the alien's meaning. "I'll answer your question if I can."

"Not-tlict you. Not-tlict this." It tickled at the boy's midsection with one hind leg. "Difference. Yes? Difference. No?"

This was perhaps the clearest thought she'd heard come out of a tlict so far. "Difference no. The merchandise is a human being, just like me." She angled a look at the prone figure beyond the tlict, and frowned beneath an unexpected stab of pity. "He's just had a harder time than most of us up to now." How to explain feral children to an alien? And was it even worth really trying?

Hard-bladed toes clattered on the decking as the tlict sidled toward the airlock door, chewing on its translator.

"Worry. Worry. Larry touches. Gertrude breathes." It poked a hind foot at the airlock controls without turning to see what it was doing. Or maybe it had spatial sensors beyond the obvious eyes. When the hatch slid open, the tlict scampered inside, still facing Rahel and the boy. "Good breathing. Wise air." It opened the outside hatch the same way as before, then tumbled out into the docking bay at what for a tlict must have been a dead run. "Worry. Worry. Goodbye."

Rahel brought her arm down to peek under the now-darkened gauze pad as the hatch hissed shut behind the larry. "Are tlict always this arbitrary?" she asked the mazhet.

Ayr's skirts rang in what might have been a mazhet shrug. "Tlict are tlict."

Rahel sighed and went back to her first aid.

"Well, I'd say your delivery of this merchandise is accomplished." Satisfied that the bite still oozed somewhat prodigiously, she slapped a clean wad of padding over the wound and raised her arm to chest-height again. "You can get the agreed-upon fee from Noah's Ark—they're good for it. Just tell Saiah Innis that I—"

The *dhaktu* interrupted her with a delicate clearing of his throat.

Rahel glanced up at the three quiet mazhet, thought about what she'd just said, and smiled thinly. "Oh, yeah. Forgot about that. Here . . ." She trotted into the cockpit to fetch her notebook off the console. Keeping her left hand clamped firmly over her forearm, she scribbled, "Saiah—It's a boy! Attached is quote of fee promised mazhet. Pay, but don't ask questions. Will explain once I'm offstation." She didn't bother signing it. He'd know who it was from.

She popped the data chip and carried it back down to the mazhet. "Transmit this to the address at the front of the message." Ayr tipped its head in acknowledgment when she passed across the chip. "The funds ought to show up in your accounts within twenty-four hours of the Ark receiving the transmission."

All three mazhet swarmed into a knot to slip the chip from hand to hand. It finally vanished into the event horizon of green-and-aqua's robes, and one of them announced with a clatter, "This is equitable." They swept into the airlock in a single cloud of silks and bells and ribbons. The four errant duacs jogged after a moment later as though only just realizing their masters were leaving. From far off down the hall, Rahel heard Toad wail with grief at the loss of her alien playmates.

"I guess that means there's just you and me."

Small and fragile in his unnatural sleep, the boy curled up with a whimper and covered his face with his hands.

She didn't really want to, but she snoozed him again before the first shot had a chance to wear off. A boy wasn't like other animals, she reasoned. He had wants and imagination, not just thoughtless genetic imperatives—he would know her handling of him was indelicate, would recognize himself as powerless, would never forget the details of what she did to him just as he would never understand her reasons. Better to take care of as much as possible, with his fears and other emotions safely tucked away in slumber. Maybe then he'd view the indignities she subjected him to as mysterious acts of providence, and not specifically something Rahel had done.

Before touching him, though, she finished cleaning and sealing her bitten arm, adding a broad-base antibiotic and a rabies booster just to say she'd thought of everything. Then she ran to the lab and gathered enough tools, handling equipment, and sampling gear for everything she could possibly want to do. On the way back, she stopped by her quarters long enough to quickstep around Toad and dig a T-shirt out of her clothes locker. Once she'd filled a shallow laboratory bucket with water and rags, she headed back for the main compartment with Toad prancing behind her with a mouthful of extra towel.

Toad's contributions to the proceedings only slowed things down a little. "Get away from there." Rahel elbowed the puppy back from the boy's face when Toad abandoned her towel so she could explore him. Complaining, Toad circled Rahel to find a less obstructed position, then resumed her cheerful licking. "He doesn't want your kisses. Now get over here." Rahel, however, hadn't yet enjoyed much success convincing Toad that normal, conscious people didn't exist just to be her undying friends. She didn't sustain much hope of having better luck with a snoozed-out feral boy.

Rahel didn't know what sort of tools people used to fasten on a restraining collar, but a pair of industrial-strength power clippers sheared off the device with no particular effort. She slipped the hateful thing from underneath the boy's neck, then tossed it into the bottom of the crate where it wouldn't be in their way. He might still be looking at scars on his neck and shoulders from Nadder's bondage. It was too soon yet to tell.

She took a blood sample from a vein in his neck, a tissue scraping from the sores left by the restraining collar, and a membrane swab from his sinuses. Bad enough that she had to knock him out instead of taking the time to win his trust—at least she could hide whatever discomfort the scrapings caused among the damage inflicted by Nadder. It didn't make much difference how much he ended up hating the black-marketeer. Rahel, on the other hand, still had to get home with the boy.

Running back to the jumpship's lab with her samples divided between both hands, she slapped together a quick set of slides and fed them into the testing station. "Check the blood and mucal smears for antibodies, antigens, parasite residue, and possible infectious agents. I'll need a vaccination set for him, plus medication for any diseases or parasites you find in his system."

"Species of sample donor?" the AI asked.

"Homo sapiens." She snapped closed the last set of slides and sent them after the others. "These are dermal and subdermal tissue samples from the same specimen. Get me a DNA spin and cross-match against the entire Noah's Ark database. I want to know what breeding population his genetics are from, and an estimate on his age, if you can give me one. Log all of this under Feral Aral, Interface Acquisition Number 1."

"Okay." The AI shuffled the slides into queue somewhere deep in its works. "Blood and mucal analysis complete. Results dispatched to Screen Two. I can display the requested genetic results in approximately ten hours sixteen minutes."

"Sounds good." It wasn't like she wouldn't still have the boy tomorrow. "Let me know as soon as you've got them."

Scientific curiosity taken care of for the time being, she assembled the vaccination set recommended by the AI and took it out to the boy. Toad had flopped to the floor full-length in order to groom between his toes. Pausing to ruffle the puppy's ears—"Thanks for the help"—Rahel administered the injection, squirted parasite medication between the boy's teeth, then pulled the bucket over to start on the unpleasant task still before her.

If this boy had ever been bathed, it was so long ago as to not count anymore. Water ran off his chest in scattered beads, repelled by the oil and filth before it could even dampen his skin. Rahel swallowed her disgust and soaped her cloth into a dripping, frothy cream between both hands. Draping it across the boy's arm for a moment produced somewhat better results: a patch of stained, pinkish skin appeared in response to her gentle scrubbing, and a smelly crust of dead cells and rancid sweat came off on the cloth and turned it blackish. She dunked it into the bucket to rinse out the worst of the grime, then attacked the soap again before slathering cloth and water all over the rest of his arm.

Little by little, the details of his previous life exposed

themselves—like brush strokes on an ancient painting, previously hidden behind a lifetime of neglect. Scars like fine, white lacework on his hands, his knees, the fronts of both narrow shins. Palms as rough and hard as dried leather, the soles of his feet even harder and thicker than that, and not so much as an intact nail on fingers or toes. Worn but sturdy teeth with no sign of breakage, misalignment, or dental caries. Long, startlingly dark eyelashes. Eyebrows the same tarnished gold as ginger honey, and fine, brittle hair that would probably be the same color once it grew back without the filth and tangles. She had to tell herself over and over again that even a bad haircut didn't last forever before she could bring herself to shave his skull down to a pale fuzz. Well, that and the occasional glimpse of something buglike that she *hoped* was either lice or fleas.

Once she'd bathed him, dried him, and swabbed him head to toe with a topical insecticide, she cleaned and dressed the wounds around his neck and wrestled him into the overlarge T-shirt. The teal-and-white shift hung down around his knees. Combined with his new haircut, it made him look like an underage Krishna monk with no fashion sense.

"Well, Spud, what do we do now?"

Toad looked up from mauling the power clippers, just in case the comment meant she was about to be played with or fed.

Rahel leaned over to relieve the puppy of the shears, exchanging them for the closest legitimate chew-toy at hand. "The way I see it," she said, bouncing the toy against Toad's nose until the puppy snapped and snorted with joy, "I've got two choices—lock him up in the shipping crate again, or give him free run of the jumpship." She finally let Toad wrench the toy from her hand and proudly trot a few meters away. "Both of which options suck."

In her heart, Rahel never liked putting animals in crates, even when she knew in her head why she sometimes had to do it. But her cargo now was a human, not a basilisk, or an oryx, or even a high-functioning bonobo—and for all their biologic composition, humans just weren't like other animals. Assuming that spending every leg of a seven-gate trip in almost total isolation didn't irreparably damage his psyche, he was still sure to suffer from whatever distorted visions his imagination fed him about what waited at the end of his confinement. Most animals had a better time of it if you left them in the dark and quiet, not stressing them with your presence. Human animals, however, could supply plenty of stress just with their own thinking if there wasn't enough input to keep their over-evolved brains occupied.

Which brought them to running around the ship at will. Suddenly, the boy's kinship with the rest of Terra's fauna seemed a lot closer than it had moments before. He might or might not be housebroken; Rahel had a four-month-old puppy, so bathroom habits were the least of her worries. Jumpships contained a great deal of equipment, though. There were places he shouldn't get into, buttons he shouldn't push, compounds and instruments he shouldn't touch. If he'd been a chinchilla, she wouldn't have cared where he scampered. But this animal was a human—worse yet, a human child. There wasn't a door on this ship he couldn't learn how to open, not a button or panel or storage bin he wouldn't be able to reach. If she let him run loose, he'd very likely kill himself before they made it to the first gate. Where would all her concern for his freedom and comfort have gotten them then?

In the end, she carried him back into the lounge and tethered him to a table. He'd have access to every part of the room except the door, and the lounge offered both a carpet for soft walking and a grotesquely colored couch. She tossed all the extra blankets and pillows into the room at random. Maybe he'd want to make a bedding pile for himself. Maybe he'd want to hide behind the sofa. Giving him such harmless options was the only freedom she could grant.

She fastened an EV tether to the leg of a built-in table, then attached a soft-cuff bracelet to the boy's wrist. Toad supervised with her head under Rahel's armpit. Rahel made sure the cuff was tight enough to restrain him but not tight enough to chafe or to feel like a punishment. Then she burned off the latch so that nothing short of a surgical laser could get the restraint off again. She didn't know the boy well enough to estimate his intellect, but she'd seen orangutans fiddle their way out of soft-cuffs just like this one. She wasn't taking any chances.

The boy came awake while she was checking the last of the cable connections. Crawling out from under the table, Rahel stood to find the boy squatting at the other end of the room, heels flat to the floor, hands linked in front of his shins. He didn't look up at her, instead fixing his attention on the soft-cuff encircling his wrist. He picked at the edges, following the curve until he reached the ball joint that connected the tether. Then he closed his hand around his wrist and sat, eyes downcast, face obscenely still.

A splash of wetness darkened the teal stripe in his T-shirt, quickly overlaid by a second drop, then matched by a third. Still, Rahel didn't recognize the uneven splatters for tears until the boy heaved a thin, stuttering sigh and began rocking silently.

She snatched at Toad's collar when the puppy tried to toddle over and investigate. *Leave him alone,* Rahel told herself as she hefted a squirming Toad and soft-footed toward the door. *He's lost everything else—at least you can leave him his privacy.* The boy sobbed with his arms around his knees and his eyes squeezed fiercely closed. Maybe he hoped that when he opened them again, he'd be back in whatever world from which he'd been stolen.

Toad's groan of frustration stopped Rahel in the doorway, surprising her more than the puppy's desperate struggles. Toad had never seen a human cry before. Maybe it was that utter strangeness that made her so alarmed at the boy's behavior. "My fault for raising you to be such a good girl," Rahel whispered. She rubbed her nose against the puppy's skull, then let Toad clatter back down to the floor and jitter across the room. The stocky terrier slipped up to the boy with head and tail slung low, ears drooping as she waggled her rear end.

Rahel watched the puppy slide her head under the boy's arm to nose at his chin. Just like dogs, humans evolved within a pack structure. Status, discipline, and social intercourse were a part of both species' most basic genetic wiring. It was why dogs made such good companions, and why humans so easily passed themselves off as naked, tool-using, two-legged dogs.

But maybe the needs of canines and humans overlapped more than Rahel realized. If Toad had been manhandled and ignored for as many weeks or months as this boy had been locked up on his own, she would have exhausted herself with happiness for anyone who would interact with her, especially if that someone let her run around and chew on things and in general act like a dog. Rahel wondered how long it had been since the boy had been allowed to act like a human, no matter how uncivilized that behavior might be.

Creeping only as far as the end of the sofa, Rahel lowered herself to the floor with her back against the armrest. She listened to Toad groan and whimper, and made sure that a shoulder-width of her back remained visible if the boy cared to look up from his weeping. She wouldn't intrude on his grief by looking at him, but at least she could try to tell him that she was there in case he needed her. That he could retain whatever he recognized as the singularity of himself, but as long as Rahel cared for him, he wasn't completely alone.

When the airlock buzzer jolted her awake some unknown stretch of time later, Rahel at least knew what ship's function had startled the hell out of her this time. She pushed groggily up on one elbow and blinked around the lounge while Toad climbed to her feet and stumbled around the end of the couch in search of a less active sleeping place. "What is it?" Rahel croaked, scrubbing at her eyes and trying to remember why she'd curled up to sleep next to the lounge sofa.

"There are four beings requesting entrance at the main airlock."

She rose up on her knees to look for Toad and found the puppy on the other end of the room, flopped onto her side among a pile of blankets, pillows, and boy. "Can you tell from visual who it is?" she asked the ship, somewhat more quietly.

"Yes. It is Larry."

Rahel jerked a startled glance toward the invisible overhead realm from which the ship's voice always came. "Larry?" *Four* of them? In the middle of the night? Or maybe it wasn't the middle of the night anymore. She gripped the arm of the sofa to drag herself stiffly to her feet. "What time is it, anyway?"

"Station time is 1157 hours."

Almost noon. She'd been asleep longer than she thought. "All right, let them in." At least the tlict were unlikely to care about her rumpled clothing and disordered hair. Still, she finger-combed what hair she could away from her face while quietly closing the lounge door behind her.

The staccato chatter of alien feet on metal decking greeted Rahel when she reached the end of the corridor. The four tlict click-clacked around the main compartment, skirting the fetid shipping crate, stooping to groom each other's belly fur, and randomly scratching themselves with their tiny lower arms as if unable to catch an elusive flea. Walking far enough into the chamber to catch at le— larry's attention, Rahel clapped a hand over he— hide a jaw-stretching yawn.

"Good morning." Then, remembering— quote, she amended, "Good afternoo— yawn again.

The tlict froze, spiders mes— communal silk. From just ins—

rusty cream-and-brown as opposed to his companions' olive green—caressed its own back with its hindmost legs and juggled a translator into position.

"Good breathing," the translator's passionless voice proclaimed. A background buzz, like distant voices muttering, blurred the otherwise stilted diction. "Wise air. Good breathing."

Rahel nodded. "Right." It was too early in the morning to sort out tlict syntax. "Are you—" She gathered all the aliens up in a single gesture. "Is one of you the Larry I met earlier this morning?"

Two of the other tlict tiptoed over to join the translator, and the ambient mumbling faded. "Larry-this. Not-visit. No. No." A touch from one larry's upper manipulator arms brought the third tlict over, as well. "Larry-that. Gertrude breathing. Larry-that. Not-current. Larry-this. Not-tlict you retrieve. Yes. Yes."

Rahel pulled back a careful step. "Retrieve?" She wasn't sure she liked the sound of that.

"Yes. Yes." How many of them were supplying the answers? she wondered. How many could hear and understand what she was saying? "Gertrude tastes this," one or more of the larries insisted. The translator blatted once with static, then cleared again. "Not-tlict you. Breathing strangeness. Answer. Worry. Answer. Strangeness." The tlict all knotted together, lower arms striving to interlink. "Answer. Gertrude."

Gertrude. Rahel scrubbed at her face, suddenly climbing toward full wakefulness as she analyzed the partial sentences collecting around her. "Who's Gertrude? Another Larry?"

Only with an alien could that question come close to
‧ ۱g sense.
‧ ‧" Three bloated abdomens cringed close to the
‧ ·v. Gertrude. Not-roaming. Gertrude. Not-

"Gertrude," Rahel said, her stomach chill with understanding, "is a female."

"Not-Larry. Yes. Gertrude. Yes."

A female tlict. The creature the mazhet had said she would never live to see.

"She's not planning to eat me, is she?" Rahel stuffed her hands into her trouser pockets, finding the snooze pistol still pushed into the folds of fabric. She closed her fist around it protectively. "I mean, I don't usually visit people who are planning to eat me."

"Gertrude. Worry. Answer." The translator tlict pushed back between two of the others. "Not-tlict you. Answer. Not-ingest. Answer."

She nodded slowly, but didn't take her hand off the snooze pistol. "In that case, I can probably stop by long enough to talk with her." Would the mazhet pay for details of the first human-tlict coffee klatch? She'd have to ask when she and Gertrude were done. "Just let me get my boy—"

"No!" "No!" "No!" "No!"

The objections cascaded one atop the other, underscored by an orgy of tlict writhing and stomping. As the long silver translator rolled free of the bundle, its metallic voice squealed, "No! Not-tlict merchandise. Not-follow. No. No! Gertrude worry. Not-tlict you. Answer. Worry. Not-tlict merchandise. No!"

"Okay! Okay!" She beat back an urge to retrieve the translator for them, unwillingly repulsed by the very alienness of their display. "I'll leave the boy here. But you have to bring me back before too long. He can't stay completely alone."

"Yes. Yes. Not-tlict you. Follow." One of the twitching green larries plucked up the errant translator. It passed between all four of them on its way back to its original holder. "Answer. Worry. Answer. Strangeness. Yes. Yes. Gertrude breathes."

"Let's keep us both that way." As they stepped into the

airlock, Rahel wondered if a snooze pistol would even work on a tlict.

With luck, she'd never have to find out.

Smells. Wet, frigid, alien smells. Smells that made her mouth taste like ginger, smells that clung like spider silk to her hair. Something hiding in the odors made her heart turn over with grief—but it wasn't a smell Rahel could sense with her nose, just a feeling that swelled up inside her from nowhere as she followed the larries through the unchanging corridor. In the cold, voiceless darkness of the tlict jump-ship, she mistook the melancholy for reality. Then they passed out of whatever area produced the sad aroma, and she felt only confused and manipulated, and more than just a little afraid.

She should never have agreed to come here.

Frost flowers salted the walls where the corridor finally widened into a cathedral-sized chamber. A scaffolding of struts and steam smothered an unseen light source, throwing the cables and elaborate grillwork spanning the ceiling into a sparse, shadowed flatness that reminded Rahel more of wrought iron than jumpship design. She stopped when one of the larries picked at her shoulder. A cloud of her own breath washed back in her face with clammy staleness, and she was startled by how different it smelled from the rest of the air.

"I hope you guys don't expect me to go on without you." The rush and roar of some gas-pumping device deadened her voice even in her own ears. "I can't see, and I don't know where you want me."

"Follow. No. Follow. Ending." Words like whispered vapor drifted down from above, so soft they might have been only in Rahel's imagination. She craned her head upward in search of a speaker, but the larry behind her pressed all four thorax arms against her back to keep her from moving away.

"Good breathing," the fragile voice pronounced. A puff of

Change. Yes? Yes?" An expanse of bony arm stretched out above Rahel, then recoiled at the last moment as though unwilling to actually touch her. "Larva-you. Adult you. Alone. Not-change. Not-information. Not-change."

"Humans never . . ." Rahel spread her arms uncertainly. "We never change. We keep the same form all our lives."

"No!" Front legs pumping, Gertrude's barbed elbows scraped sparks against the metal walls. "Larva. Adult. Not-same. Can't-same. Never-same." Drops of light showered around her, singeing the larries with a smell like burnt roses.

"There are differences as we become older," Rahel admitted. Backing out through the open door was probably not a good idea, no matter how attractive it might seem. "The way humans think, the way we move. All of that is different by the time we're finished growing. Brand new babies may share the same physical form as all other humans, but they aren't as well-developed, and they aren't nearly so large."

The rust-and-cream larry used its lower arms to wrench one primary limb up close to its mouthparts. Gertrude flicked the male away from her with a foot. "Not-tlict larva. Not-tlict grow." Her great crest tipped from side to side, testing the torpid air. "Big. Grow. Not-change."

Rahel nodded. "That's right."

A splash of ammonia-bitter stench flared through the room. The rust-and-cream larry jittered off in a circle, leaving his arm splashing in a pool of mustardy blood on the floor. Rahel jerked back into the doorway with her stomach riding a wave of acid up into her throat.

"Not-adult. Not-tlict." Something in Gertrude cracked like breaking glass as she pushed upright. "Abomination."

"It's our nature!" Rahel shoved both hands into her pants pockets, suddenly wanting the snooze pistol even though she no longer believed it could help her. "It's the way evolution made us—we didn't get any choice!"

Gertrude snatched another larry out from under her,

swinging it above her body almost as high as the ceiling. "Abomination," the translator whispered coolly. "Abomination. Not-tlict. You."

Skating for purchase on the smooth deck, Rahel pushed off against the doorjamb and tumbled as much as ran into the open corridor. A tlict body shattered against the bulkhead behind her. She felt the splash of fluid from its ruptured organs, heard the crash when it slid down the wall, choked against a surge of bile when the stink of the larry's death chased her down the corridor. Horses panicked at the smell of blood; Cape hunting dogs could be whipped into a killing frenzy. Rahel didn't wait to find out what the tlict would do when perfumed by the scent of their own deaths.

She bolted the dark corridor with snooze pistol in hand, alert for the clatter of tlict feet on metal, primed to shoot any spindly movement ahead of her. No one and nothing tried to stop her. While the route proved significantly shorter at a dead run, Rahel suspected she had the slow diffusion rate of smell through atmosphere to thank for her clear escape route, and not some sudden clemency on the part of the tlict. She slid into the airlock without slowing, slapping at the controls several more times than necessary. Even so, she could see tlict wandering into the corridor she'd just fled while the airlock hatch banged closed.

Running all the way back to her docking bay was simply impossible. Rahel knew that even as she banged on the outside lock door to try and make it open faster. The Interface was larger than most planetary cities, webbed together by transit tubes and slideways, and spiraling outward from its central hub like an intricate crystal helix. So when the tlict jumpship disgorged her, she jumped from the hatch without waiting for the gangway and made a head-down run for the nearest tube portal. As long as Larry didn't catch her before the next train screamed into the station, she could be half an Interface away by the time her breathing slowed.

Plunging up the ramp to the transport level, Rahel caught

the bulkhead to swing herself around the corner and into the tube train vestibule. An orange light throbbed above the row of open tube doors, and a sexless, speciesless voice announced in conflicting languages: "This transport now departing for Docking Rings One, Four, and Nine, and for Central Hub Levels One through Seven . . . This transport now departing—"

"Wait!" Fear of failure—of being caught, of being killed by aliens who couldn't even explain what she'd done wrong—shocked her muscles with adrenaline and kicked her heart so fiercely she nearly went to all fours trying to scrabble the last distance. "Wait-wait-wait-wait-*wait!*" Her final lunge jammed one shoulder between the closing doors; then a twist wrenched her torso into the narrow opening, and another half-second's squirming squeezed the rest of her inside. Duacs scattered with yowls and jangles when she thumped to the train floor among them.

"Proctor Tovin." The glottal rattle preceding the *dhaktu*'s greeting was nearly lost in the shower of ringing that marked the tube train's slide into motion. "The mazhet welcome your barter."

She levered up on her elbows and earned a wet duac nose in her eye. "I'm glad somebody does," she grumbled, recoiling from cold snuffles at her nose and mouth. Pushing the duac's head irritably aside only made room for another cat to nudge in and take its place. Rahel finally had to struggle over onto her bottom so she could sit up and use both hands to fend off the curious paws and tongues and whiskers. "You know, I don't even let my dog give mouth kisses."

The duacs didn't seem impressed.

Climbing to her feet, she swiped half-heartedly at the sand and cream hairs clinging to her trousers, then glanced about at the silent slim statues crowding the train. The simple volume of mazhet pressed into the car was enough to drive a person colorblind. Rahel pinched the bridge of her nose, abruptly weary with a headache she hadn't realized she was nursing. "Did I just bull my way into some kind of private mazhet dining car or something?"

"The mazhet do not eat in public," the train's single *dhaktu* informed her. Rahel couldn't tell if one of the vibrant alien merchants had first clicked that little bit of data or not. "This vehicle is for transportation services only." A be-ribboned and turbaned mazhet with the scarlet robe and chain-link veil of a caravan *dohke* drifted its hand through the *dhaktu*'s silky topknot. "Do you wish to initiate barter? The mazhet may construct such facilities as needed."

"That depends." She shivered at the thought of where she'd just been, and scrubbed at her arms to try and warm them. "I have need of information."

The *dohke* blinked dark glass eyes lazily. "The mazhet possess all manner of information."

Which didn't surprise her in the least. "You even have the information I want, I suspect." She flicked a finger through a string of duac earrings and cocked her head across the train car at the *dohke*. "Can you tell me how long the mazhet have had dealings with the tlict?"

"No." The *dohke*'s only sound was the sparkling ring of its shaken hand. The *dhaktu*'s voice was ruthless.

Rahel resisted spitting a frustrated oath toward the floor. "How well do you know them, then?" she persisted. "I mean, if I had questions about how to handle my dealings with them, would the mazhet be able to supply me with answers?"

Another wave of ghostly chiming whispered through the car as it slowed to match up with another station. "Much about the tlict is not knowable." Sparks of light danced off the spangled arm the *dohke* raised to the wall beside it, gold coins fluttering like candle flames in the leftovers of the car's momentum. "Speaking to the color of your odor, it would seem your dealings with the tlict run quite deeply already."

"My odor?" She lifted her shirt front to sniff at it, then

realized what the *dohke* must be saying just as the train doors sighed open on either side of her. "You mean I *smell*?"

"Larry tasting." A dull tlict translator voice joined the clatter of multiple feet on the floor of the car. "Not-tlict you. Abomination."

Panic shot through her like lightning. Darting aside, she stumbled over scattering duacs and fetched up hard against a wall of mazhet in her effort to distance herself from the tlict. The larry, his upper thorax already pushed through the open doors, struggled to cram his forward legs in as he flashed both primary arms with gripping-spines extended. Rahel ducked down and back, into the silk aurora of brilliant mazhet finery—

—and both tlict appendages snapped off above the elbow. Gripping-spines, melted into a row of blackish knobs, splattered like chocolate where the arms hit the floor. Rahel didn't have time to recoil, nor did she even think to, before the tlict jerked back out the doors as if kicked. When the doors whisked shut to hide it, Larry had already thumped his abdomen flat to the station floor, legs and arms and thorax curling into an awkward fist, like a spider left to dangle in the heart of the web where it had died.

Rahel crept forward on all fours. Beneath her hands, the narcotic thrumming of the train's drive engines felt as reassuring as her own heartbeat. "I . . . I'm . . ." This time, the duacs made no effort to pad over and investigate.

A twinkle of movement picked out both the *dohke* and its attendant *dhaktu* as the translator helped slip some alien firearm back into the mazhet's sleeve. Rahel hadn't heard the gun fire, hadn't seen the muzzle flash, hadn't even felt the kiss of its thunderbolt passage. She took a deep breath and blinked away the image of the tlict's melted appendages and the gaudy ribbons of blood that strewed the floor around it. Doing barter with the mazhet no longer seemed the safe, trustworthy business it once had.

The *dohke* clicked in rhythm with its quiet ringing. "You have spoken with Gertrude." It wasn't a question, and neither the *dohke* nor its brightly dressed *dhaktu* bothered to look at her.

Rahel nodded stiffly, then crawled unsteadily to her feet, careful not to reach out toward any of the mazhet for assistance. "I—well, yes," she finally stammered. "Gertrude sent for me."

"Irrelevant." Tapping the heads of three duacs in turn, the *dohke* touched its eyes one by one, then rang its veils by brushing hastily at its mouth. "That was unwise."

Rahel couldn't keep herself from snorting. "Tell me about it."

"What information did you convey?"

"I . . . I'm not sure . . ." She scoured her hands against the legs of her trousers, then dragged her sleeves across her shirt as if that could help dislodge whatever smell the tlict had basted her with. "I'm not even sure what we were talking about. She had a lot of questions about the feral boy the mazhet bought for me last evening, and about how humans tell the difference between children and adults." She looked up at the *dohke*, shrugging helplessly. "At least, that's what I *think* she was asking. And what I think I told her."

The *dohke* laced elegant fingers into a single filigreed ball. "Did you reveal to her that humans may not necessarily be born self-aware?"

"What 'may not'?" Rahel judged from the *dhaktu*'s wrinkled forehead that her answer told them more than she'd meant it to. "I think we touched on the basics of society and observational learning. Why?"

Mazhet closed around her in a whirl of maddening color. Thin, cool hands grazed fleeting patterns on her cheeks. "You must leave the Interface." The *dhaktu*'s voice rose from somewhere out of sight behind the *dohke*'s left shoulder.

Rahel twisted side to side, only to find herself frowning up into the same impassive features wherever she turned. "Why do you think I was in such a hurry to squeeze myself into this transport?" It occurred to her that mazhet body odor reminded her faintly of cinnamon.

"Your ship will require a departure code to cast moorings from the station. You may use the mazhet code 3572019 and apply for immediate departure."

The numbers ricocheted into and out of her memory as she tried to split her attention between the wall of mazhet and any mnemonic that might help her remember the sequence. "The Newborns said I'd have to apply for a departure code twelve hours before I planned to ship out. Do they let you guys just keep a list of departure codes on hand or what?"

"The mazhet have a special arrangement," the *dohke* informed her with a lift of its chin. "Code 3572019 is valid for immediate departure. The mazhet extend it to you as an equitable service." Another of the mazhet clapped its hands twice, smartly. The *dohke* added with a bow, "Your employer will be invoiced for the execution of this contract."

At the moment, she didn't even care what kind of expenses that invoicing might entail.

"Aren't you guys gonna tell me what I did to flip the tlict out before I go?"

They stared back at her, even their bells and jewelry silent. Their infuriating calmness made her want to scream. "I'll pay you for it!"

A dozen voices rose up like a chorus of manic rad-counters, and Rahel found herself uncertain of who to talk to or where to look.

"What the tlict think of, how the tlict feel—much of this cannot be translated to creatures outside the web of tlict genetics." Human words reeled out of the racketing chaos almost too quickly for Rahel to follow. She wondered if the *dhaktu* spoke for one of the many mazhet, or all of them, or if it really mattered. "This the mazhet can say: Tlict at birth possess no minds. They possess only hunger, and a need for air and sunlight. In the first day of their lives, tlict children eat more than seventy thousand times their own mass, and excrete only once. So rapid is their growth, they achieve adult proportions within seventeen days of birth. At this time, they exhibit the Change."

Larva-you. Adult-you . . . Change. Yes? "They turn into adults."

The *dohke* and thirteen other mazhet nodded gravely. "Tlict children who do not mature continue to eat, grow, and reproduce themselves, but they never inherit the intelligence—the sentience—"

Rahel suspected the *dhaktu* inserted that clarification on his own.

"—which the tlict judge holds them separate from all senseless, unaware animals. Including their own mindless young."

Every shudder, scuttle, and tortured half-sentence ground together in her memory like slabs of crushing stone. Caught beneath the weight of her redefined knowledge, Rahel poked through the rubble of what had come before. "I told her we grew up, looking just the same from baby to adulthood. I told her"—she scrubbed her eyes with the heels of her hands and groaned—"that we were animals, every last human in existence. Just like paramecia."

"You told her worse than that." The *dhaktu* said it, but it sounded like most of the mazhet actually uttered the response. "You told her that humans are unChanged children, abominations who would feed themselves to the destruction of everything else around them. You told her that humans cannot be lived with or trusted."

Rahel glanced up into the nearest mazhet countenance. "What do the tlict do with the children who never make the Change?"

The *dohke* alone gave her the answer. "On the eighteenth day, the adults kill them."

"I've got to get off this station." She made a desperate circle within the knot of mazhet. "*Everybody*'s got to get offstation." Everybody human, at least. "Is there some way to get word out to the other human visitors? Through the Newborn administrators, maybe?"

The *dohke* inclined its head. "Shall this be accepted as an addendum to your contract with the mazhet?"

Rahel was horrified to think how much her blunder was costing. "Yes!"

"This is equitable." The *dohke* flicked its hands in a double chime. "It shall be done." Then it proffered one palm with delicate mazhet flourish, and waited.

"What?" Not sure what else to do, Rahel slowly slipped her own hand on top of the alien's. The *dohke* curled its fingers around her wrist to turn her hand palm-upright. "What?" she asked again. One involuntary tug as the *dohke* accepted some small, narrow tool from another mazhet proved she couldn't pull herself free, so she didn't try again. "If you don't mind, I'm kind of in a hurry."

"The departure code." Mazhet tool touched skin, and pain cut through her palm deep enough to sear the bones. Rahel barked a short scream and this time tried to yank herself free in earnest. Even throwing the whole weight of her body into the pull didn't break the *dohke*'s grip, and mazhet hands at her shoulders and elbows discouraged her from fighting further. She squeezed her eyes shut and clenched her jaw, barely noticing the tears that stung her cheeks while the *dohke* etched seven numbers into her palm so precisely she could see their shapes carved in fire at the back of her brain.

"Now," the mazhet said at last, releasing her with chill indifference. "You will remember."

I'll never forget. Rahel hugged her fist under her chin until she choked up enough courage to crack her eyes and peel her fingers away. Seven shiny black figures marched with rulerlike alignment across her unburnt palm. Like a freshly printed flimsy, or calligraphic ink. Except these numbers didn't rub off when she smudged at them with her thumb.

"After all that . . ." She closed her fist with a shaky sigh. "This number had better be a good one."

The train doors shushed open onto the corridor tracing the foot of her docking bay. "The mazhet do not lie. Nor do the mazhet dishonor a barter." Mazhet and duacs moved gracefully aside to open a kaleidoscopic path toward the exit. "But move quickly. The tlict may do both, and do both with equal facility."

Her hand still throbbed while she waited for the airlock on her jumpship to admit her. First thing after casting moorings, she'd poke and prod whatever she could reach in her palm with the ship's smartdoc. Maybe she could find out how she could have no cuts or bruises and still hurt so damn bad. *But not before I'm moving,* she advised herself when the door finally slid open and let her inside. Odds were, nobody complained much about pain from inside a tlict gertrude's belly, so it really wouldn't matter if she didn't first make good her getaway.

The *clitter-skitter-scatter* of toenails all over the decking announced the approach of Toad's greeting dance. Rahel laughed as the puppy galloped over in an ever-contracting sequence of spirals and bounds. She finally snugged herself up against Rahel's legs tight enough to blow wet snorts into her hands while simultaneously thumping her butt and wagging her tail in alternating rhythms of worshipful joy. Puppy hair and breath smelled strongly of dog-food grease, and Toad's belly looked round enough to hide a casaba melon.

Rahel shook the dog's big, ugly head and drummed her hands against Toad's rib cage. Toad raised her nose with a grunt, then belched indelicately. "Someone's been a piggy with the dog food." Rahel grabbed a double handful of loose skin and moved it back and forth across Toad's shoulders. "What're you doing in the storeroom, anyway? I thought I left you—"

In the lounge. With the feral boy.

Swinging around the doorway to find the soft-cuff and tether intact but empty didn't surprise Rahel nearly as much as finding out the boy had opened the lounge door with nobody to help him but Toad. Her own damn fault, she admitted with a curse. Feral or no, he was still one of the brightest species to ever grace the galaxy, and this jumpship had been designed to accommodate people with a lot less motivation than he had. She should never have made the mistake of expecting him to accept his captivity so readily.

"Boy!" Stumbling over Toad to get back into the hallway, she trotted with the puppy on her heels into the passenger sleeping area, Toad's playroom, and the lab. "Come on, boy, don't do this to me! Where are you?" Because she couldn't leave unless she knew he was on board. The thought of ruining humanity's relationship with the tlict, running up a lifelong debt with the mazhet, and getting Noah's Ark kicked off the Interface without at least going home with the one thing she'd legitimately paid for was a little too crazy-making, even for her tastes. *"Boy!" Please, God, let him still be on board.*

"I have the results of the gene spin and cross-match you requested for Feral Aral Number 1," the testing station AI informed her when she darted through the lab to glance into the back sampling area. "Would you like a visual display or an audio summation?"

Both. Neither. She didn't have time to pore over the genetics of a specimen she wasn't even sure she still possessed. Still, she couldn't make herself run off without getting at least the most basic of answers. Pausing to fidget guiltily in the doorway, she called, "Give me the short version. Where's he from?"

"Unknown. Feral Aral Number 1 displays no genetic affinity with any *Homo sapiens* population currently cataloged by Noah's Ark."

Shock jerked her back into the room when she would have dashed away after only half-listening. "But that's impossible." As if the AI would lie. As if genetics could lie. "He is *Homo sapiens*, isn't he?"

"Yes."

"Then he's got to have a closest ancestor in the database."

"Feral Aral Number 1's closest ancestor falls outside my genotype modeling parameters by greater than twenty-five thousand generations."

"Oh, my God . . ." This little boy, with his childish stature and narrow build, came from a bloodline that hadn't crossbred with Terran humans for better than 750,000 years. When Nadder said she didn't carry genuine animals, she was lying—this boy was more genuine than anything else Nadder could have sold her.

Rahel knew with sudden, bitter certainty that there was no way she could leave the station without the rest of Nadder's cargo.

"Come on, Toad. I—Toad?" She looked up and down the empty corridor with a growl of frustration. It must be an annoying feral thing to wander away when no one was watching you. "C'mere, Spud! Toad?" She clapped her hands and whistled. "C'mere, you replaceable little tub of trouble!"

Echoing adolescent yaps rang out from the rearmost storage compartment. Where the dog food was kept, of course. A four-month-old terrier was nothing if not self-indulgent. Rahel jogged to the end of the hallway, already planning how she would explain to Saiah Innis that she'd somehow misplaced the greatest biological discovery of this century.

Too gorged to feed herself, Toad sat atop a spill of crunchy dog kibble and contentedly watched her friend chew on a handful with cautious uncertainty. Not the most nutritious fare, even given this boy's past history. Maybe dog food smelled good when you'd been raised by wolves. Stepping over the boy, Rahel grabbed a few seal-meals at random, then bent to take hold of his arm. "You can eat all the dog food you want once we're off of this station, but right now we've got to haul ass."

The boy lunged away from her grip, barking with surprise. Rahel dropped hard onto one knee to keep from having to loosen her hold. "Listen to me . . ." She balanced the stack of meals across her thigh and reached out to stroke his arm gently. Toad wiggled in between them to pursue her hand with sloppy licks. "I wish I could explain to you why everything that's happening is important, but I can't. You're just gonna have to listen to my voice the way Toad does and understand that I'm not gonna hurt you. Look—she trusts me." Rahel fondled the puppy's face and folded-down ears. "Can't you?"

Eyes the same dark chocolate as Toad's watched while the puppy squirmed and wiggled in response to Rahel's petting. A little of the angry hardness seeped out of the boy's tense muscles. When he cocked his head to aim a suspicious glare up at her, though, the naked intellect reflected in his eyes slapped Rahel's face with embarrassment.

"I don't know if you being stupid would make this easier or harder." Standing slowly, she let him pull himself to his feet without guiding him the way she would some recalcitrant child.

"Well, that takes care of at least one of our little problems." She backed into the corridor, then smiled when he followed with only the most requisite amount of wariness. "Now—let's see how fast you can run."

Medve's docking bay stank of alien pheromones and burning polycarbons. The scream of working lasers somewhere out of sight made the boy jerk to a startled stop, and Rahel had to tug at the tail of his T-shirt to drag him along when she started down the access ramp. He trotted up on a level with her hip, seal-meals clutched possessively to his chest with both hands, and frowned at the broken splashes of light erupting from beyond *Medve*'s landing pylons. Rahel wondered if he just didn't like the noise, or if he knew something she didn't about what Nadder played with while hiding out behind her jumpship. Toad was no help—she bumped happily along behind them with her throat full of growling and her leash clamped between her teeth. She wouldn't have noticed a problem if it bit her on the behind.

The laser light was extinguished before they'd made it halfway across the bay, throwing the dock into startling darkness and clearing the air for whispered curses and the scrape of metal against something more yielding. Rahel half-expected to find Nadder and her assistant dismantling animal crates in an attempt to do away with evidence of their crimes. But when the albino backed into view around the jumpship's nose, his welding gloves were sticky with rotten-mustard blood instead of welding flux, and the long, jointed segment he dragged across the deck behind him looked distinctly organic in nature. Rahel stopped where she was and squeezed her hand just above the boy's elbow to keep him from running.

Nadder, another length of tlict leg balanced over each shoulder, planted both feet when she rounded the jumpship in turn. Her opaque face-guard pointed at Rahel in what could only be a glare. "Why, you sneaky little eco-wench! Where the hell did you get *him*?"

The sliding slap of seal-meals hitting the deck was Rahel's only warning. She dropped Toad's leash and spun to grab the boy with both hands, closing her right fist on nothing but T-shirt when he twisted himself almost completely behind her. With one hand still locked on his elbow, though, that was leverage enough. Hauling back on the fistful of T-shirt, she leapt forward and swept her arms around him as his bare feet lost purchase on the decking. He shouted in anger, nearly crawling up her front in his effort to get away, but she managed to crook one arm around his neck just before he cracked her chin with the top of his head. He answered her with a stamp of his feet and the warm snap of teeth on her wrist.

"Don't even think it!"

The boy rolled an angry lower up at her, but, surprisingly, didn't bite down.

"You so much as give me a love nip, you little throwback,

and I'll have the vet yank all your teeth while he's got you in for neutering. You understand me?"

Before words were invented, there was tone of voice. Even 750,000 years of evolution couldn't erase that common heritage. Rahel waited until he eased his jaw open and backed his head away, then slowly loosened her own grip around his throat.

"Good boy," she said sweetly, in just the right tone to make Toad look up from the floor and wag her tail. Later, when the boy knew enough words to make explanations worthwhile, she'd worry about constructing a better reinforcement for good behavior. Right now, though, she settled for rubbing his shoulder and plastering on an artificial smile. "That's a good boy."

"That's better progress than I ever made with him. I was just about ready to wire his jaw." Nadder knocked the face-guard up over her forehead, stalking forward to peer at the boy with professional interest. He backed closer against Rahel, but didn't try to run. "So, did you actually send the mazhet out here to get him, or did their *dohke* cut a deal with you after the mazhet knew what they were buying?"

Rahel kept her hands on the boy as she guided him around behind her, just as happy to keep him touching her and out of Nadder's reach. "How I got him doesn't matter. We've got bigger problems, you and me." She nodded toward the larry parts Nadder's albino was so diligently stuffing down the matter reclaimator in the docking bay's wall. "There's gonna be a lot more of them, you know. One tlict more or less won't help a lot in the great big scheme of things."

Nadder picked up one end of a leg when the albino scurried back to her, shoving it into his arms without taking her eyes off Rahel. "You don't have the faintest idea what's going on here."

"Then I'll take a wild guess. You were doing some kind of business with Larry here when he started getting psycho. Maybe you killed him—maybe he killed himself. What matters is that you ended up with a dead tlict and no good explanation for how he got that way." Rahel watched the albino force another length of leg down the wall with a tooth-grinding buzz. "Now you're disposing of the body."

Nadder pursed thin lips into a pensive frown, tugging on the cuffs of her welding gloves, picking at the seams. Somewhere behind Rahel, the boy started gathering up the dropped seal-meals in furtive grabs. "What is it you want from me?" Nadder asked her coldly.

Rahel stooped to sweep a few of the scattered meals in the boy's direction. "I want the same thing you do—to get offstation before the tlict come to find us."

"Well, then help us clean up the rest of this mess." Nadder jerked her thumb at the rest of the tlict on the other side of the jumpship. "'Cause I put in for a departure code when Larry first tried to take Styen's head off. Traffic Control said we'd be on queue at least six hours." She spread her hands and took a few steps backward toward the hidden work area. "Or are you in too much of a hurry to wait around while we chop-chop?"

Rahel shook her head, winding Toad's leash up around one hand. "I don't have to wait around. I can go back to my jumpship and be gone in fifteen minutes." She smiled thinly when Nadder slammed to a stop and grimaced suspiciously. "I don't have to take you with me, Nadder, but you've got what I want, and I've got what you need. I thought we might find some happy middle ground before we all ended up as larry food."

"Sonofabitch." The word burst out of Nadder on a short, soft puff of laughter. "You've got a mazhet departure code!" She dropped her fists to her hips in belligerent awe.

Rahel wondered how impressed Nadder would be if she knew what Rahel had done to necessitate getting the number. "And you've got Terran-descendant genotypes that haven't seen a common Earth ancestor in seven hundred thousand years." She reached around behind her to hook a finger in the boy's T-shirt collar. Nadder lifted an eyebrow, first at Rahel, then at the boy. "I want your cargo," Rahel told her flatly. "All of it. And I want to be on board with it when you pull out."

"Bullshit." Nadder slapped the face-guard back down into place. "You can't just take all my merchandise without paying me for it. That's piracy!"

"I'm paying you with your life."

"Which won't be worth shit if I have to welsh on certain financial obligations." Nadder tossed the albino the cutting torch off her belt and pushed him in the direction of where they'd left the rest of the body. He ducked under the jump-ship's nose and disappeared from sight. "At least give me two-thirds the going rate for anything you decide to keep."

As if Rahel or anyone else she knew could quote the going rate for black-market genotypes. "One-third going price," Rahel countered. "And that's generous for illegal merchandise."

Nadder shook her head, the slow, knowing gesture of someone much older and wiser in the ways of the evil world. "Half-price." The arc light of more tlict dismantling illuminated the bay behind Nadder. "And I won't tell the authorities you arranged for a slave trade using the mazhet as your agents."

My problem, Rahel thought as she glowered at her own reflection in Nadder's anodized mask, *is that I'm just not slimy enough to make good use of my options.*

"Half-price or nothing." Nadder's voice rose to a surprising sharpness as she took two rapid steps backward and brought her hands off her hips. "Decide fast!"

Toad slammed the end of her leash hard enough to jerk Rahel halfway around toward the entrance, punctuating her barking with a cataract of wild snarls. The larries at the docking-bay doors cringed into a tangle of legs, arms, and flailing mouths. For an instant, that writhing mass looked too much like Gertrude in her too-small cathedral. Rahel jerked Toad up into her arms and ran toward *Medve* with the puppy howling over her shoulder. "Interface! Traffic Control!"

"Interface Traffic Control." The Newborn's voice echoed over the bay's invisible intercom far too calmly to have any idea what was going on. "Online."

"Departure code—" She shrugged Toad further up on her shoulder to squint at her palm between the puppy's hind legs. "—3572019. Seal off our bay and queue *Medve* for immediate departure!"

Rahel snagged the boy's hem when he dashed across in front of her, trying to aim him for the airlock and not the deceptive safety of the gap beneath the ship. "This way! This way!" He hitched up short, nearly tripping her, then ducked away from Nadder and her albino as they clambered into the airlock with their welding gear in tow. The main bay doors thundered closed, but Rahel didn't dare turn to see whether any of the larries made it through.

"Query, *Medve*," the Newborn interjected politely.

"Dammit, not now!" Rahel dropped Toad without releasing her lead and swerved to intercept the boy with her shoulder. He squealed once as she lurched upright and hauled him off the ground, then grabbed frantically for her belt to keep from pitching off her back completely. To his credit, he didn't try to bite her.

"Traffic Control recognizes 3572019 as a mazhet departure code. Please clarify the nature of your possession."

Nadder planted her hand on the edge of the airlock to hold it open while Rahel pitched the boy inside. "We bought it from them!"

The Newborn hesitated long enough for Rahel to jump in on top of the boy and Nadder to reel up Toad's leash and bring the puppy aboard. "Transaction noted," the robot finally stated flatly. "Class three transport *Medve*, you are cleared for immediate departure. Cast off moorings at will."

The inside lock door sprang aside, and Nadder shoved both hands against her albino's back even though he was already up and running for the pilot's station. "You heard the

Newbie—we're clear! Get us moving!" He wasn't even in sight by the time she added, "Go, goddamn you! Go!"

The soundless thrum of maneuvering thrusters rumbled through the jumpship's deck like a dragon's purr. Sinking back against the airlock bulkhead, Rahel let the boy skitter out from under her and all-four it into the central chamber where he crammed himself into the corner by a maintenance locker. Not that it mattered where he went now—there wasn't a ship in existence that would let him open an outside door without a suit on. He could hide under the furniture all the way home for all Rahel cared. It would certainly simplify keeping tabs on him.

Fending off Toad's curiosity with her elbows, Rahel peeled the seals off three of the dinners and skated them across the deck at the boy while he watched the food travel with dubious longing. Toad scrambled in place with excitement before bolting off after the dishes. Rahel met the boy's gaze and shrugged while Toad attacked the first plate. "So get up and fight with her. But don't come crying to me if your sister hogs it all."

Nadder laughed softly, wandering aimlessly back and forth through the airlock as she picked up welder pieces. "What're you going to do with him once you get him back to Noah's Ark?" she asked, stepping over Rahel's legs to fish out some part from behind the small of her back. "I mean, how long can he keep the lot of you busy, being just the one little guy and all?"

One little guy with a lot of big mysteries. Rahel sighed, watching him creep out of hiding to play tug-of-war with Toad over one of the plates. "Between him and the rest of your cargo, we're not going to be at a loss for things to do." She pried up the corner on another of the meal packets and sniffed at the contents to see if her stomach was hungry.

"Aw, hell . . ." Nadder hoisted the bits of bloody equipment and dragged them toward the locker the boy had just deserted. "Haven't you figured it out yet? You're not gonna take my cargo." She dumped the load unceremoniously into the locker. "You're not gonna want it."

Rahel lowered the food tray back to her lap. "What are you talking about?"

To her surprise, Nadder only laughed again and settled contentedly back against the locker door. "I've got a storehold full of animals, all right," she said, smiling. "Fifteen hundred suspension coffins, and none of 'em carrying anything more exotic than a pet store budgerigar tailored to look like a Carolina parakeet. They're fakes!" The marketeer tossed her arms wide with hapless delight. "Every last one of 'em! And I sell 'em to fashion-conscious idiots who don't know how to tell the difference. I'll even let you examine 'em, if you want to, 'cause I know what you're gonna find."

"But . . ." Rahel blinked a flustered look at where the boy crouched with Toad, picking green beans out of his ramen and dropping them down for the puppy to gobble. She couldn't remember if she'd noticed that he used his hands to eat before. She wasn't even sure if that was significant. "I ran his gene spins. You can't fake raw data like that!"

Nadder shrugged and folded her arms. "I'm sure you can't. But I never had to. I got him from the same place I got the couple Terran genotypes that probably lured you here." She sighed at the boy with a certain touch of ironic fondness, and smiled. "I bought him from the tlict."

"What do you mean you lost the jumpship?"

Frustrated, exhausted, Rahel couldn't be bothered to lift her head from her hands and see what expression accompanied Paval's disbelieving squeak across the comlink. "I left it at the Interface. It wasn't like I had a lot of time to consider better options."

"Taking the jumpship wasn't an option?"

Rahel cocked a glare at the comlink screen, and Paval returned her look with a scowl of equal annoyance. "Considering everything leading up to my decision," she told him, "no, I didn't think it was."

Paval sat back in his chair and rubbed his hands across his face as if he'd been waiting all night just to hear this depressing news. "Well, what am I supposed to tell Proctor Innis?" he asked, a little peevishly. "He's already angry about this bill from the mazhet, and everyone else is angry about whatever happened with the tlict." He sighed the deep, soulful sigh of the young. "Proctor Tovin, you're supposed to be setting me a good example, but all I end up getting is confused."

"And sarcastic." She turned half away from the comlink to check on the passenger tucked comfortably under her bed. He'd taken the blankets and all the extra pillows, and now all she could see of him was one elbow and the top of his shaven head from somewhere inside the fluffy bundle. Even Toad had been chased out of the boy's makeshift habitat when she'd tried to cuddle up with him for softness. "At least I'm not coming back empty-handed. Tell Saiah I'm bringing home an animal more valuable than anything we ever thought he sent me for."

"A Terran animal? Really?" Paval sat up attentively from more than a hundred light-years away. "How many? What kind?"

"One, of a kind Noah's Ark has never really worked with before." Rahel watched the boy roll over in his sleep, hugging himself into a ball as small as a baby and as complicated as the world. "I just hope we're up to the challenge."

AUTHOR'S NOTE

Nobody makes a greater mistake than he who did nothing because he could do only a little.
—Edmund Burke

Since 1975, the Center for Reproduction of Endangered Species in San Diego, California, has utilized the latest technology and information to give Earth's vanishing wildlife a chance to beat extinction. CRES's breeding programs have helped bring gratifying population increases in such rare species as the Indian rhinoceros, Chinese monal, Przewalski's horse, and the Arabian oryx, and their unique Frozen Zoo indefinitely preserves semen, embryos, and other living cells and tissues from hundreds of severely threatened species.

In support of CRES's good work, I have committed 10 per cent of my income from this novel to them. It's my hope that other authors might take the same opportunity to "do only a little" for some cause that they believe in. If all of us do our little, we'll find we can accomplish a lot.

If you would like more information about CRES, write:

Zoological Society of San Diego
CRES
P.O. Box 551
San Diego, CA 92112–0551

Tell them Noah's Ark sent you.

Julia Ecklar
November 30, 1993

Captivating Fantasy by

ROBIN McKINLEY

Newbery Award–Winning Author
"McKinley knows her geography of fantasy...
the atmosphere of magic." — <u>Washington Post</u>